'SUN-DRENCHED ESCAPISM...
the ideal way to revel in other people's messy lives'
STYLIST

'Wry humour...
A BEGUILING SENSE OF PLACE...
emotional depth'
THE TIMES

'GIVING *BIG LITTLE LIES* ENERGY'
GRAZIA

'A DELICIOUS READ – INTIMATE, INTRICATE, IMMERSIVE.
The kind of book you want to shut yourself away with, and read in one sitting'
RACHEL JOYCE

'A Cazalet Chronicles for the twenty-first century.
I ADORED IT'
BRYONY GORDON

'Compelling, lyrical and gorgeously crafted...
AN UTTERLY TRANSPORTIVE DEBUT'
GLAMOUR

'EVOCATIVE PROSE...
it's easy to see why *The Garnett Girls* is being likened to works by commercial fiction queens Penny Vincenzi and Maeve Binchy'
THE OBSERVER

'ONE OF THE BEST DEBUTS THIS YEAR...
a great book about a complex family'
HELLO

'RICHLY TEXTURED, IMMERSIVE AND ASTUTE'
MIRROR

'RICHLY DRAWN, deeply fallible characters in ENVIABLE SETTINGS...
a clear-eyed understanding of family dynamics and intimate damage'
PATRICK GALE

'Full of forbidden and thwarted passion...
AS FRESH A SEA BREEZE'
BEST

'Sublime writing... as DELICIOUS and INTOXICATING as a cool glass of Sancerre. Heavenly!'
VERONICA HENRY

'An assured first novel...this immersive saga probes the traumas all families conceal. **A NOVEL OF APPETITE...** readers will down greedily'
THE SUNDAY TIMES

'Utterly beautiful... a stunning landscape and **AN INCREDIBLY MOVING STORY.** I loved every moment'
JOANNA CANNON

'TRULY ONE TO GET LOST IN'
HEAT

'A wonderfully woven tale of love, friendship and family. **AN EXCELLENT DEBUT** about the unbreakable bond between sisters'
CATHERINE ALLIOTT

'WHAT A GEM OF A BOOK! I could literally smell the salty seaside air. Such an accomplished first novel'
ERICA JAMES

'THE PERFECT HOLIDAY READ... characters that I'd love to party with in real life'
HARRIET TYCE

The Garnett Girls

GEORGINA MOORE

ONE PLACE. MANY STORIES

HQ
An imprint of HarperCollins*Publishers* Ltd
1 London Bridge Street
London SE1 9GF

www.harpercollins.co.uk

HarperCollins*Publishers*
Macken House, 39/40 Mayor Street Upper,
Dublin 1, D01 C9W8, Ireland

This paperback edition 2024

1
First published in Great Britain by
HQ, an imprint of HarperCollins*Publishers* Ltd 2023

Copyright © Georgina Moore 2023

Georgina Moore asserts the moral right to be
identified as the author of this work.
A catalogue record for this book is
available from the British Library.

PB ISBN: 9780008506377

This book contains FSC™ certified paper and other controlled
sources to ensure responsible forest management.

For more information visit: www.harpercollins.co.uk/green

This book is set in 11.5/15.5 pt. Centaur by Type-it AS, Norway

Printed and bound in the UK using 100% renewable electricity at
CPI Group (UK) Ltd, Croydon, CR0 4YY

For my grandmother, who told me to write.

For you I know I'd even try to turn the tide

JOHNNY CASH, 'I WALK THE LINE'

PROLOGUE

Margo slammed the heavy door shut behind her, letting her hand linger on the cold brass of the doorknob. She felt the heat envelop her, the air thick and still with it, no sea breeze to bring relief. There was even a heat haze over the sea, blurring the horizon. Sasha's small sticky hand slipped out of hers and she was off, taking Sandcove's steep steps with hops and jumps. 'Da!' she kept calling. She was chasing her father, she was always chasing her father. Margo watched as the white blonde curls shot along the sea wall above the beach, the curve of her cheek slathered in sun cream.

Margo shouted, 'Not near the edge!' hearing the echoes of all the times growing up this had been shouted at her. 'Imi, go with her, make sure she's okay! Your father's too far away.'

Imogen obediently trailed down the steps, book in hand. She moved slowly, dreamily. Margo noticed how knotted her long hair was, there was a huge bird's nest at the back. People would think she wasn't coping if they saw it.

'Quicker than that! She's already at the walkway.'

Margo felt Rachel lurking beside her, two enormous picnic bags at her feet. Margo looked at her eldest daughter's face which always seemed to be set in a scowl these days. She was wiser than she should be at nine, clever and sarcastic. She did not help the atmosphere in the house with her sharp observations.

'What's wrong now?'

'Didn't you see? Dad just left, he didn't take anything for the picnic.'

Margo had seen Richard's pale legs disappearing over Horestone Point. He'd been holding something, most likely the cooler box. He would already be on the white sand of Priory, a glass in his hand, chatting to whoever was there. On a day like this people would be coming into the bay by boat for barbecues and picnics.

'He couldn't wait to get away from us.'

Margo wanted to go back alone into the cool and quiet of the house. But she couldn't leave Richard in charge, she would never be able to leave him in charge. She needed to say something reassuring to Rachel.

'Don't be silly – he went ahead to get a good spot.'

Margo ignored the world-weary sigh beside her. She picked up the two bags. 'You okay to take the rug, darling?' She looked out at the horse-shoe of the bay. The light was dazzling, the tide had come right in, leaving only a crescent of beach. 'Look, Rach, it's perfect for swimming.'

Later, on their striped rug, Richard handed her a glass of cold white wine. He was grinning, a ragged straw hat perched on his head, a blob of sun cream on the bridge of his nose. Margo reached up a finger to rub it in and he seized her hand, kissed it. They both leant back on their arms, watching their girls play in the sea. Imogen was patiently leaping with a squealing Sasha in and out of the waves near the shore. Rachel was swimming along the bay, strong and sure.

'It'd be grand to have a stroke like that.' Richard's voice was envious, he was a terrible swimmer. Margo had tried to teach him but he was too proud and impatient.

'I don't want her to go out of sight.'

'Stop worrying so much and drink your wine.'

Margo looked up at the spindly trees leaning at an angle over the beach, sending long shadows at sunset. This beach could feel like it only belonged to her in winter; today they might as well have been by the Mediterranean, with all the smart RIBs and speedboats crowding the water, just a short swim away from the shore. There were bronzed bodies everywhere. One thing she didn't need to worry about was Richard looking at any other woman; he only ever had eyes for her. She watched as he leant over and sloppily tipped the last of the bottle into his glass. She knew better than to say anything.

'I'm boiling, shall we have a swim?'

Mostly it was a happy day. It took hours for Richard to get drunk and before he did he played cricket with his daughters, threw Sasha high up in the air, made them all laugh with his terrible handstands in the sea. Then he slept it off in the shade of the trees. The beach had started to empty while Margo was fully absorbed in building an enormous sand village, with moats and shell houses. Rachel had pushed them all to be ambitious and was still there beside her, adding a turret. Imogen had sloped away to read her book. Sasha was burying her Da's feet in the sand as he slept. When Margo looked up, the sky was streaked with vivid pink, the tide was far out and half the sand was in shadow.

'I want a photo of the three of you with this. Come on!'

Obediently Rachel and Imogen knelt beside Sasha, the sand village behind them. Margo noticed their new freckles, their beach hair, the patch of red on Sasha's dimpled thigh, where she had missed the sun cream.

'Come on girls, big smiles!'

3

I

Sinking

Venice

Imogen watched the door shut behind William and fell back against the pillows. William liked to get his money's worth at the hotel breakfast buffet but Imogen had no patience in the mornings for tourists with heads bent over maps, as if in prayer. The solemn hush, the stealing of sly glances at residents as they entered the dining room. Tourists in Venice were so earnest. To please William, Imogen had experimented with breakfast at La Calcina but all the getting up and down for bits of hard cheese and cold meat, a stale croissant and a cube of butter on ice had made her self-conscious. And the breakfast room was gloomy with Venetian burgundy and brocade twirls everywhere. There was a certain kind of opulent Italian decor that looked good at night, but in daylight reminded Imogen of a sad and shabby Victorian theatre.

Margo had always made them have a big breakfast on holiday, so they could skip lunch for church visits. On cultural trips, Margo had kept them on their feet all day, marching out in front, her strident call of 'Girls!' turning heads on all sides. Imogen remembered being embarrassed by how English Margo sounded, how unmistakeably herself. She never seemed to care about the looks she provoked. Heartened by the thought that Margo was not with her now, Imogen threw off her sheets and, like a ghostly blur, spun around the hotel room, clattering open all the shutters. She made so much noise that passers-by glanced up from the canal-side below; the waiters laying out cutlery at the floating restaurant turned their heads. If they had caught a glimpse of her, they would have seen that she was naked. But before anyone could see more than a flash of skin, Imogen was quickly back under the sheets, basking in the sunlight that now warmed every corner of the room.

Imogen worried that their hotel room was so imposing that it was overwhelming any romantic instincts. Not just 'a canal view', the room had a private terrace overlooking all the action of the Zattere with views on three sides. Everything shimmered in the spring sunlight. First Venice had seemed like an impossible mirage rising out of the water and then it had assaulted Imogen with a riot of colour. Its cobalt skies, warm red stone, the gold of the St Mark's Basilica, the orange of the spritzes they drank. Imogen had not expected to feel so daunted by it all, or for her feelings to be so rebellious. At times just the teal stillness of the canals made her tearful. She had always known that Venice was destined to have significance for her as her parents had honeymooned there. Margo had never taken her daughters, never even spoken of it, even though they all knew that Italy was her favourite place on earth. It was one of those subjects that was off limits.

As a child Imogen had once found a photo in an envelope in her mother's bedside drawer. It showed a young Margo with a halo of fat curls. She had round cheeks, endless legs. She was smiling in a way Imogen had never seen before. Her father was out of focus but grinning too, a possessive arm draped around Margo's shoulders. He had slim hips and a lion's mane of hair. They stood by one of the sculptures in the garden of the Guggenheim. Even at that age Imogen had known that she should not mention the photo. She wanted to sit and drink in its glamour; instead she had pushed it back into the envelope, back into the drawer.

The first place she had suggested to William that they visit was the Guggenheim. She did not tell him why she wanted a photo of them arm in arm by a certain statue, but as soon as she saw their pale imitation captured by a passer-by on her phone, she knew it was hopeless to try to emulate Richard and Margo. Imogen hated her moon-like face, the fact that she didn't look one bit like an elegant young Margo. Imogen had deleted the image from her phone. She was wondering why she had kept the whole thing from William when the old-fashioned telephone rang from the marble-topped bedside table, making her jump. She picked up the receiver, pulling herself up higher against the pillows.

The voice at the other end was abrupt and sharp. 'Has he done it yet?'

Imogen was one of the few people who could tell Margo and Rachel apart on the phone. She was relieved it was her sister. Even if it was sometimes like having two mothers, Rachel was definitely easier to deal with. 'No. Please stop ringing and asking. What if William was here? And why are you ringing the hotel? I've got a mobile.'

'You never answer it. You're phone-phobic. He's at breakfast poring over maps, planning your day, and I bet you're lounging in bed. Probably naked. Some of us have been up since six, you know – I've just kayaked to Priory and back.'

'I'm allowed to laze around, I'm on holiday. How are my nieces? What's going on there?' Imogen hoped to distract her sister.

'No news . . . except Margo is planning an Easter party at Sandcove. You know, the house that's supposed to be mine. Tom's talking about

7

using his boat trailer to bring crates of beer down the slipway. Lizzie had her first ride on one of Gemma's ponies, I'll send you a photo. Margo keeps asking if I've heard from you. She's like a cat on a hot tin roof.'

Imogen hated that they were all at home discussing her, waiting for the inevitable. She also felt homesick for Sandcove. She had a picture in her mind of her sister standing in the kitchen, bare feet on the flagstones, the window open and noise from the beach floating through. Her little nieces Lizzie and Hannah chasing around the kitchen island, the way Imogen and her sisters used to as children. 'She'll be trying to outdo the Goughs.'

'I've asked her if she can make it less rowdy than last year but I doubt she'll listen to me. Listen, I've got to go, I've got a client call at eleven.'

Imogen heard William on the hotel stairs, whistling. She was glad he was happy but his whistling grated on her nerves. 'Will's coming. I can hear him whistling on the stairs.'

'If Gabriel whistled all the time, I'd divorce him.'

'Rach! Don't be mean.'

'How is Venice then?'

'Don't know. Terrifying?'

'You're a writer, Imi.'

'It's hard to explain. It's so swoony, it's a bit unreal—'

'Margo won't talk about you being there. Because of her and Richard's honeymoon.'

William walked in, twirling a huge brass key attached to a brocade tassel. *'Buongiorno Principessa!'* With a flourish he handed Imogen a croissant wrapped in a paper napkin. 'Breakfast is served.'

'I'm on the phone. It's Rachel.'

William raised his eyes to the ceiling. 'Her daily check-up.'

8

'Will's here.'

'Send my love. Call when you have news.' And just like that, Rachel rang off.

Imogen tried to eat the croissant with enthusiasm. As was often the case, her sister's impatience with William made her feel more affection for him. She decided she would no longer suggest she visit Basilica dei Frari alone, meeting William later for lunch. They should go together. William did not share her passion for churches but why had she given up on trying to convert him? Margo still had not given up on Sasha, twenty years after she had tried to indoctrinate her as an eight-year-old in Florence. Sasha sneered at the arts. Her calling was medicine and she travelled the world for a charity setting up medical crisis centres. It was Sasha's great cause and she made sure they all knew how important it was to be doing something worthwhile, sometimes making Imogen feel that her writing was self-indulgent.

Imogen thought how long it had been since she had seen Sasha, how long it was since Sasha had been home to Sandcove. Imogen missed Sasha when she was away, then wondered when they were finally together how she tolerated Sasha's sarcasm and spikiness. The baby of the family, Sasha was probably the one who had run furthest away from Margo's expectations, leaving Imogen to soak up all the leftover mother love. She tried not to resent Sasha for it, but she could not always be the good sister in thought and deed. Pushing thoughts of her family aside, Imogen tried to anchor herself more in the present. She threw off her sheets, brushing crumbs onto the floor, guiltily enjoying the fact that someone else would clear them up. Wrapping herself in a towel, she followed William onto the terrace where he sat watching a passing cruise ship, so enormous it seemed like it might blot out the sun and the whole sky.

'Goodness. That's so weird. So out of place.' She could see passengers waving from the decks, thousands of them.

9

'They can see you, Imi! Put some clothes on!'

'I don't care! Loads of waiters saw me when I opened the shutters – they got a right eyeful.' William's prudery made Imogen want to tease him. But William just smiled at her. In response, she wound an arm around his shoulder.

'Shall we have a family meeting then and plan our day?'

But Imogen could not relax, even though ostensibly the next few days seemed easy and peaceful in the sunshine. They visited Damien Hirst's *Treasures from the Wreck of the Unbelievable* and William compared her to the green head with the snakey hair. He bought a postcard so he could show Margo the likeness. Imogen did not tell him that she thought Margo would find herself too busy to listen to their Venetian tales. They ate some memorable meals, a delicious lunch of *risotto al nero* on the terrace of the Gritti Palace washed down with several glasses of Gavi de Gavi. William worried about the expense. Sometimes Imogen wanted to put away the map and just wander along the back canals and William indulged her, only very occasionally checking his Google Maps. There were ice creams, pistachio for him, cherry for her, from a stall that they visited over and over. There was the afternoon in their hotel room when they managed a siesta, or 'afternoon cuddles' as William called it. And to appease William, Imogen did not take any more calls from her mother or her sister, or even her agent.

As the end of their trip drew closer, William began to behave strangely. It was Saturday and they were leaving on Monday morning. William had asked her several times on the Friday before what she might fancy eating on Saturday night, or as he put it what might 'tickle your fancy'. Imogen had a feeling that it was to be 'the' night. The trouble was she still didn't know how she felt about getting engaged. Sometimes she didn't even want to say yes, and then she remembered everyone at home, waiting and expecting, how she had led people to believe she would marry William one day. The only place she found certainty and conviction was in her writing. The rest of the time she quaked in the face of the Garnetts' passionately held opinions.

'Why don't you choose? I don't mind. All the food has been so delicious.'

Like Imogen, William found being in charge stressful, especially given the pressure he was clearly putting himself under. He spent even longer by himself over breakfast – Imogen guessed he was researching romantic restaurants. She tried not to be snobby but could still hear Margo dismissing guide books as 'mostly bollocks'. Margo had always sung out loudly, 'Let's go off piste!'

'We haven't tried the Venetian classic tiramisu you know. Perhaps somewhere that is known for traditional Venetian puddings?' William said worriedly.

Imogen found herself snapping, 'Yuck! You know I'm not a pudding person.' Too often William's diffidence provoked her to act uncharacteristically, like forceful Margo and Rachel.

William looked discouraged. 'Sorry, I do know that. You always pick the cheese platter.'

'And rarely share it!' Imogen said to cheer him up.

William smiled at her. 'Well the owner of La Calcina suggested a canal-side restaurant famous for *sepia al nero* . . . and tuna carpaccio which I know you like—'

'Wonderful! Let's go there.'

The bellinis were so delicious at L'Academia that Imogen found she had had three before they had even ordered any food. They were delivered by a waiter who looked bored until he saw Imogen, and then he had lit up, his dark eyes shining. Imogen knew she was having one of her rare beautiful days, and wondered how it would be to be gifted with the privilege every day, like Sasha. To see people's heads turn on the street, to be served first in bars. Sasha had never known anything different and it gave her an arrogance that sometimes made her intolerable. That evening Imogen had finally glimpsed young Margo in her face. Her skin was clear and freckly, her eyes their best blue-grey. She had sneaked a dusky pink top from Rachel's wardrobe and it suited her. William kept looking at her nervously; even more so when she began to giggle at everything he said. She knew she was drinking too fast, doing anything to take the edge off her anxiety. It wasn't long until three drinks on an empty stomach meant she kept dropping things onto the cobbled street. First it was her sunglasses, then her napkin; finally the menu flew away from her, landing on the lap of a very closely seated neighbour. William apologised on her behalf and she giggled some more. William's nerves were made worse by the fact that every time she dropped something, their waiter Davide rushed over to help her.

'Thank you, thank you so much, Davide. Yes I'm fine, oh thank you . . . a clean napkin.' She tried not to giggle as Davide flapped more stiff linen over her lap.

There was an edge of impatience when William next spoke, his head buried in his menu. 'Have you decided? I think perhaps no more fizz?'

'Yes, probably wise. Don't want to fall in the canal!'

Their table was a tiny steel thing, precarious on the cobbles, even though Davide had leapt around with bits of folded matchbox, trying to stabilise it. The lack of space meant that their lantern was on the canal wall, as was their salt and pepper and soon their wine bottle.

As the sky turned pink above and was reflected in the water, Imogen tried to concentrate on the menu. She didn't much feel like eating, only drinking. She felt slightly sick, her nerves bubbling under everything. But she knew William would expect the full three courses if this was 'the night'. She picked tuna carpaccio to start and some ravioli to soak up the alcohol. Once Davide had been allowed to read out all the specials, none of which Imogen or William had chosen, and they had ordered, they were left alone together in the dusk, quiet and awkward, aware of all the chatter bouncing off the cobbles around them. Imogen looked helplessly around for a diversion.

'Noisy, isn't it?' William spoke before she could. She saw he looked anxious too, and felt a pang for him.

'So much atmosphere. Just a sign of how popular it is. And it's a Saturday night.'

'I am glad you are getting your tuna.'

'Yes, me too. The wine is delicious.'

William watched her drain her glass, sat up a little straighter, cleared his throat. He sounded stiff and formal. 'It's been such a wonderful trip. I am so pleased you persuaded me to come.' Just then Davide appeared to conscientiously top up Imogen's wine. William sighed and tutted as Davide left. 'I think he fancies you, Imi. You do look beautiful tonight, so . . .'

'I think this is just a good colour on me . . . Thank you, I mean.'

William cleared his throat and slowly moved a small velvet box across the table, as if he was making a move on a chess board. Imogen watched as he opened the box, looking intently at the ring inside, then up at her. 'This was my mother's, Imi. I hope you'll wear it and be my wife. It's what everyone wants, I hope it's what you want too?'

Imogen blushed, feeling hot and then cold. She reached to pull her shawl around her shoulders but it was stuck. She pulled again and realised that it was caught under a table leg. Tears were filling her eyes, she could not understand why she was crying when this was supposed to be the happiest moment in her life. She knew she had been quiet for a moment too long, that William was waiting. As she moved to free her shawl from the table leg it wobbled, sloshing wine over the tablecloth. She couldn't look at William.

'Are you all right? Are you crying? Oh darling! I'm so happy you're happy.'

'Just trying to get this.' Imogen gave a fierce yank and, as she did so, the table bounced towards William who leapt up, sending the lantern clattering off the canal wall and into the water with a loud splash.

There was a round of applause around the outside tables and laughter, shouts of *'Felicitazioni!'*, *'Bravo!'* Imogen and William smiled sheepishly at everyone, sat down quietly while Davide fussed around them. Then flushed and brave, William suddenly stood up again and told their audience that they were engaged. He made Imogen stand up with him and more cheers and clapping echoed down the canals, the sound of another Venetian engagement. When they sat down again they apologised over and over, offering to pay for the lost lantern, while Davide, wreathed in genial smiles, kept repeating *'Non è niente.'* Complimentary champagne arrived at their table, which they sipped quietly, suddenly shy again. The ring sat between them still on the table, still in its velvet box, until William nodded at it and said, 'Go on then, put it on, silly. I missed my moment I think, for putting it on you.'

Imogen did as she was told, slipping the ring on under the table, aware of all the eyes on them, not wanting more clapping and congratulations. By the time they walked home she felt strangely sober, and standing on the Academia Bridge, with the Grand Canal at their feet, she wondered what had happened. She hadn't said yes. She had said nothing.

'I was thinking of proposing here instead, I know you love this view. Thank God I didn't push my luck trying it, we might have found Mum's ring tumbling over the Academia.' William held Imogen's hand, turning it so the ring caught the glow from the streetlamp on the bridge. Imogen saw many diamonds sparkling around a dark centre, but she could not see much else. She would have plenty of time to look at it properly. A lifetime. She wondered why William wasn't asking her why she was so quiet.

'I'm so sorry about being a bit tipsy and for all that drama in the restaurant.' She wanted to apologise for not reacting appropriately, but he seemed not to have noticed and she couldn't get the words out.

'I'll need to get used to it now you are going to be Mrs Bradbury,' William smiled sweetly at her.

Bradbury would be her third surname. First O'Leary, then Garnett and now Bradbury. Imogen looked out at all the astounding history and culture spread in front of her, and the beauty that left her feeling restless and dissatisfied. It would be so strange to no longer be a Garnett. Perhaps it was for the best. She continually worried about letting the Garnett name down. She was sure no other Garnett would find themselves engaged almost by accident.

'Isn't it strange to think that this will probably all be under water one day?' William was staring down into the dark water below them, his face in shadow.

Imogen turned to him slowly. Not for the first time she wondered why their thoughts were worlds apart. 'I try not to think about it.' Imogen didn't want to look at the view any more, which now seemed a tragedy waiting to happen. 'Let's go back to the hotel.'

2

Limoncello

It was their last night in Venice and Imogen was on edge, still hungry for everything that Venice flaunted at night, the energy and the drama of its lit-up beauty. It was the kind of restlessness she felt with the first blue skies and spring blossom, the urge to drink the world in. William had suggested a reliably good dinner at the hotel and an early night and Imogen had to persuade him that there was still so much to see and do. She begged William to go with her on a *cicchetti* crawl along Rio San Trovaso. After a few Aperol spritzes, he began to get into the spirit of things.

They sat eating morsels of bread on a canal wall, this time careful not to have anything within knocking distance. Imogen's eyes danced over everything, wanting to lock it all in her memory. She watched William playing with his straw. She could tell he was looking forward to heading home, now he had done what he needed to do. Imogen was overcome with sadness to be leaving, feeling nostalgic for it all before it had even ended. 'We've barely scratched the surface . . . doesn't it bother you?'

William smiled at her indulgently. 'We've got our whole lives to come back. I'm sure we will. If it's still here.'

Imogen worried that William did not mean it. Venice for him was 'it' not 'her'. It had been the correct place for a proposal to Imogen, to keep her family happy. It would sound good when he told the engagement story to colleagues or friends. It was keeping her awake at night knowing and wondering why she had said nothing, why it hadn't mattered, why it had been overlooked.

William saw her frown and reached for her hand. 'Let's go back to the hotel . . .'

At the hotel Imogen left William to his bedtime routine. She felt the pull of their terrace and the busy Zattere life. Outside Venice wrapped its magic around her. There was so much to hear and see, the Italian chatter from the floating restaurant and the comings and goings of the waiters as they brought drinks on trays in and out of the hotel. Glamorous couples promenaded along the canal-side, Venetian women with imposing bone structure, wrapped in shawls, despite the warm weather. For a moment Imogen let herself imagine her mother and father walking there beneath her. They would be holding hands, passers-by sneaking admiring glances at them both. Margo would be smiling up at Richard, giving him the full beam of her happiness. A speedboat shot past leaving a wake and Imogen came back to the present. She watched a *vaporetto* chugging along to the Zattere stop where lots of tourists disembarked looking for the Venetian impossibility, an affordable pizza restaurant. Imogen lit one of her 'naughty' cigarettes, sat watching, feeling the bustle humming inside her, making her part of it all.

On the chair beside her, her phone began vibrating and without thinking she picked it up. 'Hello?'

'Imogen, at last! I've been trying you all day.'

Imogen sat up straighter, looked around her guiltily as if she was being watched. Her agent Claire was old school, and did not believe in office hours or holidays. She tended to make Imogen feel like a breathless teenager.

'Things are moving fast here. What day did you say you were back? Rehearsals start on the fifth. The director wants you for the read-throughs, meeting the cast, all that jazz. We're bloody lucky he wants you involved. Loads just cut out the playwright. And fuck me, this casting news takes things to a new level. The casting director is wetting his pants. Make sure you're sitting down for this!'

Imogen knew better than to say anything about where she was or what she was doing. Claire didn't do personal detail. 'Exciting . . . I'm sitting down.'

'They've landed Rowan Melrose for Alexandra! God, that's going to sell tickets. She's a bit young for Alexandra, not many stage creds, but she's really hot right now.'

Imogen immediately thought of Margo's reaction, how she would point out that Rowan Melrose was not a theatre actress, the caustic comments she would make. But ten million people had watched the BBC's *Anna Karenina* in its first week with Rowan in the starring role and it had seemed like half of them had fallen in love with her. Imogen knew Claire was waiting for a reaction. 'That's wonderful news!'

Claire sounded pleased with herself. 'I told you we'd be going big with this. The Playhouse really want to make a splash. Rowan's tricky, she's got a bit of a rep, but Fred can keep her in line. She doesn't want to get typecast for her looks apparently, likes the idea of playing the Romanov mother, getting a bit of gravitas.'

'Did she say anything about the play?' Imogen hated sounding needy, but she was having pangs about handing her Alexandra over to someone else. To a half-starved starlet, who most likely knew nothing about the Romanovs.

'Nope, not that I know of. You'll find out when you meet her. You're on hols, aren't you? Go out and celebrate. This is big news – huge! We'll have a unit at the Groucho when you're back. Gotta go, love.'

Imogen sat looking at the phone, wondering whether to text Margo or Rachel or both. But she hadn't told either of them yet that she was engaged. She knew that Margo was desperate for news. But once she told them about the proposal, it would be real and she would have to accept that she had let it all just happen. It hadn't been perfect or romantic, it hadn't been worthy of Venice. And now, with Rowan Melrose, she wanted to form her own view before her mother and sister told her what she should be feeling.

When she went back inside to share her news with William she found him asleep on top of the covers in his pyjamas, lying like a starfish. He was snoring, which he always did when he lay on his back. Imogen pulled the satiny quilt over him and left the room quickly, scenting freedom. She passed the hotel bar, richly red and candlelit, and let it draw her in. She ordered a glass of prosecco and found herself being towered over by a young man, who looked about twenty.

'I am Angelo. Why are you all alone, *signora*?'

Imogen tried not to look taken aback. He was Italian but his English was good, if a little stilted. He seemed so sure of himself, arrogant in his beauty. He had eyes the colour of Guinness, framed by long eyelashes that most women would have paid good money for. Something about the way he looked at her made her need to tell the truth. It reminded her of her brother-in-law Gabriel, a psychotherapist. 'My boyfriend's asleep.'

'That is very stupid of him and not very . . . *romantica*?'

Imogen smiled at him, watched with surprise as he pulled one of the leather and wood bar stools very close to her own. He was staring at her like she was the Mona Lisa and there were hidden mysteries in her face. To compose herself she took a large gulp of prosecco. 'Not everything has to be romantic.' She felt self-conscious, like she had suddenly been transported onto the set of a cheesy film.

'I think everything should be romantic for someone like you,' Angelo said imperiously.

'The other night he proposed. So he's my fiancé now,' Imogen said, so that Angelo would not think she was a sad older woman prowling a hotel bar.

'You are very beautiful. *Bellissima*.' He said it like it was an absolute truth. She laughed, this time lightly flicking her hair as she did so. She was glad she had worn it down. 'I will buy you another drink. As you have been abandoned by your fiancé.' He stood over her and ordered more drinks in very fast Italian. When a fresh glass of prosecco sat in front of her on the polished mahogany bar, and a glass of red in front of him, he looked at her intently again. 'So his proposal, was it romantic?'

'We're a bit too old to be romantic.'

'You cannot be so old, you are around twenty-six – no?'

Imogen grinned at this but for some reason didn't correct him. The bar was dark. She had slept a lot this week, her under-eye shadows banished. She probably could pass for five years younger. 'Something like that, Angelo,' she said, realising she was flirting a little and that her glass was half empty again. The bar was thinning out. The floating restaurant outside was noisily packing up for the night. Soon they were the only two people in the bar. Usually Imogen would have worried about keeping the waiters up, but tonight she did not care. Perhaps it was Angelo, acting like he owned the place. She ignored the feeling that the two waiters whispering in the doorway to the kitchen were watching them and gossiping, and let Angelo go ahead and buy a bottle of wine. He told her he had never wanted to kiss anyone so much in his life. 'But it's not like you've lived long,' Imogen teased him. 'There'll be lots of people you want to kiss.'

'Have there been lots for you?'

Imogen felt a bit taken aback when she realised there hadn't been. 'Not really. But I'm different to you.'

'How? You don't need to love or be loved? You look like you do.'

'Yes I do — of course I do. It's just you seem so sure of things. I sometimes feel like I don't seem to want things enough.'

'You never feel yearning?'

'Not for kissing. For work and my writing, yes.' She was surprised by the words coming out of her mouth.

'Well I am yearning for you now.'

Soon she was very drunk, as was he. They got bored of wine and drank tiny shots of icy limoncello, like sorbet in a glass. She chatted to him about her play, about the TV star who was going to be in it. She could hear herself, a pretentious playwright dropping names. But Angelo didn't have the Garnett habit of talking over her; instead he was giving her star billing. He was putting all the drinks on his room bill and she didn't protest, knowing that way William would not see the bar tab. She felt unsteady and knew she should go upstairs. She was risking William waking up and coming to look for her. But she was so happy where she was, laughing and feeling uncharacteristically funny and charming. When Angelo clumsily leant over and tried to kiss her with red wine-stained lips, she was shocked but aware that she had been leading him on. It was as if the lights had gone up in the theatre and the performance was over. She put out her hand flat on his chest and pushed him away from her.

'Don't go, beautiful Imogen.'

'I have to. I have a fiancé upstairs.' She could feel how strong he was, how impatient. She managed to get cold air and space between them and the victory made her leap up, nearly knocking her stool over. She tried to compose herself. She was too old now to start kissing men in bars, too old to start kissing anyone. She was engaged. For once she had a plan and she had to stick to it. She couldn't drift any more, things were decided. And something she had always dreamt of was going to happen, her play was going to be staged. She was a grown-up with a career for the first time in her life.

'You need to do this with a girl your own age, Angelo.' She sounded so prim. Not a Lucy Honeychurch in *A Room with a View*, but a Charlotte Bartlett instead. 'I'm sorry I have to go. Thanks for the drinks.' And with that she turned gracelessly, momentarily disorientated in the dark hotel bar, and by all the alcohol. 'Sorry – which is the way out?' Angelo pointed wordlessly, his face like thunder. Imogen left without looking back.

The next morning Imogen wanted to hide in bed from the Venice sunlight like a new-born vampire. The inside of her mouth felt like sandpaper, her cheeks were burning and her skin clammy. She dared not lift her head to see where William was as she could not face his gently enquiring looks. It absolutely was right that her punishment should be a morning spent hurriedly packing, settling up and having to talk to people. She would be expected to smile and be charming and arrange the water taxi and all those tedious things. Dread scuttled into her brain like an army of spiders. What if the night waiters who had served her and Angelo were still on duty? They might point and laugh. Angelo could be downstairs and might come over and try to talk to her, perhaps even try to kiss her again. What if Angelo had actually been putting all the drinks on her room bill and it had all just been an elaborate scam? Imogen groaned, imagining William turning pale as he saw the amount on their final bill, a pained expression as he asked her, 'What were you doing last night, darling?'

Instead she heard his real voice from the bathroom, responding to her only partly muffled groan.

'Everything okay, Imi?'

Imogen forced herself up to a more upright position, feeling the ache in her arm muscles. 'I feel really sick – I've got a terrible headache. Maybe it was something I ate last night?' She had to hope and pray that he had not smelt the alcohol on her.

William came out of the bathroom frowning slightly, clutching his washbag. He looked perky. 'Oh no, poor you. We ate mostly the same of those little tapas things though, didn't we? I feel right as rain.'

'*Cicchetti.*' Imogen heard herself correcting him, the way Margo would. Her excuse for irritability was that her brain was trying to escape from her skull.

'Yes, *cicchetti*. Rest for a bit, I'll go down and get some breakfast and settle the bill. You probably should aim to be all packed up by elevenish. Do you want me to sort the water taxi or have you already done it?'

Short of physically restraining William and keeping him locked in the room, Imogen did not know what other options she had other than to risk him going downstairs. 'Thanks. I'll try to be packed by eleven. At the moment I don't feel well enough to face anyone so if you don't mind doing the water taxi . . .'

'You're sure we shouldn't just share one with a couple of the other hotels? I don't want to be a killjoy but it's a big expense. I know you've got your heart set on it because Margo did it—'

'I can't share today. I feel sick, Will. I'll pay half, like I said.' Imogen knew she was being waspish, but all she wanted was for William to go and leave her in peace so she could groan out loud. 'I don't want a croissant this morning, thanks, but coffee, juice and lots of cold still water would be great.' Imogen directed her demands in a rush to

William's back, hoping he would not turn and accuse her of needing hangover cures.

Instead he shrugged. 'I can't smuggle any of those things out of the breakfast room. It'll have to be a separate order on room service. I can get them to send it up?'

She knew he was worrying about the cost. She summoned her most charming tone. 'Please.'

'Okay. I'm off now. Packed by eleven, Imi, please.'

She lay back for a while just listening to her breathing, trying to empty her mind of any thoughts. She wanted to speak to Rachel, as she always did at moments of crisis. Rachel was her tide clock, knowing her comings and goings. Rachel came up with solutions, she could make decisions. She had been making decisions for them all since she was eleven, when she had had to step up to be a replacement mother. With her lawyer's brain she would want to examine what had happened forensically. But this was precisely why Imogen could not call her, why Rachel must not know. Rachel would wonder why she had not told her she was engaged, why she had not called anyone. Then she would bluntly suggest that Imogen's behaviour implied she did not want to be engaged.

Imogen simply had to hope never to see Angelo again. She needed to get out of Venice without William discovering that she had got drunk with a stranger, had nearly let him kiss her. But at least she had stopped in time. She wasn't reckless like her mother, kissing whomever she felt like. Imogen knew of Margo's reputation; hints and snide comments had made their way to her. And she had vague memories of a revolving door of men when their father had left. But she was different. No one needed to know. Just like no one else needed to know about her silence during the proposal. She had always intended to say yes.

Like a reluctant child on a school morning, Imogen dragged herself out of bed and into a hot shower. She washed her long thick hair, which she hated doing as it was always such a big operation. Then, wrapped in two towels, snail-like she moved around the bedroom collecting her belongings, haphazardly throwing them into the suitcase on the floor. There was a knock at the door. Room service, Imogen presumed. But instead it was an imposing woman maybe ten years or so older than her. Imogen knew she was Italian at once, she was elegant in an uncreased linen suit. She was not beautiful but her features were angular, like a Modigliani woman. She had amber eyes and her jewellery was all heavy antique gold. Imogen was suddenly aware of her towel, the turban on her head. The woman looked amused.

'*Signora*, I have something that has belonged to you.' Her English was hard to understand, the accent thick. The woman held out her cupped hand, long fingers, nails painted the colour of figs. It was the kind of nail colour Margo would wear. One of Imogen's earrings lay in her cupped hand. Imogen felt so foggy, as if she was in a dream.

'Oh. Thank you – where was it?' She took the earring, gold bells studded with little pieces of turquoise, from a pair Margo had given her one birthday. They were not Imogen's style, and much more Margo, as was often the way with Margo's gifts.

'*Bellissimo,*' the woman said, inclining her head slightly at the earring. Imogen had worn them the previous night. Slowly she felt the blood was draining from her head. Could this be Angelo's wife? Oh God. Suddenly she thought she could hear William's whistling on the stairs. Cold fear overwhelmed her. The woman was still looking at her curiously. 'It was, how do you say, on . . . stuck on . . . Angelo's jumper.'

Imogen remembered the jumper in a quick flashback. The kind of jumper an Italian wears on a spring evening. Duck-egg blue, soft under her hands. She blushed as the woman continued to examine her closely. She didn't know what to say. The woman needed to go before William came back. She was trying to look past her, to see the room behind her, trying no doubt to see if there was someone else there, a cuckold. 'I'm sorry,' Imogen stammered, starting to shut the door a little. 'Thanks for bringing it back.'

'I am Angelo's mother.' The woman didn't move, only smiled as Imogen looked even more confused. 'He is just sixteen. I thought you should know. It does not matter. He seems older. *Uomo*. I know this. But he is a boy. He seems *inamorato* with you.'

He was sixteen. This was so typical. She couldn't even get an Italian flirtation right. Instead she was now someone who got picked up by underage drinkers in bars. Imogen stared back at the woman, holding on to the door, using it as a prop, the words rushing out of her. 'I'm so sorry. I really didn't know he was that young. I only had a few drinks with him, he was good company. Lovely manners.' She tried to smile at the woman, to wrap things up in an acceptable way, but there was nothing in the manners handbook for this situation. 'Thank you then. Goodbye.'

The woman turned decisively to go, still a glint in her eyes. 'You English girls . . .' she said quietly as she turned. 'Goodbye, *signora*.'

Imogen shut the door behind her and breathed out. William would be back soon and they must pack. And then they must leave Venice. She could see now that her Venice could never be the Venice of Margo and Richard.

3

Bus Pass

Isle of Wight

Margo was having a blue day. Despite the hope that Imogen was finally making steps to settle down, it was another day when she felt lonely and old. Her spirit remained the same, still struggling with the idea of being a grown-up, still mystified by the fact that she had been allowed to mother humans. It was really only when her girls were around her at Sandcove that she felt she might pass for an adult, for a mother who was at the heart of things, who was needed. The bad days came upon her stealthily with no fanfare, catching her unawares, reminding her that she was nearly sixty and would soon be ready for her bus pass. Her body sometimes failed her. There was a pain in her calf muscle which jabbed at her in the middle of the night. She would remember with nostalgia her mother telling her when she was a girl that any mysterious twinge she had was a growing pain. Now in the depths of night, she would convince herself it must be DVT. Hadn't Ali had one and she was only in her forties?

There were other small things that plagued her. She thought of them as pulls in a longed-for new jumper, snags that caught the eye and downgraded it to second best. She had to use eye drops for her glaucoma every morning. Other days her eyes watered for no reason. And she needed the loo much more often; coffee went straight through her. She seemed overnight to have become a whole stone heavier and was unable to shift it, no matter what diet she tried. She ate like a bird, knowing that it was really alcohol she needed to cut back on. Some days she felt so tired that her head was cloudy. When she was writing, the right words just would not come. Her mind would wander to memories of when the children were little and so lovely. And worst of all she found her emotions were so close to the skin, pinpricks of longing for the past, acute pangs of loneliness. She cried over books and bad movies and anything her grandchildren did made her heart swell to ridiculous, unmanageable proportions. She knew she should feel lucky that she had navigated a short menopause in her early fifities, seeing off the worst of it with HRT, and that her libido had come back with a vengeance, but it was still hard not to think of the further indignities of ageing that lay ahead. She looked younger than many her age, the plumpness in her face keeping wrinkles at bay, her girls keeping her *au courant* with the world as it was, and her sexual adventures keeping her body alert, but still she was scared that these were her last years of grace.

She was in her study at the Other Place, at her desk, surrounded by papers, old diaries and newspaper clippings, her laptop open. She was feeling hemmed in at the cottage. Sandcove in its bay, with the open horizon all around, called to her restless spirit and it was a call she resisted several times a day. She knew she was putting off working, irritable in her skin. She had been commissioned by a publisher to pull together her old magazine columns and newspaper articles into a kind of memoir but it was difficult to shape it when so much was missing from those columns she had written, with the realities of living with a drunk whitewashed out. Margo felt a fraud reading her chirpy eighties pieces, funny stories of what the girls had done as toddlers, recipes she loved, vignettes of her Soho life. Then in 1994 she was 'on a sabbatical' for the whole year. The year Richard walked out and she fell apart. She knew it was fashionable now for everyone to reveal the darkest moments of their lives, to talk about mental health, to talk about trauma. But Margo had not been trained that way. In the eighties and nineties you were showing you could have it all; as a woman you were holding it together, putting on a front. You never moaned about the impossible juggling, in case something was taken away. It was hard to accept the idea of a memoir at all. Looking back was not easy for her, facing the things she had put her daughters through.

She turned her thoughts to her middle daughter. With that strange instinct she always had about Imogen she felt that there was news, but Imogen hadn't rung her for days. Now Imogen should be on the plane home. If she was engaged then why hadn't she rung to say? Margo had always thought it would be a last-night thing from William, who wasn't known for being in a hurry. Margo had hated not knowing what was going on. It did not help that she could not let her mind travel to Imogen in that place. She could not think of Venice without thinking of Richard and their honeymoon. A time when she had been so full of happiness and hope, it hurt her now to think of it. Why did Imogen have to go to Venice and make it part of her life story, so that Margo had to keep hearing the word 'Venice'? It seemed thoughtless and out of character for Imogen. More the kind of thing Sasha would do. Margo wished she was alone today but instead she kept being bothered by Carol, who could talk for England.

'I haven't touched your papers, Mrs G. I know how you get. They're all over the desk – I couldn't dust round them. That red wine spill's a real bugger, even Vanish won't shift it. What happened? Such a shame on that pale rug.'

'It was me. I was tipsy.' Margo blushed a little at the white lie, as she flashed back in her mind to a naked man sprawled underneath her on the rug, a flung out arm knocking over a full glass of red. She made a point of looking at her watch. 'Time to make your way over to Sandcove now? Gabriel has you at midday.'

'Rachel off somewhere for "work" again? That man's a saint. Can't be many who'd put up with all the housework and babysitting he has to do.'

Margo looked at Carol over her reading glasses. 'He has you to help with the housework. Of course he has to look after his own kids sometimes. Rachel's the breadwinner, working full time. She's got a big case at the moment and papers to catch up on so she had to go into the office in Ryde. The world's changed, Carol – you need to get more with it.'

'Some things aren't right. A father looking after littlies all weekend while their mum "reads" papers is one of 'em.'

Margo used her harshest voice, which could freeze blood. 'The girls are brilliant and they need husbands that support them.'

Having been part of the family since the children were born, Carol was immune to Margo's tone. 'Imi still isn't married, is she? You've hopes for that William bloke but he's a bit of a drip. I know Rachel thinks so too.'

'William's a good man and perfect for Imogen.' Margo's voice lacked conviction. Carol gave her a knowing look.

The phone rang and Margo picked it up quickly.

'Hello Ma.'

Margo knew at once. Ma was a term of endearment used only for big moments. She felt herself smiling, relief flooding in. 'Imi! Are you engaged?'

Carol, eavesdropping and dusting, raised her eyebrows and shook her head. Margo placed a hand over the receiver and frowned at her. 'Can you dust somewhere else? I want a private chat with my daughter.'

'Ma?'

'Just Carol. Well?'

'Yes. William proposed.'

'When? You're home now. I thought you'd ring me as soon as it happened? I've been waiting by the phone.'

'Sorry. I sort of lost track of time.'

'You've done very well. He'll make a good husband. He adores you – and he's sensible about his career. Not too ambitious. He'll make a good father, like Gabe.'

'I know all that.'

'You don't sound very sure? A bit flat.'

'Just tired. Sad to have left Venice—'

'When can we celebrate? Is it too early for fizz now?' Margo stood up at her desk, suddenly full of energy, wanting to somehow banish Imogen's tone, which was ruining everything. Some papers fluttered off her desk. 'I wish I could be with you to celebrate.'

Imogen laughed, she sounded relieved. 'I thought you'd want all the proposal details.'

'No, save those for your sisters.' There was an awkward pause. 'I'm just glad he's finally pulled his finger out. One proposal's pretty much like another. The view, down on one knee, the saying yes part. Hang on – what's the ring like?' Margo felt a hesitation. 'Oh.'

'It was his mum's.'

'Ida's?' Margo's sceptical tone revealed what she thought of Ida's taste.

'A sapphire with diamonds around it. Classic.'

'Not at all you.' Margo sat down again and called out to the kitchen. 'Carol, can you get me a drink so I can toast my daughter? There's a bottle of Veuve in the fridge – I can always take what I don't drink down to Sandcove—'

'Give me a chance to tell Rachel first.'

'Fine – listen, you'll have to send that ring back and get another. You can't spend your life looking at a ring you don't like. Bring it to show me. Which weekend can you come?'

'Will thinks it's a big honour that I have Ida's ring. You know how he is about her. I can't hurt his feelings.'

Margo remembered the tiny ring Richard had given her. It had made her so happy. Richard had gone down on his knees on a cobbled street in Soho and passers-by had stopped to cheer and clap. She remembered how it had started to rain, the dark smudges on the shoulder of his jacket, as he gazed up at her. 'I sent your father's ring back.' There was a silence. Margo began pacing in the small space between her desk and the window, annoyed with herself for sharing the memory.

'I didn't know. How would I know? You never speak about him.'

'Where is that drink—'

Carol appeared, looking resentful. She was holding a crystal glass of cold champagne by the stem. 'Don't shriek at me, Margo O'Leary.'

'I'll bloody well shriek at you if you keep getting my name wrong.'

Imogen was insistent on the phone. 'What about the ring? Richard's ring?'

Margo took a long gulp of champagne and raised the glass to an imaginary audience. 'To you, Imi. Congratulations.'

'Ma?'

Margo sighed. 'Richard didn't have much money. It was a tiny diamond, you needed a magnifying glass to see it. I was crying and laughing so much I hardly looked at it – but later when there was some money I asked for a new one. That's when he bought me the huge garnet set in rose gold. Bought with gambling money no doubt.'

'I don't remember it.'

'I think I threw it away.' Margo suddenly wanted to see that ring again, it had been such a beauty. 'And now I really need to change the subject. Your father's had enough air time for this century. What about a fuck-off engagement party?'

'Please no. The last thing I want is lots of people staring and asking questions.'

Margo could hear the steel creeping into her daughter's voice. She would need to be her most persuasive self. She moved with her glass, now empty, to the doorway of her kitchen, wanting to know where Carol was, why she was suspiciously quiet. Carol was standing there in her apron and stockinged feet holding a copy of *Vogue*, flicking through the glossy pages with affected nonchalance, clearly eavesdropping again. Margo wrinkled her nose and shook her head at Carol as if to say, 'Since when do you read *Vogue*?'

'Margo, I'm serious. I hate parties – Will hates them even more.'

'Nonsense. You loved Sandcove parties as a child. Remember that one where we danced the conga in the kitchen and I let you stay up until three a.m. and—'

'That was Sasha. Sasha's your true party girl. Well she used to be – before she married boring Phil and he made her give up fun, got her into healthy living. I miss old Sasha. All those times you had to pick her up from beach parties, she just refused to come home.'

Margo wasn't really listening as she was trying to alert Carol to her empty champagne glass. 'Mmm, champagne's so lovely,' she said pointedly. Carol resignedly went over to the fridge to get a refill.

'Are you listening to me or baiting poor Carol? It's a bit early for a drink, isn't it?'

Margo could tell Imogen was losing patience. 'It's a celebration, darling! You have to have an engagement party. It'll make me happy. I can sort it all, invite everyone – all you two have to do is show up.'

'I'll speak to Rachel. Hopefully she can talk sense into you. Or Gabe. He's the only one you listen to.'

'Nonsense. You ring your sisters now. Such lovely news finally. Remember to ring Sasha, she needs to come home for this. It's been too long since we all saw her. She might come if you ask her. Let's speak soon about the party.'

Imogen had hung up with a hurried 'Bye'. Unfazed, Margo smiled seductively at Carol. 'Cas, have a glass with me? I'll need my address book – I've no bloody idea where I put it though—' Margo stopped suddenly as she saw Carol pulling on her coat.

Carol looked up from her buttons. 'You told me that I was needed at Sandcove, so I'll be off.' She looked straight at Margo. 'I've loved this family a long time. My heart's breaking for you – having no one here to share this with. I know you're lonely, even if you hide it. I can't celebrate with you though. That girl does not light up around that man – she never has. I've seen you and Richard, I've seen Rachel and Gabriel. I've known nothing like it myself but I know when it's not there.'

Margo held herself very still and straight and made herself meet Carol's eyes. Carol rarely spoke so directly, most of the time trying to keep up the illusion of being a respectful member of 'staff'. Margo kept her voice low. 'You're wrong. There's a deep and long attachment between Imogen and William. It's a happy moment for this family. I don't want us to fall out over this.'

Carol shook her head and patted Margo's arm. 'If you don't have it at the beginning, what hope do you have ten or twenty years later? It's the glue.'

One up to Carol, Margo admitted to herself, as she watched Carol's retreating back.

4

Rizlas and Tobacco

Margo saw the redhead for the first time at The Ship, a few weeks after Imogen got engaged. Leo had called, begging her to cover a Tuesday night shift. He had been left in the lurch by one of 'those bloody useless young'uns'. Leo liked to moan to Margo about the millennials who worked for him. He had no tolerance for their unexplained sickness, their oft-expressed anxiety, and the 'duvet days' they expected as their God-given right.

'Wouldn't know a full day's work if it hit them in the face.'

'Young people aren't lazy. It's just that growing up right now is a bit shit – the world's let them down.' Margo loved young people, because in her heart she still felt she was one of them.

It had been a hot day and so it was busy for a weeknight. Margo understood the need people had to celebrate the longer evenings, they made her restless for company and fun too. Some local boat builders, and three workmen from the Sanderson site were in. Ben, a talented local singer, was in having a quick pint before he headed home to say goodnight to his young family. He and Margo nodded at each other but she could see he wasn't in the mood to chat. Margo's sensitivity to people's moods made her the most popular of the bar staff at The

Ship. She was also often up for mischief and lock-ins, and a good number of the older men appreciated her looks, as did some of the younger ones. She could flirt and was more lenient than most with laddish behaviour, but it was also known in Seaview village that she had removed people from the premises with her bare hands. Margo wasn't sure where the bare hands bit of the rumour had come from but it was useful.

'Ali and I'll be at the Newport gig, Ben. Can't wait.' Margo loved live music and Ben sang the blues. He had a voice that cracked with heartache and longing.

'Cheers, Margo.'

Margo was enjoying a lull, leaning on the dark polished bar and staring out across the view through The Ship's big windows to the Solent. As the pink sunset started to die away she could see the twinkling lights of Portsmouth. Just then Tom Barrison came in with his usual swagger. Wearing a shirt under his blazer that was undone halfway down his chest, but which was pulled tight across the barrel of his stomach, he was also sporting a pair of bright yellow cords. Tom still had a good head of hair, eyes as blue as Margo's and charms that had not yet fully dimmed. He came from one of Seaview's old families and was part of the furniture at the sailing club. He was capable of being a chauvinist dinosaur but he had a fierce intellect, could laugh at himself and was one of the most well-informed people that Margo had ever met. Margo forgave him most things as he made her laugh. They were good old friends, and there was a Seaview rumour that Tom had been one of a handful of local men who had proposed to Margo after Richard O'Leary left her.

Tom leant over the bar and kissed her a bit too close to the mouth, but used to the game, Margo swerved just in time. 'New lippy? Suits you.'

'You're always a sucker for a dark lip. Malbec?'

'Not tonight. I'm still doing this effing juice detox.' Tom's voice carried across the large front bar of The Ship. 'Tomato juice with lashings of Tabasco. Dull.'

'I didn't think you'd last a day.'

'Ali keeps nagging, she wants me to lose some bloody weight. All of this.' Tom clutched with both hands the stomach that protruded from his trousers. 'She's banning sex until I've lost half a stone.'

Margo laughed joyfully. She admired Alison and her wily ways. 'Poor baby. Is Ali coming in?'

'Should be, when I left she still had a few covers to get through.'

Tom's third wife was a talented chef twenty years his junior. Tom had recently bought the Bayview Hotel and controversially had sacked the chef who had been in place for seven years and put Alison in his place. Then he had somehow managed to persuade her to marry him.

Leo moved over to stand with Tom and Margo. The building gang were getting louder and pacing the bar like caged lions. There was back-slapping and calls of 'Cheers mate', 'My round' as they got their fourth pints in. 'I reckon that lot's in for the night.'

Tom tutted. 'It's a bit of a bloody comedown, Duchess. Working in the local. Bet you didn't know she had her own magazine column back in the day, Leo? My first wife was a devoted fan.'

'What was the column about? Clothes and stuff?'

Margo hit Leo on the arm. 'Jesus, Leo! Don't be a sexist idiot. I wrote about whatever I wanted – being a mum of young kids, juggling work, literary London. Trying to have it all—'

Tom interrupted. 'Trying to deal with a husband who kept disappearing to the pub. You were pretty damned loyal about him in print.'

Margo thought about all the effort she had wasted trying to keep

Richard's drinking a secret. She gave Tom a look and turned to Leo. 'So what's new? I went up to London to see Imi for a few days.'

Leo sighed and looked dreamily back at Margo. 'Those Garnett girls. Lookers all of them – brains too. Hard to decide which one I fancy most.'

Margo slapped at Leo's hand on the bar with a beer mat. 'They're not girls any more – women. Strong, independent women.'

'Just like their mum.' Leo reached for the Malbec, poured himself a glass. Margo put her hand over her glass. He lowered his voice to a stage-like whisper. 'The Millars are still fucked off with the Goughs about their dinghy—'

Tom leant in closer. 'Yep, I heard that at the yacht club.'

Margo moved away to serve a young couple who had come in, and the next round to the builders. When she came back she found the two men talking about RIBs, dories and sculls, one of their favourite subjects. Who had something new, where they had got it, how they would like one. Tom looked up at her when she appeared in front of him, and Margo saw that he had that air about him, the air that he was going to tell a Richard story whether she liked it or not.

'Remember that night Rich was wasted and he let go of my dinghy in the surf on St Helen's? We were late-night fishing.'

'It started drifting out to sea. If only he'd been in it.'

The two men laughed as they saw the angry spirit come alight in Margo's blue eyes. She was holding herself straight and wary.

Tom turned to Leo. 'Guess what happened next?' Leo had not known Richard, but had heard the stories. He shook his head, watching Tom expectantly. 'This one dived into the sea. Pitch black. Swam after the dinghy and brought it back.'

Leo looked at Margo with open admiration. 'I'd heard you were a strong swimmer.'

Margo shrugged. 'I had a lot of practice diving into the sea, rescuing things. Especially when Richard O'Leary was around.'

Tom wasn't easily stopped once he had started reminiscing. 'I remember you two when you were just weekenders. You'd ask Maria to babysit and come in here – sat in that corner.' He inclined his head to a dark corner at the back of The Ship's bar, where a couple were twined like ivy around each other, at a table for two.

Margo kept looking at Tom, an unreadable blankness on her face. She hated that part of the pub, the air there was thick with memories. It had once been her and Richard's table. Twenty years later and she would not collect empties from that table. She only had to look at it to see Richard's nicotine-stained fingers, the mess of scattered Rizlas and tobacco, his wallet and probably a beer mat shredded as they talked, red wine pooling on the varnish. She could hear his smoker's laugh, see the way his eyes danced when he looked at her, the way he would sometimes just stare and stare at her. His eyes had changed colour as fast as the sea, from blue to green and back again. Sasha had his eyes.

'Thick as thieves. Everyone knew it was your table. Sinking a lot of wine but talking and talking. You didn't have much time for the rest of us.'

Leo looked at Margo, taking in what Tom had told him. 'It's hard to imagine . . . Now you're always in the middle of everything.'

Margo was thankful to have an excuse to move away again when a young woman appeared at the bar and asked for a Bacardi and Coke. Margo didn't recognise the girl who was in her early twenties and striking, with red hair to her waist and pale freckly skin. She held the change for her drink tight in her hand, the way a child might, and when she tipped it into Margo's outstretched palm the money felt warm and sticky. Margo smiled to try to put her at ease but the young woman looked back sullenly. Her bright inquisitive eyes flicked quickly back and forwards.

'Your change.'

'Thanks.'

Margo couldn't place her accent but the way the girl was looking at her was unnerving. She didn't seem to want to move away, stood looking at Margo's face as if she recognised her.

'Is there anything else?'

The girl's voice was accusatory. 'You live with Gabriel at Sandcove, don't you?'

'No, my daughter Rachel does – his wife. I'm there a lot though. Probably more than I should be!' Margo wondered why she was wittering. 'Do you know Gabriel then?'

The redhead looked at Margo as if she was considering how to answer. 'Yes, we know each other a bit. Nice to meet you.' And she suddenly spun in her trainers and marched to the back of the pub. She sat on her own, facing Margo, looking down from time to time at the iPhone in her lap. The light from it gave the girl's face a spectral glow. Margo wondered how Gabriel knew her, whether she should mention it to him or to Rachel. She moved back to Tom and Leo, trying not to let her concern show.

'Anyone know who that is?'

'Let's just say we noticed her when she came in.' Leo nudged Tom, who chuckled.

'Come on – she's barely in her twenties . . . You dirty old men.'

'But you knew that already!' The two men laughed together in chorus.

Margo felt the familiar pang of unease she always felt when a man she knew ogled a young woman. Her first thought was always for her daughters and what they might have encountered. The second nagging thought shamed her – regret for her own lost youth. It seemed so unfair that no one knew when they were young what power they had. It was one thing to be outraged by wolf whistles and cat calls as a young woman, but quite another as an older woman to face the fact that they were over for good. She was distracted by Alison's arrival. 'Ali!' Margo came out from behind the bar to hug her friend.

'Never comes out from behind the bar for us,' Tom muttered, accepting a kiss on the cheek from his wife. Even in her chef's baggy trousers, and with her hair in a messy bun, Alison was a beauty. Margo believed that the world was divided between women who looked good with messy buns, and those who did not.

'What's new? Diet Coke for me. We're off the hard stuff. I'm sure Tom's been moaning.' She winked at her husband, perched on a bar stool opposite Margo. Margo passed her the Diet Coke and grinned at her.

'I think I've persuaded Imogen to have a party.'

'Hurrah!'

'Can't have been easy for you, Duchess, them being in Venice. I remember Rich telling me about your honeymoon and how you didn't leave the hotel room for twenty-four hours.'

'Tom, shut up.' Margo's glare was a warning he had gone too far.

Alison looked warily between Margo and Tom. In the hush that followed, everyone heard the redhead stand up suddenly and shout at her phone, 'You dick!' Her face flushed with anger as she ran out of the pub. The heavy door slammed behind her with a gust of wind off the sea.

Tom turned to them with a grin. 'Clearly a bunny boiler!'

Ignoring him, Margo checked the clock by instinct. 'Last orders!' she called.

'I'll have a Diet Coke for the road,' Tom smiled appeasingly at his wife.

Margo shook off thoughts of the girl and allowed herself to finally check her phone. She had been pretending to herself all evening that she wasn't waiting for a text. One had arrived. *Are we on?* If she did last orders fast, and sweet-talked Leo into locking up, she could be home in less than an hour. She'd have to think of a reason to explain her rush to Leo or he would get suspicious. She could say she was expecting a call from one of the girls. Another message: *I want you.*

One hour, she texted back.

5

Hot Stuff

Margo had woken up ravenous, as she always did after lots of sex. Biting into a slice of toast and marmalade, she looked out at her garden, thinking about the work that needed to be done. She could see that one of her roses had come loose from the trellis in the night and would need to be tied back. There had been angry winds and rain and, now that everything had died away, the world seemed quiet and still. Margo imagined the sea was glassy, the perfect mirror for the sky. She thought of Sandcove and whether there would be damage, as there often was during storms, loose tiles or a new leak. Drake and Juno, her Border terriers, appeared at her heels. Lovingly they licked her bare feet, pushing their cold noses under her silk dressing gown.

'Go on then,' she said, flinging open the French doors that led to the garden. The dogs bounced out with wagging tails. The wind blew in the familiar briny sea smell she loved. She greedily breathed in a lungful of air as a colony of seagulls lifted off a nearby cottage roof. Keeling and screeching, their cries overhead were the sound of home. She just wished she could see the sea from her cottage. At Sandcove every morning she had woken to the sea through her bedroom window, her own window onto the world. The vast sky over the sea had so many moods, sudden or subtle changes, it was easier to understand her own quixotic moods against its backdrop.

It was a good morning though and nothing could dim her spirits. She felt as young as a teenager. Probably because her whole body still hummed from the orgasm she had only half an hour ago. She marvelled at the strength of the aftershocks. It had been the kind of orgasm that felt like it had rewired her. Some disappointing orgasms stayed in the groin, but this one had reached out from her core, spreading to all her nerve endings, to her fingertips, her toes, even her hair follicles. Jack had fallen straight back asleep but she knew he would need to leave soon and she was already preparing for that, planning distractions to fill the rest of her day. She needed to call Sandcove, see how Rachel's hearing had gone, her night out with friends in London.

She called up the stairs to Jack. 'It's eight. Time to get in the shower. Can I make you something?'

A voice muffled by duvet called back, 'Coffee.'

Margo smiled to herself and crossed to her kitchen, switched the kettle on, reached for her phone.

Gabriel answered, 'Margo.'

'Smart arse.'

'You always call this time on a Saturday.'

'You're making me sound predictable.'

'Just a bit.'

'How was the hearing?'

'The judge agreed there'd been abuse – the husband is now a "restrained person".'

'These bloody men . . . good. Did she have fun?'

'Cocktails in Soho, the works – Garnett style. I'm not sure she's been to bed – she was on an early train to Portsmouth. I told her to have a nap, she was green. Come over later for dinner?'

Margo could hear Lizzie or Hannah crying in the background. She thought, once again, what a model of a modern male Gabriel was. She knew that Rachel hated it when she praised Gabriel for sharing childcare, being a hands-on parent, that for Rachel's generation it was expected. But Margo's father had been a shadowy figure who was always at the office, and Richard had been terrified of domestic drudgery, and had run away whenever he could. 'I'll be there. What are we making?'

Margo climbed the stairs with a mug of coffee for Jack and set it noisily on the bedside table. Jack did not stir. His black curls snaked across the pillow. Margo loved to see his curls wild, before he tamed them with wax. She thought he used too much hair product and told him so. She waited for him to open his eyes which were the colour of bracken in autumn. She wanted to slip out of her silk and climb in beside him, press her whole nakedness against him, feel him stir and grow hard, start the whole dance all over again. But she would have to wait.

'Jack — you need to go home. I have things to do.'

Finally he moved, propped himself up in the bed, yawned and stretched. 'Woman! Let a man rest. You wore me out.'

Margo rang a fingertip across one of the tendons in his arm. 'I doubt it.'

Jack grinned at her. 'Where are you off to? Come back and shag me instead.'

Margo had to move quickly as he made a grab for her. 'Shouldn't you be going?' Margo didn't ever ask directly but she guessed that Jack's wife must be visiting family on the mainland. He rarely stayed overnight. She saw his eyes skip over hers at the question. He pushed the covers aside, and she turned her head so he wouldn't see the effect he had on her. She didn't want him to know how much she wanted to keep him here in her bed.

'Okay woman, I'm going. I wouldn't say no to a bacon sarnie.'

That evening, when Margo arrived at Sandcove, she came through the back door, which was always open. She paused in the boot room, her eyes falling on the expensive Barbour Richard had rarely worn, hanging on the iron coat hooks along the wall. Somehow it had escaped her ruthless clear-out. She sat down for a minute on the oak settle that had been abandoned there, along with other bits of furniture Rachel didn't want. Margo had bought the jacket for Richard somewhere stiff in Jermyn Street, the kind of shop he wouldn't have been seen dead in. It had been one of her attempts to get him to embrace island life, to wear something other than his moth-eaten velvet jacket or the hideous cracked leather jacket that stank of pubs. He'd looked at her like she was mad when she'd presented it to him and then worn it a handful of times to make her happy. She closed her eyes and let the familiar smell of the room remind her of happier times, excited children about to go out into the snow; flippers and masks flung down, squeals as wet swimming costumes were peeled off. In summer there was always a gritty coating of sand on the floor and in winter it smelt of the wood stacked in the corner for the fire. Slowly she stood up and turned her back on the jacket.

Gabriel stood in the middle of the kitchen, wearing an apron and holding a carving fork as if he was about to conduct with it. He smiled at Margo and it was a smile that reached his eyes. He was one of the few men Margo thought could carry off an apron. The one he was wearing said 'Hot Stuff' on it with a picture of a chilli pepper underneath. It had been her Christmas present to him; that same year he had given her a 'Queen Bee' apron. They teased each other and they

48

argued, Gabriel asked her personal questions or about the past, the way few else dared to. They understood each other and each knew that Rachel and the children were the priority that ruled their friendship. As Gabriel welcomed her into the kitchen, they began to move around each other with their perfect choreography. Rachel teased them, calling them 'the old married couple', but their partnership mostly suited her as she hated cooking. There was something about the ease of Margo and Gabriel's domestic chemistry which soothed and calmed Margo. She was her best self, relaxed and funny. Rachel and Imogen loved to pull up high stools at the oak island and watch the magic they made. Colourful bowls from the Bonchurch pottery would slowly fill with jewel-like ingredients in front of their eyes. Margo and Gabriel agreed on the importance of presentation, although Gabriel left the table settings to Margo who loved to get her grandchildren to write and colour in name place cards, collect flowers from the garden to display, or even scatter petals. They would be allowed to choose from Margo's collection of tablemats and tablecloths, still stored in the blue Welsh dresser at Sandcove. Knowing their mother's love of table decoration, each Christmas her daughters gave her glasses – gold goblets, crystal champagne flutes etched with flowers, tumblers in bright colours, shot glasses with gold rims.

That evening it was just the three of them for supper. Gabriel had fed and bathed Lizzie and Hannah and as it was a Saturday they were allowed a film. Rachel was up in her home office trying to catch up on work. Gabriel had started an Ottolenghi dish which was one of his staples and together he and Margo added the finishing touches while sharing a bottle of rosé.

'Now Imogen's engaged, can't you relax a bit? Take a step back – let the girls get on with things?'

Margo saw that Gabriel was half teasing her and decided to ignore the question. She picked up a battered orange Le Creuset casserole dish from her days at Sandcove and brandished it at him. 'What do you want to do with this squash? You should invest in some new cookware – this is ancient.' Margo set the dish down with a clatter, as if it had offended her. 'It doesn't go either.' With an arm sweep Margo indicated the state-of-the-art steel kitchen. She had not been able to hide how much she disapproved of the modern kitchen, the one thing Gabriel and Rachel had changed at Sandcove.

'It needs roasting – bottom oven. You know your daughters can't let go of the past. They hold on to things for sentimental reasons. Like old Le Creuset. I'm always falling over the past in this house. We might be able to make some changes if—'

'Is it possible to have a conversation with you without it turning into a therapy session? If I wanted therapy I'd pay for it.'

With a knowing smile, Gabriel took the dish from Margo and put it in the oven. 'When Richard left, you should've talked to someone. The girls wouldn't have suffered as much if you had. Losing a father was one thing, but losing you too . . . It's not too late to talk to someone now.'

'Everything's fine in this family.' Margo turned and moved away, still carrying her glass. 'I am going to check on my grandchildren.'

Gabriel heard squeals of happiness from the den. Margo's voice higher, softer, and her peals of laughter. 'You'll be back when you need a refill!' he called after her.

It did not take her long to reappear in the kitchen. 'That new *Jungle Book* is too scary for Lizzie.' She held her glass out to him imperiously.

'She doesn't really watch it, but she wants to do everything Hannah does.'

'Imogen was like that with Rachel.' Margo had a clear memory of Imogen at ten or eleven, refusing to get her hair cut, wanting it to be as long as Rachel's. Gabriel moved to the fridge to fetch the bottle. He heard his phone vibrate and went over to look, pushing his dark hair off his forehead. Margo watched him, waiting impatiently for her wine. Gabriel's phone vibrated again.

'Why does your phone keep doing that? Rachel's upstairs, isn't she?'

Gabriel turned the phone over and turned back to the sauce that was bubbling on the stove. 'We've had some enquiries today – just Sarah letting me know.'

'I thought the practice was full?'

'Pretty much, but Sarah's hoping I could see one more client on Tuesday mornings – she's full.'

Margo put down her glass. 'What about school drop-off?' She saw him clench his jaw and realised he was annoyed.

'I do drop-off every morning – is there no way you could help out one morning a week? You're right on the doorstep.'

'I'm hopeless in the mornings. And selfish. I did say when I gave you Sandcove that just because I was up the hill didn't mean I would be hands-on—'

'Okay – I don't need a lecture.'

Margo frowned at Gabriel's tone, but continued to hover close to him. His phone vibrated again. Gabriel moved to it, pressed the screen. Before he could swipe, Margo caught a glimpse of a text message that was just three fire emojis in a row. 'Who the hell is telling you you're hot?'

Gabriel laughed loudly. 'It's Jonny. Trying to tell me about some girl he's met – he thinks she's fit.'

'Jonny's fit,' Margo said solemnly, intending to make Gabriel laugh.

'Margo!' Gabriel lightened his voice, pretending to be shocked. But Margo's crush on Jonny was an open family secret. Jonny was Gabriel's oldest friend. They had both started boarding school together aged six, both far too young to be sent away from home. Gabriel, shy and sad at the separation from the mother he idolised, immediately gravitated towards Jonny's boundless enthusiasm and bravado. Both boys were handsome, one dark, the other blond. Jonny was usually competitive with everyone he met, but with Gabriel he felt an almost instant brotherly bond and they became inseparable allies. Jonny had confided in Margo how he struggled at home as an only child under the dictatorship of a father who undermined him, pushing him constantly to be more 'manly'. Margo thought Jonny's mother could have helped him more; instead she seemed to put being a devoted wife before being a mother to Jonny. Funny, clever but lost, Jonny had gravitated to the Garnetts when Gabriel started his love affair with Rachel and he found his natural place amid the boisterousness of a big family.

Jonny remained a regular visitor at Sandcove and flirted with everyone but most brazenly with Margo. She had had sexy dreams about him during his visits, and sometimes it was hard to look him in the eye for a few days afterwards. She hid her lust badly by teasing him, and they sometimes sat at the kitchen table after the others were in bed, indulging in a ping-pong match of wit and whisky. Jonny often said that if he had had a home as happy as Sandcove he would never leave. They all knew that Margo was a large part of the attraction Sandcove held for Jonny, as was Imogen whom he tended to like a little sister, and Sasha whom he treated warily as his equal, and who was the one person who was capable of riling him.

For a brief time Margo had worried that Sasha and Jonny were falling for each other; there was a summer when no one missed the glances between them, the long walks they took. It hadn't come to anything and Sasha had met Phil and got married so quickly. Now they all had to endure Jonny's parade of saucer-eyed, waifish girls. The girls seemed as surprised as Jonny was to find themselves visiting Sandcove, where they would then be left to fend for themselves. Margo would declare them 'hopeless', too vapid and keen to please, and unable to drink more than half a glass of white wine, or eat more than a lettuce leaf. Of course she desperately wanted Jonny to find the right girl while being secretly relieved that he hadn't yet, and grateful that none of her daughters had fallen under his spell.

'It's okay for me to fancy him,' she said to Rachel once. 'But imagine if you'd fallen for him. You might have chosen him over Gabe.'

'You taught me to be sensible about men,' Rachel had replied drily. 'Poor Jonny, he likes to think he is some sort of playboy but anyone can see that once he finds the right woman of spirit, he'll be her devoted slave.'

Margo pulled herself out of her Jonny reverie, hearing her oldest daughter galloping down the wooden staircase that ran like the main artery all the way through Sandcove. Rachel did everything with spirit and it reminded Margo with a pang of all the energy she used to have. Rachel swept in, her long dark hair pinned high on her head, her pallor and the dark smudges under her eyes doing little to distract from the symmetry of her face, her poise. She wound her arms around her mother. Margo rarely initiated hugs but she would accept them as her due from time to time.

'Well, Ma. We can't tease you or call you Mrs Bennett any more! All the Garnett girls soon to be married off, not a spinster among us.'

'Very amusing, daughter. Have some wine. I've already had a bit. Lizzie wanted you earlier, she said only you would do. I said you were working and not to be interrupted but that you'd give her lots of cuddles and stories at bedtime.'

Rachel pulled up one of the stools. 'Poor girls, I've neglected them today. Lizzie's going through a clingy phase. I'll need to make it up to them tomorrow.' She took a big sip of the wine Gabriel had poured for her, steeled herself. 'Imogen doesn't want a party.'

'It's William who doesn't – I know it. He and his mother can't deal with parties. They stand in the corner, drives me mad.'

Margo saw Gabriel and Rachel exchange looks and watched Rachel shake her head. 'You can't be mean about William – you're the one who's pushed them together.'

Margo pulled up a stool next to Rachel. 'All I did was suggest they move things on – come on, he's been hanging around for ages. He'll be a good husband. Just no use at parties.'

'What if she wants a very bad husband?' Gabriel asked with a smirk as he started to slide bowls across to them.

Margo stood up to refill her glass and began to pace. 'I had a bad husband – I wouldn't recommend it. Imogen has always been the sensitive one – you know she needs someone kind. She's finally getting some attention for her plays . . . William'll support her – he'll be there at home when she gets back late from rehearsals. I can't see him being jealous, or worried about cooking a simple meal or—'

Rachel interrupted. 'Don't you worry that Imogen's marrying him just to please you? To feel safe?'

'She lost her father at six. Of course she wants to feel safe.'

Both women ignored Gabriel and Margo gave Rachel the full beam of her piercing eyes, the blue of summer seas. 'Those aren't the worst reasons for getting married. Come on – let's eat.'

There was the patter of small feet on the flagstones and Lizzie appeared, her long nightgown trailing the floor. The adults all turned to her and she looked shyly at the ground, pressing her bunny against her cheek. Margo's curls had skipped a generation but there they were on Lizzie, bouncy and wild. Margo found it unsettling at times, this mirror image of her childhood, triggering old Sandcove memories of her and her sister Alice. 'Mama, don't like tiger.'

Rachel got up and went over to Lizzie and scooped her up in her arms. 'Silly tiger. Let's go and read *Guess How Much I Love You.*'

Margo turned back to Gabriel and her food. 'There's gossip from the village. Those weekenders the Bradburys are adding another floor to their house – there's going to be drilling and works for months. The Hewitts are up in arms.'

Rachel paused on her way out of the kitchen, raising an eyebrow. 'Weren't we once weekenders?'

6

We Are Family

'It's okay for some. I never got an engagement party.' Sasha's voice was loud and several people turned to look at her. It was the hushed beginning of the party when guests were spread out awkwardly, waiting to see who would arrive, what would happen next. The room encouraged reverence with its polished parquet floor, mirrored bar and low velvet armchairs in jewel-like colours. Expectations would be high. Margo's parties were always a riot.

'You didn't want one.'

Sasha could see her and Imogen's reflections refracted across several mirrors. Sasha's hand stole up to the nape of her neck. Margo had gasped when she had seen her new pixie cut, the white blonde feathers of hair. Sasha had enjoyed shocking them all. As sisters they had always had their long hair in common. Growing up they had looked like ship's figureheads, with hair loose to their hip bones. Sasha watched as Imogen plucked at the clingy material of her dress and then turned her back on her reflection. She looked uncomfortable, and for a fleeting moment Sasha felt sorry for her.

'How do you know I didn't want one? Rachel said you didn't want any of this but Margo bulldozed ahead. Because you're the favourite. Let me guess – Margo chose your dress. It's not very you, is it? It doesn't even look finished.' Sasha looked back at her own reflection, the tailored black jumpsuit and spiky black heels with their flash of red sole. Tonight Jonny had stopped in his tracks when he saw her, turned away from the girl on his arm just to look at her. Phil had been seething beside her, but she had ignored the energy coming off him, smiling provocatively at Jonny. Phil was always jealous about something or nothing and he was going to be angry this evening whatever she did. He hadn't wanted to come, hated the claims her family made on her. The only child of divorced parents, his upbringing had been insecure and lonely. He didn't understand siblings or ever feel comfortable in large Garnett parties or gatherings. He was happiest when he could have her to himself. At the beginning of their relationship the intensity of his desire had been flattering, had convinced her his love was the real deal.

'Where's Phil? Usually he's stuck to your side.'

Sasha had been looking forward to a moment alone with Imogen but they had fallen into their usual sisterly pattern, sniping at each other. Sasha knew she should be kinder but the weight of the secrets she was carrying felt oppressive when she was around her family. She already had a tension headache. 'Somewhere avoiding Margo? He's in a foul mood because we're staying here tonight. It's costing us a fortune for a room the size of a coffin. He hates this place, says it's overpriced and pretentious. You know how he is about "arty" types.'

'I did say you could stay at mine.'

'With Margo and you getting soppy going over old memories and drinking whisky? No thanks. That's the thing about being off the booze, parties are fucking boring after ten p.m.'

'You were more fun when you drank.'

Sasha ignored Imogen, feeling Phil's eyes back on her. She scanned the room and saw him scowling in the doorway. 'I need to go and look after Phil.' A group of guests suddenly rushed across the room, forming a tight circle around Imogen, their voices going off like fireworks. Sasha had always hated Imogen's RADA gang, the way they all tried so hard to appear Bohemian, the way they projected their sing-song voices.

'Where is the lucky man? Where are you hiding him?'

'Your mother's such a character. She's had us all in stitches.'

'She's such a party girl.'

'Wow, you look sensational.'

'Don't think I've ever seen you in a frock before, Imi, hot stuff!'

Sasha caught Imogen's eye and inclined her head to tell her she was slipping away. Sasha wondered where William was, he should be by Imogen's side. Imogen wasn't Sasha's responsibility but even so, Sasha hated to leave her sister with that hunted look in her eyes. There had been a brief time as teenagers when their friendship groups on the island overlapped and they had gone to parties together. Imogen had always wanted to borrow Sasha's clothes, which hadn't suited her, and she had stuck to Sasha's side like a limpet. Sasha had done all she could to shake Imogen off so she could snog boys, wear their jumpers and smoke their weed. Her happiest teenage moments had been spent on beaches huddled in some boy's jumper, looking hazily into the embers of a fire. Beer bottles littered across the sand, shouts and splashes from the sea as drunk boys went skinny-dipping. Imogen had ruined Sasha's cred with the local boys, her elongated vowels reminding them all that the sisters were from the big house, from the Garnett family, the family without a father. The one with the mother who wrote for magazines. Sasha looked around the room for Margo, anger flaring up. It was easy to blame Margo for most things and the engagement party had been a typically selfish act. Sasha saw William at the bar, his back to the party, chatting to Gabriel. As she picked her way carefully across the shiny floor, trying not to slide in her heels, she caught Jonny's eye again. There was trouble there if she wanted it.

'What the hell are you two doing? William, get out there and help her. You can't just hide at the bar.'

Gabriel jumped in, hearing the edge in Sasha's voice. 'Imi will be happier if there's dancing. All the Garnett girls love to dance. William, go and rescue her from the luvvies and do a couple of circuits of the room – then we can get the real party started.'

William set his drink down carefully on the bar, resigned. 'Okay, here I go. Into the fray.'

Sasha tutted at William's retreating back. 'He's like an obedient Labrador.'

Gabriel threw his head back and laughed. 'You Garnetts are all so mean about William – he's a nice bloke. Why are you grumpy? I love the new hair – you look like a goddess. I see Jonny's noticed.'

Sasha looked up into Gabriel's green eyes, feeling the warm glow of his attention. 'Phil doesn't want to be here.'

'He'll warm up – I'll go cheer him up. Rach says you're coming for the family weekend? I'm really happy. We don't get to see you enough. Rachel misses you. Please just try not to fight with Margo?'

Sasha looked away. 'Why does she do it? These grand gestures. Force us all together and make stupid speeches.'

'God knows. Trying to make up for you not having a father?'

'She can never make up for that.'

A few hours later and the Margo liggers and hangers-on were drifting back into the Soho night. Sasha had moved through them that evening, greeting the ones she remembered, catching glimpses of what her father might have been like in the colourful collection of poets and ageing hacks. They all looked older than Margo, the late nights drinking and smoking etched on their faces. Neglect hung in the creases of their old tailored suits. Sasha had turned her back on the world of letters, but still she felt the pull of this rabble, the seediness. Many had known Margo and Richard when their table at the French House was the one to cluster round. Growing up, there had not been a lot of stories about her absent father; her mother refused to talk about him, and Sasha eagerly soaked up any tales she overheard. Tonight she stayed vigilant, eager for the crumbs sometimes dropped when Margo was out of earshot.

At her eighteenth birthday she had overheard someone telling a group of listeners about the time a drunk Richard had decided to serenade Margo from the top of a tree, and had fallen out of it, breaking a leg. At a Sandcove Christmas party, Tom had told the story of Richard buying everyone in the pub a drink, the night of his and Margo's wedding anniversary. These stories were precious parts of Sasha's identity. She was always left wanting more, and with the Soho crowd she wanted to creep out of the shadows and ask a million questions about Richard. If she could understand the way Richard had once been, then maybe she could understand why she did not fit in. Tonight she only heard one thing, caught on the air, just a whisper. A little bent old man, in the strange combination of a cravat and leather jacket, said, 'He just disappeared. The poems stopped too. They were all about Margo, so people say once he left her, he couldn't write any more. Such a waste.' Sasha locked the whisper away safely to treasure later.

The party thinned out again and suddenly there was room to breathe. Just the Garnetts and their close tribe were left now. Sasha loitered by the dance floor, Phil standing sentry, and smiled as she watched her aunt Alice letting her hair down and enjoying a few cocktails. Alice was one of the few people whose advice Sasha would take. She loved this new incarnation of Margo's sister, now she had finally got rid of Uncle Seb. Alice had once been a browbeaten wife – a peahen next to Margo's peacock. Her marriage to Seb had been a long, slow and mostly separate one; then he retired from the bench and no longer had the excuse to spend the weeks up in London. The cracks had widened and Alice had faced the fact that she had married a bully. Eventually Sasha and Margo, united for once, had convinced Alice to ask for a divorce; she lost her Bembridge house, but gained a new life running a bookshop on the green, something she had always dreamt of doing. As single women Margo and Alice had become close again, back to the way they had been before sixteen-year-old Margo had run away from home.

Sasha had hung out for a while at the party with Alice's twenty-something twins Evie and Lucas until they had disappeared into the main part of the club to find the famous smoking terrace. Jonny had told them there was a whole gang of 'gorgeous' fashion students out there squeezed onto each other's laps and a band from Manchester that was just about to 'make it big'. Jonny seemed to be coming and going constantly, and every time she saw him their eyes snagged on each other, with an unspoken invitation from him to disappear into a wilder night, just the two of them. She kept avoiding him and he had left the party and then reappeared with two new girls following behind him. They were giggling over the celebrities they had spotted in the downstairs bar. Jonny had started the dancing in front of Sasha, dancing badly with both girls at once. Sasha had tried not to smile, aware of Phil there with his arm draped possessively across her shoulders, watching her.

'Why have you got so much red lipstick on?'

'Don't you like it?'

'It's a bit slutty. Why can't you just dress like everyone else – wear a dress like your sisters?' He looked her up and down.

Sasha swallowed down all the things she wanted to say. 'Dance with me?' She watched Phil shake his head. He never danced now he had stopped drinking. Gabriel had asked the DJ to turn up the volume and Sasha could feel the bass reverberating inside her, the rhythm pulling her. Her hips started to sway as she watched Rachel slide onto the floor, cheers going up all around. Imogen followed onto the floor holding hands with Margo, whose dress swept the ground regally. There was pure joy on Margo's face. However different the Garnett women were, they all loved to dance. Their childhood had been filled with kitchen discos at Sandcove where they would leap and twirl together. Sasha could only remember love and laughter in those moments. 'We Are Family' came on, requested by Gabriel, and Sasha gave Phil a reckless shrug and followed her sisters into the middle of the dance floor with a whoop. She felt wild spirits blowing up inside her, the memories of so many nights, the raves and the drugs, being lost yet free. She grinned openly at her family, for the first time happy, her hand moving out to take Rachel's. They were a pack again, the four women. They all danced so differently. Sasha knew she was like a marionette, all jerky movements. But she threw herself into it. Imogen was self-conscious, smiling shyly. Margo swayed elegantly to the music while keeping a beady eye on what was going on around her. Rachel had been a gymnast as a child, the only one who could do cartwheels and the splits. Her dancing was eye-catching and sexy and Sasha smiled to herself when she caught Gabriel watching his wife. They moved together, united in that moment, wreathed in smiles, letting the spectators see them in all their glory.

Then the song ended and so did the moment. Rachel and Gabriel began to slow dance, and soon they had the floor to themselves. They looked like they were in a Hollywood movie. In the early days, Sasha had felt that she and Phil had a marriage that might rival her older sister's perfect partnership. They had fun and a shared love of travel and adventure. He believed in her work, and even started working for the same charity so he could follow her around the world. He had made it clear that the position, some way down the hierachy from her director role, was beneath him, but that he would take the job so that they did not have to overcome a long-distance marriage. Now, though, something in their relationship was being eroded. She knew it must be her fault; Phil said she ruined most things, drove people away. She needed to find her husband and try to appease him, otherwise a whole night in a tiny room with him would be an ordeal. The silence like a suffocating blanket, the steady drip of throwaway comments about her selfishness, her awful behaviour. If she had been drinking she would have become the bad fairy, stalking through the party like everyone's worst nightmare, embarrassing Phil. They had agreed to give up together and he kept her on the straight and narrow, reminding her of all the foolish things she did when she drank. He had moved away while she had been dancing, making his disapproval known. Sasha went over to Alice, who had sat down for a moment in a low velvet chair and had kicked off her heels. Sasha knelt beside her.

'Too much dancing, and these silly shoes. Margo persauded me to wear them, God knows how you all glide around in them, they're killing me.'

'Just dance barefoot.'

'It's not the beach, Sasha. Are you okay? You look tired, beautiful but tired.' Alice reached a hand out to touch Sasha's hair. 'This is so chic, how did Margo take it?'

'I haven't given her a chance to say anything.'

Alice moved an arm around Sasha's shoulder. 'Oh, you two. I wish you would talk. Margo misses you so much, sweetheart. This silence and stubborness between you needs to end, it's upsetting the whole family.'

Sasha patted Alice's hand and stood up. 'Today's all about Imi. I need to be good and quiet and know my place. And I need to find Phil, have you seen him?'

Alice shook her head, a crease of worry on her forehead. 'Is everything okay with you and Phil? He had a face like thunder before, he couldn't make it more obvious he doesn't want to be here and you seem so on edge.'

'Phil's fine, he's just grumpy, he hates crowds.' Sasha gave her aunt a weak smile as she moved away. As she crossed the room looking for Phil she heard noise from the fire escape, where the smokers were all gathered. Sasha stepped out there and took a cigarette from the pack Jonny wordlessly held out to her, having first checked that Phil was not within eyeshot.

Jonny smiled at her as she fumbled nervously with his Zippo. 'Naughty cigarette time?'

'I need something. Not drinking is fucking hard.'

Jonny's voice was husky and low, close to her ear. 'Just get back on it. I miss drunk Sasha. So much.'

'I'm sure you do.' She gave him a quick look from underneath her lashes, saw on his face what he was thinking, what he wanted. They had drunkenly snogged at a few parties, before and after Phil. No one knew. As far as Margo was concerned, Jonny was out of bounds for her daughters. At the beginning this made him even more appealing to Sasha. Now, if she was honest, it was about something much more than baiting her mother. Sasha wasn't proud of what she had done but when she was with Jonny she wanted to be bad. His hand brushed hers and she knew it wasn't an accident. Sasha took a step away from Jonny, not wanting Gabriel to notice the tension between them. Gabriel's good opinion mattered to her. The crowd outside was rowdy and excited, refusing to accept that the evening was winding down. Jonny had smuggled out bottles of champagne and was passing them around.

'God, Margo is putting it away,' Gabriel slung an arm around her. 'Imi might need to bundle her into a taxi soon. I can't see William getting to go home with Imi tonight if she's got Margo in tow.'

'Poor guy – the night of his engagement party. Shouldn't he be getting some?'

Sasha's eyes had adjusted to the dark on the fire escape and saw that Imogen, Phil and William were talking in a quiet threesome down on the next landing. She quickly dropped her cigarette.

'Shut it, Jonny. They're just down there.'

She descended carefully, not wanting to get a heel stuck in the metal mesh of the stairs. Imogen looked up and a smile broke over her face, as if she was set on making up for their squabble before. She was drunk. Sasha looked at Phil who was not making eye contact with her and went and snaked an arm around his waist. She made her voice falsely bright, smiled at them all.

'Imi – I'm so happy for you. It's great being married.' Sasha looked up at Phil and he leant over and stamped a hard kiss on her lips. She knew he had not forgiven her. This was his way of showing his ownership, aware of Jonny watching from above.

'Guys, it's an awesome thing when you find your partner for life. Even if they do turn out to be a total handful,' Phil added.

'Thanks, that's lovely.' Imogen's voice slurred a bit. 'It's amazing you came home for the party. Can't wait for this weekend. Only two sleeps.'

Phil smiled coldly. 'I don't know what any of you see in that old house. It's always bloody freezing. No one seems to notice that it's falling apart. Why do old English families live in tumbling-down houses and waste all their money on parties like this one instead of repairs? I thought Gabriel and Rachel might splash some cash. All they've done is put in that chef's kitchen which seems way over the top. Once you've lived in Australia, it's hard to see the appeal of an English beach.'

William loyally moved closer to Imogen. 'I love the island beaches.'

Phil ignored William. 'Let's hope Margo isn't going to be a nightmare this weekend.'

Sasha saw Imogen's hurt expression. 'It's hard, Imi, Margo never makes Phil feel welcome. And all the pointless rules. Breakfast at this time, drinks at six. It's like stepping back into the Edwardian era.'

'It's just not true, she loves having you both. We hardly ever get to see you.'

'You are so sentimental when you're drunk. You and Margo are exactly the same.'

'Please come for Christmas.'

'We're waiting to see what time off we get. We have some dialogues coming up in Palestine at the end of the year. If we get a couple of days we'll try.'

William smiled politely. 'We can't do that bonkers swim without you, Sasha, you're the bravest.'

The Priory Bay Boxing Day swim and BBQ was a Sandcove tradition started by their father. Sasha had no memory of her father swimming, but there was a photo somewhere of Richard on the beach, his skinny white legs disappearing into the sea. Sasha had no idea why Margo had kept the tradition up when almost everything else about Richard had been ripped out of their lives. 'You just have to get on with it, otherwise Margo crows,' she said running her hands through her short hair. 'Remember last year we raced back and I won – Margo was so pissed off. She needs to face the fact that she's an old lady now. It's embarrassing the way she goes on pretending she's as young as we are. And all that shagging around – as if none of us knows anything about it.' Sasha felt a shift in the air and looked up as William turned pale. Margo stood at the top of the fire escape looking down at them. Imogen grabbed Sasha's arm to stop her saying any more and then all she could see was Margo's back.

'God – did she hear?'

Imogen narrowed her eyes. 'Looks like it. You're such a bitch, Sasha.'

William turned to Imogen. 'Imi, you should go to her. I think I might head home to mine. Is that okay? Margo'll want to sit up drinking whisky. I'm sure she'd much rather have you to herself.'

Imogen's voice was sharp. 'Poor old Ma. She's taking a battering from you lot. William, just go home – I'm happy to do Margo duty. After all, she has just spent a fortune on this party for us.'

Sasha watched as Imogen wobbled up the steps with William trailing behind, his head bent. No one said goodbye to each other. She could feel Phil's silence beside her like a physical thing. She attempted a joking tone. 'William's in trouble now.'

Phil looked disgusted with her. 'You're not even drunk and you've upset everyone.'

'You were saying stuff about Margo too—'

'Not so she could hear. Now she's going to sulk all weekend. You'll have to make it up.'

'Fine, I'll try to talk to her at Sandcove.'

'You should tell her what you know too.'

'I can't. I don't want to – she'll hate me.'

Phil's voice was scornful. 'You're hardly her favourite child now. If you don't do it, I'll do it for you. I mean it. I'm sick of it – it's all you think about, all you talk about. I'm going. Are you coming?'

Sasha knew she couldn't stay, knew it wasn't being offered as an option. Her voice was meek. 'Yes, I'm coming.'

Two For One

Isle of Wight

Sasha always woke early at Sandcove. The morning sunshine lit up her old bedroom through the white muslin curtains. Margo had not been the kind of mother who invested in blackout blinds and thick curtains to help her children to sleep. She felt children had to adapt to their surroundings, not the other way around. There was never a stairgate and sometimes a child had tumbled down a flight of stairs, but mostly they had learnt to go slowly. Richard had fallen down those stairs more often than the children. The orchestra of noises of home woke Sasha early too. Old pipes clanked as they came awake. Every summer someone suggested that the boiler be replaced before it packed up that winter, but every time it hung on for just one more year. Outside there would be the whirr of a motor, the chug of a boat. The seagulls, their different types of call, the staccato bursts and then the long 'keeee-oh', high-pitched and plaintive. Sailboat cables hitting their masts with a clang, halyards flapping. All of it filled Sasha with nostalgia, that sense of anticipation about the day ahead, the desperate need to get out onto the stretch of sand outside Sandcove. She missed the girl she had been, when she had liked herself and woken up unfettered by her disappointment, by the secret she knew and the wall that it made between her and her family.

When she had gone to bed, her mother had been in full extravagant hostess mode, taking charge of Sandcove as if it was still hers. She had been holding court to the Barrisons, Leo and Alice. Rachel, her face pinched and tired, had barely been able to look at Margo. Sasha wondered how late her mother had stayed up in the end, ignoring Rachel's hints. Once upon a time Sasha would have been drinking and arguing with Margo, also in trouble for encouraging her to stay up late. Rachel had told Margo to move the party to her own house but Margo never listened when she was in her cups. Imogen had been in tears, she always got upset when Rachel and Margo went head to head. And Phil had been gruff and distant at dinner, and had slipped away to bed early.

Sasha heard a voice out on the beach and she lifted herself up on her elbows, trying not to disturb Phil who was lying in the single bed pushed up against hers. She drew the curtain to one side, looking out to the sea glittering in the bright sunshine. She started to peel back the covers slowly when her phone vibrated with a text: *No. 47 15 mins?* She typed back *Yes*. Sliding off the bed, she hurried into skinny jeans and an old Breton T-shirt of Rachel's she had borrowed and never given back. Its frayed cotton softness was comforting. Pushing a pair of huge dark glasses on her head she opened the door, knowing exactly how far she could open it before it creaked, glancing back to make sure Phil still slept on, then shut it gently behind her. She could feel a few hours' freedom beckoning her, a chance to shrug off Phil's gloomy presence. She resisted the urge to take the stairs two at a time but as soon as her feet hit the red tiles of the ground floor she flew out of the front door, a habit she had kept from childhood.

From the sea wall she ran down the slipway and onto the sand, taking her flip-flops off, feeling it squelch cold and wet between her toes, sighing out loud with the pleasure of it. She looked back up at Sandcove which rose above her, its Edwardian double-fronted facade slightly crumbling around the edges, patches of white paint peeling from window ledges. It wasn't a beautiful house, but it had a friendly face, with its lower half clad in red brick, and its upper half criss-crossed with mock timber, triple-paned windows reflecting back sky and sea. It stood detached and imposing, with its symmetry still, its majestic chimney, and it was the house in the bay that was nearest to Priory woods. Sasha sometimes thought that it looked like a town house that had been picked up by a tornado and set down in a wilder place than it was used to. At the back of the house was a wild garden, a children's paradise, with a swing in the old oak, and the perimeter marked by delicate silver birch, and hills behind. There was a decked terrace at the front built over an open boat store, where the jumble of kayaks, dinghies and fishing nets gave the house a year-round holiday feel. She had heard Rachel and Gabriel talking about the brickwork that needing repairing, the missing roof tiles, how long the house would need scaffolding for. Still nothing got done.

Sasha had spent a long time running away from Sandcove and the island, hating how parochial it was, the same white middle-class people talking endlessly about yachts and tide times. But Sandcove would always have a place in her heart, and she felt sad for it now, the way it was drifting into ruin. Margo had always told them as children that the pointed dormer windows were Sandcove's eyes and as a child Sasha had imagined them winking at her, wise and knowing, the keeper of their secrets. Often as a teenager, Sasha had wished that Sandcove could tell her what had really happened between her mother and father, why her father had left. Now she knew it was childish to think of Sandcove as a place with a heart and soul. It was just a draughty old house. She was the one with secrets.

Sasha set off at a trot across the blank sand, weaving in and out of the swash, trying to let the sound of the surf soothe her. She had once been so sure of her feelings for Phil. He'd been so carefree when she had met him in Australia, a muscly surfer boy looking the best he ever would with a tan and dreadlocks. He had a tattoo of a heron on his shoulder and played the guitar by firelight at night on the beach. He had filled her need for a bad boy, someone to shock Margo with. But he had become a duller version of himself back in England, his long hair shaved off. His love and focus on her began to feel claustrophobic and, once he was no longer stoned all the time, he moaned about everything. The feelings Sasha had once had for him were lost under her fear of his quick anger, his interrogations, the continual pointing-out of her shortcomings. These days she rarely found an escape from dark thoughts about her marriage, her brain always whirring, her anxieties sometimes overwhelming.

Walking on the beach, she tried to empty her mind and let her breathing slow. It was just one foot in front of the other. Soon she was scrambling over the pebbles that marked the boundary wall between Seagrove Bay and the hill climb into Seaview. She took long strides up Pier Road, arms swinging, past the back gates of some of the smart houses that lined the sea wall, and into the village. Sasha crossed over the top of the high street, her eye drawn as it always was down the steep hill of pretty Victorian villas to the sea. The bottom of the high street was the crossroads to so many of Sasha's childhood memories. To the right, steep steps carved in the sea wall down to the little beach of coves so perfect for rock pools and crabbing, to the left a promenade high above the sea, past The Porthole pub to the sailing club where all three of the girls had learnt to sail, and onwards to the open spaces of Springvale beach.

Sasha took one last gulp of ozone and salty air, before she pushed the door into No. 47 and was hit by the fug of cooked breakfasts and steam from the milk frother. She blew a kiss to the owner, Jane, who was behind the coffee machine and moved to the back of the café. Rachel was in their usual spot, a sofa tucked in the corner, with Margo's dogs lying at her feet. The table was littered with newspapers.

Rachel looked up. 'Say you'll share a bacon sandwich with me? I've been sitting here trying not to have one. The smell is too much.'

Sasha fussed over the dogs. 'Has *she* dumped the dogs on you now as well as the house?'

'Very funny. But yes. When she was finally ready to leave last night, we couldn't find Drake. So she went without them. I'm not sure how I got out this morning without waking the kids but I'm going to make the most of the peace.'

'I'm going to get a cappuccino, I'll order a sandwich if you want.'

'Please.'

They tucked into the enormous bacon butty, sipping coffee, pushing the scavenging dogs away fondly. Rachel dutifully returned waves and smiles from passers-by. She seemed a little on edge, her eyes tired, probably still smarting after her row with Margo the night before. Sasha rarely had Rachel to herself, she had to try to talk to her.

'Where do you think Dad – Richard – is now? Do you ever wonder?'

Rachel put her coffee cup down. 'God, you're as bad as Imogen. Who cares?'

'What do you mean?'

'She's always badgering me about him – trying to piece things together.'

'I think Margo drove him away.'

'You really need to move on, Sasha. He was a useless drunk. I remember what it was like living with him.'

'What if he wanted to see us? Wanted to be part of our lives? What would you do now if he found us?' Rachel's anger whenever they discussed Richard made Sasha nervous about confiding in her. Rachel would be horrified by what she had done.

'He didn't want to see us. The private investigator found him and even then he wanted nothing to do with us.'

'What if he's changed since then?'

'We're better off without him. I would never see him. I know you think something's missing – you want a father. But he couldn't even be bothered to show up when you were born.'

Aunt Alice had told Sasha her birth story, after much persuasion. There were no photos of Richard holding her as a baby. He'd been on a two-day bender; Margo had gone through labour with only Alice by her side. He had turned up once at the hospital very drunk, and hadn't been allowed to see Margo, the ward sister had ordered him away. He had left a present wrapped in Christmas wrapping paper, a single Baby-gro in a pack marked 'Two for one'. It had hurt Sasha's heart to hear it all those years later. Her birth had seemed to mark the beginning of the end for Margo and Richard. Not long after she had been brought home, Richard had flounced out of the house and turned a shed in Sandcove's garden into his writing room. He had complained about all the noise in the house, how even at the very top, the children's shrieks and cries floated up and destroyed his concentration. He was once a poet, but he wrote less and drank more and once Sasha was born he was mostly in the shed, if he was home at all. Alice had told Sasha that drinking friends would visit him there and often he would sleep off those nights in the shed too, on a collapsible camp bed propped up in a corner, or simply the floor. It wasn't difficult for Sasha to conclude that her birth had been the final straw for her father, that he had been driven away by domestic life.

Sasha's voice wavered. 'We don't know his side of the story, don't know what he was feeling. What he was going through.' Just then the side door of No. 47 flew open and there was a flutey call of 'Girls!' It was one of Margo's cronies, one of the posh sailing club lot. Irritation flashed across Rachel's face; Sasha's chance to speak to her sister evaporating. The woman was an outdoorsy type with a windswept grey bob and wind-roughened skin. 'Great news about Imogen! Finally engaged. Margo must be thrilled.'

Sasha bent her head over her coffee, refusing to engage, leaving it to Rachel.

'We're all very happy.'

'Any excuse for a party! Sasha, is that you? Hardly recognised you with the new do.'

Sasha was forced to look up. 'Yes, it's me. Hi.'

'Brave to cut it all off. How nice for Margo to have you all at home. Well, I'd better get on, tell Margo I'll see her at book club.'

She bustled away and Sasha shook her head at her sister. 'How can you bear it? All these nosy people knowing your business. You used to hate it.'

'I still hate it.' Rachel shrugged. 'But Hannah and Lizzie love it here, all the things we loved as kids. Hide and seek in a big old house, the Wendy house, afternoons at the beach hut. They can learn to ride on the beach, learn to sail. It's a good place to bring up a family.'

'It wouldn't be, for me.'

'Let's not go over this again. We should head back. We'll both be in trouble. Is everything okay with you?'

'Why?'

'The party wasn't your finest hour. Margo's upset, Imogen's upset. Things seem tense between you and Phil.'

Sasha avoided her sister's eyes. 'What's new? I'm always the one in trouble. The black sheep. I shouldn't have bothered to come this weekend.'

'Just apologise to Margo.'

'What about you and Margo? You were at each other's throats last night.'

'We see each other most days. Our rows blow over. She never sees you and she misses you. She can't understand why you are so angry with her – why you say such hateful things. There's not much worse in Margo's world than being called old.'

Sasha felt a twist of anxiety in her stomach at the thought of speaking to Margo, trying to wallpaper over the cracks again. Facing the guilt that she could not seem to manage a relationship with her mother, the way Rachel and Imogen did. Rachel was looking at her for an answer. 'Okay. Fine.'

On the walk home they linked arms and dragged their feet a little, the dogs bouncing around them, fetching sticks in and out of the sea. As they got closer to Sandcove, Sasha began to worry about how angry Phil would be that she had left him.

'Phil's going to be angry that I went off without him.'

Rachel stopped in the sand, pulling Sasha to a stop with her. 'He might be a bit pissed off, but not more that that?'

Sasha wanted to confide in Rachel but she didn't know how to find the words. They all thought she was strong, they wouldn't understand how she had let things get to this place. 'I make him angry quite a lot of the time.'

'What about?'

'Just silly things – stupid things. Things I do.'

Rachel's face was serious suddenly. 'That's not good. Are you saying you're frightened?'

'Just worn down . . . exhausted.'

'Talk to him, tell him it's not acceptable. Say you won't put up with it any more. I can talk to him?'

'No, no – it's fine. Please don't, Rach. I'll deal with it.'

As soon as they stepped onto the tiled floor of the house Sasha felt the chill in the air, the uncharacteristic hush. Margo, Gabriel, Imogen and Phil were all gathered in the kitchen waiting for them.

'Morning,' Sasha said as cheerfully as she could. She wondered where the children were, had hoped they would be running around, a welcome distraction. 'Where are Hannah and Lizzie?' Her eyes met Phil's and he did not smile. He was standing awkwardly near the door, as if he was planning to escape.

'They wanted their mother so we let them watch cartoons in the den to distract them. Do you want coffee or have you had enough at No. 47?' Gabriel was at the stove, the only one in the room smiling at her.

Margo turned to Sasha with a frown. 'Phil wondered where you were. Poor thing hasn't had any breakfast yet – he's been waiting for you.'

Phil shifted from one foot to the other as they all turned to look at him. While Gabriel and Imogen were still in their dressing gowns, Phil had showered and was fully dressed with his walking shoes on. In all the time Sasha and Phil had been together, he had never come down to breakfast at Sandcove less than fully dressed.

'It's fine Margo, really. I'm not much of a breakfast person.' Phil's tone was polite but icy.

Rachel stalked over to the coffee pot and helped herself. 'For God's sake, Phil's a grown man. If he wants breakfast, he can have it without Sasha. Why are you here so early anyway? Seems like you only left a couple of hours ago.'

Margo gave Rachel a grand look. 'I came for my dogs.'

Sasha looked around the kitchen at her family and wished she was anywhere else in the world at that moment. The cappucino and bacon sandwich were sloshing around in her stomach, and she felt sick. Imogen smiled at her in solidarity.

Imogen stood up. 'Right, let's make a plan for the day. Then I'll go to see where William's got to. He said he was only going for a short walk . . .'

Sasha used Imogen's distraction to move over to where Phil stood, ramrod straight. 'Sorry you didn't know where I was.'

He didn't look at her. 'I knew you'd be on one of your early morning jaunts with Rachel.'

'I didn't want to wake you.'

'Come on.' Phil lowered his voice to a hiss so no one else could hear him. 'You expect me to believe that? You always do exactly what you want, no thought for anyone else. Selfish like the rest of your stuck-up family.'

Sasha could feel his anger bubbling up and turned away before she inflamed things.

'Family meeting! Where should we go?' Imogen pulled up one of the stools by Margo. 'I'll start – Bembridge windmill, walk and picnic?'

Margo scowled. 'Are we really going to inflict the windmill on William again? How many times can you look at some wheels going round? Gabe always hits his head in there.'

Gabriel laughed. 'True.'

'How about Newport – cinema and pizza? The kids'll be happy, and I can have a nap in the dark too. After being kept up all hours.' Rachel did not look at Margo as she spoke but there was an edge to her voice.

Margo ignored the dig. 'Newport's miles away. It's a gorgeous day, why sit in the dark? We're supposed to be having a typical island weekend for William and Imi, you can go to the cinema any time. I vote Carisbrooke. The kids love climbing the battlements. Charles the First was imprisoned there, it's got an amazing history which William'll like. His poor daughter Elizabeth was also locked up – she was found dead with her head on the Bible her father had given her. Only fourteen.'

Sasha watched as Imogen wrapped her arm around Margo's shoulders as she spoke, as if it was the easiest and most natural thing in the world. 'You've always loved that story. Remember that rubbish play I wrote about her?'

Sasha remembered Imogen had been only twelve when she had handed her play proudly to their mother, and how Margo had returned it covered in red pen. At first Imogen had cried but then she had sat with Margo in the big sitting room at Sandcove in front of a fire and Sasha had eavesdropped jealously as Margo had talked to Imogen like she was a grown-up, about the ways the play could be improved. Margo had given Imogen such focused attention. It was then Sasha had understood that some talents and interests were valued more than others in her family. She had decided not to try to compete with her sister. Margo was baffled when, seemingly out of the blue, Sasha had turned to the sciences.

Margo looked like she was miles away. 'I know what it's like to be locked up. Your grandmother once kept me a prisoner at Sandcove – for a whole summer.' The family exchanged amused looks, united by Margo's sense of the dramatic.

Imogen elbowed Margo. 'Ma, it's hardly the same as Elizabeth Stuart. Being grounded as a teenager. We could do the Romanov trail in Cowes?'

Rachel turned to Imogen. 'I'm sick to death of the Romanovs. We followed their every step when you were writing that play. No more.

The beach hut? Tables and chairs out on The Duver, the kids can play on the beach while I drink wine.'

Imogen, hiding her hurt, stage-whispered to Sasha, 'It'll be a miracle if we ever agree.'

'We can go to the hut any time. If I can't have Carisbrooke, Mottistone? The gardens'll be glorious – roses everywhere. We could climb to St Catherine's Oratory.'

Everyone ignored Margo, who as the family's only gardener always lingered for hours in the manor house's gardens at Mottistone.

'As William isn't here, let's ask Phil. Anything *you'd* like to do?' Rachel turned pointedly to Phil.

Sasha realised she'd been quiet for too long, that she should speak before Phil was made to. He hated it when the family spotlight landed on him. 'What about Jonny's favourite? Compton Bay and a beach picnic? Margo can make us all laugh with her body boarding.'

More of the tension lifted as the family exchanged grins. Margo had always embarrassed her children by body boarding in a bikini, some part of which would often come away as she leapt on and off the board.

'As the surfer in the family I'll point out the bloody obvious – the sea's as flat as a pancake.' Margo looked smug as she gestured to the open window and the sea beyond.

'God, come on!' Rachel turned to her husband. 'Gabriel, you take charge! You usually choose well.'

Sasha watched as Margo bowed her head to Gabriel in acknowledgement. Margo would never respect Phil in the same way. He remained an outsider, tainting her position too. That was why she hated to be back home, being reminded that she was peripheral. She only remembered some of these places from childhood but it was clear that the rest of her family took these trips all the time, meeting up in the rarified atmosphere of Roman villas and castles and ornamental gardens. The island was like some kind of ridiculous Disneyland for grown-ups. It was even worse this time because Jonny wasn't here to pull faces at, to make her feel like she had an ally. Jonny hated the Sandcove obsession with outings, he refused to join in unless there was a beach and picnic involved. But he'd sent her a text after the engagement party saying he couldn't spend a weekend watching her with Phil. Something had changed since that night, he had dropped the pretence that their flirtation did not involve strong feelings. In another text he had told her how much he had wanted to be the one taking her home that night. She had archived that one.

'Yarmouth for lunch at The George? The new chef's supposed to be good. Walk it off round Newton Creek and wear out the girls.'

Margo jumped off her stool. 'That's not a bad idea. We can stop and have tea and cake on the way home at Mottistone.'

As everyone disappeared upstairs to finish getting ready, Sasha reached out for Margo's arm, to hold her back.

'What is it? The others are waiting.' Margo's voice was haughty.

Sasha looked down at her feet, crusted with sand. 'I'm sorry about what I said. At the party. I didn't mean it.' Sasha could feel Margo's blue eyes on her, her mother's stillness. Margo was not often still, it meant Sasha had her full attention.

'You did mean it. And you're probably right. I'm trying to be younger than I am.'

Sasha looked up, finding her nerve again. 'And what about the shagging around?'

'Sasha! There have only been a handful of men—'

'Since Dad?'

Margo's eyebrows went up. 'Since when has he been "Dad"?'

Sasha wished she was brave enough to tell Margo then and there that she had found him, seen him, that she knew all the things her mother didn't want her to know. But behind Margo's challenging look she saw pain. She didn't want to hurt her mother more. She wasn't the total bitch they all thought. She corrected herself. 'Richard.'

'I wish I knew why you are still so angry with me. I know I let you down when you were little, when you needed me most. But all I've done since is try to make it up to you. You think you'd be able to be more yourself with your father, that he would understand you. But there's part of me in you, Sasha. I didn't always fit, I didn't always want to be in this house or part of my family. I can understand if you let me.'

Sasha saw that her mother was welling up, could hear emotion in her voice. She heard the answering wobble in her own voice. 'What do you want me to do?'

'Let me back in, be part of this family – come home sometimes?'

'But you hate Phil.'

'No, I just don't know him. What's more important is how you feel about Phil.'

'What does that mean?'

'You don't even want to stand near him.'

Sasha wondered how her mother saw everything when it seemed like she was so wrapped up in herself. 'It's nothing – just a stupid row. We'll be fine.'

'You don't need to pretend you're fine all the time. Not with your family. That's the point of family.'

Sasha thought it was hardest of all with family, to be yourself, especially when silence and secrets divided you.

'I thought the point of family was to squabble endlessly over what outing we are going on.' She smiled sardonically at Margo.

'That too. Obviously.'

8

Date Night

Rachel sat at the kitchen table, a martini in front of her. It looked too pretty to drink, the frosted antique glass with a gold rim, the green olive suspended. Gabriel was working through a cocktail book she had given him and Friday was always cocktail night. Even though they rarely made it out, they tried to make Friday-night cocktails a moment when they sat facing each other and talked about the week. Tonight they were managing to go out too. Rachel had dressed up, leaving her dark hair down. Gabriel loved it like that and so tonight was a concession for him. She was even wearing earrings, gold hoops inherited from Margo, and a silk skirt which swished as she walked. She didn't love dressing up the way Margo and Sasha did, it felt a bit frivolous, but she knew the times it was expected. All was quiet; Gabriel was putting the children to bed at the top of the house. The sash windows that faced out over the sea were open as high as they would go on this warm summer's evening. One of them was unreliable, and needed a wedge in it to stop it coming down like a guillotine at odd moments. Rachel dreaded the expense of having to replace it, but there would be howls of protest if she suggested practical new windows. Margo had some mad notion that the windows were the eyes of Sandcove. Of course she had believed it too as a child, but that was the point of growing up, you stopped believing houses had souls.

As if it was an outraged sign from the house the old rotary phone in the kitchen rang and stopped, then rang again and stopped just as Rachel reached for it. 'Don't tell me the phone's on the blink too,' Rachel said out loud. The phone rang once more and Rachel snatched up the handset. 'Hello?'

'I've got a bloody useless connection.'

'Is something wrong?'

Sasha sounded distant and tense. 'Can't I call to say hello?'

'Of course.' Rachel thought of the tricky weekend they had all had at Sandcove, Sasha like a coiled spring. She realised she had been waiting for Sasha to confide in her again.

'We're having a break in Bali. I found a beach that reminded me of that one in Thailand – where the beach hut was and we had that delicious satay.'

Rachel was transported back to the time she and Sasha had travelled together. She had been twenty-one, Sasha seventeen. Sasha at seventeen had been fearless. She had led them merrily into all kinds of trouble. Rachel had felt like the poor relation, a plodding and cautious chaperone, looking on as Sasha dazzled. She remembered ice-cold bottles of beer, slippery with condensation in her hands; sand as white as sugar on miles of deserted beach. There had been an evening when they had gone out night fishing and she could still remember the pools of light the lanterns cast on the ebony sea. Each night they had lain on top of the sheets on their twin hotel beds, the fan whirring overhead, the chorus of cicadas and geckos keeping them awake, and had talked until the early hours.

'God, that beach was stunning. I'm jealous – wish I could be there with you.'

'Why didn't Imogen come with us to Thailand?'

'She never wanted to leave home. I'm so jealous of the places you get to go to for your work. We should travel together again. Perhaps I'll just come and visit you somewhere – leave everything behind.'

'You'd never do that.' Sasha's tone was dismissive. 'You're too good and too responsible – too tied down.'

'You're probably right. When are you next home? How's things with Phil?'

Rachel had been disappointed when a ridiculously young Sasha had announced she was marrying Phil. They had all hoped he had just been a fling she had picked up in Sydney but he had stuck, like a piece of chewing gum on a shoe. Gabriel thought some of Rachel's dislike of Phil was childish, jealousy that he had taken Sasha away. Rachel had been a mother to Sasha when Margo had taken to her bed and she knew this made her overprotective. But Rachel also found Phil's small eyes sly and watchful. It wasn't good or kind of her to think it but Sasha was beautiful, a nine or even a ten, and Phil was an average seven. He didn't hide his impatience with the Garnetts, and his mood swings were extreme. One minute he was charming and easy-going, the next he was like a caged tiger, and everyone knew to give him a wide berth.

What was really wrong was that Sasha seemed to have lost her light. She was still loud and passionate, but now anger was driving her, and her confidence was brittle. She never stayed long enough for them to see how she really was, she just blew in and out again like a storm cloud, Phil stuck to her side. Margo always dismissed Phil as just a devoted drip but after the last trip Rachel had been left wondering if there was something more sinister about him.

Sasha's voice was hesitant. 'It's okay, I can't really get into it now.'

'Come here, just you. When none of the others are around. We can talk properly.' Rachel could feel Sasha slipping away from her. 'Lizzie was asking after Auntie Say Say the other day, she wanted me to show her on the globe where you were.' Sasha was the favourite aunt, loved as much for her beauty and energy as for her exotic postcards and presents.

'Give her a big kiss from me. I've got to go.'

Rachel was still sitting by the phone thinking about Sasha when she heard Carol's key in the lock, and she steeled herself for an onslaught of local gossip. Carol was part of the family but sometimes Rachel longed for a babysitter who didn't know the whole family history and who didn't report things back to Margo. Someone who hadn't babysat her. She pulled herself up to look busy. Carol's gimlet eye rarely missed anything.

'I thought you said her ladyship was out this evening at some sailing boat do?'

'I think that's what she said.' Rachel was cautious, her instinct was always to protect Margo's privacy.

'I went past the sailing club and it's quiet as the grave. And then I went down past the Other Place and the curtains were drawn but with light round the edges and I could hear that opera she's always putting on. High-pitched woman – la la la la la la.' Carol's attempt at a trill faded into a hacking cough.

'Queen of the Night – Mozart's *Magic Flute*.' Rachel wished Gabriel was there with them so they could trade amused looks.

'Mozart, that's right. Anyway, then I saw Jack Walker coming out of the Other Place. What do you make of that?'

Rachel looked back at Carol, keeping her face blank. Margo and Jack Walker. That would not be good. Rachel wanted to swear loudly but realised Carol was watching her. 'Jack's a client of mine. You mustn't tell anyone – I can't talk about the case. Jack dropped some paperwork off for me with Margo. It's best he's not seen coming to Sandcove.' Rachel was pleased with her quick thinking.

'Goodness! I know you can't say but I hope he isn't in any trouble. His father's such a good man and left him that boatyard. Everyone's wondering if he'll make a success of it. You do look nice – your hair's so straight isn't it, not like Margo's curls. Have you taken off a bit of weight? I know you were trying.'

'I wish – this skirt's just flattering.'

'Gabriel adores you, that's all that matters. We can't all be natural beanpoles like Sasha. You know I thought when you moved in here, and Margo up the road, she'd help a bit more – be a bit more hands-on.'

'She was always very clear with us on that.'

'But what does she need her evenings for? I can't fill mine now I'm on my own.'

Unbidden, a memory of Margo floated up. Rachel had found her hiding round at the back of Sandcove, where the bins were kept. She was passionately kissing a man, an arm snaked around his neck, pulling him closer. Margo was pressing the lower part of her body hard against him. Rachel had been thirteen, not easily shocked after all their family had gone through. But she knew the man, it was Mr Spencer, father to Ronnie and Liza, both at her school. And he was still married to Mrs Spencer. Rachel had hurried back inside. She never mentioned it to her mother or her sisters or to anyone. Just one of the many Garnett secrets she carried to protect them all. She sometimes wondered if that was why she was anxious about drinking, why she always kept such a tight rein on herself. Gabriel thought it was obvious why, having an alcoholic as a father and a mother who had been lost to drink for a while too. But Rachel knew it was also to protect all the secrets she kept, all those secrets that one day could just spill out if she wasn't on her guard. Now it seemed Margo might be involved with Jack, a man Rachel knew a great deal about.

'She's always busy – you know that. On every committee. Book club, her nights at The Ship – the sailing club. She's trying to write too and she's behind deadline.' Rachel busied herself, her back to Carol, setting the kettle down on the range, collecting a cup and saucer from the dresser.

Carol sat down heavily in the parrot chair with a loud sigh. 'She hasn't seemed to write much since she left Sandcove. She feels a bit claustrophobic in that cottage – keeps saying she can't see the sea.'

Rachel felt the colour rise into her cheeks. 'It was her decision to leave Sandcove – it wasn't my idea. We didn't steal it or push her out. She's here most of the time anyway. Just not when I need a babysitter.'

'She didn't want you all in London, miles away.' Carol took the tea Rachel handed her and shook her head sadly. 'Like my daughter is. You'd think she'd visit me more than once a year. Look at Sasha – she's forgotten she grew up on the island. It breaks Margo's heart, not that she lets on. I always thought Imogen would settle here. Such a home girl.'

Rachel realised her nerves were very close to the surface. Usually she could let Carol's chat wash over her but today she could feel her temper rising. If Margo was involved with Jack Walker, things could get complicated. She shouted up the stairs to Gabriel, knowing he would understand her code. 'Carol's here, darling. Let's get going.'

'I used to sit in this same chair and watch your mother heading out with Richard. She was always so stylish. You girls have got that from her.'

Rachel had lost count of the times she had been told that she got things from Margo. It was hard to know what was left over, just hers alone. She sometimes fantasised about being far enough away, where no one knew Margo, and she could live without people telling her how she was like her mother. 'Have you had dinner? There's some leftover fish pie in the fridge.'

'I remember this one night when they were going to a party at the Olivers'. You must have been about two. You didn't want your mother to leave, clinging on to her legs. Your father couldn't keep his eyes off Margo, she was wearing this blue dress, flashing quite a bit of leg. I don't think his drinking had got bad, they were still having so much fun together—'

'Carol, you know I'm not interested in hearing about him.'

Carol looked put out. 'You can't just pretend he never existed. He was such a charmer – he just had a problem. A disease.'

'I can pretend he never existed. Just like Margo does. He may as well be dead.'

'Don't say that! As a little girl you adored him.'

'I don't remember – I only remember hating him.' Rachel's voice was cold and final. She reminded herself that Carol had helped keep them alive the year Margo had locked herself away in her bedroom. Carol had raised one very ungrateful daughter on her own after a teenage pregnancy and then finally in her thirties she had married a dull man whom she hadn't seemed to like much. He had died leaving her widowed ten years ago. She was lonely and had always lived vicariously through the Garnetts.

'Kids are settled. Lizzie might need one more kiss from Mummy and I can't find her bunny. Hello Carol.' Gabriel appeared in the doorway and swept over and kissed Carol's cheek, making her blush with pleasure. He grinned at Rachel. 'You look gorgeous.'

'Such a looker, like her mother. They all are. As for Sasha, I'm always telling my Dawn, she could easily be a model. Where are you two off to tonight?'

'Two Buoys. Fingers crossed they have the fish and chips on the menu. Taxi's on its way. It's Bob coming, said he wanted to see his favourite Garnett girl.' Gabriel started stowing his keys, phone and wallet in his pockets.

'He says that to all of us. Let's hope half of Bembridge isn't going to be there. So we get a chance to talk to each other.' Rachel knew she was being grumpy, that it wasn't the right tone for a 'date night', especially when they had become so rare, but she couldn't help herself. The possible collision of her work life with Margo's private life was a complication she could do without. Sasha's call had reminded her that she didn't really know what her little sister was thinking or feeling. And she had let Carol wind her up. Living in a close community, where everyone knew you, knew your family and all its stories, sometimes made her feel she had no sense of who she was any more. She could feel the siren call of London. She had a hearing next week and the thought of it calmed her. If there was time she could see some of her friends. Wander around unseen. Look at shops that sold something other than windcheaters and nautical stripes.

Gabriel looked over at her to read her face. 'We'll just ignore them.'

She smiled at the idea of Gabriel ignoring anyone. All the ladies of a certain age loved him and the rest all wanted to tell him their problems, to wangle some analysis for free. He always seemed to have time for people. And yet she knew a lot of it was not compassion but just nosiness, researching patterns of behaviour and gathering insights he could use to help his patients.

Date night was supposed to happen weekly, but it had kept slipping until it was now more like every six months. Gabriel had once been such a staunch advocate, but he had forgotten to arrange one in a long while. Rachel had pushed hard for this evening, feeling out of sorts and hoping that Gabriel would help set her back on the right track. He had been distracted recently, only saying he was worried about an unstable patient when she pushed him – client confidentiality meant Rachel knew she couldn't ask any more questions. Even when he was drunk, Gabriel remained scrupulous about the rules. She needed to be careful about her clients too, but she needed his advice more.

As soon as they had been seated in the restaurant, the words tumbled out. 'Margo's seeing someone really inappropriate. Jack Walker. His ex is a client of mine.'

Gabriel frowned at her. 'I'm not keen on discussing your mother's sex life on our date night. Can we talk about us? How *we* are. Do you want some wine? I know I do.'

Rachel watched Gabriel pick up the wine list. 'Since when do you need wine to get through an evening with me?'

Gabriel breathed in slowly as if he was inhaling patience and looked at Rachel. 'They've got a good wine list here, I'd like some. Do you need to read more into it?'

Rachel knew she was scratchy, feeling uncomfortable in her own skin. Probably hormonal. She tried to recentre herself, take pleasure in being with Gabriel, the pristine white linen that stretched between them. No children. 'Sorry – I'm out of sorts. Carol was driving me mad.'

'Why do you let her get to you so much? She's harmless – a bit of a busybody. She's basically given her life serving you all. It's sad when you think about it.'

Rachel reeled back at the sudden steel in Gabriel's voice. 'That's a bit harsh.'

'I can't help observing it. The way you and Margo and your sisters rely on people like Carol, and Tom, and Alice most of all. And yet they are firmly kept on the outside of the Garnett inner circle.'

Rachel could feel the evening spinning off in a direction that could upset them both and she didn't want that. She wanted comfort and alliance from Gabriel, not challenge and argument. Gabriel was looking out into the restaurant over her head, beckoning the waiter. He ordered a bottle of Malbec and sparkling water, before she'd had a chance to say anything. Rachel tried to catch his eye. 'You're being outrageous! Fuck's sake. You didn't ask me what I am having or what I want to drink. I want sea bream and *white* wine.'

'Keep your voice down – have the steak instead. Look, the whole white wine with fish thing isn't gospel.'

'I cook steak at home all the time. I can't believe you.' Gabriel let his eyes settle on her and Rachel felt something relax again between them as they looked at each other, an acknowledgement that they were both being childish.

After a while, Rachel decided to try again. 'Can I please ask you about Margo and JW? I need some advice on how to handle it.'

Gabriel stretched his hand across the table and placed it over Rachel's. His face had relaxed after a few sips of wine. He had taken his phone off the table and put it in his jacket pocket. 'Is JW the one who's in the band? Married with a kid?'

'Yes. I've a client who's claiming that he's the father of her child. JW's refusing any involvement, refusing a paternity test. We've filed the suit and the court will request him to have a DNA test. If he refuses he could end up with a default ruling saying he's the father regardless of the test.'

'How do we know Margo's involved with him?'

'Carol just saw JW coming out of Margo's. What other reason is there? He's gorgeous and only forty-something. Margo has history with younger men.'

'Perhaps they're just friends. Or is she a fan of the band?' Gabriel smiled at his own joke.

'It's not funny. I've had a feeling recently that she's got something going on. She hasn't been as needy.'

Gabriel took a large gulp of wine. Rachel watched as he caught Lydia Slater's eye across the room and gave her a big smile. 'If it's just a fling, does Margo need to know about JW?'

'The child is one. So this happened recently, while he's been married.'

'But there's no future between them, so why worry? Don't turn around but Lisa has just come in. She's with that new barman from the Inn. Looks like they're on a date.'

'You're such an old woman . . .'

'You and Margo never gossip about anyone in Seaview?'

'Don't you find it stifling? Living on top of everyone. I miss London – and my career.'

The waiter came over with their starters, the hum of the restaurant vibrated around her as it filled up. She'd had a whole glass of Malbec and she could feel it spreading through her, loosening her. The waiter poured her another, too fast and too large, and she let him. Gabriel was looking at her with concern now, she suddenly had his full attention. He hated it when she talked about missing London and she had said it deliberately. His flippancy about her feelings recently was scaring her. She looked away from him down at her crab ramekin, bright orange against the stark white plate.

'How could I miss it when I get to be out on the water most days, to swim in the sea? We live in a huge house with a garden right on the beach, we could never afford that space in London—'

'I know how well it suits you and the girls.' Rachel could hear the self-pity creeping into her voice. 'But I was going to be a partner. Now I'm buried in a tiny practice.'

'You would've had to slow your career down wherever you were – while we're trying for another baby.'

Rachel had a few mouthfuls of the crab ramekin starter, but it felt cloying and rich, coating her tongue. She took another large sip of wine to cut through it and noticed her glass was nearly empty again. 'I don't want to try any more. I'm sorry.' Rachel hadn't meant to say it so bluntly, but her tongue had been loosened by the alcohol. She saw the shock on Gabriel's face. He put his knife and fork down, sat up a bit straighter. 'I can't do it again. I can't have another miscarriage. Two in a row. It makes me too sad. I think about the lost babies all the time, the spaces they make.' Rachel knew as well she could not see the blood again, all that blood. She sensed from deep inside her that her body would not give birth to another child. Gabriel was looking at her like he didn't know her. 'I'm sorry, I know you wanted a boy. The Garnetts only seem to have girls. I've let you down.' Rachel felt like crying as the silence stretched between them.

Gabriel finally reached across the tablecloth for her hand again. 'I know those miscarriages were so hard. I'm sorry – I'm so happy with the family I've got, you know that. I love my girls. If you really don't want to try again, of course I'll support you.' He smiled at her, just a small frown knotting his brow. Rachel understood that in the delicate marriage negotiations she now had no more cards to play. Talking about moving back to London, about her career, would be steps too far. Gabriel would be crushed with disappointment, she knew all the dreams he had shared in their early years together, of a big family, four or even five children. Not for the first time she felt he would have done better with a more selfless wife. One who didn't want to work, who only wanted domestic chaos around her, a more fertile woman. But she had never hidden from him who she was, he knew where she came from. He had chosen her. She mustn't apologise again. She was about to reach out to him, ask him to talk to her more about his feelings, when the waiter interrupted with their next course.

Once he had gone, Gabriel changed the subject with a decided tone. 'Talk to Margo when you can. You Garnetts always seem to leave the important things unsaid. If you know something that might hurt Margo you must tell her.'

Rachel wanted to ask Gabriel if he was okay, if he was angry with her, if he still loved her, but a shutter had come down over his face, and now there were customers on both sides of them, pressing in close. It was a small restaurant and the tables were close together. It was easier to talk about Margo again. 'Next time I'm alone with her I'll see what I can find out. I wish these things didn't always fall to me. I never expected to be so closely wrapped up in Margo's life . . .'

Gabriel shrugged at her. 'It's the way it's always been since your crazy childhood. You mothering everyone – you sorting out the mess.'

'With your help.' Rachel knew she was flattering him now, trying to win back ground.

'You didn't have my help as a child. And you don't need my help, not really. You make your own decisions – you're strong, Rachel.'

Rachel wondered how Gabriel made this sound like a bad thing. Suddenly she was very tired and could not pretend any more that the evening's mood would change. 'I'm not sure I feel that strong. I feel like I'm never around enough for the girls, Lizzie is always so sad when I leave for work. I'm tired – there's so much to do on the house.' Rachel hated the wheedling note in her voice but more than anything she wanted Gabriel to take the responsibility for Sandcove off her, to make the decisions, to have the rows with Margo for her over the changes that were needed. But Gabriel seemed to have just stalled with his kitchen.

'It's only the roof that's urgent. The guy who did the Slaters' is coming round to look at it. He'll give us a quote, we'll take it from there. You're saving a bit each month—'

'Trying to.'

'You need to try a bit harder.'

'Okay.' Rachel had no more energy to point out how much fell to her already as the main breadwinner. And Gabriel took charge of everything domestic, so she did not really have a leg to stand on. 'Shall we bother with pudding, or shall I get the bill?'

9

The Railway Hut

Rachel had no idea where Sandcove's RIB was moored up, she hadn't seen it on the slipway. Gabriel was always lending it to people and so she had rung Tom and persuaded him to let them take out one of the hotel's RIBs. They were sleek and fast and Tom needed some prawns from Admiral Dan's in Ryde so he was happy to send Rachel and Margo on an errand. Rachel had finally given in and asked Margo to teach her how to pilot a RIB. She was sick of always having to rely on Gabriel, and she had inherited Margo's love of speed.

The club was quiet apart from a few people on the terrace and Rachel saw Margo sitting with James Ripley. James was Old Seaview money. Now in his seventies, he had known Rachel since she was a child. The clouds had all scattered, leaving only blue sky and heat. The shallow water in the bay was transparent. Rachel longed to swim, she hoped she could persuade Margo to stop at Priory before home. The heat on her skin made her feel holidayish.

James smiled at her. 'Rachel, my dear. You look pretty today. You off somewhere with your mother? It's a bad day for sailing, I'm afraid.'

'Just to Ryde. I'm having a lesson.'

Margo nodded. 'She's getting good. I thought we'd swing by Bembridge on the way back. The seal's been spotted again.'

James put his newspaper down. 'I saw the seal when I was out in the harbour on Tully's boat. It was just lounging in shallow water. Enormously fat. The place I've seen it the most is Newtown creek.'

Margo's face lit up. 'We were just there when Imogen was down for the weekend. One of the best places on earth. So many kingfishers!'

'Were you in one of the hides? I saw an osprey not so long ago—'

Rachel tried to hide her impatience to be away. 'Please not bird-watching . . .'

Margo stood up and linked arms with Rachel. 'Okay, we're going.'

Rachel loved to be with Margo on the water, the place her mother was truly happy. Margo had been boat mad since she got her first dinghy, *Camelot*, her escape route from home and her mother. Margo had become a sailor, a canoeist, a diver, a water-skier, anything to use the water all around her. As they motored out of the harbour through the channel marked by the buoys, Rachel's heart was inflated by the shimmering blue all around her, the wind lifting her hair, the space and horizon. Soon they were picking up speed, the wake behind them cutting the glassy surface. From the sea the island was small, a fairytale island with its golden sandy bays fringed with green woodland. Along the coast, Springvale now with the first few families setting up on the beach for the day ahead, past The Ship, bright blue in the sunshine, and round the corner for Puckpool. She could see Appley Tower, the huge stretch of golden sand that marked the beginning of Ryde and the water was suddenly busy, all the bustle of the ferries, people out on RIBs and yachts and the horizon now interrupted with the forts, the Spinnaker Tower and huge tankers. Margo began to slow down and stepped aside so that Rachel could take the wheel.

'Tom said there's a mooring next to *Carpe Diem*. Visitor pontoon. Keep the port and starboard buoys in sight. You're doing well. Look, there's *Serendipity*. God, Dan's looked after that boat. He used to come out with me in it when we were just kids.'

'Are we having lunch?'

'Yup. You're coming in a bit fast – hit reverse. Salt?'

'Too posh.'

'Fenders ready.' Margo gestured with her arm to one of the restaurants overlooking the harbour. 'The Lobster Shack? Throw out the rope, I'll jump off.'

'It was pretty average last time.'

'You're fussy today! I could get fish and chips from Ed's – we could have it out of the paper on the sand. You used to love—'

'That was Imogen's favourite thing, not mine. You're always muddling us.'

'Sometimes I think all those antidepressants I took messed with my memory. I have so many gaps.'

Rachel wondered if Margo was in a rare confessional mood. It was unusual for her to speak about that time, especially to Rachel who was the only one who properly remembered parts of it. 'Perhaps it's selective memory loss?'

'Very funny. Shall we do Tom's errand, get back in the boat and go to Bembridge? The Railway Hut? Toasted cheese, sausage and onion sandwich? We can moor up at Fisherman's.'

Rachel hugged Margo. 'You remembered *my* favourite.'

Bembridge Harbour was dazzling in the midday sun and the crescent of houseboats was a circus of bright colours, of flagpoles and plant pots, names all proudly displayed on slate or driftwood. When Rachel was a little girl she had loved walking with Richard around the bay, looking at all those names, singing out her favourites. Richard had known many of the people who lived in the houseboats and called out hellos as they walked, which Rachel had hated, wanting his whole attention on her. This was one of only a handful of happy memories she had of her father, before her suspicion of him, her anger over his drinking and absences from home, began to colour everything. A lot of those old houseboats had gone now and in their place there were smart new floating houses with two stories and decking and names like *Gypsy* and *African Queen*. It was high tide and, as Rachel and Margo made their way from the pontoon round to the café, they walked in silence watching and listening, snapshots of different views of the water appearing between the houseboats. The Redwing dinghies were all out on the water and the harbour was full of the chug of motors coming in and out of the harbour mouth, St Helen's Fort standing sentry behind.

The Railway Hut had been there for as long as anyone could remember; it was said there had been a café in that spot as far back as the 1940s when there was still a railway at Bembridge. It was just a green wooden shack, with a front door on the Embankment Road and a back door out onto the harbour, where children lurked in summer jumping up and down in front of the poster displaying the ice creams. There were buckets and spades and fishing nets for sale and dusty postcards in a spinner, slabs of pink and white fudge, even a secondhand book stall inside full of old Jilly Cooper novels. Rachel grabbed the last free wooden picnic table outside the café. There was no clearly defined garden, the outside tables just seemed to be part of the beach and a sandy path alongside the café cut through the marram grass, up into the dunes. It was busy with dog walkers, and children following their parents, trailing spades. The path was tempting, with the spiky blue of sea holly scattered among the sea grasses, the yellow of evening primrose. Rachel thought about the swim she wanted, the clear green water just round the headland on Bembridge beach. No one local swam in the harbour as there were rumours that at least one of the houseboats still had not invested in onboard sewage treatment.

They ate hungrily side by side watching everything, in the same way they had sat outside the café a hundred times or more. Margo had a photo on her desk of the three sisters sitting at one of the Railway's picnic tables. They were huddled together, eating chips with matching bright pink wetsuits on, about a year before Richard had left and their lives had changed. They sported matching cheeky grins and freckles. Rachel could feel the happiness of the day just by looking at the photo.

'I nearly bought one of the houseboats when I gave you Sandcove.'

Rachel froze with a chip on the way to her mouth. 'You were never serious though?'

'Sometimes I wish I had.'

'But you love Seaview, you grew up there.'

A look came into Margo's eyes. 'But I would have escaped the memories. Are you finishing my chips? Is that wise?'

Rachel turned and looked at her mother hard, dug her with an elbow. She hated it when Margo commented on what she ate, her eagle eyes noticing when she was eating too much. 'Don't start.'

'You need to be careful in your forties. You don't want to get fat.'

Rachel had noticed that her clothes were tighter, that there was a pair of jeans she hadn't worn in several months. She had been putting it down to stress, the pressure of all the things that needed to be done at Sandcove, the new tension between her and Gabriel. 'I'm a year off forty and I'm already fat.'

'Don't be silly. Just be more careful. Gabe is so handsome – it's unfair but men get more attractive with age.'

'Are you saying that you think he'll run off at the first signs of me getting a bit chubby?'

'I'm not saying that. But even the best of men can't be trusted.'

It was the same old argument. Margo's lack of trust in men, her belief that they were all capable of what Richard had been capable of. All through her teenage years Rachel had tried hard to not let Margo's cynicism rub off on her. When big love hit her she had glowed with belief and faith in Gabriel, sure she had found something that Margo could not understand. Now she stood up crossly and clumsily moved off the seat she was sharing with Margo to one further away. At that moment the owner's granddaughter appeared with a tray with two mugs of milky coffee, the only kind you could get at the Railway. She was oblivious to the chill between the two women, noisily clattering away the mess.

'Let's get this cleared up for you. Looks like you've enjoyed it all anyway.' Elise was always cheerful with her big white teeth, her straightened blonde hair and permanently tanned skin.

'Right, two coffees and Tony sent over a Tunnock's for you, Mrs Garnett. He remembered they're your favourite.'

When Elise had gone Margo pushed the teacake over to Rachel who pointedly pushed the cake back, before breaking into a rueful smile.

Margo smiled back and rested her head in her hands. 'I remember the time I brought Richard to the island, just after Dad had left me Sandcove in his will. I felt bad as I knew Alice thought that she should have got it. Our mother had just died in it – it felt creepy. The weather was terrible, Richard clearly thought I was mad – he wouldn't swim or let me take him out on a boat. He moaned about the sand getting in his clothes, he said it was all parochial. It was like he'd ripped my heart out. We had a row and I ran here to Tony who was always kind to me. Richard found me crying on Tony's shoulder, and went mad – he thought something was going on. Tony never liked him after that.'

Rachel widened her eyes at Margo. She couldn't imagine Margo with placid, amiable Tony. 'Tony's lovely but you were hardly going to do anything with him.'

'He had some hair then.'

Rachel laughed and then looked at her mother, trying to judge the mood. She seemed nostalgic, it was rare for her to tell stories about Richard. Rachel wondered if it was the right time to try to ask her about Jack. 'You're right though, I'm eating too much. Comfort eating. I can't seem to feel on top of my life right now.'

'Is it work? Gabriel?'

'Gabriel's being distant. He's always on his bloody phone. I some-times think he's having an affair but when would he have the time? And it's Gabriel. How do people find time for affairs?' Rachel watched her mother.

'He's not having an affair! You just need more time alone. Are you having enough sex?'

Rachel shook her head at Margo who was speaking too loudly as usual. 'Ssh. That's all fine. What about you?'

'What do you mean, me?' Margo frowned.

Rachel told herself to be brave, forced herself to carry on. 'I mean do you have sex? Affairs? You never tell us about your life. Even now we're grown-ups. We're not idiots – there's gossip. You're involved in our lives but we know nothing about yours.'

Rachel watched as Margo tipped her sunglasses from the top of her head over her eyes. 'Come on, Rachel. I'm sixty later this year. There have been a few men since Richard, but years ago.'

Rachel continued to look at her mother steadily, not letting her gaze drop. 'If there's someone you're seeing, couldn't we meet him? At least know about him?'

'There isn't anyone, drop it. We're talking about you and Gabriel. I can take the kids more, I know I'm not the most hands-on grandmother.'

Rachel heard the finality in Margo's voice and realised she would not be able to get Margo to speak about Jack. She sat silent, pointedly.

'I'm not that bad.'

'I don't want you to be different – we have Carol and Alice to help out.'

'If you think something's up with Gabriel you must do something. Don't leave it. I was an idiot like that – I ignored all the signs.'

'Maybe it's me. I miss the way my career was, before Hannah and Lizzie. I've lost my drive. It's just endless admin, small children. I feel like I'm just struggling through doing it all badly. All the time spent on ferries—'

'It's not new – I felt it too. Your generation acts like you're the first-ever mothers to work.' Margo pushed up her glasses again. 'I know you'd die for your children but motherhood is hard. I could've had you all taken away from me. If it hadn't been for Alice, for Tom, for you. If social services had known how bad it was . . .' Margo's words tailed off.

Rachel realised she was tearing a paper napkin into tiny shreds. 'I remember.'

'I wish you didn't remember.' There was a pause and Rachel could feel Margo's eyes studying her. 'Is there something else?'

Rachel had felt the pressure inside her to talk to Margo about Sandcove building all day. She had been trying to find the words for months now. 'I'm worried this sounds ungrateful. But this isn't the life I want to be living. It's like I've borrowed yours. I mean the island, Sandcove. You and Gabriel chose it and I just went along with it, hoping it would suit me. But it doesn't.'

The bustle around them drifted out of focus. Margo did not look shocked.

'I feel bad just saying it, I know it's selfish – I miss my friends—'

'You've got friends here! Friends you grew up with. I can stop having parties at Sandcove.'

Rachel shook her head. 'It's not that. It's annoying but it's more than that. *You* have friends here. Most of mine moved to the mainland. All the people in and out of Sandcove, they're *your* people. I don't even want that kind of home – people coming and going. I'm away too much for work; when I'm home, I just want Gabe and the girls to myself.'

Margo sounded defensive. 'I didn't force you! You and Gabriel decided it was a great thing for the kids. The space, the outdoor life. Riding, sailing. All the things—'

'All the things I ran away from. I couldn't wait to go to boarding school. I know Imi hated that school and being away from home but I loved it. None of us were as good as you at all those things. That was always hard – being compared to you.'

Rachel knew the independence she had pushed for had sometimes put a distance between her and Margo; she had made her mother feel unneeded. Part of it had been survival, after losing her childhood. Then in her teenage years, her independence had masked her struggle to live up to Margo's expectations.

'You're so much better than me at most things! When you wanted something you'd get it. The English cup or the lead part in a play. That school was bloody tough – I'd never have coped in a place like that, I'd have broken all the rules. You bent the rules to your will. You changed the school from the inside. Now I watch the way you juggle everything in awe.' Margo paused to catch her breath, mastering her feelings and Rachel felt an answering flare of emotion. 'If you really want to change your life – I'll have your back. Even if I hate it.' Margo gave Rachel a small smile.

Rachel felt a rogue tear roll down her cheek. 'Oh Ma. Thank you. It's really helped, telling you. I need to be brave and tell Gabriel. I feel guilty, though, the girls are happy here, Gabe's happy here.'

'Maybe there's something to bargain over? A compromise. God, I can't bear the idea of you all not being at Sandcove. Having to think about what to do with Sandcove. I'm not going to think about it yet.' Margo stood up suddenly, looked over to the café. 'Shall we cheer ourselves up with an ice cream?'

'I'll go. Magnum?' Rachel watched her mother suddenly distracted by someone she knew heading out across the harbour on a paddleboard.

'How many bloody hints do I have to drop? Please can you all club together and get me a paddleboard for Christmas.'

'And I suppose you want us to store it for you too at Sandcove?'

'Where the hell do you think I'm going to put it?'

10

Blue Moon

Her room was a tip but there was no way she was tidying it. She could rely on Carol to loyally clear away the old mugs and plates covered in toast crumbs, crisp packets and sweet wrappers. And once her mother had finally stopped behaving like a total bitch, she might give in and do some of Margo's laundry. She was having to wear the same dirty jeans and smocked top with Marmite down it that she had been wearing since the weekend. She could not leave the house like this. Not that she was allowed to leave the house.

She sighed dramatically for her sister's benefit. 'I need to borrow some clothes.'

Alice stirred slightly from where she was slumped on Margo's floor, her bare legs stretched out into the piles of dirty clothes that lay abandoned there. 'You're thinner than me though. As you always love to remind me.'

Margo propped herself up on one elbow on her bed and smirked at her sister. She had to keep Alice sweet. In the current state of warfare at Sandcove she needed an ally desperately and so far Alice had proven herself to be steadfast and surprisingly cunning. 'Not that much thinner. Those new hot pants sit on my hips which is fine. Gives me a more waif-like look.'

'What do you need clothes for? You're trapped, remember.'

Margo fell back on the bed. 'Fuckity fuck, I hate this house.'

'It's a nice house.' Alice was always scrupulously fair.

'It's a prison in the middle of bloody nowhere. There's no fun, no cool people, just *her*. Ruining my life.'

'She's having a gin right now with Anne. In the sitting room.' Alice was the information service at Sandcove. The sitting room overlooked the front door steps, Margo would not be able to get out without being seen. The back door had been locked since Margo had been found sneaking in through it late one night several weeks earlier.

'I have to get to a phone.' Margo sat up again and looked pleadingly at Alice. She widened her blue eyes as far as she could, and with the dark shadows around them, the effect was dramatic. Her hair, thick dark curls, hung around her shoulders, knotted and matted at the back, giving her the air of a tragic Carmen.

'If you go out, you'll need to brush your hair.' Alice was playing for time. She had no idea who she could ask to pull in a favour for her sister. Margo had offended everyone in their circle.

'There must be someone nearby whose phone I can use. I just need to hear his voice. What if he's forgotten me?'

'He won't forget you.' Alice could not imagine anyone who was under Margo's spell ever recovering. No doubt poor handsome Richard, who she had only glimpsed once or twice with his arms wrapped around Margo on Seagrove beach, was torturing himself too and wondering how he could break in to the Sandcove fortress. For some reason Alice felt sorrier for him than she did her own sister. Margo always got what she wanted, in the end.

'London's so far away. And there are so many girls there.' Margo reached for the notebook beside her on the bed and opened it at a random page. It was where she wrote down the things that Richard had said to her over the last few months, either in person or on the phone. Her eye fell on some lines, she read them greedily, needing the reassurance. *This is just so real. We have to be together. It is the only thing that matters to me. You are my girl, always.* Margo felt the tightness in her chest, the sick feeling that stopped her eating. Time was so slow in this house; she could feel her life ticking away. Her life away from him.

The girls heard their father's voice on the stairs. 'Alice! Supper time.'

Quickly Margo shoved the notebook under her mattress. He wasn't calling for her. She was invisible now. No one called her name any more, they had stopped asking her to join them for dinner, as so often she refused to eat or refused to speak. The only time anyone spoke to her was to tell her she couldn't do something. The tension crackled all day long. Margo imagined dark monsters lurking in every corner of the house, the childhood home that she had once loved so much. The door creaked open. *Everything in this house is old and creaky*, thought Margo. Her father stood there, blocking the light. A nervous smile hovered tentatively on his face. Margo felt sick with guilt every time she saw that smile, but it also made her angrier.

He cocked his head slightly to one side. 'Tidy in here.'

There was silence. Alice moved one of her legs like a windscreen wiper across the wooden floor, moving a pile of clothes with it. She noticed that her legs badly needed shaving. The silence in the room thickened.

'Fleetwood Mac hasn't lost any of its appeal?'

Margo sighed loudly. She had been listening to *Rumours* on her record player for two weeks. 'Chain' felt like it was her personal anthem. 'What do you want, Dad?' She made her voice cold.

Her father stayed in the doorway and his shoulders visibly sagged. 'Just to tell Alice that supper is ready. Are you still on your hunger strike?'

'*She* doesn't want to look at me at the table so I'm just doing her a favour.'

Margo pulled her knees in towards her on the bed, wrapping her arms around them. She wouldn't make eye contact with her father.

Alice began to slowly, apologetically, get up off the floor. 'I could smuggle something up?'

Margo just shook her hair, face now buried in her knees. Alice and her father turned to leave. 'Dad?' Margo lifted her face; suddenly it was ablaze, beautiful in its fury. 'You know if Mum doesn't let me see Richard, if she doesn't let me go to London, I'm going to run away.'

Her father came into the room, sat on the end of Margo's bed. The mattress sagged beneath him and more clothes slid to the floor. Margo put her head back on her knees.

'Margo, your mother loves you. She's in a lot of pain. She just wants you to do your A- levels. You have so much ahead of you. She's worried – we both are – that if she lets you have this relationship with a much older man—'

'For God's sake, he's only five years older than me, Dad! You're four years older than Mum.'

'It's quite a significant gap at your age, Margo. He's a grown man of twenty-one, independent and an adult, you are just a . . .' He paused, aware of all the conversational traps they kept falling into, over and over. Margo stood up suddenly, pacing the floor between her bed and the window.

'A fucking child! Yes I know you both think that, want to believe that—'

'Please don't swear, Margo, you know your mother hates it.'

Wearily her father lifted himself off the bed and turned to the door, not looking at Margo again. 'If you could just try talking to her, Margo. For my sake if nothing else.'

'You know what she's like. She doesn't listen. She's giving me the silent treatment right now, psyching me out.'

Alice turned to their father. 'You can't think it's fair, Dad. Keeping Margo locked up like this. Grounding her. Not letting her use the phone or leave the house . . . it's so . . . draconian.'

Edward Garnett smiled at his younger daughter. 'Good word.'

Margo flopped back on her bed. Trying to get their father to admit that their mother had finally gone mad was a losing battle. 'Don't waste your breath, Alice. Dad'll never rat out Mum. Loyal to the core, a good Army man. I'm the black sheep who's letting down the family.'

'You always were so overdramatic, Margaret. From the day you were born.'

Margo's voice was icy with the world-weary sarcasm of

someone twice her age. 'Yes, let's blame poor baby Margaret for it all. Let's not blame Mum, shall we, Mum who couldn't bond with her baby, who abandoned her to a nurse as soon as she could? It couldn't possibly be her fault, could it, that I turned out this way?'

Alice wished Margo would stop. She always went too far. She couldn't bear their poor gentle father to be hurt any more than he was already. He was out of his depth in the war that raged around him.

'Where do you get this stuff from?' Edward Garnett leant against the doorframe, facing out of the room, as if he longed to escape. Then he recoiled slightly as he saw his wife, who had appeared on the landing.

'Elizabeth.'

'Edward, come away, this isn't helping anyone. Alice, come and have some dinner.' Mrs Garnett didn't acknowledge Margo or step into her room, she simply led the rest of the family back down the Sandcove staircase for dinner in silence.

'What do you think you'll get?'

Alice and Margo were both lying on a bit of decked terrace at the front of the house, which covered Sandcove's boat store and looked directly over the beach. They had both begged for Margo to be let outside as the sky was cornflower blue and the glitter on the sea called to them through all the house's many windows. They lay in their matching crochet bikinis, newly freckled, the smells of Alice's Charlie and Margo's coconut oil mingling with barbecue smoke from the beach. The sea wall and slipway were busy with families going up and down with nets and buckets, children trailing crabbing lines. People had settled in for the day with their windbreaks and inflatables.

Margo ignored Alice's question. 'Of all the things that cow has done, not letting me on the beach or in the sea is the cruellest. Dad wouldn't even let me take the canoe out last night, I mean what trouble can I get up to in a canoe?'

'You'd head straight for the beach party. Last time you were found skinny-dipping with Winston by his parents.' Alice shifted a piece of her bikini material over the round curve of her breast. 'My boobs have grown.'

Margo lazily turned her face sideways to look at Alice critically. 'All of you has grown.'

'Thanks a bunch.'

'Are you eating all my food at family meals?'

Alice dug a finger into her sister's ribs. 'Not funny. You have no idea what those meals are like, the painful silences. I have to eat extra potatoes to make it bearable.'

'God I hate them both. Dad's no better. Why doesn't he stand up to her?'

'You didn't answer my question. Your O- levels? I'm dreading you getting all As. Imagine having to follow that—'

'Calm down. There are more important things than exams.' Margo picked up her book, *The Mill on the Floss*. Alice looked at it.

'I'm reading *Silas Marner*.'

'Good place to start. Then *Adam Bede*. I really liked the opening scenes of this, but to be honest the heroine, Maggie Tulliver, is doing my head in a bit.'

'She looks like you in that cover illustration.' They both

113

looked at the book, which showed a young woman in profile, dark curly hair, full lips.

'I don't look that vacant and tragic, do I?' Alice giggled. Margo looked out to sea. 'Winston's coming in on *Blue Moon*.'

'Love that boat. You know he asked me out?'

Margo looked sideways at Alice, her eyebrows raised. Winston's family were Old Seaview and the kind their mother approved of. 'Blimey. Little Miss Popular.'

Alice blushed like she always did. 'Might have something to do with the fact that I'm nice to him.'

The sisters grinned at each other, Alice's a demure, freckled grin the boys called 'cute', while Margo's wolfish smile showed all her straight white teeth. Margo looked back at *Blue Moon* which was anchoring. A gang of teenagers were unloading what looked like bottles of cider into a dinghy to bring ashore. Margo whistled. 'Looks like you're in luck – Winston must be having a beach party. Idiots anchoring in Seagrove – it's heaving. Should have carried on round to Priory.'

Margo saw Alice looking over at the boat. There were lots of familiar faces. If Alice joined them she would be the centre of attention – having one Garnett girl there would be better than none. They had not been seen for a while. Word had spread quickly that Alice was keeping her troubled older sister company throughout her imprisonment. Margo tugged Alice's arm. 'Go to the beach – join them. Wear my turquoise sundress, you'll look fab.'

'Are you sure?'

'We don't both need to be miserable. Go and drink vodka for me and kiss boys.'

Alice gave her sister a guilty smile and hurried into the

house. Margo let a sigh escape and self-pity flood her mind. Where was Richard now and what was he doing? Was he thinking of her? Everything she felt, everything she saw, was coloured by her feelings for him. Even the beach, so familiar from childhood, was changed forever by a memory of Richard. When Margo closed her eyes, imprinted on the inside of her eyelids was an empty beach and Richard waiting for her on the sand. It looked like a melancholic painting, the ash-coloured sea, the last glints of light like ribbons in the sky, one man all in black with the grey fort behind him. She could not see his expression, but she could see that he was trying to smoke a roll-up until he gave up and threw it into the wind. He had come for her, all the way from London. That had been at the beginning of the summer, the summer of captivity. Such a long slow summer, six weeks away from London. Her mother had decided to drag them all to Sandcove for the entire holiday, knowing that Margo would be safer there. Margo often wondered how much worse it would have been the summer before, the impossible heatwave summer, when she had given up on baths and instead taken endless warm sea dips.

They had met at the beginning of the year, which was why her mother felt she could call it 'just a whirlwind'. Margo's father had taken her to a book launch for a writer he knew, thinking that it might interest his precocious daughter, top of her class in English and determined to be a journalist. Margo had quickly spotted Richard across the room, the second youngest person there. He was so tall, he was already slightly stooping at twenty-one. Margo had not known many men but even she knew that he was not handsome in the dangerous way, the way that would lead other women to look at him on the street, or press their phone number into his hand. But he saw her and their eyes met and immediately she knew that he was the first person who might really see her as she was. There was a slow dance around the corners of the room until they braved a meeting in the middle. Neither of them said anything interesting or original but somehow the axis of the world was tilting. Margo felt energy fizzing all around Richard; she was soon to learn that he lived life as if it was a race to the finish line, only slowing down for love and poetry. His eyes were a kaleidescope of blues and greens. They talked and talked, Margo about her plan to study English at Oxford, Richard about the small literary magazine he was working for unpaid in the hope they might publish his poetry. He took large gulps of wine before and after every word in a way she had never seen before. Her parents only had wine with food, sipping it, sometimes a cocktail before dinner. Richard drank like it was air, holding out his glass insistently whenever a waitress passed.

Margo's father, an academic and absent-minded man, had not noticed what she was doing so they talked uninterrupted for about an hour. Margo had time to notice how skinny Richard was, his thighs as slender as hers. She noted the birthmark on his neck, that his wild hair hid big ears, that his head was a lion's head. His laugh was sudden and joyous and he could suddenly sound Irish, his voice thick with velvet. Margo's eyes kept being drawn to Richard's full lips. Her thoughts were so impure that they shocked her. He presented her with a battered notebook, scrawled through in black ink with scraps of poems. She wanted to stop and read them all.

He held out his fountain pen and commanded her to write her phone number down.

Margo was scared suddenly. 'I bet you do this all the time. Take girls' numbers at parties.'

He was taking the measure of her. 'Sometimes. If they're as fine as you.'

There was a pause as Margo looked at the pen he was holding out to her, the ink blot on his fingers. 'I'm only sixteen.'

He didn't flinch, but smiled a crooked smile at her. 'You look older.'

'And my mother's a nightmare.'

'They often are. Your oul' fella looks harmless enough.'

He was a man of the world, she was out of her depth. She took a step back but it was like trying to pull magnets apart. More than she wanted anything else, more than Oxford, more than writing, she wanted to see him again.

He spoke as if in reply to her thoughts, something he was soon to make a habit of. 'I feel different this time. It doesn't feel like just another conquest.' Margo blushed, unable to meet his eyes. 'Also you look lovely in those dungarees. I've never seen anyone at one of these parties in dungarees.'

'I wore them to annoy my father. He thinks everyone should be in tweed.'

Richard's smile lit up his face to his eyes and she could not help but smile back and reach for the pen. There was no surface to lean on and so he turned. 'Use my back.' She noticed he smelt of cigarettes. The intimacy of feeling his body heat through his velvet jacket made Margo's stomach dip and dive like a rollercoaster. Her heart was beating faster than it ever had before. Even though she would go over this moment, awake and in her dreams, she wanted her father to come and claim her and take her home, so she could be a child once again. She neatly folded the paper in two and handed it to him.

'You don't have to call,' she mumbled, suddenly clumsy and graceless. 'And my mum'll probably answer anyway.' She looked around her, planning her escape route. The party was thinning out and her father was near the door. She turned and gave him a quick smile. 'I'm going to go now. Looks like my dad needs rescuing.' And she dived into the noise of the party, away from the magical space that had held them.

She heard him call after her. 'Don't despair, Margo Garnett! I'll be calling you.'

Through her Richard reverie, Margo watched Alice bounce down Sandcove's steep brick steps onto the sea wall and then down the slipway onto the sand. She looked much younger than fourteen in her borrowed dress and Margo felt a pang. She hoped that Alice could cope alone with that gang of idiot public-school boys, who were always the worst for trying to maul you after some ciders. She would come back with the scent of smoke in her hair, lip gloss smudged away, someone's jacket wrapped around her. Boys her age now seemed intolerable to Margo which was why she was so rude to them all. She only wanted one man's quick brain and lean muscles.

Later that evening, driven by stifling boredom, Margo was forced downstairs with a pile of washing. She dragged it down the stairs behind her in a bin bag, enjoying the thwack it made on each step behind her. She felt like a thwarted child, when she wanted to feel like an adventurous woman, leaping towards love and life in London. The situation could not carry on. Her mother was pale and pinched. Alice was eating everything. Margo was eating nothing. Her father had recorded *Fawlty Towers* on his new Betamax machine, and was watching it over and over, but no longer laughing at Manuel. The house was eerily silent, more so than usual with Alice out and Margo was on high alert for her mother when she inched into the kitchen. There was no sign of her, just a crusty lasagne dish soaking on the draining board, and the smell of melted cheese made Margo feel nauseous.

Margo was caught off guard when she walked into the utility room off the kitchen and came face to face with her mother, the ironing board the only barrier between them. Margo saw her mother stiffen. She dropped the bin bag on the floor and her mother looked at it.

Her mother's voice was strained. 'I wasn't going to tell you, but—'

'What?'

Her mother's eyes rested on Margo's filthy bare feet, her bright blue toenails. Her voice was weary, as always. 'Are you washing at all? I mean I can see you are about to do some washing—'

'What's the bloody point? I can't see anyone. I'm a prisoner.'

'Margo.' Her mother's voice was a whipcrack.

Margo looked down at her toes too and then at her mother's stockinged feet behind the ironing board. They seemed oddly vulnerable. Margo always thought of her mother in shoes.

Margo tried to sound more accommodating. 'What were you going to tell me?'

There was a long pause as if her mother feared what was to come next. 'Richard rang for you.'

In her sudden hopefulness Margo thought she saw some hesitation in her mother's face. 'What did he say? Why didn't you call me?'

'Not much to me, of course.'

'Can I ring him back? Please, Mum, I beg you. Just one quick phone call?' Margo felt tears spring into her eyes. She had kept up a wall of hardness for so long. She watched as her mother turned aside; she didn't want to see Margo's tears.

'You know I want you to forget about this mad infatuation. It's just a crush, Margaret, and an inappropriate one. We've all had them as teenagers. But you need to listen to us. You're only sixteen and you've A- levels and university ahead of you.'

In defeat, Margo let her tears of frustration fall freely. She wasn't sure she had any fight left. She turned to leave, just pausing for one moment. 'Can you at least tell me what he said?'

'He said nothing. He heard my voice and said he would try another time. I told him if he had any sense he would stop trying.'

Margo raised her chin a fraction. 'He won't stop trying.'

Her mother looked down at the ironing board, smoothed the cover with her hand. She looked so smug to Margo. 'He's a man, Margaret. Men give up. He's after what they're all after. Once he realises it's too hard he'll get on with his life living in a bedsit. Which I know you think is so romantic, but let me tell you that is no life for any woman, to be at the beck and call of a failed poet.'

Margo let fresh hatred for her mother blaze through her. The sarcasm, the judgement in that polite clipped voice, the fussy way she stood there smoothing the ironing board. So knowing and so superior. Margo did not bother to choke back the venomous words that fired out of her mouth. 'Do you think I want to be like you? Cold and unfeeling? All manners and nothing else? Buried under all this?' Margo waved an arm wildly around. Elizabeth Garnett bowed her head, biting her lip. 'He isn't like other men. He hasn't touched me, he won't, he refuses to until we have your blessing. He loves me, which is more than you do, you have never loved me. Why should I listen to you?'

There was silence as they both absorbed the words that could not be unsaid. Her mother now looked more like a hunted animal. They both heard the door of the TV room open, Edward Garnett's tread on the stairs. Margo only ever saw him hovering in doorways. 'Don't do this, girls. Don't say things you don't mean.'

His voice was sad and Margo flushed when she looked again at her mother and saw she had wet cheeks. She wasn't even sure her mother had noticed. But there was no way back now, Margo had felt her resolve harden when her mother called Richard a failure. 'I won't ask again. Please will you let me go back to London and live with Aunt Mary until term time? I promise to keep the eleven p.m. curfew. I won't stay over at Richard's. Not until I can go on the pill. Aunt Mary said she would take me in, if you said she could.'

Her father was looking at the carpet, embarrassed, her

mother lit up with fury. 'Ha!' Her sarcastic laugh cracked through the air like a gunshot. 'We're supposed to trust you after Bonfire Night?'

'I fell asleep! How many times! I've told you over and over – why can't you just believe me! For God's sake.' Margo turned to escape but was blocked by her father. She looked him in the eyes, pleading. 'Dad, please. If you won't let me live with Mary, I'll just run away. The only place I'll be able to go to is Richard's bedsit. I won't have any choice. I just want him as my boyfriend, you're the ones blowing it up into a massive deal, making it about me leaving this family.' Margo sobbed suddenly, thinking of banishment from Sandcove, from Alice and her father who was standing there so fearful and small. Her threat hovered in the air, the unsaid now said. Her mother's biggest fear.

'Go to your room, Margaret.' Elizabeth Garnett had turned her back, stood facing the small corner window that looked onto the back garden.

'Of course,' Margo spat out her words. 'What a truly brilliant and original way of dealing with me! Congrats all on such wonderful parenting.' She swept past her father, gulping back sobs, running for the safety of her room.

Later that night Margo lay on her bed, curtains open. An indigo sky stretched above her full of brilliant stars. The push and pull of the sea, usually so soothing, tonight made her feel trapped, cut off on her island in the sea. Something had shifted in her that night. Fortune's wheel had turned and she felt ready to leave. She had heard her mother weeping but it had only shut her harder and faster behind the protective wall of her anger. Alice crept into her bedroom at around midnight, her face shining. She sat on Margo's bed and Margo pulled herself up to look at her. The smells of sea, smoke and cider clung to Alice, and her face was the face of someone who had just been kissed. They whispered to each other.

'So you snogged him.'

'He kissed me!'

They beamed at each other. Alice held out her hand. Folded tight in it was a letter in an envelope. Margo felt her heart start to beat faster, but she was scared to hope.

'What is it?'

'A letter, silly. From Richard.'

They both looked at it.

'How?' Margo murmured, reaching out slowly for it. Alice, still smiling, stood up a little unsteadily. The sundress was rumpled now, her curls as unkempt as Margo's. Margo would always remember how girlish and pretty Alice looked that night.

'I'm going to go – let you read it in peace. You should know something though. When he came to the island that last time, you know when he camped on the beach?'

'Yes.'

'And he met all the gang when Bob had the party.'

'Yes.' Margo, normally so impatient, was so still, waiting, hanging on Alice's every word.

'Richard asked everyone then. He even asked that idiot girl Lucy who's a bit thick and who snogs everyone.'

Margo moved the hand with the letter onto her lap, began to unfurl the envelope; her heart felt as if it was blowing up like a balloon when she saw the familiar black ink, the scrawled writing 'Miss Margaret Garnett, c/o Winston Bond, The Look Out, Seaview'.

'Asked them what?'

Alice's face was still shining with excitement and cider. 'Asked them if he could send a letter care of them. To you. And Winston said he could.'

Margo and Alice stared at each other open-mouthed.

'I like Winston more now.'

'Yes, me too, the others all said no—'

'Because they hate me.'

'Not that, but because they were scared their parents would find out.' Alice turned towards the door, her midnight mission accomplished. She paused for one moment, looked back at Margo. Her voice was serious. 'He really loves you.' They exchanged a look across the room and Margo wondered if her sister knew what was around the corner.

'Night night.'

'Night Alice.' Margo was desperate to rip open the envelope but she paused a moment, called after her sister. 'Alice, thank you.' And Alice smiled as she slipped out through Margo's bedroom door.

The next morning Sandcove was full of Elvis songs. They blared from the kitchen radio, and the one in Edward Garnett's study and the one in Margo's bedroom. Elvis had died in the night. A shocked Margo had wanted to phone Richard, who did a very brilliant Elvis inpersonation. Alice, still fuzzy from her late night, dozed in bed wondering why on earth everyone was playing Elvis songs. Elizabeth Garnett sat on the deck smoking cigarette after cigarette, very pale and grave. Occasionally passers-by would say hello to her and something unoriginal like 'God, isn't it awful?' or 'Imagine, only forty-two.'

Margo knew she should go to her mother, offer her some comfort, but she couldn't fake it. She knew that her mother would be devastated. She was the same age as Elvis, and had had a passionate crush on him all through her teen years. Her mother tended toward anxiety and hypochondria and she would be thinking about her own death, how if Elvis could die, anyone could die. The details were splashed all over *The Express* on the kitchen table and that would have upset her too. Elvis, her God, collapsed on the loo, only found by his girlfriend in the morning. Margo thought how strange it was that none of the sadness could touch her. Not now she had her letter. She read it over and over and each time she did it hardened her heart a little more against her mother.

Girl I just can't get you out of my mind. We need to be together. I cannot think or eat or sleep when we are apart. Even the black stuff doesn't taste the same. We will be together. I won't let you down. They are wrong, your oulds, we can still do everything we need to do together. More in fact. We can be great together. I know we want their blessing but Jesus we have tried so hard to make them see reason. Send me a message M and I'll come for you. And this time I won't leave without you.

She was going to go to Winston, now rehabilitated in her eyes as a kind of hero, under cover of night and call Richard. She knew she couldn't take one of the monogrammed suitcases that sat in a neat pile on top of her mother's wardrobe. She would need to take what she could in black bin bags and leave the rest. She wouldn't be able to fit much anyway in the boot of Richard's car, an unreliable red Fiat Spider which he always seemed to be crashing, usually when he had drunk a bit too much. So many dreams of her freedom centred around that car. They would get in it, just the two of them, and go anywhere they wanted, roof down, wind in their hair. She was going to run away with Richard. No one was going to stop her.

II

Coup de Foudre

London

'Are you sure you've left enough time? You know you Garnetts never do.'

The morning of the rehearsal was inauspicious. Over breakfast, her nerves bubbling under everything, Imogen had quarrelled with William over taxi timings. Later when she had run out to grab a sandwich for lunch from Liz's café on Goldhawk Road she had been caught in a sudden shower so now her hair was frizzy, almost as wild as Margo's. Margo and Rachel both rang to wish her luck, making her jittery and late. On a loop, she just kept thinking, *my rehearsal, my play*. Her play *Standart*. She was thirty-two and her play was going to be staged at The Playhouse. It felt like it should be a monumental day, but she felt jangly, and then the taxi was late, and she didn't have enough time. Suddenly from having all the time in the world, she was running late. She wished she was poised and composed, but feared even as a playwright with a play in rehearsal, she would never be those things.

When she rushed into the rehearsal room underneath The Playhouse she found Rowan Melrose standing right in the middle of it, and at the clunk of the big soundproof doors, Rowan turned, as did the group clustered around her. Rowan couldn't know who

Imogen was and yet her face lit up as if in recognition. There was no other way to think of that moment, other than as a cliché. Their eyes locked. Imogen felt the breath catch in her throat, and the blood pump to her cheeks. She knew she was staring back like some crazed fool and yet she couldn't break the spell. The director came over to welcome Imogen and to introduce her to everyone. But her whole body was alert only to one thing and that was where Rowan was, and whether Rowan's eyes were still on her. Imogen was meeting the actors, stumbling through her greetings, not paying attention, and then the director was introducing her to the person she suddenly wanted to be near more than anything else in the world.

'And this is your leading lady, this is Rowan of course. Your Alexandra.'

Imogen knew that face, had watched it every Sunday for a month on her television screen. She took the outstretched hand in hers, noticing the long white fingers, the childlike wrists. The hand was cool and firm and when Rowan took it away, Imogen realised she was trembling slightly. So this was how a *coup de foudre* felt. She felt like she had popping candy underneath her skin.

It wasn't just that Rowan was beautiful. Yes, her blonde hair fell like a sheet of silk. Yes, her green eyes were flecked with gold and Imogen had noticed on the television that sometimes they looked almost turquoise in certain lights. Yes, she was tall, a bit too thin like most actresses, and elegantly draped in an oatmeal cashmere jumper. It was all of that but more. She seemed to glow; the magnetic pull of her was electrifying.

'Imogen Garnett,' Rowan said, smiling almost shyly. 'I cannot believe I have this part in your brilliant play. You're a genius.'

Imogen wanted to hear Rowan say her name over and over. Could she answer without stammering? When she spoke she needed to sound normal, not to embarrass herself. 'It's lovely to meet you. I'm so looking forward to hearing you read the part.' Her words expressed nothing of what she was feeling. She wanted to grab Rowan's hand and run from the room. People were watching her, expecting things from her, but there was nothing that could have prepared her for the physical effect of Rowan's presence.

Fred Baxter was calling everyone to order and Imogen found herself being led to a circle of chairs where the read-through was to take place. Stephen Williams, who was playing Tsar Nicholas, sat next to her. She was three seats away from Rowan, which meant she only had to listen to her voice, not look at her while she spoke Imogen's lines. Fred was introducing her play to the actors, describing it in brief, and it was all so hard to believe, she was not sure she had ever felt happiness like it. He was talking about her characters as if they were real people, to a company of actors. She half-wished Margo was there with her to hear it.

'So most of you should have had a chance to read the script. If not, no drinks on me at Colette's later.'

There was some giggling, shifting in chairs. Margo had told Imogen that Fred Baxter's drinks after the first rehearsal were legendary and suddenly Imogen could feel her insides fizzing with the prospect of Colette's, and Rowan and drinks.

'The play is based on a trip the Tsar Nicholas and Tsarina Alexandra made with their four daughters and son to the Isle of Wight in 1909, where they met with King Edward the Seventh during Cowes Regatta week. So far, so historically accurate. At the time Alexandra was thought to be under the influence of Rasputin, and in this play Imogen takes us beyond known history and explores the idea that Alexandra was infatuated with Rasputin, a woman on the brink of a sexual affair, a desperate woman who wanted more than anything to save her son. Imogen, would you be able to tell us a bit more about why you chose to write a play about this moment in history?'

Margo had warned Imogen that this might happen and so she had prepared, but she had not known that the pressure to shine, to do justice to her play, would be so intense. She shifted in her chair, coughed, felt all eyes on her, and sensed that Rowan had swivelled in her chair to look at her.

'I won't stand up – if that's okay, I'm nervous enough!' Warm smiles greeted this. 'I have a family house on the Isle of Wight, Sandcove, and the island means a lot to my family.' Imogen hadn't meant to start this way, to be so personal, but they were the words that came to her. 'My mother, Margo Garnett, is a journalist – she loves history. I was lucky enough to be told stories in a way that made them stick in my mind and to be taken to lots of places of historical interest. I remember being about ten and being taken to St Mildred's Church in Wippingham where there is a memorial to the Tsar and his family and learning of the fate that lay in wait for those daughters, when they were still so young. Perhaps it spoke to me because I have two sisters, I don't know. We would go to Cowes and Margo took us to the Yacht Club, to the Regatta, and told us how the doomed Romanovs came by their yacht *Standart* to the island. I imagined how impressive it would have all looked – the Spithead crowded with boats, the two great royal yachts moored near.'

Imogen paused letting her audience conjur the scene. 'There would have been fireworks and parties and crowds of onlookers, waiting to catch a sight of the royals. All that would have seemed so tempting to the little boy Alexei, the brother with haemophilia who wasn't allowed on shore. My imagination was fired by the idea of this family, how overprotected they were, the girls only allowed once to walk around in Cowes. There were local reports of their beauty, how they giggled together under their parasols. I guess those Romanov daughters were my first way into the story, as they are with most people, the old photos of them all in white lace, their beauty and the murder that was around the corner.'

Imogen paused, took a breath, saw her audience was listening raptly.

'But then as I read more and as I got older it was the Tsarina who caught my imagination. The influence of Rasputin. And so in this play the trip comes at a point for Alexandra when she does not want to be parted from Rasputin, she is desperate to be near him, and she's realising that it is not only for Alexei's health that she needs him, that she has her own needs. People try to warn her that Rasputin is a sexual predator, and a drunk, but she can only feel his charisma, can only see him as her saviour. Rasputin is offstage in *Standart*, but he's always the hidden shadow. Alexandra is also struggling with the guilt that though she had finally produced a son, that little boy would most probably die of the disease that claimed her brother and uncle. She passed on the disease.'

Imogen could feel the emotion building in her, the way it always did when she thought of the Alexandra she had created in her play. She tried to keep her voice steady. 'This play is about a woman struggling with depression, unable to see a way out, but also chained by duty, the demands of the trip. The quandary of her real affection and loyalty to her husband Nicholas. The play is also about mothers and daughters. Alexandra's guilt that the care of Alexei has taken her away from her daughters, that she has abandoned them emotionally. I wanted to explore the idea that death was waiting for them all, so did all of their struggles, their domestic dramas, did it matter in the end? But also how you just have to keep living, to keep living under the threat of death.'

There was a hush when Imogen finished and she could feel herself blushing.

'So beautifully put.' It was Rowan. 'Fred, we'll need a group outing to the Isle of Wight and Sandcove and all the other places Imogen mentioned!' The group laughed and Rowan smiled at Imogen, the kind of full-wattage smile that had probably left a slew of lovelorn victims in its wake.

'Right, my loves. Best foot forward. Let's show our playwright what we're made of.'

And like that the group was called to order, heads bent to scripts. Imogen was left staring out across them, her insides knotted with nerves and something else altogether.

Colette's was loud and it had the frenetic feel of somewhere crowded with the glamorous young, all with money to spend. By day people came here for a flat white, to people-watch with a newspaper unread before them. By night the bar was a notorious pick-up spot for well-heeled West Londoners. The balm of a summer's evening only added to its louche atmosphere. Real champagne spilled out of coupes, making tables sticky. The doors constantly swung open as packs of revellers moved on to the pavement for cigarettes, then moved back again. The ten 'Standarts', as they were now collectively named by Fred, had squeezed onto a corner table. Fred began to fill glasses standing up, refusing a chair. Suddenly, before she even had a chance to reach the glass Fred handed her, Rowan was beside her, their bare arms touching. Imogen could smell her perfume, citrus and woodsmoke.

Rowan flicked her hair, its silken strands caressing Imogen's face. 'Budge up, playwright darling!'

Rowan was trying to edge onto the tiny wooden chair with her. Imogen shifted over a few inches to accommodate Rowan, feeling sweat starting to prickle up around her hairline. Shouts rang out around her, calls for more drinks, insults were traded, people talked over one another; everywhere buzzed with noise and movement. Fred and a couple of the cast were already heading for the pavement. Imogen watched, frozen, sitting as still as she could, feeling Rowan pressed right against her. She could feel Rowan's voice vibrating in her ear, her tight thigh muscles pressed against her own. Her bottom squashed against Rowan's suddenly felt too big in comparison. Imogen tried to breathe, to relax, realising that although Rowan was so close, all her attention was focused on the group. Rowan was showing off, playing to the crowd. It reminded Imogen of Margo's performances at parties. Imogen took a large sip of her champagne, and another, and felt the alcohol's alchemy working quickly, as it always did when she was happy and excited. She could feel her nerve endings, waves of heat from inside her, and sometimes Rowan's breath on her as she turned to answer a question.

'Cigarette.' It was an order, not a request. There was challenge in the flash of Rowan's eyes but something else as well. Imogen, a novice still in matters of sexual attraction, realised in a lightning bolt of understanding that Rowan wanted her. Her, Imogen. The playwright. She was the object of Rowan's attention for the night. It may not be much more than that but for now it was enough.

'I don't really smoke.'

'But you do sometimes? When you're feeling naughty?' Rowan emphasised the word naughty and licked her lips. She was looking at Imogen's lips. Imogen felt a flood of wetness.

'Sometimes — come on then.' Imogen was up before she lost her nerve, weaving in and out of drunk people, pushing through with the odd 'Excuse me', her face and insides on fire. She could feel Rowan close behind, saw some of the looks over her shoulders as people spotted the actress. Some openly staring, or shouting, 'Oi Rowan', or more stupidly, 'Look, it's Anna Karenina!' Imogen didn't let any of it slow her down, kept pushing until she was through the swing doors and out into the summer evening air. A harem of girls with bright red lips and off-the-shoulder tops stood together laughing their outdoor laughs and air-kissing. The businessmen in suits watched the girls, waiting for their moment. There was sex everywhere.

Rowan ignored the whispers and catcalls as she joined Imogen on the pavement. She stood there in just a white T-shirt and jeans, the T-shirt moulded to her braless body. Imogen looked at Rowan's bare arms, tanned and smooth, as she handed her a cigarette, and at the way her bicep flexed when she leant over to light it for her. 'Is everyone looking at me?'

'Yes, but you must be used to it?'

'I can't seem to see anything but you tonight.'

Imogen kept the gasp in. There was tension in her chest, she could hardly breathe. This was happening then and she knew she wasn't going to run away. She pushed the sudden image of William's worried face away. This could be nothing, a flirtation on a summer's night. Champagne and kissing a girl. Ticking things off a list before she got married. She made herself meet Rowan's eyes which were still locked on her, intently, like Imogen was her prey. She could shrug and play the game for longer but her blood was racing with desire. She took a drag of her cigarette, feeling the head rush. Then she stepped towards Rowan, the crowds around them, the London traffic, all fading into the background.

'Me too.'

12

Dear Playwright

'I can't believe you bagged Anna Karenina. You've always been the good Garnett. Who would've thought?'

Imogen looked away from Jonny, felt the telltale redness spread across her chest and stayed silent.

'Stop looking so tragic! It doesn't have to be a big fucking deal. So what if you kissed a girl and you liked it?'

Imogen leant over the table and swiped Jonny with her linen napkin. 'Stop making bad jokes.'

'You know me, if I didn't joke around, spend all my money in restaurants, go on a string of meaningless dates, I'd have to face up to the fact that I hate my job – my life.'

'Tell your father you don't want to work in the City any more. Just stand up to him.'

Jonny shrugged, gave Imogen a hard stare. 'Yeah, 'cause you stand up to Margo all the time – it's that easy.'

They were interrupted by a surly waiter slamming down their starters. Imogen looked down at her goat's cheese salad. The salad leaves were wilting. Jonny prodded his two small pieces of smoked salmon.

'Oliver's has lost the plot. I'm not bringing any more dates here.'

It was Sunday lunchtime and the brasserie on Fulham Road was rammed with rich Europeans feeding their children chips and ice cream. The resulting sugar highs were not conducive to a relaxing meal, especially when there were secret matters of the heart to share. All the noises were amplified by the tiled floor and the central bar where blondes with facelifts and men in suede slip-ons knocked back mid-afternoon cocktails and flirted as if their lives depended on it. Imogen would have preferred an anonymous chain restaurant. She kept dreading one of the Standarts appearing.

'Shit, Imi. Please tell me this isn't a thing?'

Imogen looked at her food. She could not bring herself to try a mouthful. Since the night at Colette's she had hardly eaten.

'We're going to need some more booze.' Jonny drained his glass, reached over and grabbed Imogen's plate and started wolfing down her food. 'The love sickness diet. See it in all the women I date.' He grinned at her, then waved his arms in the general direction of the restaurant, failing to get attention. 'Jesus. Let's get back to what happened.'

Imogen finally met Jonny's gaze. 'We were in Colette's—'

'Colette's – banging pick-up spot, love it,' Jonny interrupted.

'Jonny, stop trying to sound like you are down with the kids. Also no one really believes you are out on dates all the time. Don't interrupt – this is hard enough.'

'Got it.' He reached out and grabbed the sleeve of the surly waiter as he went past. The waiter stopped reluctantly.

'Another bottle of prosecco, please. And if you could deign to clear these plates?'

Imogen tried to look as if Jonny was nothing to do with her. In restaurants he behaved like a spoilt City brat. 'We were in Colette's. I'd had loads of champagne.'

'Is this going to give me a massive hard-on?'

Imogen went on as if she had not heard him. 'She told me to meet her in the loos. So I went. I don't know what made me go—'

'It's called lust.'

'I was terrified waiting for her, worrying who was going to come in, wondering if she would chicken out, or if I should go into a cubicle rather than just standing there like a lemon. And then she came in.'

The waiter stood over them easing the cork out of the prosecco. When he poured it into Imogen's glass it fizzed over the sides.

'That's not cold enough mate.'

The waiter pushed the bottle into the ice bucket. 'You want ice?'

'No thanks mate, you can go. This is edge of the seat stuff, Imi. Then what?'

Imogen took a large sip. 'She grabbed me by my arms, asked me why I was trembling, and then she kissed me. Over and over.'

'This is so hot. You with your whole big-eyed serious thing and that minx Anna Karenina going for it at Colette's.'

Imogen played the images from that night constantly in her head. Feverish, dreamy snapshots. Rowan's soft mouth, her clever tongue. The kisses that were somehow both tender and wild. The slow smile that spread up to her eyes. How she had asked, 'Are these kisses making you wet, playwright?' Imogen had buried her head in Rowan's shoulder; the cashmere jumper smelt of her scent and cigarettes. Rowan had run her fingers up and down Imogen's bare arms and Imogen had felt as if her legs would collapse underneath her. The clawing in her pelvis. She could summon it all, and did, every moment alone.

'Where's the rest of our food? I've had about three mouthfuls. Then what?'

'We got caught by one of the Standarts.'

'What the fuck is a Standart? Fucking luvvie!'

'My play, you idiot. *Standart*. You've even pretended to have read it. The director has nicknamed the actors the "Standarts".'

'Next you'll be talking about yourself in the third person. So you were rumbled, then what? When's the hot action bit back at Anna's, I mean Rowan's, flat?'

Imogen shook her head at him. 'There wasn't any. We were interrupted by Elise. She's playing one of the Tsarina's maids. She didn't say anything but she definitely saw us spring apart. I don't think she's a gossip—'

'Don't be an idiot, Imi. It's the theatre. They're all mad gossips, don't you remember Margo saying actors can't be trusted? She went out with that actor for a bit to make Richard jealous, before they were married.'

'I know nothing about that.' Imogen wasn't surprised that Jonny knew something about Margo she didn't. Margo talked most when she had been drinking and she was often drinking with Jonny.

'She'd had a few when she told me. Richard suddenly freaked out about the commitment – being responsible for her, because she was young and had run away. To annoy him she went out with this actor for a bit. It did the trick and Richard got down on one knee—'

'In Brewer Street. I know that story at least.'

'After that Richard said he didn't want her to be an actress. She'd been having lessons. He was too jealous of the good-looking actors. Don't you think their love story is like some country song? The drinking and hell-raising.'

For once there was too much going on in Imogen's own life for her to want to talk about Margo and Richard. She buried her head in her hands. 'Oh shit, so everyone will know.'

'Yup! I bet she's got a bit of a rep — always seducing straight actresses or playwrights or whatever.'

Imogen looked up quickly at Jonny who had gone back to angrily gesticulating into the restaurant, trying to summon their food. 'You're not cheering me up much.'

'And *finally* some food.' Their sullen waiter dumped down some fishcakes swimming in sauce for Imogen and steak frites for Jonny.

'Hang on, my friend! Some Dijon mustard, some mayo and another bottle.' Jonny had to raise his voice above the din, then caught the eye of a woman in the corner of the restaurant and winked at her. He turned to his food with a sigh of satisfaction.

'How on earth are we on our third bottle?' Imogen pushed her plate aside. 'I can't eat this, I feel sick.'

'It's not like you to be so dramatic. Margo and Sasha, but not you. What's going on with Sasha by the way? She was being odd at the party. She's not texting me back.'

'None of us know. She's still so angry with Margo about everything. I can't talk to her about it. We just end up squabbling about stupid things.'

'I'm convinced it's that bloke of hers. He never lets her out of his sight. He's like a prison guard. I'm actually worried about her.'

'Do we need to keep talking about my family? Margo keeps saying she wants to come to rehearsals. She knows Fred and can easily invite herself. She'll see me and Rowan together and just know. You know what she's like.'

'Yes.' Jonny nodded, his mouth full of food. 'Eyes in the back of her head.' He said it admiringly and Imogen tutted.

'You and your alliance with my mother.'

He shrugged. 'What can I say, she's a game bird. Margo'd hate hearing this but she's looked out for me in a way my mother never has.' He caught Imogen staring into the middle distance again. 'So how did you leave things?'

'We didn't really . . . We sort of got swept away as everyone was leaving. There was a gang going west in a taxi who took me under their wing. I mean I was quite drunk, things are a bit hazy, I think they were just trying to look after me.'

She had told herself this but it had felt like they were forcibly tearing her and Rowan apart. Imogen remembered her last sighting of Rowan on the pavement looking strangely lost, her big eyes and forlorn expression. Then an hour later there had been a text: *Dear Playwright, I loved kissing you tonight, R x.* Imogen hadn't answered it, just stared at it thinking of endless combinations of words until suddenly it was too late and she had fallen asleep. She couldn't tell Jonny, it was too private, and too damning.

'Massive anticlimax. What's happened since? You haven't done anything mad like tell William?'

'Of course not. But . . . well I want to see her again.'

Jonny looked at her levelly. Imogen confided in Jonny like a brother because he stayed calm, and wasn't easily shocked. He joked around, but underneath it all he took her seriously. Now Imogen had said how she felt once, she felt like she needed to say it again.

'I want her. I don't know what to do. I'm supposed to be planning my wedding.'

Jonny rubbed his eyes, refilled their glasses, pushed his plate aside, so he could put his elbows on the table and rest his head in his hands. 'Have you seen her since?'

'There has been one rehearsal and it was horrendous. I couldn't look at her. I was pathetic.'

Imogen had been sick in the loos before she could go to the rehearsal room, and even then the whole time her stomach rolled and dipped and she could only steal glimpses of Rowan under her eyelashes. Rowan had seemed distant and pale. They didn't speak but Imogen obsessively pored over each word Rowan said to the others, seeking any hidden messages Rowan might be trying to send. She finally understood the expression 'heart in mouth'. She was constantly terrified that Rowan thought their kiss a mistake or had been just playing a drunken game with the new girl. But another part of her knew the truth was even more frightening than that. And then the phone that Imogen had kept close to her all through the lunch vibrated.

Dear Playwright, we probably need to talk about the other night and clear the air. Dinner this week at mine? R x

13

Still Waters

Isle of Wight

It was early evening at the Other Place, the garden doors were open and Margo was standing in her kitchen, with just a satin dressing gown covering her nakedness. She poured ice cold rosé into a wine glass, took a bottle of beer out of the fridge. Dusk had left ribbons of coral in the sky and there was still some heat in the August evening. She was in the afterglow of sex, her muscles tired but her brain still. Palestrina was playing in the background and she could hear children still outside in their gardens, enjoying a long summer's evening, after a day at the beach. The gulls no longer seemed mournful but celebratory, wheeling through the sky. The phone rang and jangled Margo out of her mood.

'Sandcove – I mean—'

'Are you *still* doing that?'

'Oh it's you.' Margo inflected her voice with surprise.

'It's only been a week or two.'

Margo raised her eyebrows, moved with the phone to the striped wing chair that faced the garden. 'Three weeks.'

Imogen laughed on the other end. 'Sorry it's been so busy, I know you've left a couple of messages.'

'Yes.' Margo softened her voice, having made her point. 'I've been dying to know how rehearsals have been going. Were the rehearsal drinks epic?'

'God yes. Took ages to recover. You were right.'

'You're mean not to have invited me to at least one rehearsal. I would've been there like a shot. Did you have to talk about the inspiration behind the play?'

'Yes – I talked quite a bit. About you and the church and how I first got into the story. I think it went well.'

Margo imagined Imogen standing up in that basement room, talking about the places that meant so much to their family, everyone hanging on her words. Pride ballooned inside her. This was her middle child, the one who had always been most unsure, the slowest to launch herself. Now she had her own play in rehearsal. 'How's Rowan Melrose doing? Has she had any tantrums yet?' Margo waited but there was silence on the other end of the phone. 'Imi?'

'Sorry, William's just come in. Can I call you another time?'

'I'm sure William won't mind you being on the phone for a few minutes with your mother. Especially as you called me. It might not have been convenient for me.'

'Don't be crabby. Did you have something else on?'

Margo heard the arrogance of youth in her daughter's voice, the disbelief that she might have a life. 'I've got Ali and a few others coming over for book club.'

It was a white lie, book club was on Wednesdays. She looked out at the back of Jack's head. He was wearing just boxer shorts, one of her Moroccan shawls draped around his shoulders, long muscled legs stretched in front of him as he lazed in a garden chair, reading a book she had recommended. The gaps in his reading were shocking, but that was some men for you. He must want his beer, she knew she wanted her wine, and it was warming up just sitting there.

'Well I'll let you go then. Call me tomorrow morning. I'll be at my desk staring into space. Bloody writer's block.' She let a note of self-pity creep into her voice. Her daughter, even though she seemed distracted, swallowed the bait.

'Oh Ma, let's talk about that soon. There are so many themes in those columns that you could use to tie it together. I'm sorry I'm not myself, I'm not used to rehearsals and all the socialising, too many late nights. Honestly it's been amazing. Just hearing the words come to life.'

'What about your leading lady?'

'She's good. She asks me lots of questions about the character, how Alexandra is feeling. She seems quite intense about the part.'

'You sound like you're not sure about her?'

'She's quite distant, quite actressy – I don't suppose I'll get to know her well. It's all chauffeur-driven cars and parties, her life. '

'TV can ruin people. Is Fred keeping her in line?'

'He lost his temper yesterday because she kept complaining about the air conditioning and sent one of the stage hands to find her jumper, right in the middle of things. And she got sushi delivered for lunch because she hates the catering. And then picked off the rice!'

'She sounds like a nightmare. You are due a visit, please. Will you come as usual for Regatta weekend?'

'I don't think I can – sorry, Ma. Rehearsals are behind because Rowan had to miss some days, she had a magazine shoot. She might get the cover, which'll be great press for the play. Fred says we might need to rehearse at the weekend. Rowan says she wants to practise lines with me as she's behind.'

'They're relying on you a lot. It's unusual for the writer to still be needed at rehearsals. I mean maybe a bit at the beginning but now?'

'Fred is very pro it for tone and motivation and if he wants to change dialogue.'

'I see. I should go and get ready for book club.'

'Don't be like that. I'll come home when I can.'

Jack was now pacing the garden with a lit cigarette. The smell drifted in, carrying with it all the associations she hated. Jack knew she didn't like him or anyone smoking. She knew she shouldn't make a fuss over Regatta weekend or feel sore that Imogen now seemed so distracted and busy. Traditions had to change gradually. She ignored the little twitch in her heart muscle, she mustn't be childish. She would make the Regatta weekend this year all about her grandchildren. Gabriel always got into the spirit of it.

'Don't worry about Regatta. You absolutely must do whatever you can to help that play be a success.'

'I might still be able to come. I'll call tomorrow.'

Imogen rang off. Margo sat still for a while, the phone in her lap. It wasn't often that she and Imogen had a conversation that left her feeling distant from her daughter. Imogen was so excited by her new life. Which was a good thing. She called out to Jack in the garden, making her voice lighter than she felt. 'That was Imogen, I'm bringing drinks. Were you smoking?'

'When do you need to go?'

Jack looked at her from under the sweep of his dark hair. They had moved inside and his legs looked so dark and long against her miniature white sofa. They were entwined around hers. The sight excited her always. She felt the familiar pull in her pelvis.

Jack looked at his phone. 'Shit, now probably.' He smiled at her and there was softness in his eyes. 'You look gorgeous.'

She wouldn't let him be serious. 'That's what a good screwing does to me.'

'Sorts me out too. I don't want to go—'

'But you have to.' She struggled with the clichés of their situation. She had told Jack at the beginning that she only wanted fun and sex. She told herself that that was why his situation and hers were the perfect fit, as long as she didn't think too much about what it was doing to other people's lives. It was why she had chosen Jack, because he was safe, already taken. She had had the great one love with Richard, lived the drama of star-crossed lovers and it had nearly killed her. She would never let herself give in to those feelings again.

Jack looked as if he was trying to work her out. 'What's up? Was it the phone call?'

'I wanted to be invited to her rehearsals, it's such a big moment. I know the director too—'

'Come on, you've got to let her just get on with it. Back off a bit.'

'I'm not that kind of mother.'

Jack laughed, reaching for her hand. He stroked her palm with his thumb, calloused from sailing ropes. 'I ring Mum about once a month if she's lucky, can't stand the old bat.'

'Are you comparing me to your mum?' Margo made a pretend move to disentangle herself, to leave the sofa, but Jack held on to her hand, pulling her back down with a sharp tug.

'Just admit it – you're too overprotective. With Imogen, way more than the other two. She's doing what you wanted, marrying the bloke, what's his name—'

'William.' Margo couldn't help smiling.

'So now just let her get on with it.'

Margo relaxed back on the sofa and they smiled at each other. 'You're too handsome, that's your problem. And you know it. You get away with being impertinent.'

'I know how ticklish you are too.'

'If you ever tell anyone, I'll have to kill you.'

'I'm right about Imogen though. You didn't want them choosing drunk, sexy poets who'd bugger off – fair enough after what happened to you. Now they're settling down, you should butt out.'

'I helped her with that play though! I was the first to tell her about the Romanovs, too—'

'So what? It's her thing now. If you keep making everything about you, how is she ever going to be her own woman?'

'You think you're so wise.'

'Some of the stuff you do – it's mad. Not being funny but relying on safe, ordinary men is pointless. Even those men have secrets. Still waters and all that.'

Margo watched as Jack started to hunt for his clothes. It was the only time she saw him looking vulnerable, half-naked, crawling around the floor.

'We started upstairs.'

Jack flashed her a look. 'Oh yeah. Usually you can't wait that long. That reminds me – talking of still waters. I meant to tell you – I saw Gabriel arguing with a fit redhead on Ryde high street last week.'

Margo's heart jumped. Jack's face was the same, smiling, relaxed. The redhead. She thought immediately of the stranger at The Ship. Jack had headed upstairs, she could hear the old cottage floorboards creaking as he moved around above her, collecting his socks and jeans from the floor. It could be anyone, Margo told herself, someone who had just bumped into him on the street. There could be a million reasons. She tried to keep the anxiety out of her voice as she called upstairs.

'Strange. I wonder what it was about?'

'What was what about?' Jack's attention had already wandered; he was checking his phone, no doubt he had several missed calls. Margo blocked the thought.

'Just wondering who the redhead was.' Margo cursed herself for catastrophising, remembering Gabriel and the text messages in the kitchen at Sandcove. The way the girl had stared at her in the pub. There was more than one redhead on the island. Something told Margo that it was the same girl.

'No idea. Looked a bit full on.' She knew Jack would not gossip, everyone knew Gabriel was so devoted, mad about Rachel still, sometimes embarrassingly so. She thought of the way they had danced together at the Groucho, her pride as everyone had stopped to stare. But only recently Rachel had confided in her, talked about Gabriel being distant, worrying about him having an affair. Margo stayed very still on the sofa thinking, pulled a rug over her legs, now Jack's body heat wasn't keeping her warm. She hated the fact that she didn't want to be alone. She started talking to keep him there.

'I might have a party during Regatta. I always used to at Sandcove and they were legendary.'

Jack sat down next to her on the sofa to pull on his boots. 'Can I come?'

'You know you can't.'

'You'd get off on having me there, knowing what I'd be doing to you later.' Jack slipped a hand onto her bare leg under the rug, pushing it up to her thigh. Margo felt the goosebumps, put a restraining hand on his.

'Remember the time we fucked on top of all the coats at Alison's house party?'

'My children were not at that party, Jack.'

'You like risks, I know you do. All those stories I've heard.'

She knew Jack was just teasing her but she felt an edge creep into her voice. 'I won't ever risk embarrassing the girls. They might think they know about my sex life, but it's something else to be confronted by it. What we're doing — well it's against the rules. You're much too young for me *and* married.'

Jack flinched as he stood up, then looked down at her, his face serious. 'I was just messing.' He bent down and softly pressed his lips against hers. 'Don't worry about the Gabriel thing. There's probably a good reason. Sounds like Gabriel's nuts for Rachel and who can blame him.'

Margo smiled and punched him in the arm playfully, then flung her arm around his neck, pulled him down for a long kiss with tongues. Then she let him go.

'Night M.'

'Night J.'

She heard the latch and the front door slam and she nearly called out 'Ssssh' but then remembered that there were no children to wake. She was alone with her thoughts.

14

West London Girls

London

Imogen felt cocooned from the world, a soft dappled light falling around her and the feel of Eyptian cotton against her skin. She was lying in a rumpled bed that smelt of sex. Then there was a sharp blast of air as Rowan slipped back into bed, cold legs suddenly sliding in next to hers, a hand creeping over Imogen's stomach. Imogen had never liked anyone touching her stomach before, had felt self-conscious about its jelly-like wobble. Now in two whirlwind weeks she had given Rowan licence to touch her wherever and whenever she wanted. She did not recognise herself, she was either humming with lust, or comatose from sexual exhaustion.

'I've got coffee and almond croissants from Colette's.' Rowan's voice close to her ear, the silky caress of hair, coffee breath. Imogen was learning that Rowan could get anyone to do anything. Colette's was the nearest place that served decent coffee to her mansion flat behind Sloane Square. She had persuaded them to let her take it away.

'I'll get fat,' Imogen protested smilingly, pulling herself up onto the huge square pillows that Rowan was propping behind her. The duvet fell away from her bare breasts, nipples alerted by the change in temperature. Imogen saw Rowan noticing, the greedy light in her eye, head bending. Imogen gave her a push. 'Oh no you don't. I'm eating before you start any more of that – I'm starving.'

'Spoilsport.'

Rowan peeled off her silk cami, her lifted arms highlighting her ribcage, small breasts pointing skyward, her concave stomach, the dip of her hipbone. Everything in Imogen stirred at the sight of Rowan's body, she wanted to reach out again, suddenly disinterested in breakfast. But Rowan carefully passed a paper coffee cup across the white sheets and she took it and began to sip it as if it was medicine. Last night they had drunk quite a few martinis in the Blue Bar; her head was fuzzy, she needed the coffee. It was hard keeping up with Rowan who seemed to pirouette faster and faster across a London Imogen was just discovering, one that looked like a movie set. The Royal Boroughs of Kensington and Chelsea were laid out before Imogen like a cloak of dreams. A movie reel of kissing until breathless on a cobblestone mews after a house party, with the dawn chorus tuning up. Of being chased by the paparazzi down Beauchamp Place. Of sunshine on white terraced houses, and picnics in square gardens. Of designer restaurants where no one ate very much but everyone drank a lot and who settled the bill was always a mystery. She spent a lot of time in immaculate Ladies' cubicles with Rowan's fingers deep inside her, having to bite her hand to swallow her screams. Rowan loved to press Imogen's face up against a wall whenever there was a chance someone would hear.

It had been easy so far to keep William's innocent faith in her. It revealed to Imogen how separate their lives were. She told him she was throwing herself into theatre life, rehearsals and parties, getting to know the actors and actresses so she could better rewrite their roles. She told him she had to network. The director had taken her under his wing, was introducing her to all the people he knew. They rarely saw each other in the week anyway. William's flat was the other side of London, the shabby end of Queen's Park, and he was a North Londoner through and through. Imogen had played along with the idea that she might compromise on where to live, while knowing that she never would leave her part of London. She had been born in Queen Charlotte's hospital and she was a West London girl to her core. And though they were meant to alternate weekends at each other's flats, they mostly stayed at Imogen's. William's flat was one of those where the mod cons were taking over. It had a shiny chef's cooker, a microwave, sound system, a flatscreen TV which dominated a whole wall and power points wherever you looked. 'This makes me glad I had no sons,' Margo had said when she had seen it, in one of her stage whispers, the kind Imogen had spent her childhood blushing over.

Once Imogen had started to lie to William she found more and more lies tripping off her tongue. Weekends were harder to negotiate but she had told William that Rachel would be staying over on Friday night, as she had a trial in town. For Saturday she invented an old university reunion, asking him if he wanted to come. William had found an excuse and had stayed on his side of London. Rowan told Imogen she had taken to lying like she had taken to sex and then distracted her by flooding her mind and body with pleasure. As soon as she saw a shadow of anxiety flit across Imogen's face she jumped on it, treating it like a rival. She resented Imogen's family who seemed too colourful, too involved with Imogen, always on the phone. Rowan needed exclusive and continual attention. She told her huge circle of friends and hangers-on that she had finally found 'The One'. Imogen kept trying to slow Rowan down but she was strident, unapologetic in her love.

'It's all happening so fast – I can barely think,' Imogen had stammered after a drunken Rowan poured love sonnets into her ear one night. 'I have a whole life, I can't just abandon it. I don't know what I feel. You need to understand about my family. They won't get any of this . . .'

Mostly of course she meant Margo. Margo, whose calls Imogen was not answering. Margo who was usually so often in Imogen's thoughts and whom in her old life she had spoken to most days. A film or book recommendation she wanted to share. A thought about a character in her next play, the one that lay abandoned on the MacBook in her underwear drawer. Imogen wished she could share with Margo the scenes and settings of her new world, the people she was meeting. Most of all she longed to tell her about the extraordinary things that were happening to her body and mind. All the missed conversations with Margo were building up in Imogen like a dam about to burst and through everything there was the tinnitus of guilt. She had always been the most available Garnett, the one who would drop everything if she was needed. Now she tried to fool herself into believing that no one would notice her sudden absence.

The touch of Rowan's fingers brought Imogen back from her reverie. She was running them up and down her arm like she was playing a piano, the softest of touches.

'Where did you go?'

Imogen looked at the crease of concern between Rowan's eyes. Apart from that her skin was line-free, smooth and unblemished. Just a sprinkle of freckles across her nose and prominent cheekbones. She smiled reassuringly, leant forward and touched her nose to Rowan's. She could see Rowan's eyes now up so close, watching her.

'Just thinking about the day. We should get up. You've got that interview and I'm meeting my agent about my new play. The new play I've written nothing of since I met you, Rowan Melrose.'

Rowan groaned, throwing aside the covers. She made to get up, then threw herself face down back onto the bed. 'I'm worth it though, aren't I?'

Imogen laughed and watched Rowan stretch out naked across the covers like a cat. Her body was taut and athletic like a young boy's, her bottom flat, her legs long. It was like looking at a beautiful sculpture of caramel-coloured marble. 'How are you that colour?'

Rowan propped herself up on an elbow and looked at Imogen archly over her shoulder. 'I have an all-over spray tan every two months.' She looked at Imogen like she was silly for not knowing. 'When I was Anna I wasn't allowed to. I had to be pale. I love sunbathing but my dermatologist said I had terrible sun damage from my teens when I roasted myself. Ageing is such a bore.'

Imogen thought of Margo who at the slightest hint of sunshine would be outside and who would imperiously wave away sun cream. It was true Margo had lines, sunspots and more freckles than she should, but her face suited her. It was a face that loved the outdoors and which reflected a life spent on beaches and boats. Imogen felt a pang of longing for that face.

'You're gone again. I've never known anyone so obsessed with their family, it's weird, darling. Why don't you just ring that mother of yours and your sister too. Apologise for being crap and make a date to go home? Then they'll be off your case. I can come home with you,' Rowan looked at Imogen mischievously. 'I'd love to see the setting for *Standart* and your precious Sandcove. You could tell the Garnetts that you've befriended your leading lady and she wants some background and character inspiration, something like that . . .' Imogen must have been looking at Rowan strangely; her voice tailed off and she sat up suddenly, hurt. 'Why are you looking at me like that? Separate bedrooms – I wouldn't let on. I can hide my feelings, you know.'

Imogen tried to make light of it. 'Of course you can, you're an actress.' But she felt that the horror had flashed across her face, at the idea of Rowan at Sandcove. How could she explain to Rowan that she had only ever deceived her mother or sister a handful of times over the tiniest things? The letter she had once sent to her father simply addressed 'London'. The photo she had found of her parents in Venice. The manuscript abandoned by Margo she had sneakily read a few pages of before she was overwhelmed by the realisation that the two young characters in love were based on Margo and Richard. That was really all her secrets. Some secrets she had kept for Rachel, a few for Sasha, although Sasha had always preferred to do her own lying to Margo. That was really all until the boy in Venice and now this. Lesbianism. The word her mother always enunciated with the tone of a person who thinks it's all a bit silly.

Rowan had a much more typical relationship with her parents. An only child who had gone against all their wishes and applied to RADA. The daughter who now phoned dutifully once a month and went home to Nottingham for Christmas if she could face it. Rowan hid everything about her London lifestyle, including the string of girlfriends and her cocaine habit, from her 'dull and ordinary' parents.

'It's impossible to hide things from Margo,' Imogen explained.

Rowan moved off the bed but not before Imogen saw a slight sneer cross her face. She was irritated, or hurt, Imogen didn't know her well enough yet to know which. 'You always make Margo sound like some all-seeing sage. You never hid anything from your parents? Never crept out? Or drank the gin and replaced it with water? Never had a secret boyfriend? I get you have this special thing going on with your mother but—'

Imogen interrupted, needing to stop Rowan saying anything unforgiveable. 'Our father left us when I was six. We never heard from him or saw him again. He left Margo with three young children. She had a kind of breakdown and couldn't look after us.' It all came out in a rush.

Rowan turned quickly to look at Imogen. Her expression softened and she moved over to where Imogen was still in bed, hugged her. 'Oh babes. I'm sorry. I shouldn't have pushed you on the mum stuff. Of course you're close if you went through all that together.'

Rowan's scented hair enveloped Imogen like a curtain as she leant in to kiss her. A soft but insistent kiss. Rowan's smooth skin on hers, her whisper, 'Oh my darling girl, you're so lovely . . .' They fell back onto the bed clinging to each other.

An hour later, dumb with lust once more, anxiety dulled by endorphins, Imogen couldn't even find the energy to care that she was late to meet her agent. She texted Claire, moving the appointment on by an hour. Rowan was rushing around the bedroom trilling like a lark, happy once again, and happy to be keeping a journalist waiting.

'Don't forget lunch, playwright. Ivy Chelsea Garden, we'll be there from about one-thirty. I really want you to meet Ant and the rest of the gang, to show you off. And don't make any plans for the afternoon . . . Ant is wild.'

15

Little White Lies

Sasha lay on her sofa thinking up excuses she could use to leave the flat. Phil was in the shower so she scrolled through the messages on her phone, through her contacts, hoping to find someone she would be allowed to meet, someone Phil would approve of. Phil got suspicious if he thought she was spending too much time on her phone. Recently her messages were mostly from Rachel and Jonny, the odd work colleague. Sasha knew it would be safer to delete the ones from Jonny but she found she couldn't, for moments exactly like these, when she felt that all her friends had slowly evaporated out of her life. *Call me any time for a drink or coffee.*

This week Jonny had caught her unaware by ringing her from his office number. Starved of calls, Sasha had answered and they had talked for over an hour, Sasha pacing up and down a side street off Shepherd's Bush Road near the flat, ignoring horn blasts and wolf whistles. Jonny told her that he knew she was unhappy, that there was something wrong between her and Phil. He told her he had seen the way Phil never left her side. He asked her to come home to Sandcove for a weekend on her own, so they could talk. He told her that he wouldn't try anything, that that wasn't what she needed right now, she needed a good old friend and a shoulder to cry on. After that, the idea of Jonny had become like a lifebuoy, stopping her going under. She had always felt a connection to Jonny, a connection they had to keep hidden. They never talked about it but there was a part of Sasha which believed that the kissing, the way they clung together the times it had happened, was something spilling over, needing to make itself known.

'What are you up to?'

Sasha looked up and Phil stood behind her, blocking the window, a towel wrapped round his middle. 'You're dripping everywhere.'

'So? This place is a dump anyway. Always has been. We've got a week until Cambodia, we should start seriously looking to buy. Why don't you get up off your fat arse and we can go and see some estate agents?'

'I thought you had the rugby? I was going to meet Imogen for lunch.'

'What the hell for? She'll just bang on at you about how badly you behaved at her engagement party. The way you upset everyone, insulted Margo—'

'The lunch is so we can clear the air. She said she wanted to talk – she's my sister, I can't ignore her.'

'It's pathetic the way you go running every time they call. God knows why you even need them in your life. You know Margo can't bear to look at you 'cause you remind her of Richard. You always come back upset when you see them. Don't you have any friends you can see?'

Sasha stood up, not looking at Phil's face, knowing it would be twisted in a sneer. Just when he had pushed her far enough, he would turn on the charm, start wheedling. 'I'm going to have a shower.'

'You know that's what married people do, don't you? They buy somewhere together. It's not that fucking hard – you don't want to though, do you? Is it because you're planning on leaving me?'

Sasha kept very still, kept her face blank. When she got angry, or defended herself, it made things worse. He was standing too close to her and she could smell his strong aftershave, a smell that lingered on their towels and sheets. 'Of course I want us to buy somewhere. I've been saving for the deposit. I can pick up some—'

Phil had turned away from her, snatched her book from the sofa arm and, quick as lightning, he flung it across the room. It hit the wall with a slap, the spine split and it slid to the ground. Sasha flinched and inched further away from Phil, who was shouting. 'Don't fucking bother – you won't have a clue what to look for. You're totally impractical – just like the rest of your idiot family – living in a house that's falling down. Do you even know what square footage we need? And I don't want to live in one of those shitty mansion block conversions that all your posh friends like so much. We want something brand new, double-glazed, all mod cons. I'll make some appointments for Monday morning.'

'Okay.' Sasha felt her hopelessness overwhelm her, a weight pushing down on her chest. She didn't want to get in the shower, where he could come and stand and watch her, like she was an animal in the zoo. She knew she had no spirit left, she needed him to leave. She started to move like a snail around the flat, small, slow movements, clearing the coffee cups away, opening the curtains.

Phil called from the bedroom. 'I thought you were having a shower? As you're ditching me, I've texted Chris and Grant to see if they're up for the rugby at the Queen's Head. I'll see you back here at around four, okay? Don't be late.'

Sasha put on clothes she knew Phil hated. One of her shortest, flirtiest dresses, wedges that would have made her taller than him. Siren-red lipstick. Washed, her hair shone white blonde again. The sunshine was warm and despite the Shepherd's Bush dust and traffic, there was blue sky above her head, bright white buildings. She heard the door slam and felt herself exhale finally. She felt she had forgotten it all, the world outside the flat, the world of pavement cafés, groups of friends and laughter, busy people with lives, hurrying around her with their dreams and plans. It was a summer's day in London, and she was free. She watched a beautiful girl go past carrying a sourdough loaf, a bunch of flowers. Once she used to do those things on a Saturday morning, go out for coffee and take it back to Phil in bed, fill a vase with tulips. Now Phil didn't drink coffee and no little touches could ever make her feel that their flat was a home. She knew she could not stay in her marriage, could not let herself slowly disappear, waste her youth. She was about to do something very reckless, and the feeling was like a drug, a kick of something like hope.

Jonny was in one of his favourite spots, a seat outside E&O in Blenheim Crescent. Even though she was full of bubbling nerves, Sasha grinned when she saw him, catching him unawares. The seat was one of four carved into the side of the restaurant. Jonny was basking in a patch of sunshine, a very pink cocktail in one hand, a cigarette in the other. With his aviator sunglasses and the messy blond hair flopping over his forehead he was working his best James Dean impression.

'Cocktails for lunch?' She blocked his sun, watching him take in her long bare legs.

'Always.' He stood up and kissed her cheek; she felt the brush of his stubble, his breath on her ear. The heat of him, his height, the muscles in his arms. 'God, it's good to see you, Sasha.'

Once she was settled beside him on the seat with her own cocktail, just a few inches between them, she realised that anyone she knew might see them there together brazenly drinking in the sunshine. 'Should we be inside? I'm not keen on meeting anyone we know.'

'God no, you know how hard it is to get these seats. It's a gorgeous day and we're old friends having lunch. No one's going to tell Phil if they see us, they know what he's like.'

Sasha took a big sip, watched someone coming out of the travel bookshop with a bag full of books. A couple stopped in the road in front of them to kiss. Sasha felt herself blushing, especially as Jonny was quieter than usual and kept sneaking looks at her face.

'Do you remember that summer we sat here all afternoon? People kept joining us? We wrecked a room at that hotel, pulled the smoke alarm off the wall?'

'We ended up dancing at the Cobden Club and you persuaded them to let us smuggle out champagne in black bin bags when they were closing. What happened to that group — Danny and Mike, the twins? You don't talk about them any more. They knew how to party.'

Sasha wondered whether it was too early to tell the truth, to ruin the mood. She wanted to hold on to the feeling of being warm in the sunshine, the sweet alcohol working on her, Jonny close beside her. But he wasn't flirting, he wasn't joking around, he was looking at her like he wanted her to talk.

'They all seemed to drift out of my life once I married Phil. He didn't much like that scene, people coming back to the flat late. He was always falling out with them. Or telling me things they had said about me. I honestly feel like I don't have any friends left.'

Jonny moved his hand on the seat next to hers, hooked his little finger over her little finger. 'You've got me.'

There was a pause as Sasha looked down at their hands and thought how she wanted to thread her fingers through his, sit here openly holding hands. 'I've only got a few hours.'

Jonny sighed and took off his aviators. When he turned to smile at her, it felt like all her insides had flipped over. 'I want to ask you to come to my flat. I really do want that. But we're not going to do that. We're going to have one more cocktail each, and then we're going to go inside and eat chilli salt squid and drink Sancerre and we're going to talk and make a plan for you. And then I'm going to walk you home, right on curfew.'

Sasha held her chin up, a gesture that made her look like Margo. 'Of course, what on earth is there to do at your flat anyway?'

'If he ever hurts you – you call me straight away. I mean it. Or just get out and come to my flat.'

Sasha could feel the velvet of the banquette under her thighs, and under the starched white tablecloth one of Jonny's legs was entwined with her own. She was aware of every inch of her body, the tantalising closeness of the man she wanted. The cocktails had made everything soft focus, and yet she could feel time rushing past. The busy lunch crowd had died away, there were just a few couples left enjoying the hush and the air conditioning, staring into each other's eyes. They could see the street through the big windows, crowds from Portobello Market, lost tourists, the monied Notting Hill set pulling up in sleek cars, roofs down. Blasts of dance music, shouts down to the street from windows above.

'He won't, I don't think. It's all talk with him. I didn't see any of it coming – I'm such an idiot. It just sort of crept up on me, the snide remarks, the wanting to know where I am all the time. Hating my family—'

'Do they know?' Jonny poured more Sancerre into their glasses. They had barely touched the small white plates of sushi and tempura on the table between them. 'I saw Imogen for lunch, she didn't mention it, so I just wondered.'

Sasha tried not to show her surprise. 'When was that?'

Jonny looked uncomfortable, like he'd blurted out a secret. 'A few weeks ago. She's going through some stuff. I can't really say if she hasn't told you.'

Sasha thought about how Imogen would once have confided in her, how distant they had become. It reminded her that Jonny had these intimate conversations with each of the Garnett women while she had been stupidly hoping he was hers alone. He belonged to them all. 'We don't really talk much any more – it's okay, I wouldn't ask you to tell me. I hope she's all right though.'

'You know she's like a sister to me, don't you? It's not the same as us.'

'Whatever *us* is.' Sasha's tone was cynical and she could feel herself pulling away from him, from the enchanted bubble around them. Her mind had flashed to Richard, his latest voicemail, the one she was ignoring. What she had done behind her family's back, how much they would hate her when they knew.

Jonny was frowning. He sounded awkward when he finally spoke. 'I think we both know there's something here. But you need to sort your life out first.'

'Yeah – because that's so easy.' Sasha pulled her leg away from Jonny's, tipped the last of the wine into her mouth. She would walk home alone, she wouldn't let Jonny come with her, in case they were seen. 'I need to go.'

'Sasha, what the hell? Where have you gone?'

Sasha looked at Jonny, saw he was upset. His hand lay open towards her on the table. She looked at his arm, his brown skin, the ridiculous cotton friendship bracelet he and Gabriel both wore. He was familiar to her and yet exciting, forbidden. Walking away now, back to her grey flat, was going to be one of the hardest things she had ever done. The way he was looking at her made her want to open up to him.

'You're not going to believe me – what I've done. I found Richard – my dad. I've seen him a few times, met his wife. No one knows. Margo would kill me. I just wanted to know about him so badly, to try to understand – to see if I'm like him. And now he's left me a message – it sounded serious – I need to ring him back—'

Jonny was looking dazed and Sasha wondered if he had even taken in what she was saying. Then his eyes focused again and he was back with her, sitting up straighter. He raked his fingers through his hair. 'That's a lot to take in. Bloody hell – resurrecting Richard is going to make the Garnetts implode. Explains why you've been avoiding everyone. I thought it was because of me – you were avoiding me – you know, because of *feelings* . . .'

Sasha could not help but smile at Jonny, at the fact that despite her revelation, he was thinking mainly of her and him. 'Oh, those pesky things!'

Jonny gave her a wry half-smile. 'Don't tease me – you'll need me when the shit hits the fan.'

'Yes I will need you. And now I need to go. Curfew.' She looked around her, taking a snapshot for her memory. The sunshine lunch, a moment of freedom. She had shared her secret and she had seen Jonny's feelings. She had something to take back with her into her small, sad life. Something to make her stronger.

'Please let me walk you back. I want to hear about Richard, what he's like. We can walk and talk. Can we?'

Sasha let her fingers gently float down onto his, where they lay on the table. The softest of touches, but one that staked her claim to him. 'Walk me to the end of Netherwood Road.'

'Good, I wasn't ready to say goodbye.'

16

The Weak Link

It was what Margo liked to call 'a boon day'. The tail end of summer, with a sudden bite in the air. There had been sea fog early that morning. Now the sun was blazing, everything clear-edged as if there was a sharper lens on the world. The ozone in the air was like an injection of energy and Margo absorbed herself in a shell hunt as she strolled along the tide line. She walked through the door of The Porthole with her pocket full of some periwinkles and cockles but nothing special enough to show her sister. Alice had already bagged their favourite booth overlooking the sea. As Margo leant over to kiss Alice's tanned cheek, she noticed a new dress and a bag she hadn't seen before. It was never easy for Margo to pay compliments but she tried hard for the people she really loved. She moved Alice's pretty basket and sat down.

'Ali, you look lovely today. Great frock.'

Alice blushed with surprise, a curse from childhood. 'Thanks.'

'Where's the bag from?'

'That shop Tides in Yarmouth. I think you told me about it?'

'You look so much better since you ditched Seb. Mum pushed you into that marriage, always going on about him being from the right background. She was such a snob.'

Alice did not respond. The sisters could have been twins, both with the same thick black curly hair now touched with grey, although Margo wore hers past her shoulders and Alice had a neater bob. They had the same curvy figure, carrying extra weight in the middle, but with what their father had called 'great pins'. Their olive skin tanned easily. Margo's face was like a more vivid version of Alice's, as if a painter had gone back and tried again, this time with brighter paint and bolder brushstrokes. Margo's mouth was wider, her cheekbones sharper. Alice's eyes were a slightly less intense bright blue, and looked out at the world with more acceptance. They both scanned the blackboard of specials.

'Ooh good, they've got the crab. I'm going to get a lager shandy. I was dreaming of one on the way here. What are you having?'

'I'll have the crab too please and I need a large glass of wine. Chablis.' Margo raised an eyebrow at her sister who wasn't usually a lunchtime drinker.

When Margo was back from ordering they sat for a while in silence looking out at the Solent. They had a lunch date most weeks, and spoke on the phone every Sunday evening so there was no rush to share news. Margo felt it was their usual easy companionable silence, until Alice spoke in an ominous voice.

'We're lucky to have this time together. Living close to each other and having lives that fit together now. It makes up for all that time we had apart, when you left home. I'm not sure Dad ever recovered.'

Margo looked closely at Alice. 'Don't make me feel more guilty than I already do. What's with you?'

Alice kept gazing out of the window, avoiding looking at Margo. Margo could see suddenly that she was very upset. 'You're going to be angry—'

Margo tugged Alice's sleeve sharply. 'Alice, you're scaring me. What's wrong?'

Alice braved direct eye contact. 'Adriana has been in touch with me.'

'What the fuck?'

'Sssh.' People turned round to look in the sudden hush. 'I should've told you outside.'

'Just tell me what that woman wants.'

Alice felt unable to get the words out; her stutter, another childhood curse, flared up when she was stressed. 'She . . . she says Richard's ill. She thought you should know.' Alice watched a veil of stone drop over Margo's face. She knew exactly how it would go, knew Margo would shut down, shut her out, as she had when Richard had left.

Margo looked back out to the Solent as she let what Alice had told her sink in. Her voice was low and urgent. 'How ill is he?'

Alice looked down at her lap where her hands lay clasped so tightly together that her knuckles had turned white. 'Very ill. He's dying of liver cancer. She wants you to tell the girls.'

Pure horror flashed across Margo's face. 'You know I will never tell the girls. Jesus, dying? Really? Did he really do that to himself?'

'I know. I can't believe it. What is he? Sixty-three?'

'Sixty-four. I always thought I would look after him when he was ill.' Margo's voice cracked.

Alice felt tears of sympathy spring up. It was unimaginable that the girls were losing a father who had been absent for so much of their lives. That she had to break the news to her sister that the only man she had ever loved was dying. The bustle swelled around them, the noise harsh and intrusive. A family jostled one another right next their table, mulling over the specials. Margo threw death stares their way. When the adolescent waitress banged their plates down in front of them, they were jolted, surprised, as if they had forgotten why they were there.

Margo tried to listen as Alice nervously chattered about nothing but it was like a rusty lock had opened, releasing old memories. No one had said the names Adriana and Richard to her like that for twenty years. She kept hearing her mother's prophetic words. 'If he carries on drinking like that, he'll kill himself.' Her mother had never apologised to Margo for the things she had been wrong about. Margo *had* made it to Oxford. Elizabeth Garnett had said that Richard would never let Margo go to Oxford, never bear a separation, in case she was swept away by someone more eligible. Yet Richard had shown his devotion and followed Margo to Oxford, dossing in a house full of poet comrades when he wasn't smuggled through the window of Margo's room in halls, working any shift he could get in the bar at the Randolph Hotel, trying not to sneer at the tourists. Oxford had been three of the simplest, happiest, hardest-working years of their lives and afterwards Margo *had* made a prestigious career she loved. But her mother had been right about Richard's drinking and she had been right when she said that one day he would leave. Margo could never forgive her for that.

'I just wonder if meeting her father would help Sasha? Bring her back to us all. I feel like all the silence about their father makes the girls fill in the gaps in ways that aren't healthy.'

Margo looked at Alice, whose face was pale and serious. She thought of Sasha who had been pushing her away ever since she had been born. 'What do you mean fill in the gaps?'

'Their imaginations have been allowed to turn Richard into something so big. If they saw him, knew about him, maybe—'

Margo gave a low groan. The argument was worn ground between the sisters. 'And then they would know what their father did. How little he wanted them.' Margo spoke slowly, dragging out each word painfully.

Alice steeled herself. 'He wants to see them before he dies. I think they need the chance to know him.'

'Why should he have them now? And now I am supposed to feel sorry for him? What else did Adriana say?' Margo's voice was whippet thin.

'Only that she thought you should know.' Alice wanted to reach out, to hold on to her sister who looked at that moment older, beaten down.

Margo moved a piece of lettuce across her untouched plate. 'Do you want mine? I'd hate Judy to think there's something wrong with it. It pisses me off, this intrusion back into my life – we all knew he would kill himself eventually. What's the big fucking deal?' Margo looked at her sister for agreement, saw hesitation. 'What aren't you telling me? How long was this little chat you had with Adriana?'

'She was traumatised, poor thing. I could hardly cut her off.'

Margo put her head in her hands. 'I would have. You're too nice – you always have been.'

'You mean you think I'm weak. She didn't ring you though. I'm going to get the bill.' Alice felt the familiar anger overwhelm her, it was always there under every conversation with Margo, ready to rise up. The feeling that Margo thought her life was more important than Alice's, that she was the more interesting sister. The stronger one. Alice started to lift out of her seat.

'Sorry, Alice. If there's more – please just tell me.'

Alice sat back down, her face very pale. 'Richard's been sober for twenty years now. That's what Adriana said.' Alice watched Margo's face and began to talk pointlessly. 'I mean the liver cancer now could well be related to all those years of alcohol abuse. Most likely it is. And the smoking, he smoked like a chimney.'

'God. Twenty years sober. A life neatly divided in two.'

Alice sagged as if all the life had drained out of her, now her secret was shared. 'I'm so sorry, Margo.'

'Go and get the bill. I need to leave.' Margo sat very still once she was alone, waiting for the hurt to engulf her, waiting to crack open. She could feel the darkness all around the edges, waiting for her. She could not let it happen again, let herself go under. *Richard O'Leary, I always hoped you would die.*' She said this inside her head, over and over, like it might change something.

Margo left Alice as soon as she could, unable to bear the look of sympathy on her sister's face. She went back alone to the Other Place to work but it was impossible. In her study, a shaft of sunlight hit her desk and dust motes danced in the air above it. A messy stack of papers, a half-drunk cup of cold tea and some toast crumbs on a plate. Everything just as it had been and yet everything was different. She had thought it would be harder to be at Sandcove with its memories in every corner. But this place didn't feel like hers and she knew that if she read over the words she had written this morning she wouldn't recognise them as her own.

She paced the room, restless with a kind of rage she had not felt for a long time. It consumed her. It wasn't the grief she was expecting or even acceptable sadness but an evil kind of jealousy. A jealousy as sharp and as insidious as if she was a girl again. She had not been able to save Richard. Her love had not been strong enough. Someone else had saved him. She had fought his illness for so long and none of it had been enough. She wasn't enough. Their family wasn't enough. She had left her home, turned her back on her mother and father, left Alice behind, all for him. And it was never enough. She felt stupid for believing they would survive, for putting their children through it. Stupid for believing he could be sober, be a normal father. She had naively believed love could change everything. She hated feeling stupid, the clever scholarship girl who had made it to Oxford without her parents' support, just the erratic cheques her guilty father sent behind her mother's back. And now those feeling of inadequacy had returned with a vengeance and it was overwhelming. Because as it turned out she was so obviously the weak link in the chain, the fault in their design.

For an hour or so Margo just walked around the Other Place trying to outpace her thoughts, trying to make the clock hands move. She made cups of tea she didn't drink. Plumped the cushions, fed the dogs. She put the drier on again needlessly. She half-emptied the dishwasher before getting distracted by a toppling pile of newspapers that needed to go in the recycling. In the end the crushing silence drove her out of the house again. She had a Residents' Committee meeting at the sailing club at six and she would walk slowly there along the beach and prepare herself for company in this small place where everyone knew your business and, worst of all, your history.

The meeting was in full swing when Margo arrived. Lots of the committee were brandishing large glasses of red which they raised in salute at Margo with 'Hello's and 'Jolly good, Margo's here.' The joviality made Margo want to retreat and hide. The setting sun had turned the Solent pink and it seemed to be encouraging a wild mood.

'Could be the Med,' she heard James Ripley say.

A couple of Seaview old-timers were using the meeting as an excuse to sink some drinks in convivial company. Behind the bar, Lacie looked like she had seen the end of a lock-in the previous night. She nodded at Margo who stood looking dazed at the bar, letting the swell of chatter wash over her.

'You all right Margo? Usual?'

'Gin please. Make it a double.'

Margo suddenly had the comforting realisation that she could get gloriously drunk tonight, she was near home and her friends wouldn't care. She could call Jack later and get him to meet her. Once she had drunk all thoughts of sober, dying Richard O'Leary out of her head. She could drink and fuck it all away. The hit of gin on an empty stomach lifted her spirits. It was a relief to have a plan for the evening, and with a gulp of gin she turned to take in the room and to find someone who would be up for flirting.

Much later she staggered out into the cooler night air, her boots echoing on the empty pavement, her breath an alcoholic fog in front of her. The door swung shut on the rowdiness behind her, and then it was just her and the sound of the sea. She nearly slipped on a jagged paving stone but managed to prop herself up on a parked car. And then suddenly there they were. Further up the street in a pool of nicotine yellow light from a streetlamp. A moment she had always dreaded. They were just on their way home from somewhere, the toddler asleep in the buggy. Margo thought about how late it was, how the child should be at home in its own bed. What on earth was his mother thinking keeping him out so late? She knew he was three – Eddie. Before she could avert her eyes she saw the swell of the woman's stomach and Jack's hand slipped into the back pocket of her jeans. Perhaps she did not know everything there was to know about Jack Walker. It did not much look like a marriage in trouble.

If she was lucky a nightcap of whisky might knock her out, on top of the other booze. She turned her back on Jack and his wife. Things felt smashed into a million pieces. And she did not want to look it straight in the eye, but a cold resolution was growing inside her. She could not see Jack any more. Even through the haze of the alcohol and a mist of tears, she saw that she could not do that any more to another woman. To a wife. To a family. Do what had been done to her. The wife was having another baby, hoping to bring Jack back to her. Margo remembered how each of her babies had brought the fresh hope that Richard would finally stop drinking, try to be part of the family. She was such a terrible hypocrite. She must stop now before her daughters found out, understood once again how weak she was. She moved away from the scene and down Seaview's hill towards her empty bed.

17

A Dark Horse

Rachel was hiding at the top of the house as the noises of yet another one of Margo's house parties floated up to her. There were sharp bursts on the doorbell, and the clatter of her excited children running up and down the tiled hallway. Rachel often wished that the old bell pull would stop working. It was a sound she had heard constantly as a child, announcing that their father was drunk and had lost his keys again. He would pull it down long and hard, trying to make Margo appear. Sometimes they would hear his voice, thick with drink and charm, calling her name. Rachel would beg Margo to let him in, just to make the sound stop. If Margo made Richard sleep in the shed, Rachel remembered lying awake, worrying about him in the cold. Even though she wished him dead she worried about how he never had a coat.

Tom's deep belly laugh cut through her thoughts, Margo's dogs barking a welcome. Rachel knew it was childish the way she had turned back into the moody teenager skulking in her room. But Margo seemed to be at Sandcove more now, since the talk they had had at the Railway Hut. It was as if Margo was treating Rachel's feelings about living at Sandcove as an excuse to slowly take it back from her, right under her nose. There was a recent carelessness about other people's feelings in

Margo, and Rachel did not know why. She had been weak when they had set up the terms of the arrangement, she should have taken a harder line with Margo not being able to simply 'borrow' Sandcove when she felt like it. It hadn't helped that none of it seemed to bother Gabriel. He could accept Margo the way she was most of the time, and he flourished under her beneficence. He had taken Sandcove as a gift that came with Margo. But then Margo was not his mother.

As a teenager Rachel had been fierce and independent, busy away from home with a big circle of friends, with sport and drama and academic success. All her achievements felt like they were motored by anger. She did not want to be a failure like her father. She did not want to be weak like her mother either. Rachel remembered the relief when she was twelve, when Margo had finally got out of bed, had shaken off the depression that had claimed a whole year of her life. And yet when Margo tried to resume her role, Rachel was vile to her, punishing her. Imogen was always the favourite. When Margo looked at Imogen, Rachel saw raw exposed love on her face; she wished Margo would look at her that way. And although she knew Gabriel was right when he said that Margo looked at her as an equal with admiration and respect, she still yearned for the primal and fierce love that Margo and Imogen shared. She saw how bad things were between Sasha and Margo, how they clashed, how things stayed unsaid, anger and sadness on both sides. In comparison she knew she had made good progress with her mother since she had been that angry teenager. Even if it was still something they both worked at, she was proud of where they had got to. Which was why Margo's recent insensitivity hurt her, especially since she had opened up to her, admitted feelings she had not shared with Gabriel. The new wild and restless energy in her mother reminded Rachel too much of old Margo, the one she had hoped they would never see again.

Rachel began to pack up her work before her mother came up to find her, moving some of her files into the desk drawer. Her eyes fell on the shiny pink childhood diary she had stowed away there. It had fallen down the side of the old leather sofa, the one which was too big for Margo to take with her when she left Sandcove. Rachel had wanted rid of the sofa, it held too many bad memories of finding her father, stinking and unshaven, asleep on it in the mornings. Memories of him gatecrashing their movie nights. 'Budge up girls and make room for your old Da. What movie are we watching then?' He would be sweaty, red-faced, stinking of booze. Everything would be ruined and Margo would get up and move away in glacial silence. There were other times when Margo would stand her ground, shoving Richard, shouting and swearing at him, telling him to sleep it off in his shed. There was more violence, Margo slapping and punching, Richard once or twice finding the focus to land a huge shove which would send Margo like a skittle across the floor. Rachel would be screaming at Richard, baby Sasha crying, Imogen running to Margo, silent tears on her face, trying to help her up.

At Rachel's insistence they had given the sofa away and when the cushions came off and the whole thing was tipped on its side to move it out, Rachel saw a flash of something pink. She saw the huge scrawl on the front, '*MUM do not read*', and snatched it up. She often wondered whether Margo knew of its existence or if it had spent twenty-something years buried in a sofa. She had read it cover to cover that very night. Sometimes she smiled, sometimes hot tears streamed down her face. She felt love for her younger self, admiration for what she had endured. From then on she kept the diary in her desk, and checked in with young Rachel from time to time. It helped her understand her family better, the legacy she and her sisters lived with and why she had got into a pattern of trying to save them all.

Listening to the noises downstairs Rachel thought how she had hated the chaos of her childhood. Even now she still found it hard to go to sleep if parties, or drinking, carried on below her, or around her. There had been a constant sharp-edged tension in Margo as she waited and worried about Richard. Margo's parties at Sandcove gave Rachel the same feeling of chaos, the loss of control. She did not know who would be invited, what rowdy shape the evening would take. Rachel wanted something different for her girls. She shut her desk drawer and reminded herself that she should be feeding them supper now. They would be happily neglected, standing on chairs to get crisps and chocolate out of the high cupboards. They loved Margo's parties, the way their parents' focus shifted away from them for a while, let their bedtime slip. But for them the chaos was only ever temporary.

Standing up stiffly, Rachel looked over the Sandcove decked terrace, saw Tom and Leo smoking cigarettes behind Margo's back, giggling together like two children. Further off on The Duver, Gabriel was walking towards Nettlestone Point. Her stomach dived. On his mobile at 6 p.m. on a Friday evening. What would his excuse would be? 'A call from a patient,' he would say. A crisis, something so dreadful none of them would be able to imagine it, and confidential of course. Gabriel could be patronising when he talked about his clients. Her dread flared up again. Something was wrong with Gabriel, with their marriage. She had made it worse by telling him that she would not have any more children. Since that night a wall had come up between them. He would leave her and she would be in this broken-down house on her own, miles away from London and her friends. Living a life she had really only chosen for him. He would leave her, because everyone knew that what was men did. When the babies came and the sex dwindled they soon began to cast around for an escape from domesticity.

Yet she knew Gabriel believed fatherhood was the most important job he would ever have. She had chosen him because he seemed different to other men she knew. His love had been the thing that had finally anchored her. He had been patient and kind in the way he wooed her and many a night he had listened to her cry angry tears over the father she had lost and how her childhood had been brutally cut short. She knew he was the kind of man her mother wanted for her but that wasn't primarily why she chose him. She chose him because he didn't seem to be restless, driven by absences. He was sure and strong. He didn't want a big fat corporate pay packet, he wanted to help people. His parents were still together, his mother had devoted herself to her husband first, her two sons next. Gabriel wasn't spoilt but he had a very strong sense of what family life should be like, family meals were sacred, as were fresh air and sport. Raised voices and petty arguments were frowned upon. But he had embraced who Rachel was and had never tried to change her. He never complained when she was shut up in her office preparing for a case. When they had lived in London, he had been a brilliant strategist when it came to her career, had helped her plot her path to partnership at the law firm, had made her push as hard as her male colleagues. She knew she was in danger of making Gabriel sound too good to be true when she talked about him to friends or family. He did the washing, cooked the meals, and kept the wheels turning with all the domestic chores she hated.

Recently though it felt like one of the wheels had come off. She would be in a room with Gabriel but feel like he had escaped somewhere else. He kept his phone close, as if it was an extra limb. Rachel would wake up sometimes in the morning and find he had left their bed. He was coming to bed later too, watching TV programmes he had never been interested in before. And then there were confidential calls at strange times of the day. He was physically at home just as much so Rachel did not see how it could be an affair, and yet it would be just like Gabriel to only be having an emotional affair.

'Rachel darling, we need the lady of the house! Imi's here.'

Margo's sing-song voice rang up the stairs, a sound so redolent of Rachel's childhood that it still made her want to dig her heels in and refuse to move. But she needed to go downstairs and try to gather the reins of her life again. And she needed to see Imogen's face. She wanted to know why her sister had been so distant of late and she needed to protect her from Margo's inevitable grilling. Imogen would hate that in front of company.

'Coming.'

As Rachel turned the corner onto the final flight of stairs, Margo was gripping the wooden bannister at the bottom. Her knuckles were white, the gold rings digging into the flesh of her fingers. She moved close to Rachel when she reached the last step. Rachel could see Margo was excited, about three drinks along. She had been drinking more recently, which made Rachel nervous.

'Where on earth have you been? You've got guests. You can't just leave me and poor Gabriel to look after everything.'

Rachel neatly side-stepped her mother and moved ahead of her. 'They're your guests. And "poor" Gabriel is on his mobile on The Duver right now.'

'Please don't be difficult, Rachel. Not tonight.'

Rachel turned and saw the slightly glassy look in her mother's eyes, the high flush on her cheeks. Margo was incapable of listening at times like these, she was only focused on the next thing she had to say. 'What do you need me to do?'

'Something's up.'

Rachel felt the tension in her stomach bubble up. She looked closely at her mother, who had a kind of manic sparkle tonight. She had stolen a snakeskin blouse from Rachel's wardrobe but she was wearing it with one too many buttons undone. Her mother behaved so sluttishly when Jonny was around.

'What are you on about? Where's Imi?'

Margo lowered her voice to a theatrical whisper. 'She's left William behind.'

Relief flooded through Rachel. This was nothing to do with her. Margo and her eagle eyes had not yet spotted anything wrong closer to home. 'So what? It's not like you hang on William's every word.'

'That's not the point. There's clearly something wrong. Imogen hasn't set a date for the wedding or made any progress and now we're having a celebration for her play opening and she hasn't even brought her husband-to-be? Instead she's brought the snooty actress from her play, apparently they're the best of friends now. Did you know they were friends? You're going to hate her. She's brought three pieces of luggage with her. All Vuitton.'

Rachel stood looking at her mother, thinking. Margo loved a drama, was always prone to exaggeration, but her instincts were always sharp. 'Seems a bit odd. I've heard nothing about a friendship or anything really about the play. We won't find out any more standing here. Try to behave for Imogen's sake.' And Rachel pulled her mother in the direction of the sitting room, her curiosity piqued by the idea of Anna Karenina at Sandcove.

'So what's up next? Any action flicks? I can't believe you're a blonde.'

Rachel elbowed Jonny, smiling. 'Sorry Rowan, Jonny has a thing for blondes. I can't believe you were fooled – it was obvious she wasn't dark-haired.'

'Did you think?' Rowan looked up from the kitchen table where she was picking the smoked salmon off the blinis that Margo had handed around. Rachel noticed that the line of Rowan's perfectly plucked eyebrows arched without creasing her forehead.

'Are you not eating those?' Margo asked Rowan, pointedly looking at the mess of abandoned blinis on the table. 'Shall I put them in the bin for you?'

'Would you mind? It's just a wheat intolerance. I bloat really badly. Rachel, you were saying you didn't think I made a convincing brunette?'

Rowan's tone was sweet, but Rachel thought her eyes were cold, like a shark's. Rachel feigned politeness. 'Sorry, I didn't mean to cause offence. It's just I have a brunette mother, and have you seen her eyebrows and eyelashes?'

Everyone looked over at Margo whose hair had gone even wilder from the heat of the oven. Rachel was hit anew by the force of Margo's attractiveness.

Rowan smiled graciously, although Rachel could see it was forced. 'You didn't tell me your mother was so beautiful, Imo.'

'It's "Imi". I'm old and past it now,' Margo snapped.

'Margo, you are in your prime.' Jonny inclined his head chivalrously towards Margo, who smiled gratefully at him.

Rachel turned to her sister hoping she would chime in. But Imogen just smiled weakly and had another sip of gin. Rowan was looking at Imogen too but her tight smile did not reach her eyes. Where was bloody Gabriel when you needed him to smooth things over?

'I think we should eat soon otherwise we'll get well and truly legless.' Rachel tried to catch her sister's eye.

Margo was defensive. 'It's all ready. I was just waiting for Gabe – you know how fussy he is about how he serves things. Where's he gone now?'

'He was on the phone last time I saw – I need to fill him in on the goss from the reunion.'

Rachel looked sharply at Jonny. 'He's looking after the others in the sitting room. What reunion? Why didn't he go?'

'I've no idea, ask him yourself. Aren't you supposed to be married? Something to do with a tricky patient he didn't want to abandon. Any more red for a thirsty soldier?' Jonny loved to refer to his soldiering days but he had been kicked out of Sandhurst after a couple of months. The final straw had been him losing his rifle on an exercise. He had left it behind a tree, planning to go back for it later.

'Is there any vodka? It's the only drink I'm allowed.' Rowan used a wheedling voice with Jonny, used to enslaving men.

Jonny stood up and looked over at Rowan's empty wine glass which had been filled with Chablis several times and laughed. 'I hate to tell you this but you've already had quite a lot of vino. Have you got an intolerance to wine too?'

'We don't keep vodka in this house.' Margo's voice was thick with disdain and Rachel saw redness creep across Imogen's pale cheeks.

'It's the calories.' Rowan looked around at them all coolly, unfazed by Margo's tone. 'As an actress I have to watch my weight.' Rachel felt like Rowan was looking at her pointedly. 'I've learnt to like vodka because no director can smell it on me. They think you should behave like a church mouse when you're working.'

Rachel saw her mother's face before she turned her back and knew she was thinking of the empty vodka bottles, hidden all around Sandcove. Margo had always woken when the house was asleep to try to hide the evidence but Rachel had lain in bed listening to her, wondering why she bothered; everyone knew their father was a drunk.

Finally Gabriel appeared and Rachel could see him immediately register the atmosphere in the kitchen. 'All okay? Alice and Tom are having a ball in the sitting room. I'm going to go and top them up . . . Not that they need any more.' Like a good host he scanned the room for empty glasses and Rachel felt a twinge of love. 'Rowan, you haven't got a drink, what can I get you?'

Margo's voice rang out commanding and cold. 'She'll have whatever's going, I'm sure. Everyone à table!'

Once they were in the womb-like comfort of Sandcove's dining room, tensions eased for a while. Margo had decided to ignore Rowan and the daughter who had dared to bring an uninvited guest. She was more cheerful as she had dictated the seating plan, with Tom on her left and Jonny on her right. The room was dominated by a Georgian dining table with rounded corners and a lustre that reflected the candles dotted along it. It was the kind of room where voices rarely rose above a respectful hum. However drunken Garnett dinner parties got, no one behaved badly within the dining room's silk-lined walls. They waited until Margo ushered them out to the sitting room or kitchen. With a different styling, the room might have been intimidating, but flowers and candles and the red walls gave it a seductive charm. The perfect Christmas room. Old portraits in ornate frames hung along the picture rail. As a teenager Rachel had been adamant that the portraits were too ugly to be Garnetts – some long-dead ancestor must have picked up a job lot at an auction and passed them off as family. Margo said that was Rachel all over, cynical and probing, a typical lawyer.

'A toast!' Jonny stood up unsteadily.

'Oh Jonny.' Margo pushed her chair back to watch him. 'You really do love the sound of your own voice.'

'Speech, speech!' Tom jumped in, joyously tapping a knife on his water glass. 'We love a Jonny toast.'

'Watch my tumbler, Tom! They're Waterford lead cut. A wedding present.' There was a small pause while this information sank in. Rachel glanced at her sister who looked a little drunk.

Imogen frowned at her mother. 'I thought there wasn't a wedding? You always said it was a Gretna Green job. No photos, conveniently.' Her voice slurred, accusatory.

Rachel and Gabriel's eyes met across the table. Margo's face went blank and Rachel could tell that she was angry.

'God I would love to elope, how romantic.' All eyes shifted to Rowan, who looked like Galadriel in *Lord of the Rings* in the candle-light. Her tone was wistful and she looked at Imogen as she spoke. Imogen had not moved her eyes from Margo, as if challenging her to speak.

The blankness lifted from Margo's face and Rachel saw that her mother was going to take pity on Imogen. 'You're right darling. We did elope. Your grandmother never acknowledged that I was married, and sent any letters addressed to Miss Garnett. I think Dad felt bad and sent the glasses secretly later on. Richard used them for whisky.' Shadows crossed Margo's face as she spoke. To Rachel it felt like the whole room must be able to see the pain etched there.

Gabriel didn't let the awkward silence sit for long, playing the good host again. 'Get on with it then J, I've got pudding to see to.'

'You are such an old housewife, Gabe. I just want to say thank you to the two beautiful hostesses Rachel and Margo. And even though you're a bit of an old woman, thank you for some seriously great grub, G-Unit. And here's to Sandcove because you all know I bloody love it here. And to absent friends.'

Tom and Leo cheered, and Rachel saw Imogen flash Jonny a small smile as he sat down, which vanished as she saw her mother gently tapping her glass with a teaspoon.

'Dear Jonny has missed the most important toast of all.'

Oh God, thought Rachel. Sometimes her mother was just set on mischief, whoever it was going to hurt. All they could do was watch and then put the pieces back together. Rowan had raised Margo's hackles.

'We must toast Imogen and her engagement to William. We're not sure why William couldn't be here tonight—' Rachel saw Imogen flinch, and then raise her head to interrupt her mother.

'I told you. He has the flu.'

Margo continued as if she hadn't heard. 'Let's raise a glass to Imogen and absent William and here's hoping that we get a wedding date soon!'

'Yes, get on with it love,' Tom called out in agreement. 'We all want the party.'

'Leave her be, you two. What's it got to do with any of us?' Alice's tone was firm. She didn't speak as much as the other Garnetts, but when she did her word was final. Rachel smiled gratefully at her aunt and then at Rowan who looked annoyed. Rachel wondered if it didn't suit the actress to be out of the spotlight. Rachel watched Alice go over to Gabriel who was at the sideboard decanting more wine, and whisper something to him. Rachel thought they were like stagehands, those two, behind the scenes of every performance, ironing out all the problems. Gabriel came back and stood very close behind Rachel's chair, reaching over her to take his wine glass, and resting a hand on her shoulder.

'Ahem.' The chattering died away. 'It's nearly cheese and pudding time and port and brandy time for Tom and Leo—'

'Damn right.' Leo looked over at the decanters on the sideboard.

'But before that let's raise a glass to our guest, the beautiful Rowan Melrose. Rowan, you are very welcome at Sandcove.'

Everyone dutifully raised a glass including an impenitent Margo. Once the chatter had started back up, Gabriel bent down to murmur to Rachel.

'This is fun. Your mother has the devil in her tonight.'

'I'm not sure what's going on with her. Thanks for trying to make Rowan welcome.'

'I've made your favourite pudding.'

He kissed her neck and it was as if she had imagined the last few months. For a moment she felt the familiar halo of intimacy around them. It wasn't until the small daily gestures of affection disappeared in a marriage that you noticed them or knew how much you relied on them to break up the grind of work and childcare. They were the bedrock of marriage, those small private moments of connection.

In a lightbulb moment, Rachel suddenly saw clearly that Rowan was desperately seeking those moments of connection from Imogen. She kept moving her chair closer to Imogen. Kept trying to make eye contact with her. Flicking her hair nervously, raising her voice, attentively asking Imogen if she needed anything. Could Rowan Melrose be in love with her sister?

Rachel found Jonny and Imogen later in the boot room. Jonny had his arm around Imogen who was crying. As she walked in, Jonny glanced up and they shared a look, and Rachel felt like Jonny was a brother to them in that moment, in that exchanged look of responsibility and care. She hadn't realised that Imogen would confide in Jonny before her, and she tried not to let it hurt her. Jonny stepped aside and Rachel slid in. Imogen barely acknowledged the change.

'I'm here Imi.' Rachel spoke sternly to Jonny who was hovering: 'Keep Rowan away.' He nodded and went, a man who had learnt to always do the Garnett women's bidding.

Rachel waited with a patience she had learnt from her mother. Margo was the most impatient person until there was a crisis and then it was as if her internal clock suddenly slowed, allowing her to resolve things for her daughters with complete attention. Imogen's sobbing eased. 'What's going on?'

'It's not good.'

'That woman's in love with you.'

There was a pause and they could both hear the sounds from the rest of the house. Leo laughing, Tom's voice booming out in answer. Margo playing Chris Rea's 'Stainsby Girl', a song she always played when she was feeling sentimental. They had all worked out that it was about her, she was the girl who could break your heart in two. Richard must have sung it to her. When they were at peace, when Richard had made one of his 'giving it up' promises, Margo and Richard had stayed up together in the evenings in the sitting room, listening to Richard's huge record collection. Sometimes Richard would sing to Margo and Rachel would hear the call and answer of their voices floating up through the house, and wish it could always be that way.

'She thinks she is. I've been sleeping with her.'

'I did wonder. Goodness.' Rachel didn't know what to think, what to say. Did this mean Imogen had been a lesbian all along? Shouldn't she or any of them have been able to tell? Could it be a phase or an act of rebellion?

'I'm a terrible person.'

'Of course you're not.'

'Are you shocked?'

'We all thought you needed some kind of sexual adventure before settling down with William. Margo thinks it too, though of course she won't say it. Does William know?'

'No. I've been hiding everything from everyone. I can't bear it. All the lies.' Imogen's small voice cracked.

Rachel pulled her sister into a hug. 'That sounds stressful. Poor darling.'

Rachel stroked Imogen's back while she thought about what they should do. 'Margo mustn't know until you've resolved everything. We can't talk any longer now, it's too risky. Let's get everyone to call it a night before Margo murders Rowan. Can you creep away to No. 47 in the morning?'

Imogen looked up at her sister, her face clearing a little. 'Yes, Rowan won't move before eleven, especially if she's been drinking.' They smiled at each other.

'Oh, well maybe we should get everyone to call it a night except Rowan and Jonny and he can keep her up a bit later. I thought he'd be all over her but he seems to be keeping her in line. She's quite full on, isn't she? You must never let anyone bully you.'

Imogen got up slowly and stiffly from the tiled floor, using her sister's hand to pull herself up. 'I know. I'm trying not to. I think I might be a bit out of my depth. It's like she has come in and taken over my life, like a tornado, scattering bits of me far and wide. I can't seem to do without her. At first we were so good together, but now nothing I do makes her happy. Unless we're in bed.'

Rachel didn't find it hard to imagine Rowan as passionate and intense in bed, the lean muscles and silky hair, the demanding ego. And it surprised her too that it wasn't too much of a leap to imagine her sister in Rowan's arms, soft and giving, finally waking up to her womanhood. Imogen wrote so much yearning into her characters, their physicality was centre stage in her plays. Rachel had never seen it in Imogen's relationship with William. She saw that Imogen was looking at her anxiously, waiting for her to say something.

'I'm not shocked. If that's what you're worrying about. But, you are a dark horse, Imogen Garnett.'

18

Queen of Fucking Everything

No. 47 the next morning was a comforting fug, thick with the enticing smells of bacon and freshly ground coffee. Rachel and Imogen were early enough to avoid the Sunday rush and got the back room to themselves. Jane greeted them cheerily, and presented them with two plates of full English. The time felt stolen, like they were teenagers again. Years ago Jane had fed them when the Sandcove cupboards were bare. As teenagers, they had run to No. 47 for iced buns and to meet friends. Rachel watched Imogen who seemed reluctant to speak, to bring her problems into the daylight. The night before, Rachel and Imogen had slipped away to bed but they hadn't managed to get Margo away and there had been music and raised voices until late. As they were eating, the café's doorbell rang, and they both froze, forks mid-air, hoping no one they knew was about to join them.

'Morning, Jane. Did I see two of the Garnett girls head this way?'

'Not sure, Eve – I was out back.'

Rachel and Imogen smiled at each other.

'I'm sure I saw Imogen Garnett walking down Seagrove beach. All that straggly hair. She must be home for the weekend – I hear she's finally engaged? He's very quiet that man of hers – not handsome like

Gabriel. Margo's been desperate to get all those girls husbands . . . My usual to take away, please.'

Rachel narrowed her eyes at Imogen and frowned. Neither dared breathe.

'She just wants them settled with good men, you can understand that.'

Rachel raised her eyebrows at Imogen, feeling an urge to giggle.

'I suppose . . . Their father was a waste of space. Poor Margo. Can you pop a sugar in that? Actually two heaped.'

'Here you go. Tell Bill I've made a batch of the blue cheese quiches he likes.'

Once the bell jangled, the girls breathed again, sighing loudly with relief. Jane, red with embarrassment, put her head around the door. She raised her eyes heavenwards.

'Sorry girls, I could tell you wanted to be on your own but you shouldn't have had to hear that. It's always a risk with this back room, people are such gossips.'

Rachel went over to hug Jane. 'We love you Jane, thank you. You always look out for us.'

Imogen smiled at Jane too. 'We'd be lost without No. 47.'

Only a few minutes later, the bell went again and there was a commotion at the front of the café, raised voices. Rachel could hear Alice, she sounded strange, panicked. Both girls rushed to the front of the shop. Alice was panting, Jonny's too-large windcheater slung over her pyjamas. When she saw Rachel and Imogen, tears sprang into her eyes. Rachel's heart skipped a beat when she caught sight of Gabriel through the café windows on the high street waving his arms at a bemused-looking tourist.

'Oh God, Alice?'

'Rachel, it's Lizzie.' Alice struggled to catch her breath, to calm down.

'Fuck, what? What is it?' She grabbed Alice's shoulders hard, almost shaking her.

'When I came down for a cup of tea this morning, I saw her out on the beach. She must've followed you. I ran out as soon as I saw her but she's disappeared. I didn't know which way to go . . .'

Rachel's stomach dropped, her head spun, she saw clearly a tiny Lizzie all on her own, getting closer and closer to the water's edge. Gabriel turned and caught her eye through the glass. She saw her terror reflected back at her, he was the only one who could possibly know how dread was immobilising her. Gabriel pointed to show he was heading down the high street to approach the beach from the other side; his activity and intent broke her out of the spell.

'I must get out there. Who's helping, who's looking? Where have you looked?' It was like her world was suddenly in slow motion. The darkest thoughts were crowding out any sense or reason. Every parent's greatest fear. Had she left Sandcove's door on the latch? Woken her with the third creaky stair? She could have drowned already, her tiny lifeless body floating out to sea, away from her.

Imogen reached out and gripped Rachel's arm, keeping her back. 'Think, Rachel, before you rush all over the place. Think about where she'd go.' Imogen looked steadily at her sister. The door to Jane's was ajar now, passers-by realising there was a drama, hovering on the pavement outside.

Jane stepped forward. 'I'm shutting up, let's organise some search parties.' She raised her voice above the babble, throwing her apron down, brandishing her bunch of keys. Rachel, Alice and Imogen followed her out onto the high street where about fifteen or so people were gathered.

'Everybody! Please can you help. A little girl of four is out on the beach alone. Called Lizzie, she has brown curls. This is her mum, Rachel Garnett. Rachel, what was she wearing?'

Rachel's face crumpled as she looked at Alice. 'Was she still in her pyjamas? She'll be so cold.'

Alice put her arm around Rachel but addressed the crowd. 'Yes, unicorn pyjamas. Perhaps some of us should head to Priory Bay.'

Rachel's face creased up with horror. 'She won't get round the rocks. Oh God, what if she tries the path—'

Imogen took her sister's arm. 'Let's you and I go that way now. Alice, you must go and get Margo *now*, in fact someone ring her *now*.'

Jane started to tap numbers into her mobile. 'We need the Bembridge lifeboat out now, just in case.'

Imogen tugged Rachel by the arm. 'Rach, come on, run!'

As they ran away, they could hear Alice running behind them. 'I'll go to Margo and check the house in case Lizzie's headed back.'

And they could hear Jane shouting, 'Some of you head to Spring Vale! I think the father went that way, but he'll need help.'

Rachel let herself be dragged across the sand back towards Sandcove, her eyes scanning back and forth along the horizon, feeling her gaze pulling towards the sea. The sea had been the background to most of her life. Reading the tides came as easily to Rachel as telling the time. She read the weather across the sea, saw squalls and rain come in, hot days break clear and calm. Sunsets and sunrises. Although she did not fear the sea, and swam far out in it most days from March until September, she had been brought up to respect it, to understand its dangers, to be a strong swimmer. They all knew stories of tourists swept away. A child out alone by the sea, a small child, was a very real tragedy waiting to happen. Even if that child had been told over and over not to ever go into the sea alone, without a grown-up. When Rachel looked at the sea now, she saw a grey implacable enemy. Why had Gabriel made them live here? Where was Lizzie? Rachel just wanted a glimpse of her little head.

'Margo's on the slipway — she's got her binoculars.' Rachel heard Imogen, looked up to Sandcove and saw her mother. She was waving at them. Rachel could see that she was frantic. They moved closer to her, as the wind was whipping away their words. The wind seemed to be building, there was more foam on the shoreline, more white caps on the waves.

Imogen was shouting at Margo. 'Can you see anything? What way should we go?'

Margo shouted back. 'Let's head to Priory, you two take Horestone Point and the woodlands. I'll go via the rocks, the tide is out enough. Alice, stay at the house!'

Rachel nodded and moved faster towards the walkway that led to stairs up to the woodland on the cliff above Priory. She knew how muddy it would be, how hard for Lizzie to make it up without falling. The wooden steps on the cliff side were slippery with a slick coating of mud. She looked hopelessly in the mud at the top for tiny footprints. Lizzie couldn't have come up here, she was sure. In several places, the cliff just fell away. She had told both the children it was a dangerous place. She looked down at the beach, struck anew by the beauty of Priory's white sand, the crescent bay ringed by trees. It was so strange to still recognise beauty when the blood in your veins was icy with dread. No sign of Margo. 'She isn't up here, I know she isn't.' She turned to look at her sister whose face was streaked with mud and whose eyes were large with fear.

'Oh God, Imi, where is she?'

'Let's head back down to the beach and find Margo, there may be news from the other search parties.'

'I've got such a bad feeling.' Rachel's voice cracked, sobs swelling up in her throat. Imogen took her hand impatiently.

'Don't say it, don't even think it.'

The sisters scrambled back down the wooden staircase, Rachel scanning the sand frantically for small footprints. Priory Bay was supposed to be a private beach owned by the hotel above and out of season it was only a few local dog walkers who knew about its hidden stretch of sand. Little footprints would be easy to see.

'There are no footprints here, there's no way she's made it this far. We're wasting our time here.'

'Hang on.' Imogen had stopped and Rachel, who was looking down, walked into her.

'What?'

'It's Margo, she's waving at us from the rocks. I can't see whether – but it looks like—'

Rachel looked and saw her mother was cradling a small girl – her small girl – in her arms.

'Oh God.' Rachel bent over and dry-retched onto the sand. She coughed and heaved. Sobs of relief escaped from her.

'She's found her! Clever Margo.' Imogen grinned, stroked Rachel's back.

'Thank you, thank you. Thank God.'

'That was the longest hour of my life.' Margo was enthroned in the corner armchair in the Sandcove kitchen. She was holding the mug Tom had given her emblazoned with 'Queen of Fucking Everything'. She had a shawl draped around her shoulders as if she was an invalid. Rachel sat cross-legged on the tiled floor at her feet, Lizzie curled up on her lap, hiding her face in Rachel's jumper, shy at all the sudden attention. Rachel stroked her fine curls, soothed her, 'There, there.' Rachel could feel murderous thoughts about her mother overwhelming her, her incessant crowing, the way she was making everything about her.

'I just had a feeling she would be in the secret hide-out. Call it grandmother's intuition.'

Rachel wanted to know how Margo knew about the secret hide-out, why she always made it her business to know everything. Gabriel, sitting at the kitchen table and looking ten years older, voiced Rachel's feelings.

'We didn't even know they had a secret hide-out.'

Imogen, opposite him, laid her hand on his. 'It seems so weird that we've been through this and Sasha has no clue. Shouldn't we ring and tell her?'

Rachel's voice was flat and cold. 'What's the point, it's over now, Lizzie's safe. Sasha barely checks in any more, hasn't anyone noticed? She doesn't want to be part of this family, she hates Margo. Why bother her with it?'

There was a shocked silence but Rachel didn't want to stop, she didn't feel sorry. She had so much more to say.

Imogen rushed to speak before Margo. 'You've had a shock, you know you don't mean that.'

Margo gave Imogen a silencing look and stood up, placed her mug carefully down on the dresser. 'You're being silly, Rachel. Of course Sasha's part of this family. I suggest we all go home and give you some space. It's been a tough morning.'

Rachel couldn't stay silent. She felt rage at Margo's smug face, and the way she tried to pretend things were fine. She tried to keep her voice low so that she wouldn't scare Lizzie. 'You want to give me some space *now*? You didn't care about that last night – taking over the kitchen, inviting who you wanted, keeping everyone up late – being a total bitch to Imogen's guest.'

Imogen, Alice and Gabriel all started to move, scraping their chairs back. They all recognised the signs of a fight brewing.

Gabriel's voice was harsh. 'Rachel, that's enough. Margo found Lizzie today.'

Margo held up a hand as if to stop him. 'It's okay, Gabriel, I don't need thanking.'

Rachel flashed Gabriel a look. 'Stay out of this, Gabriel. You're supposed to side with your wife, not your mother-in-law.' Rachel stood up slowly, bearing Lizzie's weight. 'Alice, please take Lizzie for a nap.' Alice took Lizzie out of Rachel's arms and left the room in silence. The kitchen was still with tension. Rachel swept Margo and Gabriel with a look of disdain. 'I'm so sick of you both. Why don't you two live here together, cook lovely meals together every night – tell each other how wonderful you are. I doubt you'd fucking notice if I wasn't here.'

Margo stood facing Rachel, her shoulders back. 'We agreed we'd have a party for Imogen. It's not my fault she turned up with a stranger and the evening was a disaster. Imi, I'm afraid I think that Rowan Melrose of yours is rather entitled and spoilt.'

Rachel shook her head, her voice thick with sarcasm. 'In your world nothing's ever your fault. *"Poor Margo."* Don't blame Rowan when it was all you. Upsetting everyone – stirring – always trying to control us. Imogen can bring who she likes to Sandcove while I still live here.' Rachel felt Gabriel's eyes on her.

'What do you mean, "still"?'

'I don't want to live at Sandcove any more. I hate living here. And today we could so easily have lost Lizzie, things feel ruined – broken. I want to go back to London.' Rachel saw Gabriel staring at her, Imogen's mouth had fallen open. There was space and silence all around her; she felt very alone. Margo's face sagged, the fight ebbing out her. More than anything, Rachel needed to fight with her mother.

Margo's voice was quiet. 'As I said before, you must do what's right for you and your family.'

Gabriel had sat down at the kitchen table. Rachel watched him put his head in his hand. 'You two have talked about it?'

Alice came back into the room and looked at Margo kindly. 'Margo, why don't you go home and rest?'

'I think I will.' Margo did not look at anyone as she left the room.

Alice waited a moment. 'Don't forget she nearly lost Sasha the same way. It will have reminded her. And — well — she's not herself at the moment. Rachel, sit down, you're shaking.'

Rachel looked down at her legs which were trembling. She had lost all her strength. She saw Gabriel's worried expression.

'Yes, sit down. No more coffee — I'll make you a peppermint tea.'

Imogen had moved closer to Alice. 'I didn't know about Sasha. What happened?'

'Sasha was two. We were all having a picnic out there.' Alice nodded her head at the kitchen's bay window overlooking the beach and sea. 'Margo came inside to get Sasha a sunhat. The stripy red and white one — you all wore it. I was inside getting a cake I'd made.'

Rachel could remember what the hat felt like, its woven straw. 'I remember that hat.'

'Margo left Richard watching Rachel. He'd had a lot of wine with his lunch. He had started carrying a flask around with him that summer; it was when things went properly downhill. When Margo came back out, Sasha was nowhere to be seen.' The kitchen was quiet. 'I heard screaming, your mother was running everywhere frantically, I rushed out to help. Your father woke up, stumbled around uselessly. A bit later Margo remembered that Sasha had just learnt to lift the latch on Sandcove's back garden gate. Margo ran that way and found Sasha serving her own picnic in the Wendy house in the back garden.'

Rachel looked over at Alice, her anger spent. She felt sorry and sad. 'Margo always notices things. That's the way she loves us, noticing all the details of our lives. It can be too much though.' Alice nodded at Rachel in agreement.

Later, as breakfast was being cleared away and plans were being made, Rowan finally surfaced, still in her dressing gown, looking a little green under the hurriedly applied make-up. She hovered in the kitchen doorway, watching them all as if they were a exotic species of animal. Eventually Rachel saw her there. 'I'm afraid breakfast is done, Rowan, but can I get you some tea or coffee?'

'Is it another Garnett tradition to be up with the lark? Imo, I don't seem to have one of my suitcases. They definitely came in with me. Can Jonny find them and bring them up? Or is he still sleeping it off? I wouldn't be surprised – I drank him under the table last night. And he got very dull after midnight – kept talking about Sasha, the missing sister, who I haven't even met. Another Garnett beauty apparently and, needless to say, clever too. Black coffee, please, not instant.'

Rachel found Imogen out on the decking, looking out to sea mournfully. She sat down next to her. 'This has been the longest day – we never got to talk.'

'I'm sad you don't want to live at Sandcove. I had no idea you were unhappy. You're always busy looking after us all, we never think to ask you—'

'Gabe and I will sort it out. I'm ashamed, I behaved like a child. Especially as Margo didn't want to fight back.'

'Alice said something about her not being herself. You don't think something serious is wrong – that she's ill? I couldn't bear it if—'

'God, I hope not. She's never ill.' Rachel studied her sister's profile. 'Margo just wants you safe with William, looked after. But that's not going to happen now, is it?'

Imogen kept her eyes fixed on the horizon. 'I don't think so. It's going to be so horrible – William loves me in his own way.'

'I know he does. What will you do about Rowan?'

'I have no clue, I love the excitement and drama. But how do people live this way all the time? It's exhausting. How did Margo do it?'

'She still does live that way . . . She is fizzing with all kinds of things at the moment. I guess we'll find out what's going on when she's ready. Someone needs to help Rowan down with her bloody luggage. I feel like throwing it in the sea. Let's punish Jonny for sleeping through everything and get him to do it. Now we know – no more celebrities allowed in the Garnett family. One diva's enough for any family.'

19

One Last Time

When Margo headed back to the Other Place at dusk, she was surprised to see glints of light creeping out from the edges of the drawn curtains in the bay window. The cottage seemed pretty to her for the first time since she had moved into it. Grief over leaving Sandcove had left her half-blind to what was around her. Now standing by the little wrought-iron gate, she could see the attractiveness of the small formal front garden. She admired the smart royal blue painted door and the rose trellis around it, the rope knot door knocker that Rachel had found for her in a market in Greenwich. Her girls always tried to stop her blatantly staring into people's windows at night, but now she could stand and look at her own cottage with new eyes. She knew she had left the curtains open this morning and only two people had keys, Carol and Jack. Despite her resolution, she knew who she longed it to be as she placed her key in the lock.

Light pooled from under the shut door of her living room, and she could hear a fire crackling and smell something like a stew cooking. She tried to slow the wild beat of her heart, she tried to feel angry at Jack for trespassing. She had not seen him for a month, not since she texted him to say she didn't want to see him any more. But she needed and wanted the evening he was offering her. She could not bear another evening staring at the television thinking about how Richard wanted to see their daughters before he died, but had not asked to see her. Another sleepless night where she wandered the empty house at three in the morning with mugs of tea. Even books, usually a lifeline for her, could not still her mind or heart. The words seemed to jump up off the page, refusing to stay in readable lines.

As she stood hesitating, the door creaked open and there was Jack, a half-smile on his face. Margo could see her candles lit on the low table. She tried not to let her eyes meet his.

'I know you said you didn't want to see me.'

Margo drew herself up, trying to gather some of her usual imperiousness. 'Yes I did.' He hadn't moved towards her yet, she would be lost when he did. She could not find any resolve. 'I meant it, Jack.'

'You can't say goodbye to me for good with a text. That's pretty shit.'

'I am a shit, you know that.'

She finally let her eyes be drawn to his – she could see hope and lust reflected back at her. 'You shouldn't have done this, Jack. It's not fair. I am going through some things . . .' She let her voice trail away, she wanted to talk and talk to him and he was here and she could. But there were other things she wanted to do more.

'Please talk to me then, we used to talk about everything. I miss that, as much as anything else.'

Margo felt a flush of heat in her face. 'It's the anything else I'm thinking about right now.'

He didn't smile but looked hard at her. 'Me too.'

'I need wine.'

The space between them felt alive with possibility. She had imagined herself naked, twisted together with Jack on the rug by the fire, and now she knew that it was the only outcome she would accept.

She could find her resolve and principles in the grey morning, when he had left, and when it would be dreary anyway. What would a bit more dreariness matter? Tea for one and a still silent house.

'I opened some and it is warming by the fire, which is where you should be – with me.'

He took a step forward, looking for a signal from her.

She shrugged off her coat and held it out to him. 'Hang this up, please.'

'Why did you do it? Why did you send that text?'

Margo leant over him, reaching for the wine. Jack reached up and cupped one of her breasts in his hand. 'Gorgeous boobs.'

She smiled, pouring them both more wine. Then she sat up, cross-legged, pulling a rug around her shoulders. The fire was dying away. She didn't want to change the mood with talk. 'I saw you and your wife, on the high street, one night after I had been in the sailing club.' Jack sat up, fear on his face. Margo knew why. 'It's okay. She didn't see me. But I saw you.'

Sympathy replaced the fear on Jack's face. 'I'm sorry.'

'We live in a village, it was inevitable.'

'I wish things could be different.'

'But they're not.' Margo could feel the tension creeping back to her shoulders.

'Please tell me what's going on. You seem sad.' He moved closer, wrapping his arms around her, and she let herself relax against the heat of his naked body, just for a little while.

'Richard is dying.' She let the words hang there. Jack moved so he could look at her face.

'I didn't know you were in contact with him?'

'I'm not but his second wife called Alice. He's asked to see the girls before he dies.' Margo could feel Jack thinking. He knew how adamant she was about her daughters not having their father in their lives, they had talked about it often, and he had given up arguing with her about it.

'Is it the drinking? Killing him?'

'Good question.' Margo gave a hard, dry laugh. 'You'd think, wouldn't you?' Bitterness crept into her voice. Jack held her a little tighter. 'But no. Apparently he's been sober now for a long time. It must have played its part – he's got liver cancer.'

'Jesus. How do you feel?'

Margo clutched the rug around her shoulders. 'I hate to think of him scared. He had this way of not facing things. He ran when things got hard but he won't be able to run away from this. It's hard to think of him sick and weak.' Margo paused, far away now. 'We were so young at the beginning. I was just sixteen – I didn't have a clue. I didn't know how to set up a home or what married life would mean. Neither of us could cook. I remember trying to grill a chop in our tiny oven, we sat there for hours talking with nothing happening because we had it on the wrong setting. We just gave up and drank wine. God, I was skinny, you should have seen me.' Margo pinched a roll of her stomach under the rug, and Jack reached for her.

'You're perfect as you are.'

Margo shivered a little, and Jack moved to throw another log on the fire. She watched him as he used the bellows to bring the fire back to life, the tendons and muscles in his arms in the firelight. He sat back down, and reached for her hands, tracing her palms with a finger.

'I came from a family where you were pushed out of the house at sixteen. Expected to be working.'

Margo thought about this. 'I guess my leaving home only seemed shocking because of the privileges we had. I was expected to stay at home until university was done, then marry some safe Old Etonian type.'

Jack raised his eyebrows. 'Isn't that what you are expecting for your daughters?'

Margo frowned in response. 'No, smart arse. I want them to use their brains a lot and find men who like their brains.'

'He was older, Richard, wasn't he? He must have known how to do things?'

'He was never a grown-up. He never knew what time it was, he was always late, always dreaming. He loved late nights staying up telling stories. That's how the drinking crept in and started to steal him away. I didn't really notice – I was working all hours as a journalist by then, and I would join him somewhere in Soho at night. I was pretty good at drinking in those days, I could match him drink for drink—'

Jack interrupted with a wide grin. 'Not so bad these days either.'

'Cheeky. We lived and breathed Soho.' Margo drifted away, as a memory came back to her of her and Richard running barefoot down Dean Street, holding hands and laughing. She couldn't remember where they were running to, or from, or where they had left their shoes, but she remembered the feeling of nearly flying, the feeling of intense happiness that coloured everything. 'We never spent a night apart and if there was no party to go to we would have our own private party, the two of us at the kitchen table at East House.'

'East House? Fancy,' Jack jibed, letting his jealousy show. Margo ignored his sneer, she suddenly had such a clear memory of a little chipped bath up on a platform, filled with champagne on ice for a party.

'I haven't thought about East House for ages, it was our attic flat in a mansion block, overlooking Battersea Park. We could see the treetops from our bed. His mother chose it for us.'

Jack laughed at Margo's tone. 'You didn't like her?'

Margo shrugged, took a sip of wine, shook her curls. 'She was always interfering. Always wanting the best for her son. Which didn't include me. She chose the flat, because the address was smart enough to please her and we'd be close to her in Chelsea. We got in so much trouble over bills, Richard would just stuff them in a drawer and I didn't know about bills, I just thought everything was paid for somehow.'

Jack stretched himself out, like a cat in the firelight, propped himself up on his elbows. 'You've never told me about this part of your life before. When was this? The fifties?'

'Very funny. It was seventy-eight. I can still remember the phone number. It was written in the circle on the middle of the Bakelite phone, the one we have at Sandcove now. Richard lost his keys a lot, so I was always ringing around trying to find out which pub he'd got to.'

'The signs were always there?'

Margo let her shoulders drop. She looked at her hands in Jack's, no wedding band, the lines, the age spots, the chips in the nail varnish. Showing her age. 'Probably – from the first night we met and he drank pints and pints of wine.'

Jack studied her face for a moment. 'People make worse choices. Fuck things up more. You got away.'

'I didn't get away. He left me. Disappeared one night. He knew before I did that it wasn't going to work any more.'

'I always thought you must have thrown him out.'

'That's because you know me as I am now. Then I didn't know which way to turn, how to change things back. As soon as the babies came, it was like there was a glass wall between us. I could see him and speak to him but I couldn't reach him.' At the mention of babies, an awkward silence rose between them. Suddenly sad, Margo tried to steel herself to be the woman Jack saw. 'Babies sometimes come between people who have loved each other. With Richard I think he thought I was lost to a new love. I wanted to come back to him, but when I did he had slipped further away. I kept wanting more babies, because it made me feel like I had the family I had always dreamt of. And the love I found in my children made it easier to ignore the love I was losing.' Margo watched Jack as he fiddled with the tassels on her blanket, avoiding her gaze. 'You're having another baby? We haven't talked about it.'

Jack looked up. 'Margo, I can't—'

'I know we never have. But I just need to know. You once said to me that things were not quite right . . . with your wife. No intimacy. All those nights you sat waiting for me at the end of the bar in The Ship. But what about the babies? Are the babies a Band-Aid for you or are they to make up for things?'

Jack put his head in his hands and Margo felt suddenly very naked and cold. She stood up, collecting her clothes and beginning to dress. Jack looked up at her, his dark eyes imploring. 'That's it? You're chucking me out?'

'I already know the answer.' Margo, now hastily dressed, sat down on the sofa. Jack was at her feet, his back to her. She waited. His voice when it came was anguished.

'I love being a dad, I wanted another baby. They make me and Jo stronger, better. It's never going to be this.' He swept his arm around the room. 'But I don't want to let them down.'

Margo sighed, looking at the nape of Jack's neck, suddenly exposed as his mop of hair fell forward over his head. 'More than you already have?' Her own voice sounded old and resigned, tired of life.

'Don't be shitty.'

They squared up to one another, but Margo knew she had no

energy for a fight. As she measured out what she would say next, tears sprang into her eyes. He wasn't easy to give up. 'I am going to miss you.'

She saw his eyes mist up in response. 'Don't do this.'

Margo shook her head, her face grave. 'If we could just be friends – but I fancy you too much. I mean look at you.' She wanted to reach out and touch his hair just one more time but she knew it would be a mistake. 'I think you should put your clothes on and leave.' She said it as gently as she could but there was steel in her voice. 'Let's always remember our times together fondly.' She realised the words were too trite as soon as they were out of her mouth. She heard a choked sob from him and he began to move around the room gathering his clothes, his face turned away from her. 'Jack, that was stupid of me. I don't know what to say. All I know is that Richard dying – it's forcing me to face up to all the bad decisions I've made. I care about you, but this was such a bad decision. You need to concentrate on your family.' Her voice wavered. She wanted the whole scene to be over. Jack left the room to dress and when he came back, his face was a mask and he kept his eyes on the floor.

'I won't forget any of it or what you meant to me. Goodbye Margo.'

As the front door slammed, Margo fell back on the sofa, and sobbed and sobbed. For herself, for Jack and most of all for Richard, who was dying.

20

Fake Fur

London

In the daylight, Colette's looked tired. The raffia-backed chairs were coming unstrung, the rugs were stained and cobwebs hid in the corners of the ceilings. A bleach-blonde waitress was waving a damp cloth over the tabletops, leaving a residue of stray crumbs. Imogen thought how strange it was to see a place of night magic and adventure as it really was. Rowan sat beside her chattering like a starling and sipping her second espresso. Her hand was wrapping and unwrapping itself around her packet of Malboro Gold, still annoyed that Imogen had insisted on sitting inside.

'It's fine what Oliver said – about my looks being distracting. He's obviously a misogynistic dinosaur.'

'Mmm.'

'I'm so sick of all this stuff about me being better suited to film. I'll bloody go back to film then – at least you get paid properly. And they treat you like a star. Ever since Oliver's review, the rest of the cast have been turning their noses up at me. And Harold's been flouncing around showing off.'

Reviews had been coming in for *Standart* and they had been less than complimentary about Rowan. The *Guardian* had praised the story, its insights into the family dynamics of the Romanovs, and Imogen carefully cut the piece out and posted it to Margo. *The Times* had praised the actor who played Rasputin, lauded 'a new playwriting talent in Imogen Garnett' but had called Rowan 'unconvincing'. At first the audience had mainly come to see Anna Karenina, but now it was changing as word of mouth and good reviews worked their magic. The Playhouse was extending the run. When Imogen allowed herself to think about success, it felt like a mysterious alchemy that had nothing to do with her. Margo had been short and dismissive on the phone, telling her she had known all along that the play would be a success. The call left Imogen feeling flat, wondering where her biggest cheerleader had gone. Imogen was trying to write her new play, trying to let *Standart*'s reception push her on, but she had let her life weave a sticky web around her, and wherever she turned there were people and commitments immobilising her.

'Jacob's got something on the table for me but it's filming in Russia – another boring Russian writer who I've never heard of. I'll get stereotyped if I go Russian again. I feel like I need something really modern. And I can't be away from you, playwright, not when you need me so much. That family of yours only care about themselves. They're as self-absorbed and as melodramatic as your Romanovs.'

Imogen was only half-listening. There always seemed to be some shiny new place beckoning Rowan, but Rowan was listless and indecisive. She was clinging to Imogen, needy and sometimes nasty. She loved to pull apart Imogen's family, her appearance, even her writing. Imogen felt sick with herself because she was still so lost in their sex life. It wasn't tender any more but brutal and desperate. When Imogen thought of the things they did and said to each other under cover of night she could hardly believe it was her, the mousy good girl. She wondered if other people were doing these things too. Now Rowan, who could feel Imogen drifting away from her, sneaked a hand into her lap, moved it between her thighs, squeezed.

'Let's go back to mine and back to bed? Start the day again – I can make you less grumpy.'

'I'm not grumpy – I'm just late.' Imogen moved Rowan's hand off her lap. 'I need to go.'

Rowan rolled her eyes, picked up her phone and started scrolling through her Instagram. 'Your favourite words.'

'Well I do.' Imogen tried to be conciliatory. 'Any idea which way I go? Sloane Square to Victoria and then—'

'Just get an Uber. He lives in the back of beyond.'

'I can't afford to keep taking Ubers. Unknown writers don't get paid the same as actresses. Especially one-hit wonders.'

Rowan gave an exaggerated sigh. Now Imogen's career showed signs of taking off, she had little patience with flattering or encouraging her. Their days of praising each other to the skies were long gone. Now they picked at each other like an old married couple. But an old married couple who were tying each other up and using sex toys. Imogen got out her card to pay.

'Can you try to attract a waiter? They always run over for you – they're half-dead the rest of the time.'

Rowan whipped her head up accusingly, her artfully messy bun wobbling as she did. 'You used to love it here.' Rowan did a clever imitation of Imogen's voice, high-pitched when she was excited. *'Please take me to Colette's, Rowan.'* She looked across the room, caught the waiter's eye and smiled at him, widening her eyes coquettishly. The waiter moved briskly towards them. There was silence as Imogen paid and Rowan once again did not offer to split it. When they had come back from Sandcove, during a row, Rowan had pointedly said, 'Please don't come over all penniless playwright with me. Your mother bought you a flat and your family own a beachfront mansion. It may be falling down but the land alone must be worth a million. They can subsidise you any time you want.'

Rowan looked at Imogen. 'Are you *finally* going to tell him?'

Imogen looked straight ahead, watching a couple being shown to a table. They looked like they were being polite to each other, the man checking with the woman that she was happy with where they were sitting, hanging back, letting her take the best seat. It reminded her of William, who always wanted her to be happy in the small things. Rowan never noticed the small things. Imogen had a flash of understanding as she gazed at this couple that Rowan, once she had forced Imogen to make the big dramatic gesture she wanted, would slowly lose interest in her.

'Imogen?' Rowan's tone was snappish. 'It's not fair keeping him hanging.'

Imogen started to put on her coat, a fake fur that Margo had bought her on her last trip to London. As soon as it was on, Imogen felt imbued with some kind of power. Rowan reached out and stroked the arm of the purple coat.

'This isn't very you, playwright.'

'Really? I love it.' She stood up, almost shaking off Rowan's hand. 'I don't know yet whether I'll tell him. It has to be the right moment. Please don't pretend you care about what's fair for William. You're only thinking about yourself.'

Imogen almost swept out of Colette's, although she imagined, had it been Margo, Margo would not have bumped into so many tables and chairs on the way out. She was hot in her coat and her eyes and cheeks were smarting but she felt a surge of adrenaline.

✦

It was a long tube ride to Queen's Park and along the way, in the restless crowds, and hot airless carriages, Imogen felt weighed down by the coat, and then by dread. William had asked her to lunch and his voice had been clipped on the phone. He had never asked her why she had gone to Sandcove without him, or why she was so absent these days. He had not chased her on wedding venues or bookings. She knew he had somehow kept his mother Ida away from her. The engagement felt like it had never happened, the only person who mentioned it now was Margo, and even she seemed half-hearted.

Jammed between bodies, Imogen wondered why Margo seemed so detached. She wanted to ring Rachel and ask her, but now Rachel knew about Rowan there was a new pressure on their conversations. Rachel wanted her to end things with William, to ditch Rowan, to somehow start fresh. To get everything into the open. Rowan had not been a success at Sandcove. If William didn't quite fit in, at least he tried. He responded with enthusiasm to the organised fun, the outings that took hours to plan. He tolerated the endless local characters who turned up uninvited, the excessive menu planning, the dogs and children running riot. He took without comment the huge gin and tonics Margo forced everyone to drink on the dot of six. William tried, and when it was too much he took himself off to the beach or to the book-lined study. Imogen remembered the Christmas when Sasha and Margo had argued viciously, dragging everyone into the row, and she had found William with the children, patiently making a train track. Imogen dreamt of taking someone to Sandcove who not only loved it unreservedly but also who brought a new layer to the traditions and house rules, the way Gabriel had.

When she arrived at William's flat, Ida let her in, pressing her thin lips to her cheek, looking Imogen up and down through her spectacles and taking in the flamboyant coat. Imogen often felt marked down by Ida if she ever showed too much Garnett colour, even though Ida admired it in Margo. The basement flat was cold and dark and Imogen immediately wanted to go round turning lamps on but she felt self-conscious in front of Ida. There was something wrong, the stale air was thick with things unsaid. She saw William hanging back down the long narrow corridor near the kitchen, a colander in his hands. Imogen tried to keep her voice light.

'How lovely, are you having lunch with us?'

'Yes, dear – hope that's okay.' She walked away to put Imogen's coat in the bedroom.

'I can do that, Ida.'

William came forward with his kind half-smile and Imogen hugged him tighter than she normally would, suddenly so pleased to see him, reassured by the living, breathing reality of him in his favourite navy blue jumper. This often happened when she saw him, they slotted back together like two jigsaw pieces and Imogen could relax because William didn't ask anything of her, or expect her to be anything more than she was.

Ida appeared again and hovered, watching them. 'Aah that's lovely, William said he hadn't seen you for a while, you've been so busy with the play.'

Imogen pulled away. 'Yes it's been a busy time. And now I am writing a new one, so . . .' Imogen hated talking about her writing in front of Ida, who thought it was a kind of indulgent hobby which kept her away from her son when he needed her.

'Mum, why don't you make Imogen a drink? I got you some gin, Imi. That one we always have at Sandcove, Mermaid something.'

Imogen rewarded William with a big smile. 'I didn't know you could get it off island?'

'Amazing what you can track down on the internet.' William grinned back at her.

'You young people spend too much time on the internet.'

'Mum, the drinks. I'll have just a tonic water.'

'Are you off the booze?' Imogen called after William as he disappeared back into the kitchen behind Ida. She didn't follow them as the kitchen only allowed for two people comfortably. William sometimes went on strict diet regimes if he was training for marathons, something he did once or twice a year. Imogen felt out of touch, looking around the sitting room for clues.

'Just for the moment.'

In the living room Imogen sipped her drink, and the cracking sound of the ice was comforting. She could tell that there was news. Ida was fidgeting. William was pale. Imogen watched people's feet pass on the pavement above and wondered where they were all going, what they were doing?

'Well, you'd better come out with it, William. Put the poor girl out of her misery.'

'Mum.' William's voice was harsher than Imogen had ever heard it. She set her gin down with a clatter on the veneer coffee table, and some spilt, dripping onto the carpet.

'What's going on?'

Ida jumped up from her seat and Imogen thought she was going to clear up the gin but then she saw that her face was crumpled, as if she was in pain. Ida began to pace around, keeping her eyes fixed on William's face.

'I've been diagnosed with testicular cancer.'

'Oh God, William.' Imogen heard a sob escape from Ida and William went slowly across to his mother who immediately buried her head in his jumper and wept quietly.

'I'm sorry. Mum wanted to be here to help but she's not coping that well.' William smiled at Imogen over Ida's head, raising his eyes to the ceiling, a gesture that made Imogen's heart contract. She could see it all ahead – how brave William would be. Imogen felt like a child who didn't know what an adult would do in this situation. She knew she should ask questions.

'I'm so sorry. How did you find it? What happens next?' Imogen thought about the cancerous lump and how for several months now there would have been no chance of her finding it. He must have been lonely and scared and all that time she had been in bed with a TV star. William detached himself from Ida, who muttered something about getting a tissue and left the room. He came and sat down next to Imogen. Everything felt unreal. She could see the fear in his eyes, beneath his concern for her.

'It's stage two. It means there is a lump on one of my testicles. I need the testicle removed and then chemo. It's in some of the lymph nodes.'

'I can't believe it, it's so unfair – you are so young and healthy.' Everything she could think of to say seemed like a horrible cliché. She knew other men would call them 'balls' and make crass jokes to cover their fear. She could not stop the stupid thoughts that kept coming. 'Do they . . . do they offer you a new one?'

'Yes, it's reconstructed. Don't worry, you won't be marrying someone lopsided.'

At the mention of marriage, an awkward silence arose. William studied the patch of carpet beneath their feet. Imogen quickly linked her arm through his, pressed against his side.

'I want to be with you when you go in for the operation, when you go in for the chemo. Please tell me what I can do to help – I want to help.'

Ida returned, restored to her usual tidy self. Imogen could see the vestiges of her grief underneath the neatly applied lipstick and buttoned-up cardigan.

'Of course you want to help. You're such a nice, well brought-up girl. Your mother did such a good job under the circumstances. I would have fallen to bits.'

This was something that Ida liked to parrot. Imogen could not stop herself replying this time, the stress of the situation making her short-tempered. 'She did fall apart Ida – it ruined our childhoods.' Imogen looked up and saw Ida and William both looking at her. 'Sorry.' She looked back at William, who had gone back to contemplating his carpet. 'William? Are you okay?'

'Yes.' He stood up. 'I'd like to postpone the wedding until this is all over with – until I'm well again. I'm sorry.'

Ida's mouth dropped open. She looked like a fish, Imogen thought. Ida started gabbling. 'But William, you didn't tell me you were thinking that.'

'I've only just thought it.'

'But you mustn't be hasty, love. What about Imogen? She needs something to look forward to, to plan for.' Ida looked pleadingly at Imogen. 'Imogen? And what about Margo? Margo won't be happy at all.'

William's face seemed unreadable. Imogen smiled kindly at Ida. 'You mustn't worry about me or Margo. Margo'll understand. The most important thing is to focus on William and William getting better – what William wants.'

'Mum, look, it's not as if much has been done, has it?' The comment seemed pointed and Ida flushed.

'You told me not to interfere and it's traditionally the bride's side, you know, who lead the way. I didn't want to be too pushy, you're always telling me I'm too pushy.' Ida's eyes started filling with tears again. Imogen felt William's eyes on her.

'Imi? You don't mind, do you? This gives us more time. I am not sure I'll have the energy with the chemo.'

Imogen crossed to William's side. 'Course not. I've been totally useless so far what with the play and everything. And I want us to plan together. Otherwise Margo will just direct operations and you'd hate that!' Imogen smiled weakly. 'Just don't change your mind, please.'

'Don't be daft, the thought of it all will get me through. Now let's go eat – you must both be starving.'

Imogen stayed at William's that night and they didn't talk much about anything, not cancer or the wedding. They ate huge amounts of leftover roast potatoes and sat close together on William's uncomfortable sofa, watching an old David Attenborough boxset, the most comforting thing they could find. That night, Imogen wrapped herself around him and found it hard not to think of what was happening inside him. Under cover of darkness she whispered, 'Are you scared?' and he replied 'Yes, a little bit. Thank you for being here.' And then they slept together in a tight cosy bundle and Imogen felt like she was where she should be. Her final thought as she drifted off to sleep was of Rowan's beautiful angry face and how she must be brave and tell Rowan that they were over because William needed her. It was like she had been given a purpose and new clarity.

In the morning Imogen woke very early, all her sense of purpose gone. Hopelessness and dread crept in. Her stomach felt like lead and she lay still beside William feeling stifled by the heavy duvet, the airlessness in the room. The flat was stale with the smell of roast potatoes and pork fat and Imogen longed to get up and throw open all the windows, pour herself a big glass of cold water. The radiators came on and there was the smell of burning dust. It was too early to wake William, so she lay there feeling like she was trapped in a version of hell, one of her own making. William was being so calm and brave, coping with his mother, when his mother should have been helping him. He had been gentle with Imogen, worried about upsetting her and Ida over the wedding. And he had cancer, he should have been thinking about himself. He deserved someone better than her. Imogen had to admit what she had done to someone who trusted her, who had loved and supported her for a long time. For two hours she lay there, finally looking at things as they really were. She and William were not suited for a lifelong commitment, they would disappoint each other. She had been trying to make Margo happy, to create something safe and secure. And yet, she knew she was searching for something more. The Italian boy, the summer fling with Rowan were the telltale signs. As the dawn chorus struck up, Imogen faced the lies she had told herself, the lies about her character and the lies about her wants and needs. She knew it was foolish and wrong but her heart wanted the big star-crossed love, like Margo and Richard.

When William began to stir, Imogen pulled herself up against her pillows and sat with her hands clasped in her lap, waiting. It was the worst kind of timing, she knew, but this way she wouldn't be letting him down any more. She had to be brave. This way she would be there for him through the trials that lay ahead, as a friend, as someone honest. This way she wouldn't ruin his life. She would tell him, not because of Rowan – there was no future with Rowan either, Rowan was sexy but a monster – but because it was what she should have done years ago. William was so honourable that he would never break off their engagement, even if he also felt they were not right together. She had to let him go so he could find someone who loved him with their whole heart, and he would because he was such a good, kind man. She would find the strength of ten Margos and never leave his side through his operation and treatment. But first she had to find the words to tell him that she knew they had made a terrible mistake, that the wedding could never happen.

21

Rachel Victrix

Isle of Wight

The original tiles in the hallway of Sandcove were Margo's pride and joy. The exact colour of dried blood, they had made it through all the years unscathed. Margo had guarded them ferociously and the sight of her, down on her hands and knees, scouring between the cracks with a nail brush, had been familiar throughout their childhood. Margo hadn't trusted Carol with the job, and about a week before Christmas Margo would always make sure the tiles were cleaned as part of the long and detailed process of readying Sandcove for the big day. Rachel hated the pressure of trying to replicate the magic of her childhood, trying not to forget any of the myriad Sandcove traditions. She should have recklessly gone her own way the first Christmas as owner of Sandcove, but instead she had dutifully beavered away trying to replicate Margo's Christmas, with not one crystal glass or diptyque candle out of place. She had replicated menus and guest lists and now she was stuck that way, part of her pleased to make Christmas the biggest parade for Lizzie and Hannah, their home a beacon for revellers, another part of her worn down by the commitment, longing for a short Christmas fling with a stranger. Having not cleaned the tiles in a year or so, Rachel was irritated by the hints dropped by the endless rounds of visitors. 'These tiles have seen better days,' or 'Margo kept these tiles like new, I suppose you've got better things to do.' She was examining them resentfully, when she heard the back door slam and then a rustling in the boot room.

Rachel called out, even though she knew who it was likely to be. 'Who's there?'

'Just me – brought you some wood.'

Rachel muttered to herself as she moved to the back of the house, 'Be patient.' Margo was pulling small sacks of wood across the boot room. She looked up when she sensed Rachel in the doorway.

'Tom gave me so much wood, I don't know what he was thinking. I keep telling him that the fireplace at the Other Place is tiny. So I've brought it here. You'll need extra for Christmas.' Margo straightened up, both hands in the dip of her back, a shadow of pain on her face.

'Is it your back again?'

Margo's voice was sharp. 'I'm fine. Is Gabriel here?'

'No, he's in London with Jonny. A big night out. They're hoping to get Sasha to go out with them.'

'God, not with Phil I hope, that's never going to be a fun night out.'

Rachel raised her eyebrows at her mother, who was now resting on the settle. 'Without him. Jonny's worried about her.'

'We all are.' Margo started rummaging in the deep pockets of her raincoat. 'Has she said she'll come for Christmas?'

'Not yet. I'm working on it. Jonny told Gabriel he thinks their marriage is in trouble.'

Margo looked quickly up at Rachel. 'I did wonder when they were last here. Didn't you think? I wish she'd talk to us, she's impossible. And now Imogen is being all secretive and silent too. What the hell is going on? What kind of Christmas is it going to be, for God's sake?'

Rachel thought about all the Christmases that had been created through the sheer force of Margo's will, filled with cocktails and champagne, roaring fires, garlands and candles, when other bigger things were going on. Christmas at Sandcove, its ambition and style, was always the constant in their lives. This year though, Rachel sensed that even Margo's determination to pursue every festive detail was waning. She seemed tired and strangely joyless.

Margo handed a folded-up piece of paper to Rachel. 'Gabriel wanted the boeuf bourgignon recipe for Christmas Eve. Tell him there are six bottles of vintage Bollinger in the cellar which we can use at some point. If he wants help with the canapés on the twenty-second I can come over.'

Rachel took the paper, folded it and put it in her pocket. 'Are you sure you and Gabriel want to do the party? It's a lot of extra work close to Christmas. It means the kids stay up late and are tired before Christmas even starts—'

Margo interrupted Rachel with a look. 'It's tradition. Why are you wearing those terrible clothes?'

Rachel looked down at her baggy T-shirt and leggings. 'I was thinking about tackling the tiles. Starting the decorating – Alice has taken the kids for the day.'

Margo stood up, suddenly full of purpose. 'Why don't I go home and change and then come back and help you? I'm happy to do the tiles. It'll be a good distraction. Have you got the decorations down from the attic?'

Rachel took a large breath. 'Not yet.'

'Okay, do that first. Also the fairy lights and garland for the staircase are in the cupboard in the spare room – for some reason they didn't make it to the attic. I'll be back in half an hour.' Margo moved to the back door, pulling up her hood. 'You know there's a storm coming in, black clouds over Seaview. Good idea to bolt the shed door otherwise the wind will have it off.'

Rachel watched as her mother wrestled with the back door, the roar of the wind outside. 'Okay.'

'And Rach – I'll need a sponge, a bucket with some warm water and Fairy Liquid in it.'

Margo had only just left when Rachel heard the doorbell go. It was supposed to be a rare day when she had the house to herself, and yet as usual people were coming and going. Rachel moved slowly to the front door, hoping whoever it was would just give up. Instead it was like the reincarnation of Richard, someone just holding the bell pull down, so that when Rachel flung open the door, she was already irritated. On the doorstep she found a slip of a girl, wearing cheap clothes and a belligerent expression. She was striking with pale skin and a shock of red hair. Like something out of a fairytale, Rachel thought.

'Can I help you?'

'Are you Rachel Garnett?'

Her voice was soft, childlike. Rachel looked past her to the sea wall, where the Swinburns were walking their spaniel. They were looking over, no doubt curious about who Rachel's visitor was. Rachel waved at them from the doorstep.

'Yes?'

'Would it be okay to have a quick word? I know your mum, Margo. The one that works at the pub.'

Rachel's first thought was that this was something to do with Margo and Jack Walker, the trouble she had been expecting. This could be Jack's wife. If it was she should get her inside quickly, before more people saw. She noticed that the girl's eyes were darting from side to side, that she was twisting her hands together, jiggling from one foot to another. She looked cold in her thin denim jacket and something about the girl made Rachel feel maternal towards her.

'You'd better come in then.' Some instinct made Rachel lead her into the formal sitting room, rather than the warm cluttered kitchen where their family life was more on show. The sitting room had a stately air, with its huge cream sofas, the polished piano arrayed with Garnett photos in silver frames. It smelt of woodsmoke and the sea and Margo's dogs, who still had a bed in there. Rachel took the armchair and motioned the girl to sit down on the sofa near her.

'So how can I help you?' Rachel could hear that her voice was haughty, she was doing her best lady of the manor impression. The girl perched on the end of the sofa, her eyes scanning the room, drawn to the photos. Rachel began to feel uneasy as she watched the girl's eyes travel over the photos. 'What was it you wanted to talk to me about?'

'Me and Gabriel. We love each other.' The girl's face suddenly lit up.

Rachel felt her stomach drop and her heartbeat race. The dread she had been carrying around with her, trying to push down all the time, rose up. She knew she must master her feelings in front of this girl. She might be lying, might be a crazy patient. Quickly Rachel trawled through comments she had filed away, things people had said which might explain this girl. Hadn't Jonny said that there was a needy patient, someone Gabriel couldn't leave, that was why he hadn't been to the school reunion? Gabriel had said something too about a difficult patient. Rachel clasped her trembling hands tightly together in her lap. She saw that the girl was waiting for her to speak. 'I think that's unlikely. Gabriel and I are very happily married, we have two daughters. We live here in this lovely house together. I think you've misunderstood something.' Rachel wanted to shout at the girl, throw her out of the house, call Gabriel on his mobile, but also in some deeper part of her knew she should tread carefully.

'We want to be together. He doesn't want to be here with you any more.'

Rachel's voice was imperious. 'When did he say that to you? Do you have any evidence? Text messages?' Rachel could see the girl losing her focus, losing her conviction. She pulled her phone out of her pocket, laid it in her lap, turning it over, looking at it like she hoped it might ring.

'They're private messages. Between me and him, you can't see them.'

'You're one of his patients, aren't you?'

The girl looked at her quickly, startled. 'We're friends, he said we could be friends.'

'Are you just friends? Or are you in love? You're contradicting yourself. I think you are Gabriel's patient, that you see him for therapy.'

'You have to believe me. We're going to be together. He said he would look after me. He said he would meet up with me for a drink or a chat.' The girl's eyes were pleading with Rachel, searching her face.

Rachel tried to make her voice a little kinder. She could see that the girl was less sure. 'You have misunderstood something. Gabriel is your psychotherapist. He cares for you as a patient. That's all. He would never mislead you or meet up with you outside your sessions.'

The girl stood up suddenly, her phone fell to the floor with a thud and they both looked at it. It occurred to Rachel that maybe she was in danger, that the girl might try to harm her. 'You're wrong,' the girl said, 'he wants to be with me, I know he does. I know him.'

'I'm going to talk to Gabriel tonight about how you came here. And what we talked about. What's your name?'

The girl snatched up her phone. 'I'll talk to him first, I'll ring him.'

Rachel stood up. 'When I talk to him we can make sure that there are no more misunderstandings. Are you stalking him?'

'I'm Elizabeth. Sometimes I bump into him, it's a small place.'

Rachel looked at the girl. 'It's a very small place. I think you should go now, Elizabeth.' Rachel walked behind the girl to the door, opened it and watched as she slowly went down Sandcove's steep steps. At the bottom the girl looked around as if she were lost and then finally she drifted away towards Seaview.

When Margo came back to Sandcove she found Rachel collapsed in the armchair in the sitting room. Her fist was clenched against her heart and her eyes were closed. Nothing had been done, no decorations had been brought down from the attic, no bowl had been filled with warm water.

'What are you doing in here? Are you okay?'

'Gabriel's got a crazy patient who thinks she's in love with him. She just came here to confront me. I think it's all in her head. But God, Ma, how do I really know?'

Margo sat down slowly opposite Rachel. 'Did she have red hair?'

Rachel looked at her mother. 'Yes, how did you know?'

'She's been in the pub a few times, watching me, acting strangely. Someone in the village saw her with Gabriel on the street. I was going to tell you, I'm so sorry. I didn't want to create drama in case it was nothing. What did you do?'

Rachel looked at her mother's pale, serious face. She looked like someone who was worried that Gabriel had dark secrets. 'Should I worry? Why didn't he tell me what was going on? What were they doing when they were seen, kissing or anything? You'd have told me—'

Margo stood up again, as if she could not keep still, and pushed her hands through her hair. 'No, not kissing – just arguing. I don't know what to say about it. Of course you're worried, anyone would be. You need to talk to Gabriel . . . don't leave it. Maybe he thought he was dealing with it, maybe it's just got out of control. Men mess up, maybe he messed up? I don't know. I'm a terrible judge of men. I would always have said he was an honourable man but whoever knows? Oh, darling. Sorry, I'm not helping . . .'

Rachel watched as her mother began to pace the floorboards. Margo had no confidence or trust even in Gabriel, her favourite son-in-law. For a moment Rachel felt sad for her. Richard had done this to her. 'Yes I'll talk to him tonight. I think — I hope — he'll be able to explain.'

Margo stopped pacing. 'You're right. Of course you're right. I am sure he'll be able to explain it all. And maybe I shouldn't say this but if the girl is crazy, it would seem like a good reason to talk about moving away? Which is what you want, isn't it?'

Rachel looked at her mother and thought how foolish it would be to ever underestimate her or to think she did anything other than put her daughters first.

22

A Rising Tide

It was a cold, grey day and the men stood facing the sea. Four Garnett heads bobbed in the water several hundred metres out. From the beach, onlookers could hear peals of laughter. Garnett friends and family were preparing for the Boxing Day party on the pale sand. Jonny hunched over the barbecue, beer in hand. Tom stood beside him, tongs dangling from his fingers, several cool bags around his feet. They had dragged a fallen log out of the woods and were using it as a makeshift table, ready to start a production line of burgers. A little further away, Alice and Alison were glamorous in fur coats and wellies, with tinsel tied in their hair. They were peering into a cauldron hung over a camp fire, in which Margo's hot buttered rum was warming. Margo's dogs Juno and Drake ran and chased each other, bouncing in the sand, shaking seaweed in their teeth. The twins were setting the children up with a game of beach cricket. Leo had just popped the cork off a bottle of vintage Veuve Clicquot, and had been instantly surrounded by a semi-circle of women holding out champagne flutes. Margo believed in doing things properly, even on the beach, and so Alice had been entrusted with carefully ferrying over a box of lead crystal glasses, all individually wrapped in newspaper. Rachel had tried to veto this part of the proceedings, as three or four always got broken, but she had been overruled by the weight of tradition.

Gabriel looked back over his shoulder. 'We've got the beach to ourselves. Remember that year when the Sandersons moored up and came ashore with their own picnic? Margo was furious until she started drinking with Andrew Sanderson.' Gabriel laughed at the memory.

Phil nodded but kept looking out to sea. 'They should come in now. It's fucking madness – the sea's freezing. We've got a trip to Indonesia in two days, the last thing I need is Sasha with a cold. She's a nightmare when she's ill.'

'Rachel too.'

'Imogen too!' William chimed in, and all three men laughed.

'They're like mermaids – they've found the drop. There's a ledge where it falls to deeper water. It's our lot in life to stand here, watching them, the poor husbands and husbands-to-be. Abandoned on the shore.' Gabriel attempted a sorrowful expression, but his eyes were dancing. He loved Boxing Day and all his work was done for now, the burgers all hand-made, beef with Stilton wrapped inside and lamb with spices.

William jiggled on his feet, feeling the cold, and looked sideways at Gabriel. 'Except Imogen and I aren't getting married any more.'

Phil and Gabriel whipped round to face William who stood between them, moving closer, as if protecting him from sight.

'Woah!' Phil reached over and patted William's arm awkwardly. 'Are you okay with that, mate? What the hell are you doing here then? You wouldn't see me for dust if Sasha and I split.'

'I think I've always known that Imogen's heart isn't in it. She thought she should get married to make Margo happy.' William looked awkward, let his words rush out. 'Also – I found out I've got testicular cancer – I need to have an op and some chemo. I think it made Imogen realise—'

'Mate! I had a friend who had that and was right as rain. They even gave him a brand-new ball, couldn't tell the difference.'

Gabriel had flung an arm around William's shoulder and pulled him into a hug. William leant into it for a minute but then pulled free.

'Thanks Gabe, but let's not make anyone suspicious right now. Looks like the ladies are coming out.'

Gabriel patted his shoulder. 'I think it's amazing that you and Imi can be friends. She'll be by your side through everything. They're fiercely loyal these Garnetts. We can talk about this more over cigars? I want to know how I can help. If you need advice, on how to handle Margo or anything—'

'I can't wait to see how this is going to shake down! For once the drama won't all be Sasha's fault,' Phil smirked.

'I'm not sure when Imi wants to tell people, I'm totally in the dark . . .' William's voice trailed off as Margo began striding out of the surf, her daughters trailing behind her. She emerged from the sea, narrow-hipped and brown-skinned in a bright orange swimsuit. Grinning hugely, wet tendrils of hair snaking around her neck, she looked young and happy, and all three men could not help smiling back at her.

'Boys! You should be brave and come in next time. Glorious! And now I need a big Boxing Day drink.'

Margo took a mugful of rum and drank it down quickly, feeling the heat spread through her. The sea had burnt her with its chill but eventually her body had adapted, her limbs had become fluid. She had dived under the water, letting the green depths cocoon her, sounds from the real world muffled, just the vibrations of her daughter's chatter, their strong pale legs churning the water around her. She had wanted to stay there, a salty mermaid. The sea felt like her only friend, the only constant. She had floated looking up at the big grey sky, and for a few moments her mind had emptied. Back on land, the healing had evaporated and she was aware again of playing a role, rather than really living this Boxing Day. She would have to have several drinks to be able to play the joyful matriarch in charge of revels. But she knew drinking was dangerous too.

This year, she could not stem the memories of Boxing Days past. The first ever swim and barbecue had been Richard's idea. She had been deliriously happy that year, pregnant with Rachel, her stomach like a melon. She could remember the feeling of plodding across the beach, her fat feet sinking into the sand, her footprints huge. She had revelled in feeling weightless in the sea, her ungainly body liquid again. Richard had still looked at her like she was beautiful, grinning at her all day long, sometimes touching the bump reverently. There had been relief too, he was trying hard not to drink, to stop after one or two, to come to bed when she did. A fresh start. He had run into the water that year, whooping. So alive. She could not believe that it was the same man who had complained about the cold beach, the sand in his shoes. He had finally embraced Sandcove, finally become a sea swimmer. She had thought him her perfect partner.

She looked around the beach for her dress, the cashmere shawl, her jewellery carefully knotted inside it. Soft layers that would drape her body, restore her to the elegant mother who stood on the beach as if it was a drawing room, who directed operations with a sweep of her arm. As she searched, she caught Sasha's eye. Sasha immediately looked away as if the sight of Margo offended her. In the water Margo noticed that Sasha had stayed well away from her, would speak only when spoken to. Now she was showing off loudly to Gabriel and Alice, clutching a glass of champagne. Imogen and William were in the group too, side by side, Margo had been so relieved when they arrived together for Christmas. And Gabriel and Rachel seemed united, working together on Christmas Day, the issue of the redhead now in the open. It seemed a crazy patient had got the wrong idea. Gabriel had told them it happened all the time, was one of the pitfalls of the job. Still Margo wondered and worried and tried not to say anything unhelpful.

Margo turned back to watch Sasha, pleased to see her letting her hair down, having a drink for once. If only they could talk, if only Margo could find out what she had done to mortally offend Sasha this time. She wasn't sure she had any strength left for argument or drama though. Was Alice right about Sasha needing to know about her father? Could it really help her to know he was dying and that he wanted to see her? Margo saw Alice looking at her, a crease of worry in her forehead. Margo smiled back to reassure her. It was Alice whose shoulder she had finally cried on, Alice she had asked to ring Adriana to ask how long there was left for Richard. Alice who had told her he only had a few months and then that Richard wanted to see her too. And now she just had to work out what to do, for herself, for the girls, for Richard. As she shivered and peeled the swimming costume away from her gooseflesh skin, she watched ashen clouds roll in the distance and wondered how long they would be able to stay out on the sand.

Once Rachel warmed up and had devoured a huge burger she sat down by a fire pit and took in the scene. Margo had lit candles in ships' lanterns on the sand, and had fashioned a seating area with fur rugs and cushions and some camping chairs draped with tinsel. A lot of the revellers wore paper crowns, and Gabriel had helped the children hang paper chains from the lowest branches of the fir trees, which fringed the sand. She could hear distant primal shouts from her children who were up above them in Priory Woods, building a den with their cousins. Margo was over at the other fire pit, dressed now in a long dress, with an embroidered shawl thrown around her shoulders. She always dressed beautifully for every day of Christmas and while she relaxed the rules for others at the beach party, she still made sure that she had beautiful things to wear. Her face glowed in the firelight and Rachel could see that she was telling a story. Jonny, Leo and Tom stood listening and laughing.

Sasha was in a huddle with Phil, and for an hour or so she had been drinking a lot. No one knew why she had decided this was the year to relax her sobriety, she made it sound like an impulsive decision and got annoyed when anyone asked her about it. She was being bright and funny but there was an edge of instability. Phil kept trying to keep her away from the rum, but Rachel watched as she waved him away, told him to stop nagging her. Rachel could see it wouldn't end well, but she refused to worry about it yet, wanting the chance to feel festive for a while longer. Imogen seemed to be sticking close to William's side, so Rachel hadn't been able to ask about Rowan. She just wanted to leave family secrets aside for this day and try to enjoy them all.

The last few weeks of conversations and negotiations with Gabriel had been draining and they had agreed that for Christmas they would drop the subject of the girl, of what had happened there and how Rachel wanted to move to London. Gabriel seemed chastened by all the worry and upset he had caused, penitent that he had not confided in Rachel sooner when the girl had started to seek him out, outside her sessions. But he was adamant that he had not once stepped outside the boundaries of a professional role for his part. Rachel had felt her faith in Gabriel being slowly restored and she watched him now as he crossed the sand, a burger in his hand, to sit down next to her. She briefly rested her head against his shoulder. She felt grateful for the reprieve from the tension.

'Which one did you have?'

'Lamb – it was soo good. I'm saving room for a beef later on.'

Gabriel tucked into his burger beside her as they watched everyone. 'Things seem to be going okay. You and Margo got through yesterday without any rows.'

'I decided to take your advice and just let her be Queen of Sandcove for the day. She's been a handful recently.'

Gabriel leant over and kissed Rachel's hair. 'Clever. Your sisters though? They just don't seem happy. Not that Sasha ever seems happy at Sandcove. Do you think there's something up with Imogen and William?'

Rachel turned to study Gabriel's face. 'What do you know? Out with it! You know you can't keep secrets. As recent events have proved . . .'

There was a pause as they exchanged a look – Rachel could see it was something serious. 'It's not good. William's just told me he's got testicular cancer.'

'What!'

'Yup. Poor guy.'

They both looked at William across the sand, who stood straight and still, listening to Tom. Rachel thought about how kind he was and how the Garnetts had never appreciated him enough.

'Oh poor Imi – I can't believe it. What did he say exactly? What happens next?'

'I couldn't get much out of him as you all started to come out of the sea. I told him we should talk more when we have our cigars—'

'Ah yes – the deeply sexist tradition my father started.' Rachel could feel anger rising up and knew it wasn't really about the cigars. She looked at Imogen and wondered if she was trapped with William now and it seemed like a horrible, selfish thing to be thinking at that moment.

Gabriel put an arm around her. 'It's not a tribute to your dad. Anyone can come – Margo joined us last year and we had to carry her off the beach.'

'I'm just worried about Imi. Did William say when they are thinking of telling us?'

'No, but there's more. Apparently they've broken up. They're not getting hitched.'

'Gabriel!' Rachel couldn't help sounding relieved. 'You should've told me that bit at the beginning, for God's sake! Poor William – how brave of him to still come. We've underestimated him.'

'You mean you and Margo have underestimated him. I've always had a lot of time for him.'

Rachel looked sidelong at her husband. 'No need to be smug. We all know you are such a wonderfully insightful person. When you don't get it all wrong. Like making patients fall in love with you.' She heard Gabriel exhale as her dig hit home. She couldn't help herself, letting the hurt of him keeping secrets come out in jagged bursts of sarcasm. 'What happens now?'

'Don't get involved. Let Imi and William work out how best to tell Margo and the others. They're grown-ups. How much longer can we ignore drunk Sasha though?'

Rachel thought again how lucky she had been to find someone who was able to face the Garnett dramas with humour. She lifted a hand to cup his face. 'I do love you. To answer your question from before: no, my love hasn't been changed by it. By what happened.'

Gabriel's green eyes locked on hers, suddenly serious. 'Thank God. Because I love you Rachel. I can't imagine my life without you.'

✿

Imogen was feeling as tragically disappointed as a child. Christmas at Sandcove was a beacon for her, her reward for getting through the year. This one was ruined. She had arrived the day before Christmas Eve and not once had she felt festive. It had all seemed a sham. Worst of all, she was guilty of playing her own part in spoiling it. William was waiting for her to tell her family that there would be no wedding. His patience made her feel worse. Imogen felt sick when she thought of telling Margo. It was going to be harder too as Margo seemed so very unapproachable this year. Her attention to detail at Christmas was usually perfect, but this year things had slid away. There were signs everywhere that Margo cared less and Imogen trotted behind her, reminding her, knowing she was being the annoying shadow of Christmas Past. The Christmas gold goblets needed to be out, where was the special platter for the smoked salmon? Why had Margo bought shiny new stockings to hang, when she wanted her old ratty one from childhood? And now Sasha was threatening the precious Boxing Day party. Imogen listened as drunken words tumbled carelessly out of Sasha's mouth. They were within earshot of Margo; Imogen kept glancing over to see if her mother had noticed or heard the things Sasha was saying.

'Does anyone understand her? Why she keeps this stupid tradition going? When it was Dad's thing – the man she hates.'

Imogen felt her stomach twist and gurgle; she had not been able to eat much since she had arrived at Sandcove, and she had a persistent headache. The stress of keeping secrets from Margo, the play-acting at which she was so bad. She looked over at Alice whose eyes flashed alarm.

'Sasha, I'm not sure this is the best time—' Alice tried to take Sasha's arm.

'Get off me – what about us? We were just children and we lost our dad. We weren't allowed to know about him – to talk about him. Stop trying to protect her.'

Imogen thought how alien Sasha felt to her. The inappropriate way she called Richard 'Dad'. The way she was always so angry at Margo, and the world too. How she was always rushing to the next place, never still. How she hated Sandcove. And yet Imogen could remember a time when they had almost been one person, only two years between them. Sharing a bed and all their toys, claiming one knee each on Margo's lap. Imogen remembered holding Sasha's hand on this same beach, looking after her, running in and out of the surf. She reminded herself that Sasha was still her sister. She looked around for Rachel, but she was further down the beach, cutting slabs of Christmas cake for her children and the twins, Gabriel close by.

Imogen made her voice resolute, a Margo voice. 'Sasha, there's no way we're talking about this now. You've had way too much to drink – I'll get Phil to take you back to the house.'

Sasha swivelled round too fast and then nearly tipped over. Her beautiful face contorted in a snarl, her hair was wild after the swim. 'For fuck's sake, you're always such a killjoy. The good girl routine's getting so boring. All you do is bang on about wanting everyone to be happy – keeping up appearances – making sure your darling Margo is protected. Her precious favourite.'

Imogen could feel rage surge inside her. Rage over the ruined Christmas, William's apologetic pale face, Rowan's persistent texts. She yanked Sasha further away from Margo. Sasha stumbled behind her, and Alice followed. The light had died now and it was harder to read people's expressions away from the lanterns. Imogen spat out her words. 'Everything that comes out of your mouth is bullshit, Sasha. Margo protected us – from *him*. He was a drunk and a hopeless loser.'

'You don't know Dad's side. Maybe he just couldn't bear to be

with her, she drove him to drink. Look, she's driven me to drink.'
Sasha waved an arm around her, beer from the bottle in her hand
sloshing onto the sand.

'You're just a lightweight. Stop calling him Dad, for God's sake.
He's not our dad, he never was. Can't you ever just let go of this
idea you have of him and try to love the family you have? We're here,
we've always been here.' Imogen's eyes prickled with tears, as she made
this entreaty in the dark. Alice put an arm around Imogen, tried to
reach out a hand to Sasha.

'Oh, fuck off both of you, I just want to get off this beach.'

Alice and Imogen stood holding each other, watching as
Sasha stomped off in the sand, muttering to herself. Behind them
shouts went up and they turned to see Tom and Leo dragging out the
dinghies they had hidden behind a shed on the beach.

'Dinghy race!' Tom bellowed, making everyone near him laugh.

Imogen shook her head in despair. 'Alice, I really want everyone to
go home now – I have a bad feeling.'

Rachel knew that she should pack up and take the children home
but a sleepy contentment had stolen over her, a combination of the
rum and the firelight. At this point the beach party always took on
a bacchanalian quality, with long shadows on the sand, the crackling
of the fire pit, and music which got wilder as the night went on. She
remembered bringing Gabriel home for Christmas the first time, and
staying on the beach with him until the early hours of the morning,
wrapped tightly in his arms, watching his expressions in the firelight.
She had loved how he had instantly been all the things that people
wanted him to be. With Margo, he was chivalrous and helpful but not
a pushover. With Tom, he had been ready with banter. With Imogen
and Alice, he had been gentler, a listener. It had been a masterclass in

winning over an entire family and she had fallen even more headlong in love. Since the babies, though, she never stayed late any more but always let Gabriel stay, she wasn't sure why. She wondered if this year, as punishment for keeping secrets from her, she should stay and make him go home early. Rachel knew she would do as she had last year and wait to hear their stories over breakfast; the late-night swims, the arguments, which locals had been upset, who had to be carried home.

'Do you need help packing up, Rach?' Imogen shouted as she came towards her.

'I was just dreading the whole thing.'

Imogen was quickly beside her, flushed and out of breath. Her voice was urgent, and angry. 'We need to get Sasha away.'

Rachel stood up, a little unsteady on her feet, wishing her head was clearer. 'Oh what now? Is it really that bad?'

The sisters looked at each other and unspoken communication passed between them. Rachel wanted to reach out and hold on to her sister, make her speak, but Alice was also moving towards them.

'What's the plan? At the moment Margo hasn't heard Sasha but we need to act fast.'

'Rach, she sometimes listens to you, can you talk to her, tell her it's time to go home? Try to talk some sense into Phil as well?'

Rachel looked into the distance and saw Sasha and Phil far away down the beach towards Nodes Point. 'If you two can pack up and get the kids, I'll try to talk to them both. What's she angry about now?'

Sasha felt blood rush to her face as Rachel stood in front of her, staring her down. Of course they were all ganging up on her, they always did. Even Jonny was keeping away. He had warned her not to drink, advised her to talk privately to Margo, but she did not feel like listening, even to him. He had tried once to take her arm, to whisper urgently to her, but Phil had appeared and had shoved Jonny violently aside, so that he had stumbled on the sand. The two men looked like they would square up to one another, but Jonny thought better of it and moved away. He had asked her time and time again when she would leave her marriage but she was paralysed, terrified of Phil's anger, and of how her life would look once she was on her own. It was hard to trust that Jonny would be there, that he wouldn't disappear as soon as she was vulnerable, as soon as she really needed him. She looked again at Rachel, so sure and righteous. She didn't want to hurt her, but she would have to if she stood in her way. She needed to tell Margo, tell them all what she knew. She couldn't bear it alone any more, she was suffocating under the weight of it.

'Margo hasn't noticed yet that you're being a dick. We need to get you off this beach before she does. Phil? Are you going to help at all? Your wife's drunk.'

Sasha glanced over at Phil who was openly glaring at her, hating her for what she was about to do. Sasha could feel the alcohol sloshing around in her stomach, beer churning with champagne and rum. A growing headache pounded her temples. 'Leave Phil out of it – I can look after myself. I've just had a couple of beers.' Sasha defiantly took another swig, fought to keep her legs from buckling. 'Here she is – the big fucking hero. The one who always saves the day. Of course Imogen went to get you – she can't do anything without you. The big sister who gets to live in the wreck of a house and lord it over us. The fat busybody . . .'

Imogen saw Rachel's cheeks flare up and wished she could stuff the words back into Sasha's mouth.

'This *is* my business, Sasha. You're being rude to everyone, you're ruining the party—'

'God help me if I ruin a precious Sandcove Christmas! I don't give a shit about Christmas – you're all protecting Margo over the lies we've been told about Dad.' Sasha felt her legs beginning to shake, acid bubbling up in her stomach. She needed to start moving, she needed to do something before her body gave up on her. 'I won't leave until I've told Margo what I know . . . *Margo!*' Sasha stumbled fast across the sand, angrily shouting her mother's name over and over, louder and louder, watching as everyone on the beach turned to look at her, and then slowly moved around Margo as if to protect her.

Rooted to the spot, Margo watched Sasha descending on her in the darkness like a vengeful angel. Her only blonde child, something she had been so childishly pleased about when she was born. Richard was white blond too as a child, and of course her own mother Elizabeth had been blonde. Sasha was the baby Margo had hoped would change things, but deep down she had known Richard did not want any more children. And yet Sasha had ended up being the baby he appeared to love the fastest and the deepest and on whom he doted like a lovestruck teenager. And the baby he abandoned when she was just four years old. Sasha, her troubled child. Margo saw Sasha's face, twisted with anger. She must have uncovered a secret. It had always been that way, always Sasha finding her out in some failing and bringing it into the light, even when she was only small. She remembered falling asleep once when she was supposed to be watching her and Sasha had joyously told everyone afterwards, 'Bad Mummy fell asleep.' What did she know?

'*Margo!*'

'Stop shouting – I'm right here. You seem overexcited. Have you had too much rum?'

Alice, Rachel and Imogen appeared breathless on the sand behind Sasha, like keepers whose lunatic patient had evaded them. Phil hung back, behind the others, looking down at the sand. Margo could see he knew what was to come and wanted to be anywhere but there.

'Phil, it might have been an idea to have taken her home a while ago.'

'I know. She never listens to me though,' Phil mumbled, cowed by Margo.

Sasha looked possessed. 'They need to know the truth about Dad. I can't bear being the only one any longer. They need to know the secret you've been keeping from them all this time.' There was silence as the whole group watched Sasha's face, wild-eyed and desperate.

Tom stepped out of the shadows. He was frowning, annoyed that histrionics were disrupting his fun. 'What the hell are you on about, Sasha? You know nothing about Richard.'

'You're wrong!' Sasha laughed a harsh fake laugh. 'I've met him! I've seen him four times now. We've talked at his house! I've met his wife – I know all about what happened. I know that Margo's lied to us all this time. I know she never told us what really happened. We had a right to know about our own father.'

Rachel and Alice gasped in shock. Some of the guests, embarrassed by what they were seeing and hearing, moved further away and so the circle by the fire pit became tighter. Margo saw the triumphant look on Sasha's face and knew she wasn't lying. There was worse to come. All the secrets were about to be laid bare.

'How did you find him?' Margo kept her voice calm, feeling all eyes on her. The silence of shock. All Margo could hear was the push and pull of the waves, and Sasha's ragged breathing.

'The same way you found out he had another family. I used the same private investigator – I found a card when I was helping you clear out Sandcove.'

'The information was confidential. They would never have just given it to you.'

'I used a different name, pretended to be another abandoned wife looking for Richard O'Leary. It was years later, if they thought it was a strange coincidence they never said.'

Rachel stepped forward, Imogen close behind her. 'Margo, what does she mean about another family? Is that true?'

Tom moved to prop Margo up. 'Jonny, get a seat for Margo please and another drink. We're going to need some more booze.'

Margo turned away from Sasha and looked at Rachel, her face a terrible blank. 'Yes, it's true. Only Alice, Tom and I knew, that is until . . . until Sasha . . .' Her words faded away as she gratefully sank into the chair Jonny brought her. She noticed how white Jonny's face was, how serious he looked. She pushed the proffered drink away.

Sasha looked around defiantly. Firelight flickered over her face and hair, giving her a savage look. 'He left us because he had another family. A family he decided he wanted to be with more, because Margo was such a bitch to him. Margo didn't think we had the right to know. He wants to see us all—'

Rachel stepped further forward and prodded a finger hard into her sister's chest, as if she wanted to push her over, wanted to silence her. Everyone flinched as she shouted in Sasha's face, 'You wanted to see him? To know him? After *that?* I think we've heard enough out of you, don't you? Why the hell are you so pleased with yourself? You talk about Margo lying but she was doing it to protect us. What's your excuse? You've been lying to your own family. How long for, tell me *now?*'

Sasha took a step back, her face crumpling, her defiance gone. Jonny moved forward, close to Sasha. No one had ever seen Rachel so angry before. Jonny's voice was a warning. 'Rachel, it's not Sasha's fault.'

'Keep out of it, Jonny. *How long?*'

Sasha's voice was low, and she stumbled where she stood, so that Jonny caught her elbow and propped her up. 'Four years.'

'God, you worthless piece of shit! You're dead to me, Sasha. Fuck off! I can't look at you.'

Margo looked for Imogen who was hanging back, hiding behind Rachel. Everyone was frightened by Rachel's incandescent rage. Alice moved to Margo's side, putting an arm around her shoulders.

'It's time to explain.'

They had spent so long carrying the secret, Margo and Alice and Tom, that Margo did not know how to say the words out loud. She shut her eyes. 'After Richard disappeared, I was suspicious, there had been someone phoning the house and just hanging up. Tom found out from drinking buddies that Richard was in London and so I hired an investigator. Barry, his name was, such a sweet man – he didn't want to tell me what he'd found out. I think he was a bit in love with me. He found Richard was married to another woman, with a four-year-old and another baby on the way. The four-year-old was born just a day or two before Sasha. I sent Richard a letter telling him I knew and to never make contact with us again. And then I fell apart.'

Sasha had collapsed onto the sand at Margo's feet. Jonny knelt beside her while Phil still lurked in the shadows. To Margo, Sasha looked like an exhausted child who had had a tantrum and needed her bed.

Jane stepped forward. 'We're going to pack up – it feels wrong for us to be here. Gabriel, shall I take the children back to Sandcove?'

'I'll come too.'

Margo looked around her, acknowledged what was happening, the party was over. 'Leo, Tom, Jonny, you go too please.' The men nodded quietly and moved away. The three daughters watched their mother's face.

Rachel's voice wavered. 'Is there anything else left to know?' Margo and Alice hesitated. Rachel's voice flared up with anger again. 'Margo, for God's sake, tell us! He's our father, whatever he's done.'

Margo put her head in her hands. 'Richard's dying. His wife rang Alice to tell her. He wants to see you all before he dies.' Margo felt tiredness descend, a fog over her brain. She held out a hand to help Sasha up. Sasha paused briefly and then took it. Her face was wet with tears.

'He hasn't got long, only a couple of months,' Sasha said, wiping her face with the back of her hand.

'You weren't going to tell us he was dying?' Imogen spoke at last.

Margo lifted her chin, her voice when she spoke was clear and strong. 'No, I wasn't. I can't stop you now, I know — but I don't want you to see him. I wanted him out of our lives — perhaps you understand why now? He made his choice, and he didn't choose us. I didn't want you to have to know that about your own father.'

The three sisters stood motionless, watching Margo. Imogen turned to Rachel. 'This makes him seem more human somehow. A reason at least, an explanation. How much he messed up . . . what a mess he got in—'

Rachel shook her head. 'The mess he made. He's a bigamist, a cheat — a liar and a drunk. Is he dying from the drink?'

'No. His other wife managed to get him off the booze. Something I spectacularly failed at.' Margo let self-pity creep into her voice.

Imogen turned from Rachel and looked at Sasha. 'What's he like?'

Margo held a hand up commandingly. 'Don't talk about him in front of me — never. I can't hear about him, about his new life. I'd like to leave now, I'm cold and the rum's wearing off. I'm sorry it had to happen this way. Let's go back to Sandcove. We can talk more tomorrow if we must.'

'One thing.' Imogen rested a hand on her mother's arm as if to keep her there a moment more. 'Did Richard ever write to you — explaining things, telling you why he had another family?'

Margo stopped still on the sand. 'I waited for that every day – for a long time. But I never heard from him again, only via a lawyer.'

Imogen stood still, dazed. 'I don't understand. You loved each other. Was it us he didn't love?'

Margo's voice was quiet when she spoke, the sisters all had to bend towards her to hear. 'He loved each and every one of you. A drunk can't explain his actions. It's a disease – it makes you do things. Love makes you do things you didn't realise you were capable of.'

Imogen turned to face Margo. 'It would have been better if we'd known – all this. To have been given a choice about whether we wanted to know him or not. We've all gone on thinking it was a great love story.'

Margo flinched and glanced towards Alice. 'It was a great love story – it just didn't last. Maybe I got all this wrong—'

Sasha turned towards Rachel and Imogen, her voice still loud and slurred. 'Ask him – he wants to see you both! Go and see him – please, you must – he's dying. He's said he'll try to explain things to me but he still finds it hard to talk about—'

'You're so fucking naive. He can't explain away bigamy, and a secret family!' Rachel gave her sister a hostile shove as she moved away, pulling Imogen with her. She shouted at Phil across the sand, who was still lurking. 'Can't you just look after her, Phil, like you should have done from the beginning? Keep her away from me – *for ever.*'

Margo had already moved away, leaning on Alice. It all felt like a dream suddenly.

Rachel stopped on the sand, clutched Imogen's arm tight. 'What do we do now? I mean what will you do now, do you know? Will you go and see him?'

Imogen looked into the dark, into the space where Margo had been. She looked round for the first time wondering where William was, whether he had slipped away much earlier. He would have felt awkward, no longer part of the family, but no one knowing yet. Suddenly her and William's news was trivial, an adjunct to the main drama. 'I don't know – I don't know what to do. If I did, I'd need to be sure Margo was all right with it first. She doesn't want us to go . . . But I've got so many questions.'

'I won't see him, not ever. I just can't believe it. It's so much worse than we thought. That Margo knew all that, kept it secret. I can't believe Sasha – how is she even our sister?'

'We must check on Margo, see she's okay.' And the sisters hurried together arm in arm into the shadows, across the cold blank sand.

23

Latchkey Kid

Rachel let herself in with the key she wore on a long piece of string around her neck, which she made sure was always hidden under her clothes. She had learnt that not many other eleven-year-olds had their own house key and she didn't want people to ask questions. The old tiles in the hallway were always cool after the hot sand and Rachel kicked off her sandals. She closed the heavy door with a bang that reverberated through the house. Sandcove was as still as the sea outside, as her sisters were with Aunt Alice, but she could hear Tom Barrison snoring, which was reassuring. She picked up the post and took it into the kitchen to sort. Margo would greedily snatch the post, looking through it, and throw it to one side when it disappointed her. Rachel would then secretly go back to it and make a pile of bills, making sure to talk to Carol or Alice or Tom about them when Margo was not there. Tom was in the big armchair, his hair rumpled and his stomach pushing out between his shirt buttons. Rachel tried not to look at it too much, embarrassed, and went to get a rug to gently cover him with. Then she started to make coffee the way she knew Margo and Tom liked it after a late night. The kettle whistling woke Tom and, once he had worked out where he was, he smiled warmly. Rachel noticed that his eyes were like two tiny dots.

'Hello chuck – you're up and about early. Are you making coffee for me? Angel.'

'I went to No. 47 for breakfast and Jane made me bacon and eggs. I was starving – we've got nothing here.' Rachel got out the cafetière, carefully measuring the coffee, not wanting to spill any. Margo had once shouted at her when she had found coffee grains spilt on the counter, telling her not to bother making coffee if she was going to make more mess for her to clean up. Her face had looked ugly and contorted.

Tom sat up and stretched. 'Are the cupboards bare again? Make a list, darling, and I'll get Carol to go and do a shop for you all.'

Rachel stirred the coffee, watching it swirl around. She liked the smell because it reminded her of happy breakfasts, all of them together, her mother flipping pancakes. 'Margo's not eating. I made her some toast yesterday with Alice's marmalade, which is the only marmalade she'll eat, and she had two or three bites and then nothing since then.'

Tom stood up, reached and ruffled Rachel's hair, which she hated. She had liked it when she was smaller but now she didn't think it was dignified. Also she had a perfect high ponytail this morning, smooth and sleek, and now it would be messy. She had tried over and over not to get any bumps. 'Your mother's not feeling her best, as you know.'

'You mean she's drunk too much again?'

'Yes, I suppose.' Tom sounded awkward whenever she asked direct questions, so she tried not to ask too much, even though the questions were bursting to come out. 'She's sad – she just needs some time to get back to her old self.'

Rachel carefully poured the coffee into two mugs. She didn't want Tom to go and leave her alone with her mother. 'Do you think we'll stay here on the island until she's better?'

Tom walked to the kitchen bay window and looked out to sea. 'Another hot day. I'll get the dinghy and canoes out for you if you like?'

Rachel knew he was thinking how to answer her question. She didn't want another long day pulling her little sisters in and out of the waves in the dinghy as they shrieked with joy or fear. The boredom of it, of the two of them following her everywhere, made her want to scream.

'It's just I'm worried about school. I want to go back. Margo chose it because it's such a good school and I don't think there are any good schools on the island. I just know I beat Elizabeth in that comprehension test, for the first time. We left suddenly before the end of term, before we got the results back.'

Tom turned to look at her as if she was alien to him. She often felt that people thought she was strange. 'School's not everything, you know—'

'It is to Margo. She's always said she wants the best school-ing for us money can buy. So we don't need to depend on a man or a man's money.' Rachel stood up very straight as she spoke and lifted her chin the way she had seen her mother do.

'You are a mini Margo, aren't you? You need to ask your aunt what the plans are, I'm in the dark. I'm just here to keep your mother from . . . to keep your mother company when she's sad. You know why she's sad, don't you?'

'Of course – I'm not a baby. Because our "useless tosser" of a dad has abandoned us all.'

Tom sat down at the kitchen table slowly as if his bones ached. 'Yes that's right.' He smiled at her. 'But perhaps best not repeat everything you hear?'

'Is "tosser" a swear word then?' Rachel kept a notebook of what Margo called 'wow words' so she could use them in her story writing. With everything that was going on around her she was thinking of writing a novel about men and women and how love could nearly kill you.

'Yeah, pretty much. When I'm a bit less tired I'll explain it. Are you taking this coffee up to Margo or shall I?'

'I'll go.' Rachel couldn't think of anything she wanted to do less, but she knew it was important to be brave. Margo had told her so many times. She spent a lot of time avoiding being in the same room as her mother and she got a pain in her stomach when she thought of having to go into Margo's bedroom. The curtains were always closed, the bed a mess of covers and papers and tissues. The air in the room smelt funny. Margo didn't look like she usually did either. Her face was round and swollen like she had been inflated with a football pump.

Tom got up, groaning a little. 'Good girl. My head though. All this keeping your mother company is going to kill me.' He saw Rachel's anxious face. 'It's just I'm getting too old to be staying up so late. Where does Duchess keep the headache pills?'

'In the first-aid box in the boot room. There's a key but the key is in the lock at the moment. I keep meaning to hide it again – I should probably take a couple to Margo with her coffee.'

Tom mock saluted her. 'Easy to see who's in charge here. You're doing great work, kiddo – looking after everyone. It won't always be like this, you know.' Tom was looking at her strangely and she didn't like it unless Tom was making jokes and being silly. The way he was looking at her like he felt sorry for her made her eyes smart and her chin wobble.

'I know. I'm fine though.' She bit her lip and thought hard of something to change the subject so that she wouldn't cry. 'Although you know what I really need is some new books to read. Alice and Olivia at school said they were setting us a challenge of reading a book a week.' Rachel could feel bubbles of excitement in her stomach just at the thought of new books, a great big pile of them. 'Will you take me to the library? I asked Sam Oliver and he said there is one in Ryde. Margo used to take us every Friday after school in London to Kensington Library. It's huge and there are window seats where you can hide away. That's where I read *Are You There, God? It's Me, Margaret*. I never told Margo of course because she would think it was trash. Just like she hates me reading *Sweet Valley High*—'

Tom interrupted her as he did a big stretch which made him seem like a giant. 'Sam Oliver, eh? You've been hanging around a lot with the Olivers.'

Rachel knew he was teasing her. She thought of Sam's eyes, green like sea glass. She felt her cheeks getting hot. 'They've got a lovely sailing boat.'

Tom chuckled. 'That's true enough and one of the most important things in life. You're a smart kid. Right, you'd better head up to Margo or the coffee'll get cold.'

Rachel felt something twist again in her stomach. 'Is it worth just trying with some toast again?'

'Let's just see what kind of reception you get and take it from there. Ask her if she's hungry when you're up there.'

Rachel climbed the stairs with small, reluctant steps. She could taste blood from where she had bitten her lip. It had become a bad habit, but the pain of biting down on the same pulpy flesh was sometimes a relief, it made her feel more alive. A little bit of coffee had sloshed into the saucer, she hoped Margo wouldn't notice. It was such a pretty cup with a kingfisher on it, one of Margo's favourites. When Rachel finally reached the landing she knocked as gently as she could, but it still sounded so loud to her.

'Tom, is that you?'

Rachel knew that Margo would rather see Tom than her. Sometimes the sight of Rachel made Margo so much sadder. Rachel pushed the door open with her foot. 'No, it's me, Ma, Rachel. I've brought you a coffee and some headache pills.' The room was dark, the curtains closed. 'Do you want me to open the curtains for you, Ma?'

'No. No, I don't.' Margo's voice was cold and flat. 'Just put the coffee down and leave me alone, please.'

Rachel tried to see her mother's face, she missed it so much, but all she could see of Margo was a lump under a pile of blankets and quilts, a few dark curls on the pillow. Rachel didn't understand because it was summer outside. She knew she should go and go quickly before something horrible happened, but she wanted to be close to her mother, to try to reach her, to find the mother she once was to them.

'Are you hungry at all, Ma? I could make you something? Some toast or eggs? I've become quite a good cook now.'

There was some rustling of the covers and a groan. 'Please go.'

Rachel bit down hard again on her lip, turned to leave the room.

Margo suddenly spoke again. The tone was curious. 'How long have I been up here? I don't seem to know about time.'

'It's been four months. Since we arrived at Sandcove. You just went to bed as soon as we got here. You didn't even unpack. I had to help Alice do it. We still don't have all our stuff – I want to know when we're going back.' Rachel couldn't help the words tumbling out even though she knew Margo didn't want to hear any of it.

'Go now please, send Tom up. Be a good girl.'

Rachel had retreated to her room at the top of the house, the room that had been Margo's when she was growing up at Sandcove. It was strange to think that this was probably her real bedroom now for good, not the room in the London flat which she had shared with Imogen. Before, this room had just been a holiday room, with nothing much in it, and it had smelt of holiday things. It had been an exciting bedroom to sleep in with lots of light in the morning and a view of the sea and the gulls so loud by the window that you thought they might be in the room with you. It used to be a room for waking up and knowing you had a whole day free on the beach and that Margo would organise boat trips and picnics and take them to the arcades. There was a big old carved wooden cupboard with a key in the lock and wood floors with rugs on them. The pictures were old Isle of Wight maps and black-and-white photos of yachts. There were always bits of gritty sand on the floor and in the bed, and old-fashioned sheets and an eiderdown, whereas in London they had duvets. Alice said boxes of her things were on their way from London and so soon she could have her duvet again if she wanted. She longed for her books but not her toys because now she felt too old for them. She would give them to Imogen.

Even though Sandcove felt different now that it wasn't a holiday house, she still loved her room. It didn't have a lock but it had a handwritten sign on the door saying 'Keep out' and she made Imogen knock before she came in. Sasha didn't try as she was only four and there were too many stairs. She was scared of the top of the house too, but then Sasha seemed scared of everything. Rachel felt sorry for her sometimes, she kept looking for 'Dada' around the house and now Margo didn't leave her bedroom she didn't get all the hugs she needed, you could just tell. Rachel didn't want anyone to know but she needed more hugs too and sometimes when Imogen was sitting on the bed beside her and she was reading to her she would sneak her arm around her sister and it was so nice and comforting. Imogen was good and sweet most of the time and didn't seem angry and bored the way Rachel was and Imogen would reach out to hold her hand when no one was around. She came to Rachel too to ask her if she would brush her hair which was always so knotty now Margo didn't brush it any more. Margo had been the only one who could brush it without hurting Imogen. Rachel tried really hard and Imogen would wince and not say anything and be brave and it made Rachel so sad and cross, but she didn't know why.

Rachel spent a lot of time writing in her diary, when Imogen and Sasha were with Alice, or up in her room. She left her door slightly ajar hoping Margo might call for her, but she never did. Sometimes her diary felt like her closest friend. She wished she had one with a lock, but Margo hadn't listened when she had given her that instruction and had just bought her notebooks to 'write your little stories in'. Rachel thought that Margo was being condescending, a new word she liked to use about the adults around her. The notebooks were pink and she didn't like pink, it was too girly. They had come in a pack with clingfilm around them and there were five of them so at least she wouldn't run out of a place to write for a while. She had given one to Imogen because Imogen wanted to copy her in everything and sometimes it felt comforting to have someone copying you. Rachel sat on her bed with her eiderdown keeping her toes warm and scribbled away.

Dear Diary,

IMOGEN YOU'D BETTER NOT BE READING THIS!!!!!!!!!!! OR I'LL HAVE YOUR GUTS FOR GARTERS.

I wrote a letter to Daddy today. Just letting him know about how I am sure I am going to come first in Comprehension, if only I could go back and find out. And that Carol bought me some Opal Fruits as a treat for being so good and looking after Imogen and Sasha while she did the shopping. Daddy loved the green ones. Sasha cried because I wouldn't give her the red ones, she's weird. I don't know how to send the letter to Daddy though and I can't ask. I wish I knew where Daddy was. He was a bit of a rubbish Da sometimes, but I still miss him. Remember that time a long time ago when I invited Jasmine for what Margo calls 'kitchen supper' and Margo made homemade chips and burgers which was yum (Margo is the best cook, better than Jasmine's mum, even though she always goes on those cookery courses and is really condescending). Daddy said he would be there and he would read Jasmine one of his poems. And he would do his special banana splits. But he didn't come home. Everything was desolate because Margo was cross and trying to hide it and I felt like a baby for caring in front of Jasmine, and Sasha just said 'Da' a lot and was screaming which made it the worst night EVER. She is such a baby. And Jasmine didn't want to stay and watch telly. She just wanted to go home. The next morning Daddy smelt funny and he had the scratchy stuff all round his chin and he looked like he hadn't slept. He said 'pleeeease forgive me baby'. The right wow word would be 'wheedling'. I had to forgive him Diary because I could see that Margo would not talk to him, and it was all my fault for being upset.

I wish I didn't get so upset so much, Diary. But this house is weird. At Jasmine's house everything is so normal. There is her mum and her dad and her dad is always there, sitting in his special chair and they eat a lot of fish fingers. And they are so quiet and no one asks questions or argues or does what Margo calls 'lively debate'. I miss lively debate now though.

I'd better go as my sisters will be home soon. Alice doesn't like to leave me in the house with Margo on my own for too long. But someone needs to stay with her. Everyone seems so worried about her, I'm not always sure why as she just seems to sleep a lot. So really she is just being indolent and I wish someone would be brave and stand up to her and tell her to stop. But all the grown-ups seem scared of her. See you soon.

Rachel xxx

She was just thinking of the next place she could hide her diary that Imogen would never think of when she heard the front door and Alice calling her name at the bottom of the stairs. Alice sounded stressy. You could sometimes tell, Rachel thought, that Aunt Alice really had enough on her plate with horrible Uncle Seb, and two new babies, and now she had the three of them on her plate too. She had a new frown line because of it and more grey hairs. Either that or she just needed to go and see Sally Fisher in Ryde and 'get it done', whatever that meant.

'I'm going to make bacon sandwiches for lunch, Rachel darling. Will you come down?'

Alice could actually burn bacon so Rachel reluctantly came down the three flights of stairs, making sure to creep very quietly on the landing outside Margo's room where there was a creaky floorboard. She would need to oversee the grill, otherwise she and Imogen and Sasha were going to starve, they were really all too thin. If only Carol would come with one of her cakes, a lemon drizzle or banana loaf. Or she could take her sisters to No. 47 for a bit and hope some of the Oliver kids were there, and Sasha could chase the cat and Imogen could watch the TV in the back and she could chat to Sam and maybe eat an iced bun when he wasn't watching. She would be too embarrassed to eat it in front of him in case it made her look greedy or a bit of the icing stuck to her lip. It might all be perfect for five minutes until Sasha got bored and had a tantrum and then it would be too awful. She felt bad though that Jane was always giving them everything for free, so she should ask Alice for a pound. And she remembered they needed shampoo, there wasn't any. She must add it to the list.

She stood in the door of the kitchen and looked around her, at what was left of her family, and gave a big sigh, which she thought made her sound world-weary like heroines often were in books. Margo was definitely world-weary, she had heard lots of people say so.

'Darling, did you manage to look for bottles when we were out?'

Aunt Alice was speaking in a hushed voice again. The shopping was all over the floor and table. Sasha had her dummy in, the dummy she had given up when she was three but which she had demanded to have back when Richard had disappeared, even though she was four and tall for her age and it looked ridiculous. But she screamed and screamed for it and there was nothing anyone could do. She was colouring on the tiled floor, big crayons rolling all around her. She looked up and gave Rachel such a big smile her dummy fell out and she hastily stuffed it back in, after saying, 'Rake, Rake.' Imogen was at the kitchen table doing the huge 1000-piece space puzzle, being good and quiet. No one understood where she got the patience for puzzles from but they were her new thing, she said she liked seeing it all become neat.

'Yes I found a vodka and a whisky hidden in the laundry basket. I put them in a box on the deck. There's a full box in the shed now too.'

Finding hidden bottles was Rachel's job and she was good at it. Sometimes she liked to pretend to herself that it was a game she was playing with Margo, like hide and seek. A game just for the two of them. At first no one had understood where the bottles came from as Margo never left the house and then it had been Rachel who had done some detective work and had realised that men were bringing the bottles into Sandcove. Not Tom, never Tom. He drank with

Margo if she asked him to but he did not bring bottles. But there were other men who seemed to love Margo and who seemed to think she was about to get better any day now and marry them. There was a time 'before Richard', so they must be men who had been watching her over the years and hoping. Rachel thought it was creepy and told Imogen she thought they were all a bit stupid. And they bought bottles as presents or hidden, smuggled in a jumper, because Margo asked them to. Rachel hated them all and sometimes would not let them in, or said Margo had gone away. And often she took the bottles straight out of their hands and mumbled something about 'the cellar' and the bottle was never seen again. Alice took all the bottles away with her and Rachel didn't know what she did with them.

'Well done, darling.' Alice came and put her arm around Rachel who briefly rested a head against her shoulder and closed her eyes against the picture in her eyes of the kitchen with no Margo in it. Alice squeezed her close.

'This is so hard, I know, but you are being so strong and brave, Rachel O'Leary.'

Alice didn't often make proclamations like that, and Rachel squinted up and could see her blue eyes were wet.

'You know that if it would be easier, you could all come and live with me at Swains Lodge. Just for a bit? So you can be properly looked after while Margo recovers.'

Rachel disentangled herself from her aunt. She could see that Imogen was watching her from the kitchen table with her big serious eyes to see what she would say. Imogen and Rachel had already made a pact that they would never leave Margo.

'No offence, Aunt Alice, but you have two tiny babies and

Uncle Seb would be even more grumpy if we were there. Also we couldn't leave Margo alone at Sandcove.' Rachel moved towards Imogen at the kitchen table, who nodded in agreement.

Alice sighed, looking at them. 'I could take Sasha, she's just a baby. I have Nanny Adams to help.'

They all looked at Sasha sitting on the floor, happy for now with her crayons. For a moment Rachel was tempted to send her baby sister away. No more early mornings, no more tantrums, just her and Imogen looking after each other and Margo. But Sasha wasn't scared of Margo like Rachel and Imogen were. They would find her snuggled in Margo's bed sometimes, or Sasha would hold out her arms to Margo demanding to be picked up. She could make Margo smile and the thought of her baby sometimes brought Margo out of her room looking for them all. Rachel knew these were all selfish reasons but also she knew that part of her believed what Margo had told them so many times, that they were sisters and they should stick together.

'She should be close to Margo. One day Margo'll be better and she'll expect us all to be here.' Rachel looked at Imogen who smiled at her, making Rachel feel warm and like sometimes it was okay to be the oldest, that they needed her.

'Okay, girls – let's all do our best with the situation we are in. Carol is sending Dawn to stay over tonight, she can make you all breakfast in the morning.'

Imogen shyly lifted her head up again from her puzzle. 'But Dawn burns the toast. We like Rachel's pancakes, they're nearly as good as Margo's.'

Alice laughed. 'Yes, Dawn really is hopeless, totally impractical. Apparently they had to tell her they didn't need her any more at No. 47 because she kept dropping things. Strange to think she is Carol's daughter, but at least she'll be here in the night if you need anything.'

Imogen looked at her aunt pleadingly. 'Could you maybe stay again for a couple of nights and bring the twins like last time so we can see them? I love looking after them. Maybe when Uncle Seb's in London this week?' Rachel looked at her sister and wondered why on earth she liked babies so much.

'Yes, I could do that if you'd like me to? Why are you calling your mother Margo now? You never used to.'

Rachel and Imogen looked at each other sadly. Rachel spoke for them both. 'Because – well . . . it sounds bad – but calling her Ma doesn't feel right any more. She isn't being our mum. There have always been two Margos, one who is Ma, just ours, and the other who is Margo who belongs to everyone else or who is in her own world. She's Margo now – she doesn't think of us.' Rachel felt suddenly angry just thinking it and guilty for saying it.

Aunt Alice was looking at her as if she understood, as if she knew this about Margo too. 'Don't forget, I've been her sister for a long time. I know about the two Margos. I think you're very smart the way you put your feelings into words, Rachel, and that's something Margo's taught you to do. She'll come back your Ma, I promise you. And she does think of you and love you. She's just looking for the way back.'

Tears spilled over Rachel's cheeks and she looked at Imogen and saw that she was crying too. Alice put her arms around them, pulling them both in close. Rachel looked down and saw Sasha looking up at them, a fist around a crayon. It seemed ages since anyone had held her and Rachel breathed in the smell of Alice's jumper, toast and washing powder and cigarettes. She could feel the big sobs, the ones that shook her whole body, rising up and she let them come.

It was after Alice had gone, as they were waiting for Dawn, that Margo came out of her room. Rachel had just got Sasha settled with a glass of milk in front of *Sesame Street* and Imogen was upstairs having a bath. Rachel heard the creak on the landing and came out of the kitchen, looked up to see Margo above her, still and ghostly in a long, pale dressing-gown. When she saw her, Rachel worried that she was about to throw herself down the stairs, down onto the tiles, landing like a ragdoll at her feet. This was something she worried about all the time and so without thinking she ran up to Margo, taking the stairs two at a time, and put out her arm across the space between her and the bannister.

'Ma?' Rachel stood looking at her mother who was staring into space. She did not seem to notice Rachel standing there. Rachel could feel her cheeks burning and anger rising up. 'Mum, I'm here – it's Rachel. Are you okay?'

Margo turned her head slowly towards Rachel, and Rachel could see that her mother was drunk. They thought she had been sleeping all this time but she had been drinking alone in her bedroom. Her voice when it came was slow and thick.

'Hello Rachel, is everything all right downstairs?'

Rachel wondered what made her say it. She thought it was probably how angry she was, how she wanted to reach her mother in some way. She moved towards Margo so that Margo moved back onto the landing away from the staircase. 'Everything's fine. Mum?'

Margo looked startled at the word. She stumbled a bit as Rachel continued to move her backwards. 'I should come downstairs and cook for you all. You must be starving. I have no clue what time it is though—'

'Mum, do you know where Dad is? So I can write to him? I have a letter I want to send him.'

A strange look flashed across Margo's face, as if something had snapped inside her. Her eyes went wild like a startled horse and suddenly she reached forward and pushed Rachel hard, as if she was in her way. A shove to her chest and Rachel fell backwards against the wall, hitting her back and head hard. She fell sideways to her knees, so shocked, her heart beating so fast.

'Mum, what are you doing? It's me, Rachel, don't you know me? It's just me. What have I done?' Rachel could feel the sobs suddenly coming out of her, shaking her shoulders, there was nothing she could do to stop them.

Imogen appeared on the landing above, wrapped in a towel, and shouted, 'Rach, Rach, are you okay? What's happened?'

Margo looked up and saw Imogen and her face crumpled, tears rolled off her cheeks. She looked back at Rachel on the floor, at what she had done. 'Never ask me again about that man. Never ever again. He's not your father. He's gone forever. He's dead to me and should be dead to you all.' Margo turned and went back into her bedroom and slammed the door.

It felt like a long time until they saw Margo again, which was strange as they were living in Sandcove with her. Rachel thought it was as if Sandcove had swallowed Margo and her grief whole. Time dragged. They were scared and lonely, feeling like a burden on their faithful group of carers, who came and went, taking their laughter away with them. A whole hot summer unfolded outside their window, on the slipway, so close and yet Rachel felt she could not understand ordinary people any more, with their boats and buckets, and sunburnt skin. The way they screeched in the waves, and chased beach balls. She had turned nutmeg brown, and she had grown, and needed new clothes, and yet she ignored it all, until she was with Sam Oliver and she saw him looking at her legs, and she thought her shorts were probably too short. She hated to think of the time lost. Summer passed and it was winter again, and Rachel got more and more worried about Christmas, about a Christmas without a Mummy or Daddy.

Then, one morning, Margo was in the kitchen doorway and she was smiling in a way that seemed an impossible dream. She was in one of Richard's dressing gowns, which swamped her. She looked thin and ill to Rachel but also so beautiful.

'You've come downstairs.' Rachel heard the wonder in her own voice. This time she knew she must not mention Da, she must not say the wrong thing. She saw her mother looking at each of them in turn, as if she was trying to find something she had lost in their faces.

'You're all okay?'

Rachel moved closer and bravely took Margo's hand, led her to the armchair by the range cooker. It was a chair that all four of them had been able to get on together when they were smaller, and it was covered in a bright pattern of parrots, now faded. Rachel noticed that the arms were starting to wear away and threads had come loose. It was a chair where Richard had often been found asleep at breakfast, but for Rachel it remained Margo's chair. She had breastfed each of them in that chair, except Sasha who had been bottle fed because she just would not take to the breast. Rachel thought that was typical of Sasha, having to be different. There were photos in frames on their father's desk of Margo holding each of them in turn in the chair, looking soft and ruffled, beaming at the camera. The soft, cuddly version of herself.

'Ma, we're all fine. Sit down, I'll make you coffee.'

'It's so nice to look at you all.'

Margo sat in the chair and held out her arms. Sasha, chattering happily and saying 'Ma' over and over, ran to Margo who pulled her up onto her knees whispering, 'Come here, baby.' She sat cooing into Sasha's hair, and Sasha became calm and still, wrapping a piece of Margo's hair around her chubby fist as if she would never let it go. Imogen had been moving cautiously across the kitchen, as if they had been visited by a wild animal. Seeing Sasha safe on Margo's knee, she slipped in beside her mother, perched on the arm of the chair and Rachel watched as Margo wrapped an arm around Imogen's waist. Rachel felt like a spare part, awkwardly looking over at them. It was always just the three of them and now the sums were all wrong. For some reason she did not want to squeeze onto the chair with them. She did not believe what she was seeing. She thought at any moment there would be shouts and tears again. She was worried for her sisters who seemed so trusting. They were just babies. So, she turned her back on the happy scene and began making coffee. Being useful, that was what Aunt Alice said she was good at and maybe Margo would notice now.

'What good girls you've been looking after each other –
such good sisters.'

Rachel thought that Margo did not know what she was
talking about. They hadn't been good. They had been cross
and sad and fighting most of the time.

'Your Mummy has needed such a big rest, I've been doing
so much sleeping. But I'm feeling better now, I promise.'

Rachel stayed with her back to them. She wanted to shout
out that she hadn't just been resting. Instead, she made
herself slowly stir the coffee, pour some into Margo's favourite
cup and saucer. She tried to stop her arm trembling when
she held it out to Margo.

'Not now, Rachel darling. You can see I've got my hands full.'

Rachel set the mug down on the Welsh dresser within arm's
reach of Margo, keeping her face as blank as possible. 'Would
you like some breakfast, Ma?'

Margo shook her head. 'No, thank you, darling. Maybe later.
I'm sure I might be hungry later.' Margo seemed to look round
the kitchen then, noticing the pancake batter in a bowl, the
table set for breakfast. She looked back at Rachel and Rachel
could see that her eyes were curious, finally settling on her.

'Have you been doing cooking, Rachel? How tidy you've
kept everything too. I'm impressed.'

Imogen pulled Margo's sleeve. 'Rachel's our favourite cook.
She's better than Alice! And she doesn't burn things the way
Dawn does.'

Margo's laugh, bells pealing, made them all smile. 'Dawn
really is useless. And Alice was never much good in the
kitchen. It's because horrid Uncle Seb always criticises her and
she's lost her confidence.' The moment seemed to have pulled

Margo into the real world, her world of people and stories and chat. She stood up, still holding Sasha in her arms, and turned to Imogen. Her voice was almost her old voice. 'So, you'd recommend Rachel's pancakes then, Imi?'

Imogen's grey eyes were round with the magic that was happening. 'Oh, yes. They're delicious.'

'Well then, Rach – pancakes for four! Let's all go and sit at the table and you can tell me what you've been doing while our brilliant chef over there makes us breakfast.'

Rachel felt nervous bubbles in her stomach as she made the pancakes. They needed to be perfect. The best pancakes she had ever made. She knew it was silly but a little part of her felt that right now in the Sandcove kitchen, Margo could come back to them if everything went right. Imogen seemed to be feeling it too as she was chatting like she had never chatted before, telling Margo all about the disastrous time Tom tried to make a cake with them. Margo had moved with Sasha in her arms to sit at the kitchen table and Sasha was still being so good and quiet on Margo's lap. She hadn't once asked for her dummy which was a miracle. When Rachel handed out the plates and sat down opposite her mother, Margo gave her a wide smile. Rachel could feel the warmth of it in her tummy.

'These look amazing, darling.'

Rachel didn't try to put Sasha in her booster seat and Margo kept her on her lap, alternating feeding pieces of pancake to herself and then Sasha, one-handed with a fork. In moments, the two plates in front of Margo were empty.

'I had no idea I was so hungry – delicious.' Margo stood up, still holding Sasha, and went to get her coffee from the dresser. 'So what else can you cook now?'

Rachel didn't want to sound like a show-off but Alice had taught her some recipes and she had been teaching herself too from Margo's cookbooks. 'Quite a bit now – but we miss your cooking terribly.' Rachel wondered why she had said that. She didn't want to make Margo feel bad.

Imogen jumped in. 'She can do really good scrambled egg and omelettes. We have lots of toasted sandwiches for lunch and pick our fillings. We made spag bol the other night and toad in the hole when Carol brought us some sausages from Woodfords.'

'It's never a bad thing to be proud of your accomplishments, Rachel. You girls are all very clever in lots of different things and you must enjoy it, not hide it. Have you noticed how boys never seem to have a problem showing off? Look at Uncle Tom, or Uncle Seb, always on about something they can do and usually it turns out someone else can do it much better—'

Imogen interrupted Margo. 'Like that time you beat Uncle Tom in the round the island race?'

'Exactly!' Margo smiled at them both. 'But I've also noticed, Imogen, how loyal you are to your sister. Which is such a good thing to be.'

Rachel, who was watching her mother's reactions like a hawk, saw a shadow pass across her face then. Rachel felt her stomach dip.

'I'm sorry you've had this horrible time, but it's made you rely on each other, I can see that. Hopefully in time you can learn to rely on me too again. I wouldn't blame any of you now if you didn't trust me much.'

There was a nervous stillness in the kitchen. Rachel saw Imogen looking at her, her eyes scared. Rachel knew she had to say something clever and reassuring. Something a grown-up would say. She reached across the table and put her hand on Margo's. She noticed that her fingers were now nearly as long as her mother's.

'Ma, we really need you. We've missed you so badly. We've done our best, and Carol and Alice and Tom. They've all been so kind and they've done their best too. But we need you back.'

Margo was looking down at Rachel's hand on her own and then she carefully placed her other hand on top of Rachel's. 'My lovely big girl. You've grown up so much. And I've missed so much of it.' Rachel could see the bright blue of their mother's eyes swimming in tears, and then one dropped onto the wooden tabletop. Seeing it, Margo seemed to rouse herself, shaking her hair and sitting up straighter. She wiped her face on the back of her dressing gown sleeve.

'Is there any post?'

Rachel always dreaded the post question and she felt her hopefulness sink away right down to her feet. She knew Margo was waiting for something from their father. But there never was any letter, she had been checking every day. She had tidied the post away out of sight. She stood up now reluctantly to get it. 'I'll get it.' Rachel handed her mother the envelopes all addressed to Mrs O'Leary and watched as Margo flicked impatiently through them and then brought the pile down on the table with a slap that made them all jump.

'Time to get dressed and then I'm going to take you all out somewhere. But before I do I have an important family announcement. From this day forward, I'm going back to my maiden name. Your father has left us so we don't need his name any more. We'll be Garnetts from now on.'

Rachel thought about how embarrassing that would be at school. Her mother would probably ring the school secretary and tell her to change it on everything. She would need new name tapes on all her uniform, Margo would hate that as she couldn't sew and would need to ask Carol to do it. Somehow she would have to explain to all her friends that she no longer had a father. But she might not even be going back to that school, back to London. Rachel did not say any of it aloud. Instead she stood up, stamped her foot and saluted her mother.

'Rachel Garnett reporting for duty.'

Imogen stood up quickly and copied Rachel. 'Imogen Garnett reporting for duty.'

Their mother stood up, still holding Sasha. 'Margo and Sasha Garnett reporting for duty.' And Margo turned with a stamp. 'About turn! Time for derobing upstairs! And a one, two, three, four.' And she began to march out of the kitchen and Imogen and Rachel followed behind her smiling their hopeful smiles.

24

The Way Home

London

Sasha climbed the white steps of Rachel's London house and hesitated at the top, turning around to take in the street. It was a new thing about Rachel to try to understand, that she wanted to live here, in this small terraced house, instead of Sandcove. House on top of house, car crammed next to car. A few spindly trees dotted among the paving slabs and no horizon. Friends of Rachel's would call it Notting Hill, but Rachel insisted on accuracy, calling it 'just off the Goldhawk Road'. So now all three sisters lived within walking distance of each other. And Jonny was a few streets away. Sasha knew he was already at Sandcove, he had promised he would be there waiting for her.

There was a biting December wind so not many people were out and many had probably already made the holiday dash for foreign sun or ski chalets. London was empty and grey. Sasha wished she was running away somewhere exotic. She had agreed to this trip home with her sisters because of the letter, because she knew she had to face the music sometime, because Jonny would be there. She dreaded it though, the recriminations. She had not been home since last Christmas, had not spoken to Margo since the Boxing Day drama. Everyone was still angry with her, she felt that they always would be, for the way she had brought Richard back into their lives. She just held on to the idea that there might be a moment when she would sit by the fire with a large drink next to Jonny and everyone would be distracted by Christmas, by Margo's showmanship, the way she made Christmas a festival of everything that was most Garnett, most fun.

Rachel's shadow appeared through the glass pane and the door opened with a whoosh and there was her sister, so full of familiar energy and purpose. 'I saw your feet from the kitchen. You're lurking – you must be dreading the whole thing. Imogen's here. You look cold and lost.' Rachel pulled Sasha into her arms in the doorway, and Sasha felt herself relax for a moment. 'Come and admire everything! Everything seems small after Sandcove but I think it's cosy. Gabriel's not here – he's taken the kids to see the lights at Kew.'

Rachel kept the chatter up as Sasha followed her into the basement kitchen, which felt like a smaller version of Sandcove's kitchen. Sasha had seen and spoken to Rachel a handful of times since the Priory Bay picnic and each time Sasha had apologised and Rachel had been poised and polite. So Sasha hadn't expected warmth today and she could feel her emotions close to the surface as Rachel fussed over her, settling her at the kitchen table and handing her a mug of tea. Imogen, who was lurking in a corner of the kitchen, now moved to sit next to Sasha, and reached for her hand.

'Are you okay? You look exhausted.' Imogen was looking at her with big grey eyes. Sasha knew she looked awful. She had fnally told Phil that they would not be spending Christmas together and he had kept her awake all night, threatening her, then pleading with her. Her hair was growing out of the pixie cut and was shapeless with coarse bleached ends. She couldn't eat and her face looked sunken.

'Bad night – and I can't face Margo.'

'We've all been avoiding her. Hence the summons.' Rachel moved a pile of unopened Christmas cards and pulled a to-do list towards her. 'She knew I wanted to have Christmas here for the first time – she could've just sent us copies of his letter. Making some big drama out of it. Taking kids anywhere for Christmas is a pain – I stayed up till three wrapping their stocking presents.'

Sasha had forgotten presents and was hoping Rachel wouldn't notice. So far she had pretended Christmas was not happening, she had not bothered with decorations and their rental flat remained bare. She thought of Phil in his dressing gown, hunched over the table as she left, refusing to say goodbye or even to turn and look at her. Everything about him disgusted her now, the way he was letting himself go, not washing or leaving the flat, the way he loomed over her, his face always red and angry. She was scared by his outbursts, the way his anger erupted, the way he would throw things. She was always on edge wondering if one day he would throw something at her, or use his fists on her. Worse than that though was the constant criticism which left her with no strength or confidence. She knew Jonny thought it was taking her too long to change her life, to end her marriage. He wanted her to make a dramatic statement, to flee under cover of night. But she did not want a relationship with Jonny to start that way, she wanted them to begin together with clean slates, as equals, eyes open. At least now though she had started to get Phil to see that their marriage was over, she had started the process with this trip on her own. When she was away from him she wondered how she could possibly choose to be in the same room with him ever again. Sasha pulled herself back to where she was and looked round at Rachel's kitchen festooned with lights and the children's bright paperchains heaped in the corner. Rachel saw Sasha looking at them.

'They want to take those to Granny for their rooms at Sandcove.

I'm so pissed off. Lizzie hasn't stopped talking about missing Sandcove and now we have to go back at the worst time. I wanted them to get used to London – their new lives—'

Sasha interrupted, impatient with Rachel's domestic problems. 'Why the hell didn't we just refuse?'

Imogen shook her head. 'She's grieving for him. We can't just abandon her.'

Sasha knew she had to talk, she had not had anyone to talk to. 'I went to the funeral and I was the only one of us there. It was pretty shit.'

Imogen's eyes got rounder. 'I couldn't face it. Why didn't you ring me and ask me to go with you?'

'Phil wouldn't come with me. He never thought I should be bothering with Richard. He hated me going to see him when he was dying – he said I came back hysterical. He didn't understand why I was so sad over a man I hardly knew.'

Rachel moved to the other side of Sasha. 'It was so brave of you to go on your own.' Rachel moved a plateful of Jaffa Cakes in front of Sasha. Sasha looked at it and smiled for the first time.

'I love Jaffa Cakes.'

'That's why I got them, silly.'

There was a pause as Imogen and Rachel watched Sasha eat one Jaffa Cake and then another. Sasha felt like she could eat the whole plate as her sisters watched her, the comfort of cracking the chocolate with her teeth. She saw that Rachel was sitting straight, shoulders squared, about to speak.

'I'm not going to lie – I've been so angry with you. Bringing Richard into our lives that way – I didn't want him there.' Rachel glanced at Imogen. 'I won't speak for Imogen. It was cruel, you hurt Margo – that ghastly drunken beach scene. And where have you been hiding? How can we try to understand if you don't talk to us?'

Sasha stared ahead, then sipped her tea, letting it burn the roof of her mouth. She knew Rachel was right, she had let everyone down, and now her father was dead and her heart was shattered into small pieces.

'I know I fucked up.'

'But for God's sake – of course I would have come with you to the funeral if you'd asked me.'

Sasha looked quickly at Rachel, a tight feeling in her throat. 'Really?'

Imogen placed a hand over Sasha's on the table. 'Me too. I wish you'd asked me. We love you. We want to try to understand.'

'You need a tissue.' Rachel dug through her handbag, which was hanging from one of the kitchen chairs, and passed a tissue to Sasha. 'You don't need to do everything on your own. We're sisters – it means something. We've all been through the same thing – we went through a trauma as children. No one in the whole world knows what we went through except us.'

'I went to see someone – to talk. A counsellor.' Rachel and Sasha turned, surprised, to look at Imogen. 'I know – can you imagine? Me? Trying to talk about my feelings – I hated the idea of it. He said that we would've suffered from post-traumatic stress disorder. Our alcoholic father disappearing, our mother unable to look after us.' Sasha held Imogen's hand tighter. She hadn't thought before of them all going through a childhood trauma together. Sasha always thought of herself as the one that was separate, who couldn't accept things the way they had, who was more angry, the only one who had needed a father.

Rachel turned back to Sasha. 'You need to talk to Margo. You need to try to understand her side of things. You two never talk.'

Sasha let her head fall forward, covered her face with her hands. 'She doesn't love me – what's the point? I was supposed to be the Band-Aid baby, the one that was going to glue us back together. Richard fucked off anyway. I was supposed to make things better – instead I made them worse. Every time she looks at me I know that's what she's thinking – I drove him away, the man she loved.'

'God, Sasha – is that what you've been feeling all this time?'

Sasha looked at Imogen and nodded. 'All this time.'

Rachel's voice was firm when she finally spoke. 'She loves us all. Not in the same way, in different ways. But she loves us – she wants so much for us, all the things she didn't have. Happy family life – a good marriage.'

Imogen nodded. 'Sometimes it just comes out wrong, like the way she tries to control things. She loves you so much though – I was always so jealous of you being the baby.'

'When Margo was really ill, I wouldn't let them take you away from us. Alice wanted to have you at her house for a bit. I wanted to keep us all together. You were the one that Margo would come looking for – her baby.'

Sasha stared at Rachel. 'I don't remember that time.'

'I can remember it for us all.'

Sasha looked back at her older sister and it felt like her heart might crack wide open. Love burst inside her chest, when she thought of the way Rachel had helped them all. 'I wish I could remember some of it. Thank you – for looking after us. I've never said it before.'

It was very quiet in the kitchen then. Just the hum of the fridge, a dripping tap. Imogen and Sasha both looked at Rachel who smiled back at them, strong and sure in her own home, back in charge of her life.

'We're the Garnett girls, a team! Now we need to pack up the car and get going. Sasha – where are your presents?'

Sasha grinned suddenly, feeling like the naughty younger sister again. 'I haven't had a chance to do any shopping. Margo's going to kill me.'

'I'll take you into Ryde tomorrow and we can do a quick whizz round the shops. You know how Margo is about Christmas.' Rachel stood up. 'Let's talk more in the car. I want to know about the funeral and William's treatment. Also how you dealt with Rowan Melrose—'

As they all stood up, scraping chairs against the kitchen tiles, Sasha looked at them both in turn, frowning. 'Rowan Melrose as in Anna Karenina? The blonde who was a rubbish brunette?'

Rachel's laugh was sudden and loud, chasing all the sadness out of the kitchen. 'Sasha doesn't know? Excellent!'

Later, in the car, Sasha felt like a child again, surrendering herself to the comfort of the spare duvet and pillow in the back. It was dark apart from the flash of passing lights and the gentle murmur of her sisters' voices lulled her. It was just the three of them, safe together, and on the way to Sandcove. The drive was familiar, Friday nights heading from London to the island, a journey from a simpler time. Sasha was happy to let Rachel take charge of her life, happy to be able to talk, unwatched, in the car. She could feel herself shedding layers, talking properly to her sisters again like she once had.

'He's finished his treatment now. I tried to stand by him – just as friends; it was harder than I thought it would be.'

Sasha thought about all that Imogen had been going through, how she had made no effort to be there for her. 'How come?'

'I thought it would be easy to be friends but it isn't. I felt like a fraud – like I'm play-acting at something. I wanted to be company for him, cheer him on a little. But every time I felt I made it worse, made him think about our failure, that he was really alone. He was so brave though.'

Sasha could not see Imogen's face in the dark car but she could hear that her voice was flat. 'You sound so sad.'

'I guess I thought that if I finally took some action, life would change in a big way. It was such an anticlimax – everything feels so grey. Lonely. Even Margo didn't seem surprised in the end when I told her we weren't getting married. She's said hardly anything about it.'

'Like when I found Dad – I thought it would change everything to have a father, that I could relax – understand myself. Instead it just confused me more. He still loved Margo—'

Rachel's voice cut through Sasha's. 'What kind of shit love is that though? Abandoning her and us – having a secret family?' The car went quiet. 'I'm sorry, but come on! He loved the booze most of all. I still don't understand why you two needed to see him.'

Sasha whipped her head round to look at Rachel. 'What do you mean?' She sat forward to try to see Imogen's face. 'What's she talking about, Imi? Did you go and see him?'

'Thanks a bunch, Rachel.'

'It was going to come out sooner or later. You know you won't be able to keep it from Margo. You're a total wimp.'

'I don't want to talk about it just yet, Sasha. Look, it's the tunnel – halfway.'

The car fell silent again. Sasha thought of Margo, the bright upswing in her voice when they had first gone through the new tunnel a decade ago. How excited she had been that the London to Portsmouth road would now be faster. Sasha had a memory of Margo's hand laden with rings, her dark painted nails, gesticulating. She looked at the back of Imogen's head, wondered what she was thinking. They had to talk about Richard, just the two of them.

'Can we have a beach walk tomorrow, Imi? Breakfast at No. 47?'

'I'm not invited?' Rachel's voice was gentler now.

Sasha and Imogen's voices chimed together. 'No.'

Rachel gave an exaggerated sigh. 'Okay, shut me out of your Daddy appreciation club. There's something you haven't thought of.'

Sasha pulled herself up and out of the duvet, knowing that soon she would have sight of the Solent. The stretch of water that was the way home. 'What now?'

'How do we know that Margo didn't go and see Richard?'

Sasha tried to imagine Margo by that bed, the other wife hovering with solicitous cups of tea. Margo in that small, cramped house that smelt of bacon and stale cigarettes, where the heating pumped out boiling hot and cats snaked round your legs. She leant forward between the seats, to be closer to her sisters, touched Imogen on the shoulder so she turned and met her eyes. Imogen looked sad and Sasha knew then that Imogen also lay awake at night, could not unsee the shrunken man lying so still.

'God, I hope not. It would be way better if he stayed being the drunk poet who adored her but fucked up her life. I hope she didn't see him dying.'

'Me too,' said Imogen.

On the top deck of the ferry, the three women huddled together as the wind whipped their hair out like streamers behind them. Sasha looked at her sisters and knew she would grow her hair long again, to fit back into their three. They watched as the sun set in brushstrokes of red, breathing the sea air as the island slowly came closer. There was always something hopeful about the ferry crossing; however familiar it was, it still always felt holidayish. On the sea, between the land, there was a respite from life, a freedom. People were cheerful, and children ran in and out of the play area. There were always lots of dogs calling to each other, excited by the sea air. Sasha knew they each felt differently about the island, and yet at that moment somehow she knew they all saw home.

'When are you going to tell me about Rowan Melrose? Are you a lesbian now?' Sasha pinched Imogen's arm and heads around them turned as Rachel laughed loudly, throwing her head back.

Imogen elbowed Sasha. 'What makes you say that?'

'I always wondered. You never seemed to fancy many boys – not the way Rachel and I did. Especially Rachel.'

'Oi.' Rachel turned with mock outrage. 'I didn't have that many boyfriends.'

'Yeah, right – you were always breaking hearts on the island, usually in the same families Margo had devastated. I wanted to break hearts so much.'

Imogen looked at Sasha, her voice impatient. 'Come on – you turn heads everywhere you go. Margo's always telling us – you're the beauty of the family.'

'It doesn't work like that though, does it. Sex appeal – confidence, style, knowing yourself – they all count way more.'

'You have all that, you idiot . . . I can't believe you've always thought I was a lesbian. Why didn't you say something?'

'Well, are you?'

Imogen paused a moment. 'I don't know.'

Rachel interrupted. 'We should keep our voices down – that man over there is eavesdropping and probably getting a hard-on.'

They all followed Rachel's eyes to a man on the bench nearby and then collapsed in giggles. Sasha felt lighter, like some of the tensions of her life were lifting, the further she moved away from Phil. She could see the steeple of Ryde church getting closer, the promising wild greenness of the island, which always surprised her.

'What did Rowan do when you dumped her? She was quite the

drama queen – worse even than Margo.' The Tannoy interrupted, announcing that they were coming into Fishbourne. Rachel stood up, looking down at Imogen, waiting for an answer.

'She told the rest of the company – told them I'd treated her badly, used her. She's still texting all the time – she calls me when she's drunk or high.'

'Booty calls.' Sasha held out a hand to Imogen to pull her to her feet.

'It was so glamorous, my life with her. The whole summer felt like a dream. My life'll never be that exciting again.'

'This is all you just coming out of your shell. You'll meet someone else. We can have fun guessing whether it's going to be a man or a woman.'

Sasha smiled at Rachel's tease. People and dogs were hurrying all around them, moving towards the exits. 'Does Margo know?'

'There's a lot of things Margo doesn't know! Come on, you two . . .'

Sasha followed her sisters to the stairs, remembering her last sight of Margo, her back turned to her as she left the kitchen. Imogen was hanging back, watching her.

'I'm dreading seeing her – the letter – the whole fucking thing.'

Imogen nodded. 'I know – but we'll stick together.' And the two of them hurried, trying to catch up with Rachel.

25

Negroni Time

Margo rummaged in the freezer, muttering. She could not believe she had forgotten to make ice. Her number one rule for parties was to have enough ice. All she could find were Alice's strange-looking homemade soups. Alice had soup every lunchtime, sitting at the kitchen table with the paper, and it drove Margo mad. She missed cooking with Gabriel; Alice turned down exotic food or anything that might be too rich as she was always watching her weight. Poor Alice, thought Margo, she really can't eat much at all, she should probably try drinking less.

'Alice! Where's the bloody ice?'

Alice appeared in the doorway. Margo knew she had been hovering in the hallway, pretending to be there to greet guests. Really she wanted to avoid small talk. She didn't love parties the way Margo did. Margo was always pushing her into rooms, trying to get her involved. It had been that way since they were children.

'Was I supposed to make some?' Alice always looked bewildered by the rules at Sandcove.

Margo stood up, a hand in the dip of her back. Her whole lower back had started complaining at random times and Margo was doing her best to ignore it. Why was it that one day something that had worked perfectly fine just stopped working? 'The freezer's full of your soup. Even if I'd remembered ice, I wouldn't be able to put it anywhere.'

'I'm happy to buy a new freezer – perhaps a chest one? – to replace the one that broke in the utility room?'

'Isn't it a bit odd that two old ladies like us should need two freezers?'

Jonny appeared in the doorway, still in his City clothes, his tie loosened rakishly. 'Gabe's on the blower.'

'I'll take it in here. Remember to put the other handset down, Jonny.'

Jonny saluted and winked at Alice. 'Come on Alice – come and chat to me in the living room. When are the girls getting here? Leo's boring on about boats again.' Alice followed obediently.

Margo picked up the receiver. It was the old Bakelite phone that was at Sandcove when she was a child. It still reminded her of clandestine calls to Richard. 'Did the girls set off okay?'

'They should be with you in an hour.' As Gabriel spoke, Margo heard the click as Jonny put down the other phone. She smiled to herself thinking how tempted he would have been to eavesdrop. Gabriel's voice was terse. 'You went ahead with a party? Was that the right thing to do?'

As soon the party had started, Margo had wanted it over, knew that it was all wrong. Richard's dead body was only a few days in the ground. She had wondered if she could turn this party into a wake. Could she toast him, though, in front of everyone? Everyone here had known and loved him. She thought her voice would not hold up. 'What do you mean?' Her voice was steely, refusing to let Gabriel hear her self-doubt. Her relationship with Gabriel had changed since the redhead. Margo found it hard to trust his version of events, to believe that he had not misled the girl in some way. She worried that Rachel's faith in Gabriel was naive.

'You know what I mean. The girls have lost the father they've only just found. You've called them home to read a will, and they'll open the door on a Sandcove party.'

Margo twisted the cord round and round her finger, the way she had done as a girl, all those long calls. What had she and Richard spoken about for so long? If only there was a way to recall those conversations, to have recorded them. Right now she hated Gabriel and his smugness. She hated the fact that he wasn't there in the kitchen with her making ice, making cocktails. She knew she sounded defensive. 'It's tradition. I always have a party on the twenty-second.' Once Richard had wanted it on the twenty-third and it had ruined Christmas. They had not had time to recover, to be the ebullient parents the girls expected. Richard had always taken things too far.

'I think this was the year you could've broken tradition and just been there for the girls.'

'I know how to be there for my girls. You just concentrate on being there for Rachel.' The antagonism between them crackled on the line. Margo knew she wasn't being entirely fair to Gabriel, he had done everything Rachel had asked of him. He had agreed to stop being the girl's therapist, to never see or speak to her again. He had let Rachel persuade him to move back to London. She could hear sadness in his voice and she realised she missed him.

'I didn't do anything wrong, Margo. Rachel believes me, why can't you?'

Margo poked one of her long red nails into the phone dial. She shut her eyes a moment, feeling a wave of tiredness. It wasn't fair to blame Gabriel for a secret when she had been keeping so many. 'I'll look forward to seeing you tomorrow.'

When her daughters arrived later, Margo was standing in the living-room window on her own. The party was spinning like a top, sticky negroni glasses abandoned on every surface. Margo felt it was at the stage when it was all happening without her, without her needing to play a part. Tom was playing the piano badly, a group around him singing. Woodsmoke from the fire hung hazily in the air, and the lights were dim, apart from the sparkle of an extravagant Christmas tree in the corner of the room. There were too many people squeezed onto the long sofa, an evening chorus of chatter as they all leant in to each other, fascinated with each other, the way people were after too much to drink. Alice kept hovering with platters of canapés that were barely touched. Margo hadn't pulled the curtains across yet, as she stood sentry, looking for her girls. And then she saw the three of them trundling suitcases along the promenade. They were turned towards each other as they walked, open faces, Margo could see that there was no tension, only a cloak of unity around them. She had hoped the drive together might do this. As long as they were not united against her. She felt overwhelmed by the sight of them here at Sandcove finally. The Garnett girls.

She opened the door, as Rachel charged up the steps first, leaving her suitcase at the bottom. 'Hello!' Margo called, any better words suddenly escaping her. She rarely felt shy, in fact she hated shyness, thinking it lazy. But she was feeling shy now of her eldest daughter who was looking at her like a mother looks at a naughty child. 'I'll get one of the boys to do the bags – just leave them.'

Rachel kissed Margo on the cheek, not before Margo saw her eyeing the sweep of the dress she was wearing, her amber beads. Rachel's voice was amused, rather than angry. 'Of course – it's the twenty-second. We'd better go and change.'

Imogen had stopped chatting to Sasha on seeing Margo, and took Sandcove's steps two at a time, threw herself into Margo's arms. 'Ma.'

Margo held her tight. Imogen felt bonier in her arms, her hair so long, like she had just given up cutting it. Margo mentally warned herself not to say anything. She looked for Sasha who still stood hesitant at the bottom of the steps. 'Go in, darling.' She whispered into Imogen's hair which smelt the way it always did, of wet earth and apples. Margo breathed in its scent, feeling Imogen's cheek pressed against hers like the softest velvet, remembering how she had always hugged that way as a child, as close as could be. 'Get Jonny for the bags – give me a minute with Sasha.'

Imogen did as she was told, went inside, with a quick glance and smile back over her shoulder at Sasha. Margo saw in that look that allegiances between the sisters had changed, that something had bound Sasha and Imogen back together. She went down the steps to Sasha. Margo could see the pain on Sasha's face, that she was mourning her father. They were both grieving. She reached for Sasha's hand which hung limply at her side, held it in hers, met the eyes that were Richard's eyes.

Margo struggled to find her voice. 'Let's never ever leave it that long again.'

'But you were so angry with me.' Sasha's voice was that of a child.

'I was angry – furious. I wanted to try to understand why you did it. But you left so early the next morning, before we could talk – you ran away again.'

Sasha shrugged, looked away, up the steps to the house. Jonny stood there, summoned to do the bags. He was just standing, watching Sasha, smiling. Margo followed her look.

'Don't just stand there! Get the bags.'

'What am I, the Garnett slave?' Jonny was still gazing at Sasha.

Sasha could feel heat spreading over her chest, neck, her cheeks. To hide it, she shouted back at him, 'All the way to the top floor, slave!' She turned back to her mother, hoping she wouldn't notice her blushes. 'Phil was so embarrassed, he hated it all. He just wanted to leave.'

'Phil hates family life, lots of people and raised voices, he always has. Maybe something happened in childhood—'

Sasha's face flared red again and she snatched her hand away. 'He hated it because you never made him feel like part of the family. Never treated him the way you treat Gabriel. He and I have always been second-class citizens.'

Margo felt exhausted at the thought of all the layers of hurt she was going to have to make her way through with Sasha, going back years. She pushed her impatience down, her desire for another drink. 'Phil hasn't wanted to be in this family. He hates this house. Ask your sisters if you think I'm being unfair. We all feel like he's been keeping you from us.'

Sasha looked at Margo, her face crumpled. Margo moved closer to her daughter who was shivering in the night air. 'You're cold. Why do you never wear a coat?'

Sasha ignored her mother. 'He wanted to keep me from Richard.'

'Maybe that was to protect you? It's no fun watching someone die of cancer. I remember coming home to see my mother when she was dying in this house. I didn't want to come – but I did it for my father. I couldn't believe that the tiny human in a vast bed was the same woman who'd been my enemy for so long.'

Margo felt Sasha looking at her differently. She knew what Sasha wanted to ask her.

'Imogen went to see him.'

Margo realised then what had united Sasha and Imogen, what they had seen at Richard's bedside. Imogen would be scared to tell her. 'Is she okay?'

Sasha shook her head. 'Neither of us are okay. Did you go to see him?'

Margo looked back at her, letting Sasha see her face unmasked, the pain there. 'Yes. I did go in the end. I couldn't not. I'm haunted by it now – I think I always will be. But we laid some things to rest. I can't believe I've said goodbye.' Margo's voice cracked and Sasha's eyes filled in sympathy. Sasha reached for Margo's hand. Margo let her take it and held on tight. She was so damn tired, but so glad to have the words out of her. She hadn't told Alice yet.

'Oh Ma.' Sasha's lip wobbled.

'I can see your sisters have forgiven you – and I forgive you. I see now that something like this had to happen. I let there be too much silence. All you could do was fill the gaps with all the things you needed your father to be. You've always been searching for a daddy who could make everything better.'

'You're not angry with me any more? For bringing him back?'

'I'm sad, not angry. So much was my doing, my wrong choices. I'm so pleased to have you back home.'

Sasha sighed and rested her head on Margo's shoulder. 'I always pretend I hate home, but today I need to be here.'

Margo looked up at the front of Sandcove, welcoming fairy lights flickering around her windows. 'There were so many times I hated living here – but I kept coming back because it was home. Sometimes the idea of home is bigger than everything else.'

'I left Phil behind.'

'I can see that. Do you want to talk about it?'

'Not really, not now. I'd love a big drink. I want to party. Are there negronis?'

'There are always negronis. Go easy though, please.'

'Can't I get wasted? I really want to – without Phil telling me not to.'

Margo saw a flash of Sasha's spirit back in her eyes. 'No more massive dramas though or Christmas will never recover.'

'Can I borrow a top? I didn't bring anything partyish.'

Rachel called them from the open doorway. Margo knew she was checking up on them, making sure they were not fighting. 'We need the front door shut, it's making the fire behave badly.'

'You can borrow something – go and have a root around in my room.'

At the top of the stairs, Rachel looked at Margo. 'Everything okay?'

'Aren't I supposed to be asking that?'

'I need to talk to you about something if we can find a private moment. It's about Jack Walker.'

Margo lowered her eyes from Rachel's. 'It's okay, it's all done and dusted. Another of my bad decisions. How did you know?'

'Carol saw him coming out of yours – I covered for you. He's part of a child maintenance case I was working on. I didn't tell Imogen or Sasha.'

A look passed between them. 'Thank you.'

'We need your negroni-making skills. Alice is rubbish. And how is there no ice?'

'Tell me about it.'

Margo followed the girls upstairs, hovering on the third-floor landing, drifting between the two bedroom doorways. She listened to the chatter, offering an opinion when asked. She passed a silk top to Sasha, moss green with bell sleeves, and was rewarded when Sasha's face lit up.

'I love this one! Can I wear Grandma's silver bells with it?'

They were like magpies. She watched as they ransacked her jewellery box, teenagers once more. Imogen, once such a tomboy, was a woman with her own sense of style. Margo noticed her delicate lace underwear as she slid into tight leather trousers, and a pirate-style white shirt.

'Goodness Imi, that underwear's a bit sexy.'

They all laughed as Imogen blushed. Without their men they had regressed to how they were as children. A memory came back to Margo of a summer when, as teenagers, they had all chosen to be home at Sandcove. Even Rachel, who was always travelling with friends, had come home and the three of them had moved everywhere as a pack, sometimes letting Margo be their fourth. She had been so happy she had let them take over the house, dropping all her rules. The only time she had to herself was the morning and she would bake and cook in her kitchen until midday, waiting for the house to come alive. The smell of bacon would lure them down, in their uniforms of tiny pyjama shorts and vest tops. All three of them had had Lady Godiva hair, sometimes knotted up high on their heads, and endless legs. Their careless beauty, their creamy skin was dazzling. Margo had guarded them from the unwanted attention of her male friends. The sisters had thought they had cleverly hidden the back-garden smoking from her, the island boys shuttled in and out, the bottles of beer in the bin, but she had seen it all, had let it all go. As long as they were in their Sandcove beds at night, arms and legs flung out from their covers, their deep breathing floating down to her bedroom.

Margo stood watching Rachel applying dark lipstick. 'Do you remember that summer when you were all here, all teenagers? It was so hot.'

Rachel turned and looked at her. 'Yes. I'd had my first year at university, had just met Gabe.'

'I was so glad you came home. It was such a happy time.'

'Yeah – it was the perfect summer. All our friends were so jealous that we had such a cool mum.' Sasha turned to smile at her mother. Margo could feel herself beaming. Imogen came and stood close, linked an arm through hers, mischief on her face.

'Rach, you had that fling with the Oliver boy.'

Rachel grinned over her shoulder. 'Never tell Gabriel that.'

Sasha pushed past to twirl coquettishly in the middle of the room. 'What do you all think?'

Margo raised her eyebrows at her youngest child. 'We're all relieved you decided to brush your hair.'

Sasha grinned. 'This is the first time I've felt like brushing my hair. I remember that summer too. Rachel also had another fling – with that boy who was working in No. 47 for the holiday, what was his name?'

'Joe.' Margo remembered finding him asleep on a sofa, abandoned by Rachel who had gone to bed. She saw that they were all looking at her and smiled. 'I saw everything that summer. Everything.'

The noises of the party floated up to them and Sasha skipped out of the room. 'Come on, you lot. Negroni time!'

It was a legendary party. Locals remembered the three beautiful Garnett sisters suddenly appearing, lighting up the rooms. Margo went around glowing with pride and the production line of negronis kept up apace, ice shipped in from the neighbours. By midnight Sandcove roared, the Garnett girls' high spirits having rubbed off on everyone. Jonny and Sasha took a long, slow walk to Seaview and back to collect the DJ decks he always kept in the back of his car. Tom and Leo shifted the long sofa out of the way with people still on it. Margo rolled back the rugs, dimmed the lights, and soon everyone was dancing like wild things. The fire was left to die down as the room steamed up. People began to strip off. Alison was in Tom's arms, barefoot and down to the slip she had been wearing under her velvet dress. Jane and Dawn jumped up and down like teenagers, their arms in the air. Jonny danced closer and closer to Sasha. Rachel twirled and swayed, lost in her own world. Non-dancers moved to the kitchen where Margo held court in the hum of close-packed bodies. She threw open the back door so people could smoke in the cold night air. The twins and their friends shivered on the back steps smoking weed and hoping their mother wouldn't notice. Margo thought sadly of Richard and how much he would have loved this party. She had missed her moment for a toast to him, but she could see that her girls wanted to be free for just a little while longer. Soon it would just be the four of them and tomorrow they would read the letter.

Later Alice found Margo leaning on the fridge once more. 'Time to stop negroni production, ice supplies have dried up again.' Margo looked at the kitchen clock. 'I'm not going round to the Goughs at two in the morning.'

'Sasha's definitely had enough. She's entwined around Jonny on the sofa.'

'I saw that – Jonny's looking very happy about it.'

'I've always wondered about Sasha and Jonny. There's something strong there, something they keep coming back to.'

Margo looked at Alice in surprise. 'Jonny's just a big flirt though – she shouldn't take him seriously.'

'I think if there's one girl he'd give it all up for, it's Sasha.'

'But Sasha's married—'

'Unhappily married.'

Margo thought about how good Alice was at seeing things she missed, or refused to see. She realised she didn't hate the idea of Sasha and Jonny together. It was time she stopped flirting with Jonny just to feel young. Time to stop advising her daughters on love, when it became clearer every day that she made bad choices for herself and for them. 'Underneath it all he has the best heart and so does she. I'll try to talk to her about it – and listen.'

'Good. Have you seen my two, smoking weed with Leo and Tom? I can't be bothered to say anything. I might go to bed if that's okay?'

Margo looked at her sister, who still looked as neat and pretty as as she had at the beginning of the evening. 'I'm feeling sentimental. It's the booze . . .'

'And Richard.'

'And Richard . . .'

'And having the girls here.'

Margo tutted. 'All that. But also I must say I like our new living arrangement. I'm not sure I've said that to you.'

'No, you haven't. I like it too.'

'Sandcove should always have been half yours.'

Alice looked at Margo with gratitude. 'You're drunk. It's the only possible reason you're being this nice. I've had an idea.'

'What?' Margo straightened herself up, curious.

'I think we should ask Imogen to live with us here for a bit. Just for a couple of months – while she gets back on her feet. I think she's a bit lost and lonely. I am not sure she's told us everything that's happened to her this year.'

Margo watched her sister, marvelling. Alice wasn't someone you could ever underestimate. 'I think you're right. And she does have a new play to write – I can help her. Only if she wants . . .'

'You'll need to try not to interfere in her life.'

'I know. Poor Imi, she does seem down about her and William. And that Rowan Melrose. Something happened there.'

'A sex thing.'

Margo tried not to look shocked. 'A sex thing? Bloody hell.'

'It's not easy to tell your mother that sort of thing, even a mother like you. Of course, I don't know for sure, but . . .'

'Even I know that that means you're pretty sure. How did I miss it all?'

'Too busy treating Rowan as a rival.'

Margo could feel a headache emerging. She always paid for negronis. 'My daughters have stopped telling me things, when did that happen? I used to know everything about them. I suppose I can't blame them for keeping secrets.'

'They don't tell you things because they don't want to disappoint you, they worry about not living up to your expectations.'

'My New Year's resolution is going to be to give up expectations – they've never worked out well. I think I might go to bed too. Slide out without telling anyone, before Tom starts doing tequila shots. Tomorrow we have the letter.' She looked at Alice for sympathy.

'It'll be okay because you saw him.'

Margo could not stop her mouth dropping open as she looked at her sister. 'How did you know I saw him? I haven't told you. You told me not to go.'

'I know that you went to see him because you're sadder than I've ever seen you. I told you not to go because I know you like to do the opposite of what you're told. But you needed to go.' Alice smiled at Margo, a little smugly, Margo thought.

'What did Dad used to call you? Alice the all-seeing?'

'*My little sage.* To make me feel better for not being exciting and dramatic like you. He was such a sweet father to me.'

'And he tried to be to me too, but I never let him. I'm glad he had you.'

'Why did he leave you the house? I've always wondered – wondered why not me. It hurt me.'

The two sisters looked at each other. They had never talked about it and yet it had been behind Margo's decision to give Alice half of Sandcove, to put it in both their names. 'I think he knew perfectly well that Richard would be a dead loss – that I would need somewhere, some security. He knew you would be sensible and marry well.'

'Well he got that wrong because I married a pig.'

'Alice! You never say anything bad about Seb.'

'It's negroni honesty. We're getting too old now not to talk plainly.'

Margo nodded in agreement. 'Let that be our new motto. Speaking plainly. No more secrets. This Richard letter is too late. Why didn't he write and explain when it happened, rather than leaving me in the dark all that time, leaving me to waste years hoping?' Margo felt the pain again. She needed the oblivion of sleep.

Alice's voice was firm. 'It's not too late for the girls. For the girls to understand.' She led Margo out of the kitchen to the stairs. 'I'll do the clearing up and breakfast in the morning, try to get any lingerers off and away before you wake. Have a lie-in.'

Margo kissed her sister's cheek when they reached the landing outside her bedroom.

'I don't know what I'd do without you.'

'Lucky for you, you don't need to find out.'

26

At Peace

When Rachel woke the next morning she was cold; the patchwork quilt had slid off the bed. There was no Gabriel wrapped around her. In all the time they had been together they had rarely slept apart. She lay still, scared to move her head in case the pounding got worse. Her mouth was dry and sticky from the shots she had thrown back in the early hours. She had let her hair down in a way she hadn't since the children. She had danced and danced – at one point on the kitchen table – and she had smoked the twins' joints, and cigarettes, and flirted with everyone. She was almost impressed with herself. And there were no children to worry about this morning, only Margo and her sisters, and the letter that was hanging over everything. She reached over to the bedside table to look at her phone, and saw two missed texts from Gabriel. *How's the party?* and quite a bit later on he had sent *Are you still partying??* He was being needier than he used to be and she knew it was the spectre of the redhead that sometimes still reared up between them. The fact that he had let it get out of control, hadn't told her when he should have, had kept it a secret from her. The power balance between them had shifted; Rachel had used it as leverage to get Gabriel to move back to London.

'Help me.'

Rachel turned slowly and laughed at Sasha. Her face was emerging from the covers of the trundle bed that had been set up in the corner of Rachel's old room. Aunt Alice slept in Sasha's room now, and she had the twins in with her too, if they had even made it to bed. Rachel was sure that there would be prone bodies all over Sandcove. Sasha was groaning.

'Oh God, I *hate* negronis.'

'You mean you like them too much, pisshead. Have you got Jonny under that duvet?'

Sasha hid her face again. 'Fuck. Was I really bad? Tell me. Did Margo see?'

Rachel laughed again but then found it made her head throb. 'Everyone saw. You weren't exactly subtle. Love's young dream, snogging each other's faces off. Don't worry – it was a great party, everyone was behaving badly. I loved spending time with you. Usually Phil's stuck to you like glue and I don't get a look in.'

Sasha propped herself up on an elbow facing Rachel. She was frowning. 'Ever since I met him, he's never let me alone for a minute. My therapist said he's a father replacement figure and I confused his control with love.'

'Hang on – what therapist?'

'I've been seeing someone. I asked Gabe for some names.'

Rachel did not think before the words escaped. 'Another secret he's kept from me.'

'What do you mean? I asked him not to tell anyone. Gabriel's keeping secrets from you?'

'It's nothing.'

Sasha leant out of bed to pick up the pillows she had thrown on the floor in the night. She wedged them behind her head, sat up a bit.

'I feel like death every time I move. Go on.' The old radiators came to life and started clanking immediately. 'Someone's up, probably Alice. She should bring us tea and toast in bed immediately. Remember how on Sundays, Margo would always make those big brunches? Her potato rösti! God I'm starving – I ate nothing last night.'

'You did – you got Margo to make you a ham sandwich at about eleven. She would have told me to make my own.'

'You did use to live here. Is it weird?'

Rachel thought about Margo opening the door yesterday. All the times Margo had opened the Sandcove door to her in her life, how seeing her at the top of the steps meant she was home. It felt like it was back to how it was supposed to be. 'I never wanted to be the keeper of Sandcove. I wanted it to stay my childhood home, keep it how it is in my memories – somewhere I can come back to.'

'I wanted to think of Sandcove that way but I've spent so much time fighting it, thinking of it as somewhere that drove Dad away.'

Rachel turned to Sasha in surprise, she hadn't realised she felt that way too. 'I remember thinking that about Sandcove. That Margo and Sandcove were some kind of combined force, that Richard was shut out of. He never wanted to come for those long summer holidays. He hated being cut off from his Soho crowd. Margo knew he was safer here. Now I realise she was trying to keep him alive.'

'I wish I had some memories of when we were all together.'

Rachel could remember a handful of happy times. The usual kinds of childhood memories. Richard had liked taking her to museums and galleries. She had a memory of holding his hand looking up at the blue whale in the Natural History Museum. He had taken her for an enormous burger afterwards. She remembered grabbing a fistful of mint imperials from a bowl on the way out – they all got furry in her coat pocket. She remembered how he embarrassed her by being loud and Irish, the funny words he used. He was such an odd mixture. He loved parties and noise but he also loved to study. He loved the Latin names of plants. He and Margo had been alike that way.

'I remember once in the V&A following behind them both through that huge hall with all the sculptures. They were holding hands and I was trying to keep up with them. I was a bit scared by how big it all was. They were talking and talking.' Rachel looked over at Sasha who was listening to her, rapt. She felt bad sharing her memories with Sasha and Imogen, when they cared so much and she did not. It didn't seem fair that she didn't want her memories, when they were so hungry for them. 'But you have recent memories. I don't.'

Sasha's face changed. 'Seeing him dying has pushed everything else away.'

Rachel tried to imagine what it had been like but found she couldn't see her father's face or hear his voice. The house was quiet. Rachel thought how strange it was knowing that it wasn't her place any more to go downstairs and start the day off, put bacon under the grill, shake Tom awake. For just a few more hours, she had no responsibilities. She understood it was a gift of time with Sasha. The hangovers had loosened their tongues.

Sasha got out of bed, her bottom barely covered by an old Wham T-shirt. She opened the curtains onto the garden and the hills behind Sandcove. There was only a ribbon of light in the sky and condensation on the old sash windows. There was scaffolding outside the window.

'There's scaffolding? Don't tell me some work is actually, finally going to start? It's a Christmas miracle!' Sasha pulled a dressing gown off the back of the door and put it on. It was too short for her – she looked like a French film star, with her smudged black kohl, messy blonde hair and long legs. 'They need to start with double-glazing. It's always fucking freezing.'

Rachel knew it was Alice pushing Margo to get organised. Alice had a pot of money left from her inheritance and she wanted to spend it on Sandcove, now Margo had done the right thing and put it in both their names. She wanted it to survive so they could pass it on to the next generation. 'Alice will save Sandcove. The woman's a saint. I can't believe you still have your Wham T-shirt. I remember taking you to that concert, I persuaded Margo to let us go—'

'I lost my voice screaming.' Sasha was smiling at the memory. 'You were going to tell me something about Gabriel? Please tell me your relationship hasn't gone to shit too? I couldn't cope with that.'

Rachel turned to her sister, pulling her knees up and the covers over them. Sasha got back into bed. 'There was a patient, a young girl. She came to the house to tell me she loved Gabriel, that I should let them be together. I'd been feeling for a while that there was something wrong, something he was hiding.'

Sasha was staring back at her. 'What did Gabe say? Was the girl a total nut job?'

'I think she was a little mad.'

'So, it's okay then? He didn't sleep with her, the mad girl?'

'It was something though – he should have told me as soon as the texts and calls started. It still hurts so much that he kept it from me, tried to deal with it on his own. Also finding out what we have about Richard, hiding another family, what a big fat liar he was – it's made me wonder if I'm just stupid to keep my faith in Gabriel. I worry I'm being a naive idiot. I sometimes think Margo thinks that, although she's being strangely diplomatic these days so she hasn't said anything.' Rachel felt her voice waver. 'How do I know he didn't overstep some kind of boundary? He swears he didn't but—'

'Come on – it's you and Gabe, for God's sake. He looks at you like you're his reason for being. It's sickening. If he's made one small mistake – so what? You can get over it. When I saw you two dancing at Imogen's engagement party I knew that Phil had never made me feel that way.'

'I know – I still have faith in him and I'll never do anything to risk breaking up my family. I know what a broken family does to the kids.'

Sasha nodded her head. 'We've been broken so many times . . .'

'Margo puts us back together.' Rachel saw her mother as she was last night, so pleased and proud to have them all at Sandcove. Following them from room to room, checking up on each of them, indulging them. Rachel felt there had been a change in Margo since she had said goodbye to Richard. Margo had managed not to say anything judgemental last night, had only listened when they talked about their lives.

'I'm going to have to stop blaming everything on Margo. But then I'll lose my whole raison d'etre.'

Rachel looked mock-sternly at her sister, lightening the mood. 'Yes you are. And when are we going to talk about you?'

Sasha's eyes slid away to the floor. With her hair like a halo around her head, she looked like a fallen angel. 'Phil and I haven't been right for a long time. It's hard to admit. It's so hard to fail at anything in this family.'

'What are you going to do?' Rachel watched as Sasha started to pick the skin on the palm of her hand, a nervous habit since childhood.

'I told him to go to his parents' this Christmas. I told him I didn't think it was working and he took it badly. I was frightened. His temper – he throws things.' Sasha rested her chin on her knees, shutting her eyes. 'He never lets me be. He wants to know where I am every minute of the day. This has been the worst year of my life because he's been suspicious, as if he knew what was coming. It's made him much worse. I'm not sure how I'm going to make the final break, whether I'm strong enough.'

Rachel wanted to move and sit next to Sasha, but she knew she might break the spell, stop Sasha talking. 'I'm sorry, darling. I wish you'd called me.'

'Everyone feels so far away. I know it's me again, doing what I do best – fucking things up, pushing everyone away. The way I behaved, over Richard, the lies. Phil never wanted anyone else in my life – he told me that none of you wanted me, that I was the black sheep. He fed my fears about Margo not loving me. He told me it was because I looked like Richard, she couldn't bear to look at me.'

'God, I could murder him! He gaslighted you. When you tell him you're leaving, I can be there. I can be waiting outside with Gabriel, with Jonny. Or in the flat with you – whatever you need. We should get your stuff out of the flat first. No wonder you thought you needed a father so much, if Phil told you that none of us wanted you. I always hated him.'

They laughed suddenly together, at the passion in Rachel's voice.

'What about Jonny?' Rachel watched as her sister, usually either cool or angry, blushed like a schoolgirl.

'He's waiting so patiently for me. Do you think I'm mad?'

Rachel thought about what she had seen last night. For a long time it had seemed like Sasha and Jonny were too much for each other. Now it was clear that no one else was enough for them. 'God no. I love Jonny. There's so much strength and loyalty there. You both have pasts, you'll both be so ready. You can make him see that he doesn't need to keep trying to win his father's approval, he can start living the life he wants to live.'

Alice called up the stairs, 'Bacon's on the grill. Coffee in the pot.'

'We'd better go and help or Alice'll burn something. We have to hope these are the kinds of hangovers that get better not worse.' Rachel stood up slowly and started to look for some clothes she could pull on. 'I hope Margo doesn't cry over the letter. Did you notice how much she talked about Richard last night, just little things?'

'The way she kept mentioning his name, over and over. It's so weird after all those years of silence.'

'She was drunk but also I think it's because it's all out now, we all know. It's like getting the whole of her back. Young Margo – her memories.'

Sasha reached and touched Rachel's arm. 'Do you think this letter will explain? About the other family? I tried asking but I was never brave enough – he was so frail – he seemed so sad and sorry – a bit pathetic to be honest.'

'It's probably just as Margo said on the beach: love makes you do strange things. I'm not sure we'll ever really understand. We might have to accept that some things about our family can't ever be known.'

Sasha looked down at her bare feet. 'Maybe he was just one of those sad men that can't be with a woman who's stronger?'

'I've thought that. Also could a sixteen-year-old really make a wise decision about the rest of her life?' Rachel thought about teenage Margo, how passionate and impetuous she must have been. Seizing her life in her own hands, all for love. Whether it was wise or not, it was brave. Rachel handed Sasha a hairbrush and watched as she brushed out her bed hair. Margo made comments about untidiness at breakfast even with a hangover. Rachel saw mischief wash over her sister's face.

'What?'

'It's bad of me I know, but I really want to be there when Imi tells Margo she's a lesbian.'

Rachel laughed. 'Oh God yes – me too!'

It was early evening when they gathered around the dining-room table. They had moved slowly through the morning and Leo, Tom and

Alison had only just left. Breakfast had gone on all day, with Alice patiently standing by the range, handing out bacon, eggs and toast, pouring coffee and tea. People came and went at different times and as always there was brilliant conversation, so Rachel had stayed put at the kitchen table, just enjoying it. It felt more like Christmas Eve, but one just for adults. Even Margo was in her red silk dressing gown, although they all teased her about how glamorous it was. She had brought it back from a Hong Kong trip she and Richard had taken. Rachel remembered she had been left behind with Alice and the two weeks had passed so slowly. She had gone with Alice to collect them from the airport and her parents had walked through the gates hand in hand like film stars, Margo in dark glasses, Richard tanned in a white linen jacket. Alice had had to push her forward to hug them. Rachel had felt like they were too beautiful to belong to her.

Now though, everyone else had gone and Sandcove was theirs again. After the party, it seemed so quiet. Only the seagulls, the rattle of the windows. Alice was finally resting in bed with a book, having packed the twins off to see their father. The sisters and Margo gathered solemnly in the dining room. Margo lit candles and fetched the Christmas ice bucket. There were four crystal coupes, and a bottle of vintage Dom Pérignon. She poured each glass with ceremony, carefully setting one down in front of each of them in turn. 'Hair of the dog.' She silenced any protests. 'It's what we all need. We need to toast him.' Rachel thought again how strange it was to hear Margo talk openly about Richard after all these years of silence. Rachel had been the only one who had not seen her father before he died. She was going to be living with that decision for the rest of her life, with the way it divided her from her family. She did not understand why she was less curious about Richard, why she could do more easily without him, when she was the daughter who remembered living with him.

Gabriel had told her people respond to trauma differently. But it unsettled her that her sisters and even Margo wanted to find some closure when she did not.

Margo looked down at the papers on the table in front of her. 'So – Richard has left you each something in the will. Jewellery of his mother's that he kept for you. She had stunning jewellery – she was as rich as Croesus. She was mean though, she would never help us when we needed it, even after he left . . . And there is a letter for you. I don't want to read it out, but he wanted me to hear it.'

Rachel spoke quickly, 'It's not right for me to read it. I didn't go to see him. I'd feel a fraud.'

There was a pause. The portraits on the walls looked down on them disapprovingly. They couldn't squabble now. Rachel knew she was upsetting the expected order of things. It was always she and Margo who read the letters, poured the drinks, and took charge. Rachel looked at Sasha. Her hair was a smooth sweep now around her face, her face soft in the candlelight.

'Sasha, I don't say this in a blaming way, but you're the one who brought Richard back. Imogen and Margo may not have seen him before he died, had you not found him. Without you there probably wouldn't be a letter. You got to know him best – you should read the letter.'

Sasha nodded at Rachel and moved a hand slowly across the table towards Margo, her tone resigned. 'Fine, I'll do it. But don't blame me if I cry.'

Imogen moved her chair a little closer to Sasha, stroked her arm reassuringly. 'You can pass it to me if you can't manage it.'

Sasha slowly unfolded several sheets of handwritten paper. 'God it's a bit dark in here, Margo.'

Margo silently moved a candle closer to Sasha.

Sasha cleared her throat. 'I'm just going to get on with it.'

My Girls. I know you aren't girls any more. But that's what I always called you. When I was away from home I would ring up Margo and I would say, 'How are my girls?' When I came through the door after being away I would shout, 'Where are my girls?' I don't have any rights over the word 'my' any more but I am dying. So I'm praying you'll indulge me.

Sasha paused. Rachel felt the directness of the voice, the intimacy of it like a kick in the gut. Her father had appeared to her again. She looked at Margo whose head was bowed, her hair falling like a screen around her face.

It's hard to know where to start when you have as much to apologise for as I do. For a long time all the sorries I needed to say have overwhelmed me. I've tried to say it to Sasha and Imogen in person, but I haven't seen you, Rachel. I know why you couldn't come. You were the one who saw the most and had to look after your Ma the most. Without you no one would have got through the weeks and months after I left. I was selfish and I relied on the thought of you, Rachel, relied on your strength. I knew you would help them all through. But Jesus, I'm so sorry I laid that on you when you were just a kid.

Sasha paused again and Rachel looked over at her mother, feeling Margo's eyes on her. She saw Margo nod. Rachel swallowed, she couldn't speak.

I was an alcoholic, I will always be an alcoholic and I could not be a father to you all. Even before I left, Margo had to do it all on her own, never knowing when I would show up or how plastered I would be. I could see it wearing her down. The joyful, carefree girl I had fallen in love with was disappearing in front of my eyes. Every time I let you all down, every time I went out on the lash, I pushed myself further away from you. I hated myself. It wasn't always that way. Your mother and I were mad for each other. She was so young when she left her family to run away with me. I felt like the luckiest man alive. It was just us against the world. We didn't need anything except each other. We travelled, we laughed and we wrote and we met crazy people. There was craic every night. I got to watch your Ma dance and sing, to hold her close. It was the time of my life. Margo believed in my poetry, and my poetry was always about her, underneath everything. You all know the energy your mother has to inspire, how she lights everything up around her and how high her standards are. I just wanted to live up to the way she saw me. But I always felt I wasn't good enough. For a while it felt like I was outrunning that fear. But then it would catch up with me and I could feel my need to drink growing and starting to overwhelm me once again. Margo tried to talk to me about it but I was a proud eejit. I wanted to pretend that the drink had no hold over me. You see, I knew all along that she was stronger than me.

Each one of you was so loved and wanted and I saw Margo fall madly in love with each of you in turn. She became what she was meant to be above all else, a mother. It came so naturally to her. I am ashamed to say it but I felt left out, unneeded, and I felt Margo was lost to me. She and I had planned you together, she had always talked to me about wanting a big family, Sandcove summers on the beach, teaching you all how to swim. I had told her time and time again how much I wanted it too. Margo wanted me there, but so often I wasn't. We fought all the time. She was a lioness if she thought I had hurt you. Even though I was a complete fool, Margo never stopped trying to make me part of things. She never gave up on me.

I don't know what to tell you about my other family or how to explain it. I think in my illness I convinced myself that you didn't need me, that I made things sad and unhappy at home. I convinced myself that Margo's expectations were unrealistic and then that she had given up on me. That she had stopped loving me. And I met Adriana in a pub one night and she was quiet and calm and good at listening. She saw the man I was now, the broken man. She didn't know about the boy I had been, the promising poet, or the lover full of hopes of being the best husband and father in the world. She listened to me and wanted to help me. It wasn't ever your mother's fault. It was my illness that made me feel I wasn't good enough for you all, and made me want a life where I could just be happy being a nobody. Our first baby, Cara, was an accident, born just two days before Sasha. I was wetting Cara's head the night you were born, Sasha. Not my finest hour, turning up at the ward to meet you still drunk from celebrating a half-sister you didn't know about. I was a mess but I couldn't abandon them either. Adriana and Cara felt like a chance for a fresh start, to try again, and so I decided I had to disappear from your lives. I convinced myself a clean break was best for you all.

There was never a day when I didn't feel like I had done the wrong thing or when I didn't think of you all. I would imagine all the places you might be, all the things you might be doing. I would think of you all as the best parts of me, the young me that was so full of dreams and hope. But I needed *to survive. I started to go to AA meetings, I stopped drinking and the fog slowly began to clear a little. But it was always there, the knowledge that I was a failure, that I had abandoned a family and the woman I loved. I've never had one day in these last twenty years which has been light or carefree. Not one day without dark thoughts or guilt, sometimes feeling I don't deserve to live. This cancer feels like all the stress and the fear and the self-hatred have caught up with me. Adriana tells me I mustn't think like that but I do.*

I am so glad you found me in time, Sasha, so I could tell you all these things. Somewhere at Sandcove are the poems I wrote for Margo, the letters I wrote her when our parents kept us apart. In those you will find the man I once was. They speak in a way I no longer can, and they might help you understand why Margo chose to love me. Despite everything, I still feel so lucky that she did choose me.

Rachel heard the crack in Sasha's voice. Imogen was deathly pale. Margo was leaning back from the table as if she wanted to run from the room.

If you'll take some advice from me – don't strive for impossible things. Realise what you want and go after it, but don't always believe the grass is greener. Sometimes settling into your life, realising it is the life you have chosen, there is comfort in that. Not all of us in this world need to be important. When you are dying, you realise that the magic lies in all the small daily things you took for granted. And there is horror at the fact that you will never have time to take them for granted again. Look after your Ma and look after each other and let her look after you. You were always bound together so tight, and what I did to you all will have bound you tighter. Margo will always have Sandcove for you to go back to, the place where you can understand where you have come from. I wanted to be at peace at Sandcove, the place that seems most Margo on earth, but I always felt I didn't deserve to belong to it. You all can belong there. And please know I loved you all, you never did a thing wrong. It was all me. Love, your Da.

The silence was thick with feelings. Rachel watched as her mother took a long thirsty sip of champagne and pushed her chair back and stood up. She hadn't cried, but Rachel remembered that this was how Margo's face had looked when Richard left, and she was scared, like the ten-year-old child she had once been. Scared that they might lose their mother again.

Margo held out her glass. 'To Richard.' They all scrambled up, surprised, reaching for the untouched glasses. 'To your father and the man I loved. Thank God you are at peace now.' Margo drained her glass, and Rachel and her sisters all took large sips, chorusing in unison, 'To Da.'

Rachel moved towards Margo. 'Shall we go and make some dinner? I'm hungover and starving again, I don't know about anyone else. Gabe and the kids'll be here soon.'

Margo looked at Rachel as if she had only just seen her, as if she had been lost to them for a while. She shook her curls and straightened her shoulders. Then she smiled a smile which seemed to banish the ghosts from the room. 'Good idea, darling. I was thinking a pie. With my special onion gravy. And maybe some homemade chips.'

'That'll do it, Ma, that'll do it.'

Never Enough Words

It was so quiet and still between them, she had not expected that. Her anger had evaporated, it had no place in the face of death. They were just two people who had once loved each other and who shared three daughters. It now seemed like the life of two actors in a play, so many unnecessary twists and turns. In that small room where Richard lay, his eyes dimmed, his cheeks concave, Margo could not remember what it had all been for. Why had they clung so hard to each other, pushed each other away so violently?

'Tell me about them.'

She didn't need to hold back. She could glory in all their achievements. So she talked, her busy hands with their bright nails and rings sometimes resting on his still hand. His skin was so paper thin, the veins bulging around the drip.

'Sounds like you're right in the middle of it all.' He smiled a little as he said it, his face at an uncomfortable angle on the pillow as he watched her. It was a shadow of the smile she remembered. She smiled back at him.

'I'm not sure they always want it that way. But the time when you left was so bad, I disappeared from them. They were nearly taken away from me. If it hadn't been for Alice, for Tom . . . Did you know I tried to kill myself?' She let it hang there between them. He shook his head slightly on the pillow. 'I'm so ashamed now. I think that's why I'm always trying to make up for the time I lost. For all the times I just couldn't find it in me to care. While they were just downstairs waiting for their mummy. Now I care too much, interfere too much.'

'But you've come through, M. You survived it all.' He said it as forcefully as he could, then closed his eyes. The nurse came in.

'Am I wearing him out?'

The nurse smiled kindly at her. 'Maybe. But also this is the most alert I've seen him for a while, he's been making do with less morphine. He wants to talk to you.'

Margo was not sure how she was going to leave the room, say the final goodbye. As she watched his chest slowly rise and fall, she let the tears fall down her cheeks. She thought about when they were young, when they were happy, when the future was so full of hope. Then she felt him looking at her again and she brushed the tears away.

'Why did you come?'

'I knew it would hurt, but that it would hurt more not to come in the end. I wanted to be able to share it with my girls, if they needed me to.'

'Are they happy? My girls? Do they have fellas? I didn't ask Imogen, I was too busy watching her. She was so still – she reminds me of Alice. Sasha's a force, like you, but Jesus she's angry.'

'I've got a lot of work to do there, to make things right with her. I wish you'd seen Rachel. She's the one I wish I could be more like, she's true to herself. Imogen is the only one who just wants me to mother her.'

'Don't be an eejit – they all want you to be their Ma, they always did. There wasn't much room for me.'

'You buggered off!'

'I know – it's hard to remember what came first. Feeling like an outsider or making myself one.'

There was a pause as Margo watched Richard drift away for a moment, shut his eyes. She didn't speak until he opened them again. 'They're struggling with love, the same way everyone struggles. After what happened with you I wanted ordinary husbands for them, ones that would keep them safe.'

'They wanted the other things? The things we had? Passion and friendship – a muse?'

'Is that what I was? A muse?' She sounded teenage again, wanting his approval.

'Yes that's what you were. You were everything.'

They stayed very still looking at each other until Richard's eyes closed again. She saw him press his morphine button. It was longer this time until his eyes reopened.

'Do you think it was bollocks, all that star-crossed stuff we told each other? How we were meant to be? Perhaps it was just bad judgement.'

'We had ten good years. Amazing years – remember those? More than many get.'

Margo looked back, past all the troubles. 'Yes we did – I need to hold on to that. Let go of some of the other stuff.'

'I can't believe you didn't meet anyone else. The best-looking woman I ever saw.'

'No one suitable.' Margo thought of all the men who had tried to be her second husband. 'Maybe I should've compromised. I don't seem to be good at that.'

'You still could. You're still such a fine woman.'

She shook her head a little, dismissing the idea. 'Has your second life been what you wanted?'

His voice was faint as he answered. 'There's been love and craic and ordinary family life. Adriana's kind, the kids are grand. But it's hard work staying sober every day. And it's never been easy living with the ghosts. I was thinking of you all the time. To fail that way – let everyone down – all the things I did. I know it was the disease but – and now it has caught up with me again . . .'

He was slowing down now, visibly tired, and Margo knew that soon there could be no more questions. 'Sasha says you became a teacher. What happened to your poetry? I always looked for it, searched bookshops. I hoped you'd write something. Something that would make me understand. Why I wasn't enough . . .' Her voice trembled as she remembered those lost years.

His clouded sea-coloured eyes sought hers, and his hand reached for hers. It felt as light as a feather. 'You were enough. I wasn't. I couldn't write after I left you. The words just went, there were never enough words, or never the right ones.'

As his eyelids became heavy she smiled at him, a smile full of all the love that she had ever felt for him. She whispered, 'You'll always be my poet.'

She set a silver framed photo of their three girls gently down by his bedside. They were on Priory Bay beach, arms around each other, freckled faces. If you looked closely, in one corner of the photo was a foot, Richard's foot, as he lay in the sand sleeping it off. Behind the sisters was a huge sand village, with turrets and a flag, and they were smiling big, hopeful smiles. He would see it when he woke up.

Acknowledgements

I would like to thank my first reader, James du Cann, who was the person to say 'You've got something here'. He patiently made notes on an early manuscript of *The Garnett Girls* and talked for hours with me about the characters, offering advice on delving deeper into their stories and giving me the confidence to work harder. He makes me focus on how to write better and his calm advice during the excitement of getting published keeps me grounded. He is the one who keeps family life on track when I attend festivals and events. For that, and everything else, I am so grateful.

My second reader, Becky Hunter, has been a huge support. She has a very wise head on young shoulders. An invaluable listener about writing and its insecurities, she is my favourite person to talk through the finer details of plot points, for her books as much as mine. It is one of those friendships that proves that a twenty-year age gap doesn't matter.

I get to work with the irrepressible agent, my pal, Cathryn Summerhayes, who rang me from the bath to tell me she wanted to represent me and *The Garnett Girls*. That was a lucky day as now we get to hang out a lot. To say she knows what she is doing is an understatement. Thank you also to the mighty Curtis Brown family and in particular ever efficient Jess Molloy and Lisa Babalis, who whipped *The Garnett Girls* into shape. And thank you a thousand times to Jenn Joel, an agenting goddess, who helped find Lucia Macro to publish *The Garnett Girls* in the US.

I had heard a great deal about the amazing HQ team: their loyalty, passion and ambition for their authors, and it turned out to all be true! My editor, Kate Mills, has really bowled me over with her love for *The Garnett Girls*. She has been at my side through everything with a gentle guiding hand and I trust her implicitly in all things. Executive Publisher Lisa Milton is a formidable ally to have and lights up a room. Editor Becky Jamieson has been so efficient and helpful. Dawn Burnett, who is looking after the marketing for *The Garnett Girls*, is a great source of calm wisdom and big laughs and has an excellent creative eye. The sales team is dreamy, thank you Anna Derkacz, George Green, Harriet Williams and Ange Thomson. I would take any opportunity to have cocktails with you. It has been a long-running joke that whoever has to look after my PR was going to have so much 'fun' dealing with me. Luckily, I am in the hands of a super dynamic PR team, who I trust totally. Thank you Sophie Calder, Lucy Richardson and Sian Baldwin. Finally, if you get the chance to experience a Charlie Redmayne lunch, you should take it without hesitation!

I grew up in a family where there were a lot of family stories about feuds, and love, and old houses, and my father, Alan, is a brilliant storyteller. He and my mother, Amber, did everything to encourage my love of books and reading and stories, taking myself and my sister, Chloe, and brother, Thomas, to plays, and operas, and on pilgrimages to writers' houses. My father even tolerated me borrowing his Folio editions of the classics. He taught me to respect and love books, and stayed up late to help me when I was struggling with an essay. Thank you M and D for all you did and for all the stories. This novel is about love among sisters and Chloe is the person in my life who I ring when I am in trouble. Thomas, who loves stories too and old films, is my favourite person to watch *The Philadelphia Story* with.

I am lucky to be in a group of old friends, 'The Urban Family', who still attract and conjure mad stories and fun, are the first to tell me to stop showing off but also are massive cheerleaders. I hope there is just a touch of their spirit and glamour in this novel. Thank you, UF.

The Garnett Girls is very much a lockdown novel. Stuck at home, the novel became my way of escaping to the Isle of Wight, and its beautiful beaches, as I call it my happy place. I hope that *The Garnett Girls* captures my love of the island, and thank you dear Bembridge friends and neighbours for making us so welcome when we bought our beloved holiday houseboat.

I have loved every minute of my publishing career, the authors I have worked with, the journalists and book bloggers. There is a gang of inspiring women and men who worked in my team over the years at Headline – they know who they are – and who have been and always will be a joy; here's to the Groucho terrace! To be part of the publishing industry is something I am so grateful for; working with authors and books is something I never take for granted. The support everyone has shown me, as I cross over to the other side, has been unbelievably generous. Thank you, publishing.

Finally, Sonny and Daisy. You are both incredible. Equally. Everything I do, I do for you and I love you both to the moon and back.

ONE PLACE. MANY STORIES

Bold, innovative and
empowering publishing.

FOLLOW US ON:

@HQStories